THE FALL OF TEROK NOR

For orders other than by individual consumers, Pocket Books grants a discount on the purchase of **10 or more** copies of single titles for special markets or premium use. For further details, please write to the Vice President of Special Markets, Pocket Books, 1230 Avenue of the Americas, 9th Floor, New York, NY 10020-1586.

For information on how individual consumers can place orders, please write to Mail Order Department, Simon & Schuster Inc., 100 Front Street, Riverside, NJ 08075.

MILLENNIUM

BOOK I OF III

THE FALL OF TEROK NOR

JUDITH & GARFIELD REEVES-STEVENS

POCKET BOOKS
New York London Toronto Sydney Singapore

This book is a work of fiction. Names, characters, places and incidents are products of the authors' imagination or are used fictitiously. Any resemblance to actual events or locales or persons, living or dead, is entirely coincidental.

An *Original* Publication of POCKET BOOKS

POCKET BOOKS, a division of Simon & Schuster Inc.
1230 Avenue of the Americas, New York, NY 10020

This book is published by Pocket Books, a division of Simon & Schuster Inc., under exclusive license from Paramount Pictures.

ISBN: 0-671-02401-9

First Pocket Books printing March 2000

10 9 8 7 6 5 4 3 2 1

Printed in the U.S.A.

To Denise & Mike
and more adventures in the 8th dimension

At that moment, before the sky was opened, it was all a flurry of this and that and the everyday. But with the Opening, there came a stillness, a pause in the endless avalanche of life, if you will, as if the stars themselves whispered for us to turn away from what troubled us and glimpse what waited at our journey's end. And the truth is, what the stars showed was no different from what we had already suspected: There were many paths to that final destination, and even in the Temple of All That Had Been and Was Still To Come, the place where all answers waited, it was up to us—to us—to choose our own way.

—JAKE SISKO, *Anslem*

PROLOGUE

In the Hands of the Prophets

"THERE WAS *another time," the Sisko says.*

"It is not linear," Jake answers. The twelve-year-old boy dangles his fishing line in the quiet water of the pond, rippling the reflections of towering trees, green fields, and the pure blue sky of Earth. The sun is strong, and the rich scent of the bridge's sun-warmed wood makes uncounted summers happen all at once for the Sisko.

"But it is, was, will be. . . ." The Sisko falters with the syntax of eternity. His father plays the upright piano in the restaurant in New Orleans as the Sisko plunges into the depths of the Fire Caves with Gul Dukat and first takes his captain's chair on the bridge of the Starship Defiant, *all within a single heartbeat—the same heartbeat.*

—The heartbeat of his unborn child, now grown,

now fulfilling a destiny unimaginable to the Sisko, a destiny now known to him, now unknown.

The Sisko laughs at the wonder of it all.

"You're laughing again," Jean-Luc Picard tells him in the ready room of the Enterprise, *in orbit of Bajor.*

The Sisko looks down at the old uniform he wears at this moment. The texture feels so real to him, even as it dissolves beneath his fingers and he is in his bathing suit on the beach carrying lemonade to the woman who will be/is/was his wife—still at this same moment.

"That is correct," Solok confirms. The young Vulcan walks beside the Sisko on the path leading from Starfleet Academy's zero-G gymnasium to the cadets' residences. "All moments are the same."

"In this *time," the Sisko says. He watches Boothby plant fall flowers by the statue of Admiral Chekov. "But there are* other *times. That's my point." The gardener now prunes bushes for the spring.*

"This is not logical," Solok says. His cadet's uniform becomes that of a baseball player, and he tosses a small white ball into the air, then catches it with the same hand an infinite number of times.

"Logic has no place here," the Sisko says. He reaches out and intercepts the ball even as Solok attempts to catch it. "Because logic is linear."

"Some logic is absolute," Sarah Sisko says. She stands by the viewport in the Sisko's quarters on Deep Space 9, the radiance of the opening doorway to the Celestial Temple filtering through her hair. Wormholes within wormholes. Temples within temples. An infinite regression. Or an eternal one.

"I think I finally know why I'm here," the Sisko says. "Why you . . . had to be certain my mother would marry my father, give birth to me."

“You are the Sisko,” Major Kira agrees. She stands at her station in Ops.

“You need *me here,” the Sisko says.*

“You are the Sisko,” Curzon Dax agrees, the vast spacedocks of Utopia Planitia orbiting with flawless precision beyond the viewport of his shuttle.

“You need me here to teach you,*” the Sisko says.*

Interruption.

The Sisko finds himself in the light space. Around him Sarah, Jake, Kira, Solok, Curzon, Worf, and Admiral Ross.

“You have much to learn,” the admiral says.

“Then shouldn’t I already know it?”

“Your language is imperfect for these matters,” Solok says.

“You have much to realize that you already know,” Worf says.

“That you have always known,” Jake says.

The Sisko holds up a finger, and each of his observers watches it, as he knows they will.

The Sisko regards their expectant faces and laughs again. “Look at you all,” he exclaims. “You want to know what I’m going to say next. Because you don’t know!”

The Prophets are silent.

The Sisko thinks of a thing, of a time, of a moment, makes it real.

And they are on the Promenade of Deep Space 9, as it is the day the Sisko first sets foot upon it.

The Sisko can smell stale smoke, hear the clamor of work crews. Feels what the Prophets cannot *feel, the . . . anticipation.*

He leads them to the entrance of the Bajoran Temple.

“Since you do not know time, how can you know of

other times?" the Sisko asks, so much that is hidden now known to him.

As he knows they will, the Prophets continue their silence.

The Sisko holds out his hand to them. "Welcome, Prophets," the Sisko says with a smile. "Your Emissary awaits you."

All enter the Temple then. Intendant Kira and Jadzia and Ezri, Jake and Kasidy, Weyoun and Damar, Quark and Rom and Nog, Bashir and Garak, Vic and Worf, O'Brien and Keiko and Eddington and Vash. All at the invitation of the Sisko.

It takes hours for them all to pass through, all in a single moment.

The last is the Sisko, poised on the threshold of the Temple.

He remembers his own words the first time he stands here.

"Another time."

An infinity of eternities in just two words. An infinity beyond the understanding of the Prophets.

Until now.

The Sisko enters the Temple.

Not to show them the beginning of things. Because that would be linear.

He enters the Temple to show them the end.

As it was.

As it is.

As it will be. . . .

CHAPTER 1

On this day, like a beast with talons extended to claw through space itself, the Station stalked Bajor one final time.

Viewed from high above, from orbit, the dark, curved docking arms angled sharply downward, as if gouging the planet's surface to leave blood-red wounds of flame. And from each blazing gash of destruction, wave after wave of ships lifted from the conquerors' camps and garrisons, on fiery, untempered columns of full fusion exhaust.

As those ships exploded upward through the planet's smoke-filled atmosphere, the sonic booms of their passing were like the echo of the death-screams of the ravished world they left behind. The jewel-like sparkle of the departing ships' thrusters like the glittering tears of that world's lost gods.

On this day, on this world, sixty years of butchery and brutality had at last come to an end.

But on the dark station that was Terok Nor, with viewports that flashed with phaser bursts and shimmered with the fire of its own inner destruction, there was still far worse to come.

On this day, the Day of Withdrawal, the Cardassians were leaving. But they had not left yet . . .

Held within the cold and patient silence of space, the Promenade of Terok Nor itself was a tumultuous pocket universe of heat and noise and confusion.

The security gates that had bisected its circular path had by now collapsed, twisted by hammers and wirecutters and the frantically grasping hands of slaves set free. Glowing restraint conduits that once had bound the gates now cracked and sparked and sent strobing flashes into the dense blue haze that choked the air, still Cardassian-hot.

Hull plates resonated with the violent release of multiple, escaping shuttles and ships. A thrumming wall of sound sprang up as departing soldiers phasered equipment too heavy to steal.

Decks shook as rampaging looters forced internal doors and shattered windows. Among the empty shelves of the Chemist's shop, a Bajoran lay dying, Cardassian blood on his hands, Cardassian bootprints on his back, his collaboration with the enemy no guarantee of safety in the madness of this day.

Turbolifts whined and ladders rattled against their moorings. Officers shouted hoarse commands. Soldiers cursed their victims. In counterpoint, a calm recorded voice recited the orders of the day. "Attention, all biorganic materials must be disposed of according to regulations. Attention. . . ."

But on this day, the only response to that directive was the desperate, high-pitched shriek of a Ferengi in fear for his life. And in fear for good reason.

Quark the barkeep kicked and fought and shrieked again, as the Cardassian soldiers, safe in their scarred, hard-edged armor, dragged him from his bar, soiling and tearing his snug multicolored jacket.

Quark opened his eyes just long enough to recognize the scowling officer, Datar, a glinn, who waited for him with a coil of ODN cable. In the same quick glimpse, he saw the antigrav lifter from a cargo bay bobbing in the air nearby; he heard the soldiers as they mockingly chanted the last words he would hear before he stood at the doors of the Divine Treasury to give a full accounting of his life—

"Dabo! Daoo! Dabo!"

Yet even as he faced his last minute of existence, Quark still couldn't help automatically tallying the damages each time he heard a crash from his establishment as the Cardassian forces laid waste to it.

A sudden blow slammed Quark to the Promenade deck, and a quick, savage kick from a heavy leather boot forestalled any thought of escape.

But even as he cried out in pain, Quark wondered if his brother and nephew had made it to a shuttle, and if the Cardassians had found his latinum floor vault. He gasped in shock as he felt Glinn Datar's rough hand claw at the sensitive lobes of his right ear, the violation forcing him to his feet. In the same terrible moment, Quark found himself wondering just why it was Cardassians always had such truly disgusting breath.

"Quark!" the glinn growled at him. "You have no idea how it pains me to take my leave of you."

"All good things," Quark muttered as waves of incredible pain radiated from his crushed right ear lobe and across his skull and neck.

Datar's swift, expert punch to the center of his stomach doubled Quark over, his lips gaping in vain for even a mouthful of air.

"Relax, Quark," the glinn hissed, reaching out for Quark's earlobe again. "It's not necessary for you to speak—ever again!"

Quark felt himself hauled up until he stared right into Datar's narrowed eyes. He felt his poor earlobe throb painfully, already starting to swell.

"My men and I are going to make this a real farewell." The glinn nodded once and Quark felt huge hands forcibly secure his shoulders and arms from behind. Datar addressed his soldiers as if reading from a proclamation. "Quark of Terok Nor, you miserable mound of *sluk* scum: For the crime of rigging your dabo table, for the crime of watering your drinks, short-timing the holosuites, inflating tabs, and . . . most of all for the crime of being a *Ferengi* . . . I sentence you to *death!*"

Incredulous, Quark tried to plead his innocence, but his rasping exhortations were drowned out by the cheers of the surrounding soldiers. He tried to blurt out the combination of his floor vault, the shuttle access codes Rom and Nog were going to use to escape, even made-up names of resistance fighters, but the sharp cutting pressure of the ODN cable Glin Datar suddenly wrapped around his neck ended any chance he had of saying a word. Even the squeak that escaped him then registered as little more than a soon-to-be-dead man's choked-off wheeze.

Eyes bulging, each racing heartbeat thundering in his cavernous ear tunnels, Quark could only watch as two soldiers hooked the other end of the thick cable to the grappler on the cargo antigrav.

Datar slammed his hand on the antigrav's control and the meter-long device bucked up a few centimeters, steadied itself, then rose smoothly and slowly and inexorably, trailing cable until it passed the Promenade's second level.

The cable snapped taut against Quark's neck, yanking him at last from the grip of the soldiers who had held him. Kicking frantically, he felt a boot fly free. He grimaced in embarrassment as he realized his toes were sticking through the holes worn in his foot wrappings. Hadn't his moogie told him to always wear fresh underclothes?

Even Quark knew that was a foolish thought to have, especially at the moment in which he was drawing his last breath. His fingers scrabbled at the cable around his neck, but it was too tight and in too many layers for him to change the pressure.

Dimly through the pounding that now filled his head, Quark could hear the soldiers' laughter and hooting. Even as his vision darkened, he raged at himself for having failed to predict how quickly the end of the Occupation would come.

He had seen the signs, discussed it with his suppliers. Another month, he had concluded, perhaps two. Time enough to profit from the Cardassian soldiers being shipped out, eager to convert their Bajoran "souvenirs" to more easily transportable latinum. He had even already booked his passage on a freighter and—

—Dark stars sparkled at the rapidly shrinking edge of Quark's vision, as he mourned the deposit he had paid to Captain Yates. Just then the roar of something large approaching—something loud and silent all at the same time—swallowed the jeers of the Cardassians, and Quark felt himself fall, flooded with shock that he was not ascending to the Divine Treasury but apparently on his way to the Debtors' Dungeon. How could that be possible? He had lived a life of greed and self-absorption. How could he not be rewarded with eternal dividends? He wanted to speak to someone in charge. He wanted to renegotiate the deal. He wanted his moogie!

And then the back of the deck of the Promenade smacked into the back of his bulbous head and scrawny neck.

Through starstruck vision, he saw the glow of a phaser emitter node by his chin, felt a searing flash of heat at his neck, and then the constriction of the ODN cable was gone.

"Breathe!" a harsh voice shouted from some distant place.

"Moogie?" Quark whispered. His mother was about the only person he could think of who might have any reason at all for saving him from the Cardassians.

Then Quark was roused from his lethargy by four nerve-sparking slaps across his face.

He wheezed with an enormous intake of breath, then choked as he saw who was saving him from the Cardassians.

Another Cardassian!?

This new Cardassian, gray-skinned and cobra-necked like all the others, was someone Quark had never seen before. He wore an ordinary soldier's uniform but had the bearing and diction of an officer, perhaps even of a gul. All this Quark observed in the split second it took for the new Cardassian to haul him to his feet. As a barkeep, Quark was a firm believer in the 194th Rule, and since he couldn't always know about every new customer *before* that customer walked through the door, to protect his profits he had been required to become expert at deducing a customer's likely needs and desires from but a moment's quick observation.

This Cardassian, for instance, would order vintage *kanar,* and would always know if the Saurian brandy was watered. *An officer and a gentleman,* Quark thought admiringly. Reflexively he considered the likelihood of the Cardassian also needing wise and seasoned—and not inexpensive—investment help.

But then the gray stranger locked his free arm around Quark's neck to violently spin him around as he fired his phaser at two other Cardassian soldiers across the Promenade at the entrance to the Temple.

Quark flopped like a child's doll in the stranger's grip. He goggled in surprise as he saw the body of Glinn Datar sprawled on the deck nearby, smoke still curling up from the back of his head and adding to the blue haze that filled the Promenade. *Cardassians fighting Cardassians?* It made no sense. Especially when it seemed they were fighting over *him.*

Suddenly Quark's captor crouched down and twisted to return fire to the second level. Still held in a stranglehold, Quark squealed as with an ear-bruising thump he was whacked backside-first against the deck. Crackling phaser bursts lanced past him, blackening the Promenade's deck. The scent of burning carpet now warred with the stench of spoiled food wafting along from the ruined freezers in the Cardassian Cafe.

". . . I'm going to be sick . . ." Quark whimpered.

But clearly, the Cardassian stranger didn't hear, or didn't care.

Quark felt his gorge begin to rise. Under other circumstances, he woozily decided, he might wish he were dead rather than feel the way he felt now. But he seemed too close to that alternative already.

". . . I have a stomach neutralizer in my bar . . ." Quark mumbled hoarsely. He waved a hand vaguely in the direction of an area behind his captor. If he could just get back to his bar. . . .

But there was an abrupt lull in the phaser firefight, and the gray stranger jerked Quark to his feet. He pointed spinward toward the jewelry shop—or what was left of the jewelry shop. "That way!" he shouted. "As fast as you can!"

Protectively holding onto both of his oversize ears, Quark peered through the haze at what appeared to be other figures hiding among the debris in front of the gem store. Their silhouettes were unmistakable. *More* Cardassians.

"Could I ask a question?" Quark whispered.

The Cardassian glared at him, then shoved him down to the floor again and leaped to his feet, slamming both hands together on his phaser as he fired blast after blast at a group of Cardassians suddenly charging him from the other direction.

Quark risked looking up just long enough to see multiple shafts of disruptive energy blast his captor and send him flying across the Promenade. Alone now, Quark acted on pure instinct and did what any Ferengi would do.

He sped for his latinum, all injuries real and imagined forgotten.

Scuttling like a Ferengi banker crab, half crawling,

half running across the deck, he finally reached the door of his bar.

Quark rolled through the door and jumped to his feet once he was securely inside his own domain. "Safe!" he cried out, then cursed as his one bootless foot trod on a piece of shattered glass.

Only after digging the glass out of his sole did he think of looking over his shoulder. The scene was one of mayhem. The Promenade had become a full-fledged war zone. Phaser fire streamed back and forth like lightning in the atmosphere of a gas giant. On the one hand, Quark had no problem with Cardassians killing Cardassians. Especially since it would be a few days before he could get his bar reopened, so a few missing customers wouldn't be noticed. On the other hand, could it be possible they were killing themselves over *him?*

"Get down, you fool!"

Quark whirled around at the guttural command. He had no idea where it came from, but the rough voice was unmistakable.

"Odo?" Quark asked.

Suddenly, a humanoid hand shot out of a dark corner behind the overturned dabo table, trailing a quasitransparent golden shaft of shape-shifter flesh.

For an instant, Quark felt as if he were about to be engulfed by a Terran treefrog's tongue, then the hand slurped around his already bruised neck and snapped him into the shadows.

With the enforced assistance, Quark somersaulted to a sitting position behind a tumble of broken chairs. Automatically, his barkeep mind tabulated the potential cost of the damage. Half of them would have to be replaced, at two slips of latinum each. Three, he could see, could probably be repaired for half a slip each. He might even be able to get a deal from Morn if he could be persuaded to stay on the station. But the way Morn was always traveling around, never staying put for two days in a row—

"Quark! Get your head down!"

Instantly, Quark flattened out on the floor beside Terok Nor's shape-shifting constable. Odo's half-finished humanoid face, with its disturbingly small ears, stared ahead toward the front of the bar, as if he were expecting an attack any moment.

"How long have you been here?" Quark hissed.

"An hour. Since Gul Dukat left the station."

Quark felt a rush of indignation. If Dukat was already safely evacuated, why were all these other Cardassians still here? "You were hiding *here* when they dragged me out *there?*" he said accusingly.

Odo looked at him, nothing to hide. "Yes."

"Aren't you supposed to be the law on this station?"

"I am a duly appointed law-enforcement official."

"Doesn't that mean you're supposed to protect law-abiding citizens?"

"Your point would be?"

"They were going to kill me!"

"Yes," Odo said again.

Quark fairly vibrated with outrage as he tried to find the proper words to express his fury and sense of betrayal. "Then why didn't you try to stop them?!" he finally said, adding sarcastically, "In your capacity, that is, as a duly appointed law-enforcement official."

Odo shrugged as best he could for someone lying on his stomach among a cluster of broken bar chairs.

"A shrug?" Quark said. "That's your answer? The law doesn't apply to people like me? You're not a law-enforcement official, you're the judge and jury too, is that it?"

As usual, Odo's eerily smooth visage revealed no emotion, only the weary resignation of a teacher forced to repeat a lesson for the hundredth time. "Fifty-two hours ago, Terok Nor ceased to be a protectorate of the Bajoran Cooperative Government. Martial law was declared under the provisions of the Cardassian Uniform Code of Military Justice."

Quark waited . . . and waited . . . but Odo said nothing more, as if his most unsatisfactory explanation had been fully complete.

"And?" the Ferengi said in a state approaching apoplexy.

"Quark, I heard the charges the glinn read against you. You *have* rigged your dabo table. You *do* water your drinks. You short-time the holosuites *and* inflate the tabs you run for customers who have consumed too much alcohol to be able to keep track of their spending. Under military law, the Cardassians were within their legal rights to execute you."

Quark's mouth opened and closed silently as if the ODN cable were wrapped around his neck once more. The only words he managed to utter were, "But they were going to hang me for the *crime* of . . . of being a Ferengi!"

Odo shrugged again. "Even the Cardassians are allowed poetic license." Then Odo held a finger to his lips and nodded sharply at the main entrance to the bar.

Quark looked out to the Promenade. The firefight had stopped. It was too much to hope that both sides had killed each other. Which could only mean one side or the other had won. "I hope someone steals your bucket," he snarled at the shape-shifter.

His insolence, however justifiable, earned him a sharp jab in the ribs. Unfortunately in the very location where the brutish Cardassians had kicked him.

Then three figures stepped into the bar.

Quark recognized them at once. They were the same three he had seen silhouetted by the gem store. Which meant the loser in the fight he'd just survived had been the Cardassian who had tried to save *him*.

One of the three interlopers scanned the bar with a bulky Cardassian tricorder. It took only seconds for him to point to the mound of chairs by the overturned dabo table.

A second of the three stepped forward. "Ferengi. Constable Odo. Step into the open, hands raised."

Quark looked at Odo. The shape-shifter had the expression of an addicted tongo player calculating the odds of calling a successful roll.

"Step out now," the Cardassian threatened, "and you will have a chance to live. Remain where you are, and you will certainly die."

"I'm convinced," Quark said and pushed himself to his feet, in spite of Odo's accusatory glare.

He frowned at the angry shape-shifter. "Oh, turn yourself into a broken chair or something." Then he stepped forward, hands stretched overhead, wincing as his torn jacket sleeve momentarily brushed his injured earlobe.

As Quark limped heavily toward the three Cardassians, he actually heard Odo step out from cover behind him. But then his attention was diverted by another surprising observation that had escaped him on first seeing the three strangers: These Cardassians weren't in uniforms. They were civilians. Three young males clothed in drab shades of blue, brown, and gray, without even the identity pins that might establish them as members of the Occupation bureaucracy or diplomatic corps. Two of them, though—the ones in blue and brown—carried military-issue phase-disruptor pistols, the housing of each weapon segmented like the abdomen of a golden beetle. *What is it about Cardassians and bugs?* Quark wondered. If he could just understand that about them, he'd know exactly what would tempt them to buy, and he'd corner yet another market missed by others.

But then Quark's soothing thoughts of profit were displaced by alarm as the gray-clad Cardassian shoved his tricorder like a weapon in the barkeep's face. This particular Cardassian was distinct from the others because he was bald. Quark had never seen a bald Cardassian before. In some ways, the sleekness of the Cardassian's skull made the alien look more intelligent. Except, of course, for his pathetically small ears. Not to mention the two secondary spinal cords running up the sides of his wide and flattened neck like cables on a suspension bridge. And the spoon-shaped flap of gray flesh on his forehead that made him look like a—

The light from the tricorder's small screen flashed a different set of colors across the bald Cardassian's face. "This Ferengi's Quark."

The Cardassian in the blue tunic gestured at Quark with his phaser. Quark noticed that his overgarment was torn at the shoulder and smudged with black soot, as if its wearer had ripped it on burning debris. "There are two other Ferengi on the station."

The Cardassian in blue didn't have to ask the obvious question for Quark to decide to answer it. There was no profit in withholding information for which they could easily torture him. "My brother and nephew. They left on a shuttle as soon as we heard what was happening on Bajor." Quark was confident he could carry off the lie. He had been dealing with the Cardassians—and the gelatinous Odo—long enough to have developed a reasonably effective tongo face.

The Cardassian in the torn blue tunic stared at Quark a few moments longer, as if he expected the Ferengi to suddenly break down and confess the real whereabouts of Rom and Nog. But since Quark had no actual knowledge of where his cowardly brother and confused nephew were at this precise moment, it was doubly easy to stare back with an expression of total innocence.

At last, his interrogator turned to the bald Cardassian with the tricorder. "What setting do we need to kill the shape-shifter?"

Quark stared hard at Odo beside him. *Let's see how you like it,* he thought peevishly.

But maddening as ever, Odo simply stared impassively at the three Cardassians, betraying not even a hint of emotion. The shape-shifter was as annoying, in his way, as a Vulcan.

"Wait." It was the third Cardassian who intervened now. The one in the brown tunic, so blatantly new it still bore the creases from having been folded on some display shelf, probably in Garak's tailor shop. This Cardassian was certainly not bald. His long black hair was drawn back in the same style as some soldiers Quark had seen. The new civilian clothes could mean he was a spy, but they could also mean he was a coward. Which one, however, Quark couldn't yet be sure. But because the brown-suited Cardassian didn't seem eager to kill Odo, Quark was leaning toward the latter.

"Can you take on the appearance of a Ferengi?" the

Cardassian in the suspiciously new civilian clothing asked Odo.

Odo frowned. "If I had to."

Quark scowled at the constable. From the way the shape-shifter answered, it was obvious he'd rather change himself into a mound of garbage before he'd become a Ferengi.

"Would that work?" The question came from the Cardassian in the torn blue tunic, and was addressed to the bald Cardassian with the tricorder.

"We only have one Ferengi. If we need a backup. . . ."

"All right. We won't kill you. Yet." The imperious pronouncement from the Cardassian in blue made Quark think for the first time that the group had a leader. Whatever that information was worth.

"How generous of you," Odo replied with ill-concealed sarcasm.

Responding immediately, the Cardassian leader slashed his phaser across Odo's face as if to teach him a lesson in obedience.

Though Quark had seen it before, he still cringed as Odo's face rippled into a honey-like jelly at the moment of impact, allowing the phaser to slip through his mutable flesh as if passing through smoke.

An instant later, Odo's humanoid face had reformed, his expression still one of vague disinterest.

The Cardassian bared his teeth like a Klingon, as if he were about to attack Odo again and this time with more than a single blow. But the bald Cardassian put his hand on the attacker's shoulder. "We can't keep her waiting," he said.

Her? Quark thought. Now that *was* something new.

Perhaps there was *another* leader. But who? And for what reason?

The Cardassian in brown gestured harshly with his phaser. "Turbolift 5's still working."

This time it was Odo who made the first move. He started forward, onto the Promenade, and Quark followed gingerly—with each step he could feel another sliver of glass he'd missed get driven deeper into his exposed foot. "Could I just get my boot?" he asked plaintively.

"Only if you want to die," the bald Cardassian growled.

Quark sighed heavily and gritted his teeth, stepping carefully around the sprawled bodies of the fallen Cardassian soldiers. "Interesting negotiating technique you've got there," he muttered.

"Faster," was the bald Cardassian's only reply.

Quark picked up his pace and followed Odo into the haze.

After they had passed a few empty shopfronts, Quark realized what was different about the Promenade. "Does it seem quiet to you?" he whispered to Odo.

Odo sighed. "Yes, Quark. *Too* quiet."

Quark snorted as he recognized the line Odo had quoted. "And I thought you didn't like holosuite programs."

"The next one of you who talks dies," a Cardassian snarled from behind them.

This time, Odo smiled nastily at Quark as if to say, Please continue. But Quark walked on in dignified silence.

As they stepped cautiously over the torn-down and sparking security gate leading to the Bajoran half of the station, Quark looked up to see a fourth Cardassian, also in civilian clothes, crouching on the second level. For an instant, their eyes met. It was Garak.

Quark was just about to call out Garak's name when he remembered the Cardassians' two phasers and the order he and Odo had just been given.

But the bald Cardassian had already noticed where he was looking, and now glanced up at the second level as well. Quark held his breath, but the bald Cardassian looked away, having seen no one. Garak had obviously jumped back, out of view.

Quark wasted no time trying to figure out why. No one had any reasonable explanation for why the Cardassians were leaving Bajor after sixty years of the Occupation. They were aliens, so in Quark's view—in the sensible, practical Ferengi view of things—they were obviously going to behave like aliens. As they should be allowed to do. Provided they paid their bills, of course. Alien or not, some laws were universal.

Turbolift 5 was on the Promenade's inner ring, just across from the small Bajoran Infirmary. Though the door to the Infirmary was open, Quark could see there was no sign of damage within. And why would there be? There had never been anything of value in it. All the medical supplies that came aboard Terok Nor were destined for the fully equipped Cardassian Infirmary across from his bar. The Bajoran Infirmary might just as well have been a barber shop for all the medicine that was allowed to be practiced in it.

Against all logic, the turbolift car arrived. Another event that made no sense to Quark. All the main lights on the Promenade were out. Only emergency glow panels were operating. And virtually all other equipment, from automatic firefighting systems to station communicators and the replicators were off-line. But not, it seemed, Turbolift 5.

The bald Cardassian scanned the waiting car with his tricorder, then stepped inside. The leader in the torn blue tunic waved Quark and Odo in without speaking.

Quark looked out at the Promenade as the lift doors closed. For a moment, he saw Garak again, huddled behind the rolling door of the disabled security gate across the main floor. At least, the figure had looked like Garak. But what would Garak have put on a uniform for . . . ? Quark couldn't identify the tailor's military-style outfit, other than that he knew it wasn't Cardassian.

Quark looked to Odo to silently inquire if the shape-shifter had seen Garak, but Odo was still pointedly ignoring him.

Quark decided he could play that game every bit as well as Odo, and looked straight ahead as the lift descended. The movement felt unusually rough, as if the power grids were under strain. Quark tried his utmost not to think about that. The last thing he wanted was to be trapped in a turbolift with three surly Cardassians. Unlike Odo, he couldn't count on conveniently escaping by liquefying and slurping out between the doors. . . .

Quark took another look at Odo as a sudden thought struck him. Why *was* the shape-shifter still here? He himself was trapped, of that there was no question. But Odo had already had at least a dozen opportunities to make his escape.

As Quark pondered the shape-shifter's motives, that portion of his brain that constantly counted and calculated registered that they had descended precisely ten levels. Almost unconsciously, Quark braced for the turbolift car's change of direction as it would begin to move laterally along one of the station's spokes.

But the direction didn't change. The car kept descending past the level of the docking ring.

Quark began to feel again the clammy touch of panic. Up till now, he had been operating under the assumption that there was something these three Cardassians—and *she,* whoever *she* was—wanted him to do. The fact that they wanted anything at all meant, reassuringly, that he was in the middle of a business transaction. And when it came to business, Quark knew he was definitely fighting on home soil.

But now, once again, he was heading into unknown territory. As far as he knew, the lower core of the station was the site of the fusion reactors, the power transfer manifolds and basic utilities, and its few residence levels were little more than prison cells for Bajoran ore workers. It was a realm for engineers, not business people. Even worse, he was not aware of *any* docking ports off the lower levels. The only way out of the lower core would be back up through the turbolift shafts.

Or through an emergency airlock, he thought queasily.

Quark moaned as he realized the trap he was entering. Then moaned again when he realized he had been so thrown off-balance by the lift car's continued descent that he had actually lost count of the levels they had passed. And every fool knew that a Ferengi who lost count had lost everything.

The two phaser-armed Cardassians continued to stare at him, their weapons held loosely at their sides as if daring him to break the rules and talk. But, finally, Turbolift 5 reached its destination.

The stop was so sudden, Quark felt the car rise back up a few centimeters as if it had overshot the desired deck. Then the doors opened.

The level beyond the open doors was so dark, it looked to Quark like the void of space itself.

But the Cardassian leader in the torn blue tunic pushed him forward anyway, and Odo at his side, even before a welcome pool of light from a palm torch sprang to life ahead of them.

"Straight ahead," the Cardassian leader ordered.

Quark limped on, as told. Adding to his resentful discomfort now was the fact that the deck plates on this lower level weren't covered by any type of carpet. They were just bare hull metal as far as he could tell. And since the station's lower core was terraced like a towering cake built upside down, Quark realized with a sinking feeling it was entirely possible that boundless space was really only a few centimeters below his feet.

But then, why are the deck plates so hot? he wondered.

He decided he absolutely hated Terok Nor. He'd be glad to leave it.

Alive, he added quickly, in case the Blessed Exchequer or any of his Exalted Tellers happened to be listening in.

The long, curving corridor on this level was narrower than others on the station. The ceiling lower. And except for a pale patch of light which Quark was just now beginning to perceive ahead, it seemed that none of the emergency glowpanels was functioning down here.

The spot of light from the palm torch kept skittering ahead, leading the way. On either side it was too gloomy for Quark to make out the Cardassian directional and warning signs on the bulkheads, but every few meters he passed an inner door. Some of these were open, with total darkness beyond.

If I *were Odo,* Quark thought darkly, *I'd be through one of those doors so fast the light from the palm torch couldn't catch me.*

But most inexplicably, the shape-shifter remained at Quark's side, even letting the Ferengi's injured foot set the pace.

Finally, just as Quark feared he would fall to the floor in exhaustion, the Cardassian leader ordered them to turn right at the next intersection. It was a *cul-de-sac,* where Quark would normally expect to find a turbolift. But instead, he halted before three more Cardassians, all females this time. Two were in soldier's armor, crisp, unmarked, the composite surfaces gleaming in the way Quark had come to recognize only the most elite Cardassian units were able to maintain. And despite the cold level of threat the two uniformed females presented, there was no doubt in Quark as to which female his three captors served.

She was the one in the middle, the only one in a matte-black civilian outfit that clung, Quark appreciatively noted, to the ridges of her spinal cords like a second skin.

"This is the only Ferengi on the station." Surprisingly, it was not the Cardassian in the torn blue tunic who was the first to address the female. It was the bald Cardassian with the tricorder. But in any case, Quark knew they were now in the presence of the real leader of the entire group, male and female—*She.*

The female leader studied Quark as if he were livestock at an auction. Quark straightened up, smirking engagingly, but her widely spaced dark eyes turned to Odo. "Why is that here?"

The bald Cardassian's reply was instant. "I thought we could use him as a backup. He can take on the shape of a Ferengi."

Quark's evaluation of the female shot up in value with her skeptical response. "But can he take on the *brain* of a Ferengi?"

"Terrell," the bald Cardassian said deferentially, "with respect, we are running out of options. Dukat has left. The station will be under Bajoran control in hours."

Terrell frowned as she hunted for something in the engineer's case she wore at the side of her wide belt. "Unlikely. In fifty-three minutes, the station will be a debris field and navigational hazard. Dukat activated the self-destruct." She removed a palm phaser and without a moment's pause shot Odo.

The constable grunted and slumped to his knees, gasping painfully for breath. But to Quark's intense relief, Odo was only lightly stunned.

Terrell lowered her palm phaser and glared at the bald Cardassian. "Atrig, that thing is a *shape-shifter.* It could have escaped you whenever it chose. The fact that it didn't, suggests it was spying on us."

The bald Cardassian's reaction to his leader's admonition was most revealing to Quark. It was definitely not that of a soldier. The Cardassian in the gray tunic merely clenched his teeth, glanced down, embarrassed more than anything else. Definitely not the response of a soldier. Quark's fuschia-rimmed eyes narrowed in speculation. If these two had come into his bar as customers, Quark would have instantly concluded that Atrig, Terrell's bald subordinate, was desperately in love with his superior, while Terrell considered Atrig as nothing more than a useful tool she might carry in her case.

"Of course," the bald Cardassian said, in almost a whisper, his head still respectfully lowered.

Terrell dropped the small phaser back into her case. "Just see you keep it stunned in case we do need it." Then she turned her attention to Quark. "*You* will perform a service for the Cardassian Union. If you succeed, you will have time to reach an escape pod before the station self-destructs. If you fail. . . ." Her smile was cruel.

Quark looked questioningly at Atrig. Atrig understood. "Now you can talk."

"What kind of service?" Quark demanded. *Let the negotiations begin,* he thought.

"A simple one." Terrell turned her back to him and faced a blank bulkhead. Though he couldn't see exactly what she was doing, Quark could tell she was operating some kind of small device, for the bulkhead began to move to one side, revealing an extension of the corridor.

Quark's first reaction was one of true surprise. His second was of true apprehension. Over the years he had mapped every hidden section of the station, to establish his network of smugglers' tunnels—but here was a corridor extension completely unknown to him. And beyond it, there was a light source, about ten meters past the bulkhead.

Quirk squinted at the light. It appeared to be emanating from a door whose center glowed pale pink.

"What's in there?" Quark asked nervously.

Terrell turned back to him. "Nothing for a Ferengi to fear." Then she nodded, and Quark felt himself pushed forward, toward the light, a phaser jammed between his shoulder blades.

Halfway to the door, he heard a sudden commotion behind him, then phaser fire. *Odo.* The constable must have tried to make his escape, and not been fast enough.

Quark chanced glancing over his shoulder and did a relieved double take. Odo was still staggering along behind him, supported by the Cardassian in the torn blue tunic.

But now the two armor-clad female Cardassians held a third stunned captive.

Garak.

The Cardassian tailor was no longer in the strange uniform Quark had been unable to identify, but was back in his usual civilian garb. Quark didn't stop to question the change. He had always suspected that Garak wasn't the plain, simple tailor he made himself out to be. All Cardassians were masters of conspiracy, duplicity, and deviousness. The only remaining mystery for Quark was how the contentious aliens had managed to occupy Bajor as a cohesive force for as long as they had.

Atrig grabbed Quark's shoulder, forcing him to a stop three meters from the glowing door.

Correction, Quark thought. The door wasn't just glowing. It was *pulsating.* The effect was difficult to define precisely, but to Quark it seemed as if the door alternately bulged out and relaxed in, as if it were the flank of some large creature slowly breathing. The glow intensified with each intake of breath, changing from rose-pink to dark red, and Quark saw now that the light it created wasn't uniform. Instead, the vertical surface rippled outward, like a rock-disturbed pool of water standing on its side.

But that shimmering surface wasn't liquid, Quark knew. It was a solid layer protecting those on the outside from something that these six Cardassians didn't want to face—or *couldn't.*

Yet for some reason, they believed a Ferengi could.

But why? Quark thought, even now still trying to find an angle to exploit. If whatever was causing the door to ripple and glow was some deadly form of radiation, the Cardassians could have captured anyone to . . . to do whatever it was they wanted done. It was a well-known fact to everyone on the station that no Cardassian officer would hesitate to order a fellow Cardassian soldier to face death.

So why do they need a Ferengi? And only a Ferengi?

"Garak," Terrell said with sarcastic condescension. "I don't know which surprises me more. That you haven't left the station already. Or that Dukat left you alive."

Quark looked back to see Terrell standing before Garak. The tailor's sagging body was held upright by the two female soldiers, each holding an arm. Garak shook his head as if to clear it.

"I was merely trying to warn you," the tailor said faintly. "I believe that Gul Dukat may have failed to inform you that for some reason the station's self-destruct system has been inadvertently activated. You should leave as quickly as possible."

Terrell patted the tailor's cheek. "Why, Garak, how noble of you."

"Terrell, my dear, given all that we mean to each other, I feel I owe it to you."

Interesting, Quark thought.

"And I owe you. So much."

Quark shivered at the unpleasant edge to Terrell's cool voice.

Garak merely nodded as he glanced at the glowing door. In the rose-colored light, his gray Cardassian skin took on an almost sickening, raw-meat color. "Well, I can see you're busy. So I'll be on my way."

"You'll leave with me, Garak. Interrogating you will help pass the time on the way back home." Now Terrell's voice was openly menacing.

Garak's careful civility gave way to cold rage. "You know I cannot go back to Cardassia."

"I do know," Terrell said. "That's why I'll execute you myself before we arrive." Then she turned toward the glowing door, her back to the Cardassian tailor as if he no longer existed.

Quark's eyes followed her movement to the door. He alone of the observers gasped at the change. It was as if Terrell now faced a vortex of glowing magma, blazing with light, yet producing no heat. Pulsating coils of red light snaked out from the rapidly deforming surface of the door. Some tendrils seemed almost ready to break free of the surface, as if whatever lay beyond was increasing its efforts to escape confinement.

Quark felt himself pushed forward again by the bald Cardassian.

"Terrell," Quark squeaked, his voice breaking in its urgency. "I'm going to need some information." More than anything else, he longed to run home. But he knew that wasn't possible. Perhaps he'd never see Ferenginar again. "What in the name of all that's profitable is in there?"

"A lab," Terrell said tersely. "What you're seeing is merely a holographic illusion. A new type of holosuite technology."

Quark couldn't be certain of the truth. He couldn't see any holoemitters in this hidden section of corridor. But then, they could be installed behind the illusion. Maybe—

Don't be a fool, Quark told himself.

Whatever was responsible for the phenomenon before him, it wasn't an illusion, and it *was* dangerous. There was no other reason for him to be here.

"So what do I have to do?" Quark asked.

"Go into the lab—"

Quark couldn't help himself. *"Through that thing?! You're crazy!"* He flinched as Atrig shoved a phaser into his back. "My mistake," he croaked.

"We will open the door," Terrell continued. "You will go inside the lab, ignoring everything you hear, everything you see, except for the main lab console on the far wall."

"Everything I *hear?"* Quark asked, his voice trailing off as his imagination got the best of him.

Terrell ignored his apprehension. "On the main console, you'll see a . . . power unit. A . . . type of power crystal. Sixty-eight centimeters tall. Twenty-five wide at its top and bottom. Spindle-shaped. You can't miss it."

The corridor fell into momentary darkness as the door heaved inward.

"And you want me to bring it out," Quark said weakly.

Terrell nodded at him. "Very perceptive. It's in an open housing. Simply disconnect two power leads to detach it from the console, then carry the crystal out. As soon as you do . . . you'll be free to go."

Her very unconvincing smile confirmed the situation for Quark. He instantly knew that if he did succeed in retrieving the crystal from the lab, a minute later he'd be as dead as if he were still dangling at the end of an ODN cable on the Promenade.

Quark's agile mind raced to identify the loopholes in this transaction.

But he had run out of time.

"Open the door," Terrell ordered.

At once, the Cardassian with the torn blue tunic moved to place himself alongside the pulsating door, one arm stretched out before him. With one trembling hand, Quark shielded his eyes from the increasing red glare to see what the Cardassian was trying to do.

At the edge of distortion effect, Quark saw a door control. The Cardassian in blue touched it gingerly.

Incredibly, the door seemed to melt to one side, and Quark squinted as the light level reached an almost painful intensity.

"—YES—"

Startled, Quark looked around, trying to see who had just cried out.

It was Odo.

"YES! YES, I UNDERSTAND!" Odo shouted. He struggled in the grip of the Cardassian in the new brown tunic, the Cardassian who Quark suspected was either a soldier, a coward, a spy. *"I WILL—"* Odo screamed. Then the shape-shifter began to reach out his arms, stretching away from his captor toward the blood red light of the lab.

"Stop him!" Terrell commanded.

Instantly, Atrig stunned Odo again and the shape-shifter slumped, as his semiconscious body slowly assumed its humanoid shape once more.

"What happened?" Quark demanded.

"You didn't hear them?" Terrell asked in return. "The voices calling?"

"What voices?"

Terrell's face blazed with reflected crimson light. "You'll do fine," she said. "Go! Now!"

Pushed relentlessly forward by Atrig, Quark swayed before the open doorway. He could see nothing in the lab except a swirl of light, a whirlpool of luminescence.

"Hurry!" Terrell shouted.

And then the light swirls fragmented before Quark, becoming writhing tendrils that seemed to reach out for him and—

"TERRELL!"

This time the outcry came from Atrig, as the bald Cardassian leaped through the air to meet the coil of light heading directly for the woman he loved. The light hit Atrig square in the back, hurling him across the corridor as if a battering ram had struck him.

Atrig's limp form crumpled to the deck, a glowing patch of carmine light flickering over him.

Quark ducked as two more tentacles of flame-red energy snapped out from the doorway. Beneath the crackle of their passage, he heard hideous screams. Saw the Cardassian in blue and the other in brown lifted up from the deck, wrapped in red light.

Their cries became muffled as the scarlet glow spread over them, flowing around them like a hungry wave. Then, horribly, slowly, their wildly flailing arms and legs ceased their struggle, as if the light itself were somehow thick and resistant.

Forgetting for a moment that Atrig no longer was behind him to prevent his escape, Quark stared at the faces of the two trapped Cardassians. Their gaping mouths were stretched in soundless wails. And then, like a plasma whip being cracked, the two were sucked back into the vortex of light, disappearing in an instant.

Odo—now held by no one—knelt on the deck and looked back at the light. Quark could see him silently mouth a single word, over and over—*Yes . . . yes . . . yes. . . .*

The two female soldiers still held on to Garak, showing no fear, but clearly ready to leave as soon as they were ordered.

Quark turned to flee, but Terrell blocked his way. Her palm phaser was aimed directly at his head. "*Hurry!*"

Quark stared at Terrell. It was madness to do what she wanted. It was guaranteed suicide. But as much as he hated to admit it, if he didn't do as she ordered, then that fool Odo would be on his feet and stumbling forward in Quark's place, into something that for some unknown reason the Cardassians believed only a Ferengi could survive.

Quark told himself it wasn't respect he felt for Odo. It was just that after so many years of being adversaries, he knew how the shape-shifter thought, knew his strategies. And most importantly, Quark thought, he knew how much *he* could get away with. And for some inexplicable reason, the shape-shifter had stayed at his side all the way from the Promenade, when he could have escaped and left Quark to his fate—alone.

Quark's chest swelled out as he drew in a deep breath. As the old Ferengi saying had it, Better the Auditor you know, than the Auditor you don't. *Sometimes,* he told himself, *you just have to sign the contract you negotiated.*

"Now!" Terrell ordered.

Quark released his breath in a mighty sigh, covered his head with his arms, and ran straight through the doorway into the blinding red light and—

—his cut and bleeding foot suddenly sank into a soft sludge of cooling mud.

It was raining. A soft mist, really.

Quark stood completely still, eyes tightly shut.

The air was sweetly perfumed with the fetid rot of a swamp.

The swamp.

Quark lowered his arms from his head. Opened one eye. Then the other. And then he gasped as through the dark silhouettes of reaching branches and hanging moss, he saw the soft and welcoming lights of the Ferenginar capital city shining through the distance and the dark of night.

"Home . . ." he cried, delighting in the magical way the word created a delicate puff of mist before him.

But Quark was no believer in magic. He needed to know how it was he could see his breath as a delicate puff of mist. There had to be another source of light nearby.

He looked around trying to figure out where the lab had gone, where Terok Nor had gone, if he had finally died.

But all questions were erased as he saw a sparkle of blue-white brilliance approaching through the swamp trees, as if a living diamond were floating toward him.

Quark was completely overcome by the beauty of the spectacle. He stood transfixed until . . .

"Quark? Is that you, son?"

Quark's mouth dropped open in incredulity. "Moogie?"

"Over here, Quark. . . ."

Quark shifted in the mud of his homeworld, and suddenly the glittering diamond was before him, held in his beloved mother's arms.

"Why didn't you tell me you were coming home," Quark's mother said crankily. "I would have made your favorite *mooshk.*"

Quark's mouth watered at the intense memory of his moogie's *mooshk.* And to see her right now, glowing as if she were a part of the crystal she held, her completely unclothed skin faceted with light.

"So the only thing I have to give you is *this,*" Quark's mother said. She held out the glittering jewel to him, until it seemed to float by itself, a shining, hourglass-shaped orb of promise and hope and everything anyone could ever want. "Go ahead, Quark. Take it. . . ."

Quark reached for the orb like a child reaching for a toy. Everything was going to be perfect now.

But as his hands closed on the object his mother was giving him, one tiny nagging thought came to him.

Small. Subtle. Barely worth mentioning.

Something that might only occur to a Ferengi.

"Moogie," Quark said. "Can I ask you a question?"

And as Quark's mother began her transformation, Quark shrieked louder than any Ferengi had ever shrieked, as he saw—

CHAPTER 2

—STARS FLASHED before Quark's eyes, and he slapped his hand to his expansive forehead, grimacing with pain.

"Who designed this *frinxing* bed . . ." he muttered, as he swung his feet over the edge of the narrow Cardassian sleeping ledge and tried once more to sit up, this time without banging his head on the underside of a utility shelf.

Then he looked around at the stark holding cell in Deep Space 9's Security Office and answered his own question.

"Cardassians. Ha!"

Quark had had it with Cardassians. In fact, even though the Cardassian Occupation had ended six long years ago, Quark had had it with this station. "Deep Space 9, Terok Nor . . . Federation bureaucrats, Cardassian secret police. . . . What's the difference? I ask you. . . ."

He stood in front of the holding cell's forcefield and checked to make certain the Security Office beyond was still empty. Though the lighting levels were low, set for DS9's night, the main door was still sealed and Quark remained safely alone. He cleared his throat. "Computer: Release the prisoner."

The security screen flashed with silver scintillations, then shut down. At least, it appeared to shut down. Quark wasn't a Ferengi to take anything for granted. He carefully flicked a finger toward the boundary of the forcefield, until he was certain the screen was off. Only then did he step over the lip of the cell doorway.

Quark trudged across the deck in his nightclothes, scratching where it itched. He came to the replicator, smacked his lips, then punched in his prisoner code for a cup of millipede juice, hold the shells. The cup appeared and Quark gulped the pale green bug squeezings down, looking around to check that he was still—

"Bzzzt—you're dead," Odo said, only one meter behind him.

Quark choked, then sprayed a mouthful of millipede juice, forcing Odo to step back out of range.

"Don't *do* that!" Quark sputtered indignantly, wiping bug juice off his sleep shirt.

Odo shook his head, not impressed. "Would you rather the Andorian sisters did that?"

Quark jammed the cup back into the replicator for recycling. "You're supposed to be protecting me. That's what this is, remember?" Quark waved his hands to include the entire security office. "Protective custody."

Odo pointed to the holding cell. "In there. Behind a forcefield. That's protective custody. Out here, you're fair game."

Quark rubbed at his temples, not knowing where the pain of his impact with the shelf left off, and his tension headache began. Twenty meters away, just across the Promenade, his bar was in the hands of Rom. *Engineer* Rom. Turned-his-back-on-everything-Ferengi, work-for-free, use-a-padd-to-total-all-bills, good-for-nothing *Rom.*

"Are you all right?" Odo asked.

"Do you care?"

Odo crossed his arms. "Not particularly."

Quark muttered a partially satisfying Ferengi epithet under his breath and looked around for a padd.

"Now what?" Odo asked

"I need something to read. Rom's driving me into bankruptcy and there's no way I can sleep."

"Actually, the bar has seldom been busier."

In a sudden wave of apprehension, Quark grabbed Odo's tunic. "He's cut prices, hasn't he? Go ahead, I can take it."

Odo firmly removed Quark's hands from his chest. "Rom is treating the customers fairly. Word must have gotten out, and so business is up. You should be happy."

Quark couldn't believe the foul language Odo was capable of using. " 'Fairly.' I'm . . . I'm ruined. I . . ." And then Quark could see no other way out. "All right, that's it. Protective custody is over. Thank you. I'm going to my—"

Odo didn't let him finish. And didn't let him leave. "It's not that simple, Quark."

Quark had been battling Odo for more than a decade. He knew what that tone meant. "What do you mean, not that simple? Being in here was my idea."

"It *was* your idea. Now, I'm afraid, it's mine."

Quark rocked back on his bare feet, studying Odo more closely in the dim light. "You *are* worried about me. I'm touched. But, I'm also running behind, so—"

Odo didn't move from Quark's path. "Please return to your cell."

Quark laughed derisively, smiled broadly. "Odo . . . you almost make it seem as if you're putting me under arrest."

Odo said nothing. He didn't have to.

"You can't be serious," Quark said. He knew his earlobes were flushing telltale red. "No, I take that back. You're always serious. What I meant was, you're joking. No, you don't do that either. But what you *do* do is . . ." Quark's throat tightened. He couldn't bring himself to say the words.

Odo could. "Put people under arrest."

"For *what?!*" Quark demanded. His face creased in a disbelieving grin as he said the most outrageous thing he could think of. *"Murder?"*

But Odo's silence and unchanging expression made the grin fade.

Quark's head throbbed unbearably. "Odo, you know me. How many times do I have to say it? I did not kill Dal Nortron."

"That's right. I do know you, Quark. Which is why I don't believe that you planned and carried out the premeditated cold-blooded murder of your Andorian business partner."

Quark sagged with relief. "Well, at least we can . . ." He looked up at Odo with sudden fear. " 'Business partner'?"

"Did you honestly think you could keep it from me?"

"The Andorian sisters did it! *They* killed him!"

"And they say that *you* killed him. Imagine that."

"So you're arresting *me* on *their* word but you're not arresting *them* on *mine?!*"

Odo uncrossed his arms and shook his head. "Quark, we've been over this. If I arrest Satr and Leen while they are on DS9 as representatives of the Andorian government, they will file a diplomatic protest, I will have to release them, and I guarantee they will leave the station and my jurisdiction within the hour."

"Sure! Right! So that's why they can walk around the station free as a greeworm while I'm in here—"

"Where they can't get you."

"No!" Quark exploded. "Where *I* am under *arrest!*"

Odo looked away as if preparing to leave. Quark knew that was how the changeling preferred to solve most of his problems. By avoiding confrontation.

But then, Odo looked back at Quark, and there was almost an air of sorrow about him. "Quark, listen carefully. This time, you are in serious trouble. Two nights ago, Dal Nortron won a considerable amount of latinum from you."

"It happens, Odo," Quark said tightly. "That's why they call it gambling."

But Odo did not allow himself to be interrupted. "Two hours later, Dal Nortron died—"

"Of unknown causes!"

"Under mysterious circumstances. The latinum—gone."

"Odo, think about it. How long would I stay in business if I started killing everyone who won at my dabo table? Are you kidding? I give the winners presents! I give them unlimited holosuite sessions—even *free drinks!"* Quark shuddered at the thought of it. "I do whatever I can to get them to return to that table so I can win my latinum back. I don't kill customers!"

"Satr and Leen say you had an argument with Nortron."

Quark glared at the changeling. "I have arguments with you. And I haven't killed you. Yet."

"Quark—pay attention! If I hadn't put you in protective custody, the Andorians would have killed you for revenge. They see justice in rather more simplistic terms than I do."

Now the sorrow was Quark's, as well. "Justice? So you do think I'm a murderer."

Odo reluctantly confirmed Quark's conclusion. "There is the matter of Kozak—"

"Kozak?! That was almost four years ago. *And* it was an accident!"

"Exactly," Odo agreed. "As I said, I do not believe you *planned* to kill Dal Nortron. But accidents do happen. Especially in the heat of an argument between business partners."

Quark swung his hand at Odo as if trying to clear the air. "Why don't you just string me up on the Promenade and be—" He stopped speaking, suddenly overwhelmed by a powerful sense of *déjà vu.*

A few moments of Quark staring blankly into space was apparently all Odo could take. "Quark—?"

"I was . . . having a dream. Just before I woke up. Hit my head." Quark rubbed at his forehead again. The pain seemed diminished. He let his fingers trail to his throat and ran them lightly across his larynx, as if expecting to find rope burns there. "They were hanging me. . . ."

Odo frowned. "Guilty conscience?" Quark knew he'd get nowhere arguing this any longer with Odo. He started back for his cell.

"We still have a few things to discuss," Odo said. "I

will need to know the details of your . . . 'business arrangement' with Dal Nortron."

Quark stepped over the lip of the cell. "Talk to my lawyer."

"You don't have a lawyer."

Quark shrugged. "Then I guess we have nothing to discuss until I do get one. Computer: Restore security field."

The air between Quark and Odo flashed with silver sparkles.

"Quark, don't make this more difficult than it has to be."

But by this point, Quark didn't care about making anything easier, especially not for Odo. "When is Captain Sisko back?"

"Tomorrow afternoon. If they don't run into any Jem'Hadar patrols." Odo's stern attitude softened. "That captain they were trying to rescue . . . she was dead."

"I suppose you think I killed her."

"She had been dead for three years. Apparently, an energy field around the planet she'd crashed on shifted the subspace signals through time."

"Odo, let's get our priorities straight. What does any of this have to do with me?"

"Please forgive me," Odo said icily. "I forgot with whom I was dealing. Pleasant dreams, Quark."

Odo turned like a soldier on parade and marched toward his office.

He had just reached the doorway when Quark called out to him. "Odo, wait."

Odo stopped, but didn't look back.

"Can I ask you something?"

Odo looked over his shoulder. "You can *ask.*"

Quark held his hand to his throat again, trying to recapture the elusive threads of his half-forgotten dream. "Those last few days on the station . . ."

"What last few days?"

"The end of the Occupation. When the Cardassians withdrew."

"What about them?"

"The Cardassians never liked me."

Odo turned back to face Quark. "Can you blame them?"

Quark struggled to find the words for what he knew he had to ask. "They destroyed so many things on the station . . . four Bajorans dead . . ."

"Your point, Quark?"

"Why didn't they kill *me?* I mean, that's what happens when governments fall. People like me are lined up and . . ."

"Shot?"

Quark saw an image of Ferenginar's capital city. He was there, doing something important in . . . in a swamp? "Hung," Quark said quietly. "Strung up on . . . on the Promenade . . . ?"

"Sounds almost . . . poetic," Odo said.

Quark stared at Odo, saw the glimmer of recognition in the changeling's eyes. "You've said that before. Or something like that. I can see it. I can remember it."

And then something went dark in Odo. "I don't know what you're talking about."

"Yes, you do," Quark said.

"I'll tell Rom you want a lawyer. When you're willing to talk about your business arrangement with Dal Nortron, we can talk again." Odo turned to leave.

"Where were you on the Day of Withdrawal?"

Quark called after him. "You answer that and I'll tell you *everything* about Dal Nortron!"

Quark saw Odo hesitate. "Come on, Odo, admit it. There's only one way you can resist an offer like that."

The hesitation ended. Without another word, Odo disappeared through the doorway to his office. He *had* resisted.

And to Quark, that could mean only one thing.

Odo didn't remember what had happened to him on the Day of Withdrawal, any more than Quark did. . . .

CHAPTER 3

LIEUTENANT COMMANDER Jadzia Dax stood on the deck of the *Starship Enterprise* with her back to the captain's chair. Because it was the first *Enterprise,* there was only one direction from which the final attack could come.

The turbolift.

Five minutes ago, when she had hurriedly studied the ship's schematics on the desktop viewer in the briefing room, she had found it difficult to believe that the most critical command center on the entire ship was serviced by only one lift. But in the memories of her third host, Emony, she found the explanation. The more than century-old *Constitution*-class to which the original *Enterprise* belonged had been designed primarily as a vessel of scientific exploration. The engineers of the twenty-fourth century might perceive its design idiosyncrasies, such as a single turbolift serving the bridge or fixed-phaser emitters, as design flaws. Dax's third host, however, considered such features to be the last echoes of the twenty-second century's charmingly naïve optimism toward space travel, inspired by the end of the Romulan Wars and the resulting birth of the Federation a mere two years later.

As a joined Trill possessing the memories of eight lifetimes, more or less spanning the past two centuries, Jadzia Dax understood she was more attuned than most beings to the similarities of every age. And the truth was that while technology might change, human hearts and minds seldom did. It definitely wasn't the case that life was simpler or human nature less sophisticated in the past.

But in the case of this ship, Jadzia couldn't help thinking, *the designers were behind the curve. They really should have known better.* After all, the first *Enterprise* had been launched a full twenty-seven years after the first contact with the Klingon Empire, a disastrous meeting that clearly proved that not everyone in the quadrant shared the Federation's belief in coexistence. And right now, the proof of that was about to face her in a life-or-death confrontation.

Jadzia heard the distant rush of a turbolift car approaching the bridge. She hefted the sword in her hand and with one quick step vaulted over the stairs to the upper deck of the bridge. She reflexively tugged down on the ridiculously short skirt of her blue sciences uniform, changing her balance to be prepared to spring forward the instant the doors opened. *If,* that is, she *could* spring forward in the awkward, knee-height, high-heeled black boots that were also part of her uniform.

The turbolift stopped. She held her breath as she

faced the doors with only one thought in her mind . . . *Klingons—can't live with them, can't—*

The red doors slid open. The lift was empty! Then a sudden crash made her spin to see a violently dislodged wall panel beside the main viewer fly into the center well of the bridge. The wall panel had covered the opening of an emergency-access tunnel, and now from its darkness emerged her enemy, resplendent in the glittering antique uniform of the Imperial Navy, a blood-dripping *bat'leth* held aloft, ready for use again.

Jadzia straightened up, unimpressed. "Worf, that wasn't on the schematics."

Lieutenant Commander Worf leaped down from the upper deck and moved warily around the central helm console, eyes afire. "I am not Worf. I am Kang, captain of the *Thousand-Taloned Death.* And you are my prey!"

Worf lunged past the elevated captain's chair, swinging for Jadzia's legs with a savage upsweep of his *bat'leth.*

Jadzia expertly deflected the ascending crescent blade with her sword as she flipped through the air to land behind the safety railing that ringed the upper deck to her right. Although he had missed his target, Worf's momentum forced him to continue his spin until his *bat'leth* plunged deep into the captain's chair behind him, shorting the communications relays in its shattered arm and causing a spectacular burst of sparks to shoot into the air.

"Worf, I'm serious," Jadzia complained testily. "I was just in the briefing room. I specifically called up the bridge schematics."

Worf grunted as he struggled to tug his weapon free

of the chair. "You should not be talking. You should be running for your life."

He turned away from her to give the stubborn *bat'leth* one final pull.

Jadzia saw her opportunity and took it. She leaned over the railing and swatted Worf's backside with the flat of her sword.

Worf wheeled around in shock. "That was *not* a deathblow!"

"I said, I checked the schematics. There *is* no emergency tunnel beside the viewscreen. You're cheating."

Worf flashed a triumphant grin at her, his weapon finally free. "If you did not see the tunnel on the deck plans, it means you did not use the proper command codes to access them. To the computer, you might have been an enemy, and so you were not shown the correct configuration."

"What?!"

"Defend yourself!" Worf shouted. He swung down to slice the safety railing in two, directly in front of Jadzia.

But Jadzia lashed out with her boot to slam Worf on the side of his head, at the same time she swung her sword against his *bat'leth* to send it spinning out of his grip to shatter the holographic viewer on Mr. Spock's science station.

"You never told me about needing command codes!" she protested.

Worf put one huge hand to the side of his head, looked at the pink blood on his fingers, flared his nostrils in what Jadzia, sighing, knew all too well was a sign of intense pleasure. There was nothing a Klingon liked better than a caring, loving mate who knew how to play rough. "You did not ask," he said, breathing hard, then leaped over the twisted railing to land heavily on the upper deck two meters from Jadzia.

"You're not playing fair," Jadzia told him.

Worf shot a glance upward at the center of the bridge's domed ceiling. "That is not the opinion of the Beta Entity," he growled.

Jadzia risked a sudden look at the ceiling as well. It was maddening to admit, but Worf was right. The amorphous energy beast that fed on the psychic energy of hatred and conflict grew brighter as she watched.

Worf took a step closer. Jadzia took a step back.

"Do not attempt to delay the inevitable. Escape is impossible."

Jadzia stood her ground, raised her sword. "Who said I wanted to escape?"

Worf took another step, arms reaching out to either side, eyes absolutely fixed on his quarry. "Ah, knowing you must lose, you choose to attempt to take your enemy with you. The *w'Han Do*. A warrior's strategy." Worf threw back his massive head and roared approvingly .

"Even better, I have no intention of losing, either." Then Jadzia slashed her sword back and forth in an intricate display of *k'Thatic* ritual disembowelment that had taken her past host Audrid more than eight years to master, and finished the motion by unexpectedly launching the sword across the bridge, where it crashed into an auxiliary life-support station.

Worf, who had been transfixed by Jadzia's dazzling swordplay, appeared shocked by what could only have been a careless mistake. He stared at her sword as it twanged back and forth in a shower of sparks from a shattered display screen.

The diversion worked exactly as Jadzia had planned it. As Worf puzzled over the sword, she slammed into him, shoulder first, elbow in the stomach, driving him back until he collided with a station chair and pitched backward, falling flat on his back.

In an instant, Jadzia was astride him, hands raised, fingers scooped in the strike position for a Romulan *deeth mok* blow to crush the larynx.

Worf fought for breath, the air in his lungs knocked out of him by the violence of his impact. The sweat and blood that covered his face gleamed as the energy beast pulsated above them.

". . . You can not defeat a Klingon with a pitiful *deeth mok* . . ." Worf wheezed defiantly.

"There's more than one way to skin a Klingon," Jadzia said.

Worf's eyes widened in alarm at the thought—and also, Jadzia thought, more than a touch of anticipatory excitement.

And then she swiftly brought both hands down to the sides of Worf's enormous ribcage and—

Worf howled with laughter. He frantically wriggled under Jadzia, ineffectually trying to slap her hands away as he gasped for breath.

"Give up?" Jadzia asked.

Worf's eyes teared as he snorted, "I will not surrender! I am Kang!"

"Ha! I knew Kang," Jadzia said as she dug in, effortlessly repelling his futile attempts to stop her. "Kang was a friend of mine. And *you* are no Kang!"

By now, Worf was totally incapable of speech. Any intelligent sound he attempted to make was overwhelmed by convulsive laughter.

Jadzia went for the kill. "Say *'rumtag,'* " she

demanded as she drove home her attack, running her fingers over Worf's ribs at warp nine. "Say it!"

The word erupted from Worf like a volcanic explosion. *"Rumtag! Rumtag!"*

With a whoop of victory, Jadzia rolled off her husband and stretched out on the floor beside him, holding her head up on one elbow as she watched him struggle to catch his breath and regain his dignity.

His pitiful attempt to glare at her as he said, "You tickled me" made even Worf burst out laughing again. After a few more aborted tries, he took a deep breath and blurted out, suddenly deeply serious, "Now we are both in danger."

"Something else you didn't tell me?" Jadzia asked lightly.

She was suddenly aware of the light from the Beta Entity getting brighter, and then the creature was all around them both. She felt a mild electrical tingle over her body and tugged down on her short skirt again. Then the light winked out as the energy creature disappeared.

"What happens next?" she asked, more curious than alarmed.

Worf took an even deeper breath, in an obvious attempt to restore his warrior's concentration. "Nothing. We are both . . ." He fought to stifle an incipient giggle. ". . . dead." He snorted again and rubbed his ribcage.

"Say that again."

"The Beta Entity was not pleased with the change in our emotional mood. Thus, it enveloped us and drained us of our life energy."

Jadzia screwed up her face in confusion. "That's not right. I studied this mission at the Academy. The energy creature that captured Kirk and Kang and made their crews keep fighting to the death on the *Enterprise* fed on hate. When Kirk convinced everyone to stop fighting and to laugh, to express joyful emotions, the creature didn't kill anyone. It just . . . left."

Worf had finally regained his appropriately stern expression. "This is the Klingon version of the holosimulation. And besides, it was Kang who convinced the others to stop fighting."

Jadzia raised an eyebrow and playfully placed a single finger against Worf's side. "It was who?"

Worf smiled. "It was . . . your *rumtag!*" And then he was on her, running his fingers up and down her sides, until this time it was Jadzia who was reduced to helpless laughter.

Finally, exhausted, breathless, they both collapsed together on the lip of the upper deck, Jadzia sitting up, leaning against Worf's broad chest, Worf's fingers gently untangling the intricate weaving of her twenty-third-century hairstyle.

The bridge of the *Enterprise* was silent, filled with a soft haze colorfully lit by the shifting display screens that ringed the Trill and the Klingon, a ship out of time.

"It's almost romantic," Jadzia said softly, sighing. She remembered being on this same bridge—in reality—when she and Captain Sisko had taken a trip into the past. She thought of the legendary Spock again, how close she had actually come to him. She sighed again.

Worf ran a finger along the spots that trailed from her temple. "Perhaps we should return to our quarters."

Jadzia looked up at Worf and smiled teasingly. "Actually, I was thinking that maybe we could slip down to the captain's quarters. Imagine—James T. Kirk's bedroom. Think of the history."

Worf frowned. "I would rather not. Besides, we only have the holosuite for another five minutes."

Jadzia considered the possibilities of the bridge for a moment, but five minutes was more of a challenge than she was in the mood for right now. She ran a finger along Worf's sexily rippled brow. "There's an arboretum a few decks down. Call Quark and book another hour."

"That is not possible, Jadzia. Odo has requested all the holosuites beginning at oh-seven hundred."

"All of them?" Jadzia sat up, away from Worf. "He's having a party and he didn't invite us?"

"It is for his investigation of the Andorian's murder."

"Ahh," Jadzia said, understanding. Once highly-detailed scans had been made of crime scenes, they could be flawlessly recreated with holotechnology, and the computers could be used to call out various anomalies with great precision. "Does he have any new leads?"

Worf blinked at his wife. "Why would he need new ones?"

It took a moment for Jadzia to realize what Worf was actually saying. "Worf, Quark didn't kill the Andorian."

"All the evidence points to him."

"All the *circumstantial* evidence."

Worf got to his feet. "It is my understanding that the evidence is more than circumstantial." He adjusted his old-fashioned gold-fabric sash, then turned in the direction of the turbolift.

Jadzia jumped to her feet and grabbed his arm to

stop him. "Not so fast, Kang." She forced her groom to turn to face her. "What evidence does Odo have?"

Worf rolled his eyes, replying like a five-year-old asked to recite logarithmic tables. "The Andorian businessman—"

"Dal Nortron," Jadzia said. "Let's concentrate on the facts."

"The Andorian businessman, *Dal Nortron,* arrived on DS9 last Sunday afternoon. Sunday evening, he won more than 100 bars of—"

"One hundred twenty-two bars."

Worf glowered at Jadzia. "One-hundred *twenty-two* bars of gold-pressed latinum—after *three consecutive wins* at dabo. That fact alone is enough to suggest that Quark had arranged to pay off the Andorian—Dal Nortron—through rigged winnings."

"Dabo's a popular game in this quadrant. There are two documented cases of gamblers winning seven consecutive dabos, which is within the statistical realm of probability."

"Not at Quark's," Worf said.

"Come on, Worf. Odo inspects the table every week. Quark doesn't rig it."

Worf let his opinion be known with a grunt.

Jadzia shrugged. "Go on."

"Two hours after Nortron left Quark's, he was found dead, and the latinum was missing."

"Stop right there. There's no logic to what you're saying." Jadzia waited for Worf to interrupt, surprised when he didn't. "If Quark had arranged to pay off Nortron with rigged dabo winnings, then why would he *kill* Nortron to get those winnings back?"

Worf shifted his considerable weight from one foot to the other. "Perhaps Nortron took advantage of the table once too often. Perhaps Quark wanted people to think he had settled a debt to Nortron and planned, when he had done so, *to* steal back his latinum. Perhaps he did not like the way Nortron was dressed."

"Oh well, now, that is motivation for murder."

"Jadzia, Quark is a Ferengi. Ferengi do not think the way other civilized beings do."

Even though Worf's sternly delivered pronouncement told Jadzia that her new husband was reaching the limits of his patience, she persisted. "Worf—this is the twenty-fourth century! That kind of stereotype belongs in the dark ages."

"The Andorian was found dead near the reactor cores in the lower levels. Security monitoring is limited there. Who else would know that better than Quark?"

"*You,* for one. Maybe we should suspect you. That makes about as much sense as suspecting Quark."

Clearly upset by her lack of wifely loyalty, Worf glowered at Jadzia. "I am DS9's strategic operations officer. It is my job to know the station's security weaknesses—just it is in Quark's interest to know them because of his long involvement in smuggling operations."

Jadzia softened her tone and affectionately reached up to straighten Worf's sash. "There's a difference between smuggling and murder, Worf. Especially since some of Quark's smuggling operations benefited the Bajoran resistance as well as the Federation."

Mollified only slightly by her touch, Worf regarded her gravely. "He cares only for profit."

"Granted. But not enough to kill for it."

Worf brushed aside Jadzia's hand. "This conversation is useless. You have not listened to me at all. You have already made up your mind about the Ferengi's innocence."

"Me? How about you? You've already made up your mind he's guilty."

Worf stared at Jadzia as if he really didn't understand what she was talking about. "Of course I have. Because he is."

"Worf! We don't even know if it *was* a murder!"

Worf's heavy brow wrinkled, and Jadzia could see he was waging an internal debate. She decided that he knew something she didn't and was wondering if he should tell her. Jadzia decided to help him make the right decision. There were better ways to defeat a Klingon than through combat.

She stepped closer to him, slipping her hand beneath his sash this time. The old Klingon uniforms had no armor, and the thin cloth of his shirt did little to interfere with the contact of her flesh against his. "Worf . . ." she whispered into his ear, "I'm your wife. We have no secrets from each other, remember?" Then she bit his ear lobe. Hard.

Worf took a quick breath, then spoke quickly, as if he was worried that he would change his mind. "Odo showed me Dr. Bashir's preliminary autopsy report. Dal Nortron was killed by an energy-discharge weapon. Odo believes such a weapon would be too primitive to show up on the station's automatic scanning system."

"How primitive?" Jadzia asked, stilling her hand on his chest.

"Microwave radiation. Extremely intense. It . . . overheated every cell in his body. A weapon without honor."

Jadzia swiftly reviewed everything she knew about

microwave radiation. In this case, it was her own experiences as a science specialist that took precedence over the memories of Dax's previous hosts.

Microwaves were part of the electromagnetic spectrum, one of at least seven energy spectrums known to exist in normal space-time. In pre-subspace, EM-based civilizations—that converged toward rating C-451–45018–3 on Richter's scale of culture—the primary applications of microwave radiation were line-of-sight radio communications and nonmetallic industrial welding, typically with some half-hearted attempts to create first-generation beamed-energy weapons. On Earth, it had even been used for cooking food. Primitive was not the word for it. Prehistoric was more like it, right alongside stone knives and bearskins.

Jadzia took her hand from Worf's chest, amused in spite of the situation to see her groom only then resume easy breathing. "Be reasonable, Worf. Why would Quark use an old-fashioned microwave weapon when he could have disintegrated Nortron with a phaser?"

Worf glanced over his shoulder at the turbolift doors, as if worried someone was about to join them. He took a step back from her. "Phaser residue can be detected for hours after a disintegration."

But Jadzia curled one finger under his gold sash to gently pull him back to her. "Who would have known he was missing?"

Worf smoothed his sash again, trying to dislodge Jadzia's grip. "Perhaps Quark didn't want to put the latinum at risk."

"So . . . stun Nortron, take the latinum, *then* disintegrate him."

"Just because I believe Quark is a criminal does not mean I believe he is a *smart* criminal. And would you please stop that!"

Jadzia was about to raise the stakes when she was interrupted by an announcement from hidden speakers.

"Ladies and gentlemen, boys and girls and morphs, this simulation will end in thirty seconds. Thank you for choosing Quark's for your entertainment needs. Be sure to inquire about our half-price drink specials for holosuite customers when you turn in your memory rods. Now, please gather your personal belongings and take small children by the appropriate grasping appendage. And remember, Quark's is not responsible for lost or stolen articles or for damage caused by micro-forcefield fluctuations. Five . . . four . . . three . . ."

The bridge of the *Enterprise* melted from around Jadzia and Worf, retreating back into history. Now they stood in a simple unadorned room, its lower walls studded with the glowing green emitters of a compact holoprojector system.

"Please exit through the doors to the rear of the holosuite, and thank you for visiting Quark's—the happiest place in the Bajoran Sector."

Jadzia and Worf exchanged a look of shared puzzlement.

"That voice sounded like Leeta," Jadzia said.

"I have heard that Rom is introducing new policies during Quark's . . . incarceration."

"If Rom is next in line for the bar, I'm surprised you haven't started suspecting him of setting up his brother."

The holosuite door slipped open to reveal Odo and two security officers.

"Commanders . . . I trust I'm not interrupting," the constable said.

"We have finished," Worf said brusquely. He started for the door.

"No, we haven't," Jadzia countered.

"I'm sorry," Odo said, "but I do require the holosuites for assembling—"

"That's not what I meant," Jadzia interrupted. "Odo, Worf told me that Dal Nortron died of exposure to microwave radiation."

Odo frowned. "That is privileged information. At least," he added gruffly as he looked at Worf, "it was."

"Worf was conferring with me—security operations officer to science officer."

Odo did not look convinced. But then, he rarely did. "Go on."

"A microwave weapon seems such an unlikely choice to commit a murder, I was wondering if there might be another explanation."

"I am open to suggestions."

"Well, if the body was found near the reactor levels, have you ruled out energy leaks or power modulations coming from the power transfer-conduit linkages?"

Odo blinked. "I was not aware that fusion power-conduits could generate microwave radiation."

Jadzia shrugged. "Not directly. But there's so much other equipment on those levels, a fusion power surge could set up rapid oscillations in various circuits. That's all you'd need to generate an electromagnetic field. And if the field was strong enough or close enough to something that might function as a wave-guide, it could reach microwave levels."

Odo looked off to the side as if reprocessing the

data she had just provided. "Could traces of such a field be detected after the fact?"

Jadzia ignored her husband's disapproving frown. "Absolutely. You'd need to examine everything in the area for magnetic realignment, heat damage, even signs of electrical sparking between conductive materials.

"Electrical?" Odo made a sound in the back of his throat, then nodded. "Very well. I'll send a forensics team down at once. If they find evidence of anomalous energy discharges, I'll let you know."

"And if they don't?" Jadzia asked.

Odo gave her a grim smile, as if he had successfully led her on. "Then it will be additional evidence that the murder was committed with a microwave weapon."

Jadzia was surprised when Worf suddenly grunted. "Unless," he said, and Jadzia could sense his reluctance, "the Andorian was killed by an anomalous power discharge somewhere else on the station and his body taken to the lower levels to confuse the investigation."

Jadzia was pleased that Worf had offered some support for her theory, despite his conviction that the guilty party was already in custody.

But Odo rendered Worf's suggestion unnecessary. "We can rule that possibility out, Commander. I do have enough security tapes and computer logs to establish that Dal Nortron took a turbolift to the lower levels approximately twenty minutes before he was killed."

"Before he died," Jadzia corrected.

"He was murdered, Commander. Of that I have no doubt."

Jadzia ignored Odo's increasing air of formality.

"Do your security tapes and computer logs show that anyone else was in that area at the same time?" she asked.

Odo's hesitation answered the question for her.

"I didn't think so," Jadzia said.

"There's no such thing as a perfect crime," Odo said bluntly. "I've already connected Quark to Nortron. They were involved in a business dealing together. They had a falling out. Quark killed him. Accidentally, more likely than not. But it is definitely murder."

Jadzia studied Odo closely. She had seldom heard such emotion in the changeling's voice. Almost as if he were personally involved in this case.

"Odo, did *you* know Dal Nortron?" Jadzia asked.

"Of course not. Why would you even ask such a thing?"

Eight lifetimes of experience told Jadzia she was on to something. "No reason. But I'd find someone who did know him," she said. "Someone who can tell you why he came to DS9, and why he went down to the lower levels."

Now it was Odo who was losing his patience. "To meet Quark."

"But your own records say Quark *wasn't* down there."

"Records can be altered, Commander."

Jadzia smiled sweetly. Now she had led *him* on. "Exactly. Altered to take someone out. Or to put some-one in. And if the records can be altered so easily, Quark and Dal Nortron could have met *anywhere* on the station without you knowing about it. And if they could have met anywhere, why did they choose the lower levels?"

Odo exhaled in frustration, but said nothing.

Worf tugged on Jadzia's arm. "We should let the constable get on with his duties."

"What's down there?" Jadzia asked again as she left with her husband. "You answer that question, Odo, and you'll solve the crime."

Odo did not respond, but Jadzia didn't care.

Eight lifetimes of experience gave her the answer she knew the constable didn't want to admit.

Somehow, in some way, whatever had happened to Dal Nortron, Odo *was* involved.

And the answer to *that* mystery was somewhere in the lower levels.

CHAPTER 4

THEY WERE CALLED *tiyerta nok*—literally, the life-flow of iron, or as the current usage had it, the arteries of the machine.

That was the term the Cardassians gave to the engineering access tunnels that riddled their mining station: a complex network of barely passable crawl spaces supporting a web of ODN cables, power conduits, waste-, water-, and replicator-mass plumbing, and air-circulation channels. But as soon as Starfleet had taken control and Terok Nor became Deep Space 9, the *tiyerta nok* inevitably became known as Jefferies tubes, a term some said had its origins as far back as the very beginnings of starship design. Others said even further.

But unlike DS9's other Jefferies tubes—most of which by now had been retrofitted with new, Starfleet-standard lighting sources and ODN upgrades—the Jefferies tube on this lower level was dark, cramped, and cut off from the station's main air-flow system. Not a whisper of a breeze passed through it, and Jake Sisko blinked as steady drips of sweat rolled into his eyes.

"You're crazy," Nog said. "It'll never work."

Jake was flat on his back at the end of this particular *tiyerta nok,* lifting his cramped arms directly overhead to work on the panel set into the uncomfortably low, sloping ceiling. The much shorter Nog was crouched at Jake's feet, where the tunnel height was a bit more generous, keeping a palm torch on the panel above Jake and passing along tools as Jake requested them.

"Nog, it's perfect," Jake insisted. He wriggled a multispanner against the flathead mini-tagbolt he had finally loosened, and the second of three U-shaped clasps holding the egress panel in place dropped free, hitting him right between the eyes. "Oww!" It was more a cry of surprise than pain. "These things never used to be so tight."

"Some of the old Cardassian subsystems are self-repairing." Nog spoke with apparent disinterest, though he added with a chuckle, "Did that ever surprise the Chief when he finally figured out why some of *his* repairs kept reverting to Cardassian configurations. But anyway, the plan can't work, because there's no way you'll ever get past the ambassador's bodyguards."

Jake carefully put the multispanner down beside him and groped for the intergrips. Three more minis to go. "That's what the diversion's for. When the bodyguards go to help the dabo girls, we slip into the ambassador's quarters, take the latinum—"

"What?! You never said anything about stealing latinum!"

Jake moaned and lowered his strained arms to rest

them. "Technically, we're not stealing it, Nog, we're only taking it to confuse Odo about the motive. And even if we *were* really stealing it, so what? We're murderers, remember? Cold-blooded and remorseless."

Jake squinted as Nog aimed the palm torch directly into his eyes. "Jake, my friend, you have to start getting out more. *We're* not murderers."

"Okay, okay. You know what I mean. Quark and Morn are the murderers."

Nog put down the palm torch, but even with the suddenly increased darkness Jake had no trouble sensing how annoyed his friend was. "I thought you said you couldn't use their names."

"You're right. I mean 'Higgs and Fermion.' It's just that I've been thinking about this story for so long, and while you were on patrol Quark let me watch one of his smuggling transactions—"

"Jake!" Nog hissed. "I'm wearing a communicator!" The Ferengi teenager lowered his chin to his chest and spoke loudly and precisely for the benefit of any potential eavesdroppers. "And I'm certain my Uncle Quark would never be involved in smuggling, or any other type of illegal—or even questionable—activity. Perhaps he was just playing a joke on you by pretending that he was."

"Oh, forget it," Jake muttered. Then he went back to attacking the third mini-tagbolt. "No one ever told me writing was such hard work."

"What's so hard about sitting in front of a computer and talking?"

"Shine the light *here,*" Jake said. "And that part's not hard. It's all the work you have to do ahead of time so you can *know* what to say to the computer. That's the hard—*owwh!*"

The third mini was much looser than the second, and left a dent in Jake's forehead when it fell.

"We could have used the transporter to get down here," Nog said.

Jake didn't know why he bothered to keep explaining things to Nog, but he tried again. "That would leave a trace in the station security log." He pried at the egress panel with just his fingers now; to his relief, it came out easily. "Huh. I thought that would have been stuck after all these years."

Nog, uncharacteristically, said nothing, and Jake looked back at him with renewed suspicion. "You sure you haven't been back here since the last time?"

Nog looked offended. "Why would I come down here?"

Jake smiled insinuatingly. "The 'Room,' remember?" Then Jake used his feet to push himself backwards until his head and upper body poked out through the wall-panel opening. A moment later, he had turned his body and swung his legs out and down, hung on to the edge of the opening, and then dropped lightly to the floor of a small stretch of corridor. The corridor was lit only by the reflected light coming in through a panel opening set high near the ceiling in the bulkhead behind him.

"Whoa . . . it's still not hooked up to the main power grid," Jake said.

Nog's voice echoed in the Jeffries tube before he stuck his head through the wall-panel opening and brought the palm torch up beside him, letting it play around the area. "With the war, the Chief's retrofit schedule lost its priority. Except, of course, when he needed to maintain critical functions."

Jake's eyebrows lifted in surprise. Starfleet had

made the retrofitting of Deep Space 9 a high-profile project, and accordingly Chief O'Brien had been given the authority to set up a renovation-and-repair program that would eventually move through the entire station, from Ops to the lowest level. War or no war, it was hard to believe that after almost six years, *no one* on *any* of the retrofitting teams had stumbled upon this ten-meter stretch of corridor that somehow had been sealed off from all the other corridors on the level.

Jake glanced up at Nog. "Aren't you coming down?"

"I thought you said you just wanted to time how long it would take for Quark and—I mean, for 'Higgs and Fermion' to escape through the Jefferies tube."

That *was* the original reason why Jake had talked Nog into retracing their old routes through the Jefferies tubes. He had decided to put his semiautobiographical novel, *Anslem,* aside for the time being and try something more commercial. So the new crime novel he was working on, *The Ferengi Connection,* was going to be set on a fictional Cardassian mining station still in orbit of Bajor. For that reason, he wanted to be completely accurate about how long it would take his crime lords Higgs and Fermion to secretly move from one part of the station to another. When Quark had allowed him to observe the illegal sale of Denevan crystals last Saturday night, Jake had been most interested to learn that the Ferengi used a network of secret passageways different from the Jefferies tubes. That would allow him to move through the station without being observed by Odo. Unfortunately, Nog's uncle wasn't about to give Captain Sisko's son, of all people, any details about the network, so Jake had decided to base the tunnels in his novel on the engineering ones he and Nog used to play in.

"Well, we're here. You timed it. Let's go back," Nog said impatiently. He held out his hand to haul Jake back up to the panel opening.

"No," Jake said as he looked around. "I can use this in the story. A lost section of the station. . . . Maybe this is where Quark—*Higgs,* has his secret headquarters."

"Jake, did you ever stop to think that maybe this section was sealed off for a reason?"

Jake didn't understand why Nog was being so cautious. "Nog, we used to come down here almost every day after school. If there was anything dangerous, we'd already know about it. Now get down here."

Nog mumbled something in an obscure trading tongue that Jake couldn't make out. But the young Ferengi squirmed through the panel opening and dropped with a loud thump to the uncarpeted deck beside his friend. He got up awkwardly, brushed dust from his Starfleet uniform, then aimed his palm torch to one end of the short corridor. The beam of light found only a standard, DS9 bulkhead, a dull, burnished-copper color, ridged and scalloped like the skin of a gigantic reptile. Nog shone the light in the other direction, but his torchlight uncovered only more of the same. "You know, we really have to tell Chief O'Brien about this," he said.

Jake patted Nog on the back. "And what are we going to say when he asks us *when* we discovered a lost section of corridor?"

"We were children," Nog said. "If we told anyone what we had found back then. . . ." He laughed. "My father would have served me my lobes on a platter for playing in the tubes."

"And for playing with a *'hew-mon,'* " Jake added.

Nog frowned, and Jake knew why. Despite the cannibalism rumors that still refused to die, human-Ferengi relations had come a long way in the past decade; but those relations still weren't so secure that many Ferengi would be comfortable joking about them.

"Would your father have been any more understanding?" Nog asked defiantly.

Jake snorted. "If I had told him about the tunnels back then, I'd still be confined to my room."

"But . . . we are going to tell them now, correct?"

"Maybe not right this minute," Jake said.

"Jake, we don't have any excuse for keeping this to ourselves. In fact, it might be my duty as a Starfleet officer to tell my commanding officer that—where are you going?!"

Jake ignored Nog and his unfathomable anxiety, and walked toward the only door in the corridor. "Let's just see if it's still here," Jake said.

Nog darted past him and stood in front of the lone door. "It is. Now let's go to Ops and—"

Jake smiled at Nog and reached for the door control panel. "And *now,* let's see if it's still *working.*"

"It *is* working!" Nog bleated as he pushed Jake's hand away from the door control.

Jake regarded his friend with a slight frown. "Nog, is there something you'd like to tell me?"

"Let's go to Ops, find Chief O'Brien, and . . . and I'll tell you everything."

Even in the pale illumination from the palm torch, Jake saw Nog's large ears flush. The explanation came to him suddenly.

"Nog . . . you *have* been coming down here, haven't you?"

"No. Well, yes. But, not often. A few times. Five . . . maybe eight, ten times."

Jake stared at Nog, nonplussed. "By yourself?"

Nog's mouth opened and closed but nothing came out.

"Oh, I get it now." Jake shook his head with a laugh, the sound oddly muffled in the enclosed space. "So . . . if I open this door, just what am I going to see?" He tried to remember the titles of the 'special' holosuite programs they used to 'borrow' from Quark's bar, the ones Quark kept locked in the little box under the stale pistachios no one ever asked for. *"Lauriento Spa? Vulcan Love Slave?"*

At that, Nog started to laugh, too. *"Part One* or *Part Two?"*

There was only one answer to that question. *"Part Two,"* Jake said with a snicker. Then both friends completed the title at the same time: *"The Revenge!"*

That was enough to make both double over in fits of uncontrolled giggling, both recalling how they would take the adult holosuite cylinders and try to run the graphic subroutines through their personal desk padds. At best, they were able to call up mildly suggestive silhouettes of some of the holographic performers from the programs, usually obscured by blurred color and jagged outlines. But the two young friends, certain they were close to learning the secrets of the universe—and equally certain they were going to be caught by their fathers at any minute—had stared at those flickering images for hours, trying desperately to see in them what it was that adults found so compelling.

Eventually, the laughter faded and Jake caught his

breath. "So, you really *don't* want me to open the door?" he asked.

Nog chewed at his lip. "And if I say No, as soon as we leave you'll be right back here to open it anyway, right?"

"Right," Jake agreed. That's exactly what he had decided to do.

Nog sighed in resignation. "Go ahead." He stepped aside.

Jake made a production out of pressing the door control. When the door slipped open, he comically placed both hands over his eyes.

Until he heard Nog say, "Hey, that's not my program. . . ." Jake took his hands away, looked into what had been the most exciting discovery of their childhood on Deep Space 9, something not recorded on any deck plan or technical drawing. A lost Cardassian holosuite.

Nog was already inside the room, standing on a slightly inclined rocky landscape. Beyond him, about a holographic kilometer away, Jake spied a collection of small stone buildings reminiscent of a primitive village. It was night on the holosuite, but the buildings and the land were lit by a cool, blue-green illumination. Jake couldn't detect the source of that backlighting, though it appeared, improbably, to be coming from somewhere behind him.

He stepped inside to join Nog, then turned around to look past the improbable cutout of the doorway to the DS9 corridor, to an astounding holographic vista of a night sky.

At once he identified the source of the blue-green light.

A planet filled almost a tenth of the sky in the holographic scene, the bright light reflecting from the green oceans of its sunlit half enough to wash most of the stars from the heavens.

Then he recognized the planet. "Hey, that's Bajor. . . ."

"Really?" Nog said.

Jake pointed skyward. "By the terminator . . . see those mountains?" The distinctive pattern created where three tectonic plates had collided to form a perfect X of intersecting mountain ranges was so well known as to almost be the galactic symbol for Bajor.

"Dahkur Province," Nog murmured. He looked around the holographic landscape again. "So this must be one of Bajor's moons. But I didn't program this."

"Neither did I," Jake said.

The two friends looked at each other, and Jake could see that Nog had just reached the same conclusion he had. "Someone else has been down here."

"Pretty dull program," Jake said softly. "I don't see a single Vulcan love slave."

They stood in silence for a few moments, listening to the holographic wind. Jake looked back at the village and saw flickering lights in some of the windows of the small buildings.

"Does it feel as if something should be happening?" Nog asked.

Jake shook his head. "It's not on pause. We've got wind, moving lights in that village."

"But why would anyone want a holosimulation of . . . of nothing happening on a Bajoran moon?"

Jake shrugged. "Maybe the program's caught in a loop. Or the holosuite's broken." He cleared his throat. "Room, this is Jake Sisko. Show me my fishing hole. . . ."

Unlike any other type of holographic simulation Jake had ever seen, the distinctive program switchover of the Cardassian holosuite now began. At first, the colors and the shapes of the Bajoran moon's landscape seemed to liquefy and swim into each other, and then, as if the plug had been pulled on reality, all the colors spun swiftly—dizzyingly—into a spiral vortex that made Jake feel as if he were about to be drawn down an endless tunnel. But, just as quickly as the vertigo of that transformation made itself felt, the spiralling stopped and with a strange optical bounce that Jake could almost feel, the new program took shape.

Jake and Nog were standing on a covered wooden bridge that spanned Jake's favorite fishing hole. It was his father's favorite, too, and six years ago, Jake had been delighted to discover that this secret Cardassian holosuite could access his father's programs from DS9's main computers.

Except . . .

"This isn't my program, either," Jake said to Nog. The perpetual summer sun wasn't shining. In fact, the day was overcast. In fact, it was actually raining."

"I, uh, sort of made some, uh, minor modifications," Nog confessed with a shrug. "The rain makes me feel more . . . at home. . . ."

Then Jake saw that he and Nog weren't alone. There were people *swimming* in the fishing hole. "Who are they?" He stepped closer to the bridge's railing, saw the impressive size and bulbous shape of the swimmers' bald heads. "Ferengi?"

"Uh-huh," Nog said in a strangled croak, as if his throat was slowly closing in.

The Ferengi swimmers saw Jake and Nog on the bridge, and started waving enthusiastically.

Then Jake saw how small their ears were, and he began to really understand. "Ferengi *females* . . ."

"I've never really been much for . . . pointed ears," Nog mumbled.

Two of the swimmers began climbing a wooden ladder at the side of the bridge. They were calling Nog's name, and as they stepped onto the bridge, leaving wet footprints behind, Jake was momentarily startled by the bulky, multilayered swimming costumes the Ferengi females wore. Other than their heads, their hands, and their feet, not a square centimeter of skin was exposed, not a curve of their bodies could be discerned.

Jake looked at Nog with a grin.

Nog's open-mouth smile was so broad, it almost made him look as if he'd just been stunned by a phaser. The Ferengi teenager stared at the two fully clad females without blinking.

"You're drooling," Jake teased.

Nog looked up at his friend. "Vulcan love slaves don't . . . wear any clothes," he said sheepishly. "Where's the fun in that?"

Jake took Nog by the arm, tugged him toward the door to the corridor. "Nog, you need to get out more. Let's go find Chief O'Brien."

Allowing Nog to wave a sad farewell to the Ferengi females, Jake pushed his glum friend out the door.

The Ferengi females—representing everything Nog could ever want—returned that wave sadly as Jake and Nog left, reverting to their true forms only when the door had completely closed, and the waiting began again.

CHAPTER 5

IF MILES O'BRIEN had his way, every starship, every runabout, every shuttlecraft, *and* every space station in the galaxy would be as smooth and featureless as his little son's bottom.

Not that DS9's chief engineer minded a turn in space. Perhaps because he was a happily married parent of two young, active children, O'Brien greatly enjoyed putting on an environmental suit and slipping out of the artificial gravity fields for an hour or two, just as he was doing today to float above the *Defiant,* relatively speaking, of course. And stolen moments such as these, when he could just drift peacefully among the stars, hearing only the rhythms of his own heart, his own breathing, he found those moments truly restoring.

But to *work* in space? In the twenty-fourth century? What was Starfleet thinking?

To O'Brien, who had given the matter some thought, the perfect spacecraft would be without surface texture—not one exposed conduit, not a single inset panel, and absolutely no components that could only be serviced from the outside of the ship. Instead, in his opinion at least, everything should be accessible from *within,* so that engineers and repair technicians could work safely in a breathable atmosphere, under controlled temperatures, in conditions where an unexpected sharp edge of metal would mean only a quick trip to the infirmary and not explosive decompression and a terrible, painful death.

Humans are far too fragile for space, O'Brien thought, not for the first time. Far too fragile for most things, actually. Which is why machines were so necessary. And why engineers in particular were humanity's best hope for a better future.

O'Brien smiled to himself just thinking about his engineer's dream of that better tomorrow. Gleaming starships, hulls like mirrors, blazing past the stars with their fragile cargo safely cocooned, and—

"You still breathing out there, Chief?"

The brisk voice in O'Brien's helmet communicator was as loud as it was unexpected.

"Who is this?" O'Brien demanded.

The short sharp burst of laughter that came in response to his startled request was enough to answer his question.

"Sorry, Major," O'Brien said. "I was . . . I was concentrating on the transionic power coupling."

O'Brien regretted the words as soon as he said them. He could picture the wry smile on Kira's face as she replied, "I'll say. You were concentrating so hard we could hear you snoring."

Blushing in spite of himself, O'Brien maneuvered gingerly around from the open coupling bay until he could look along the length of the *Defiant*'s upper hull, past the towering pylon and immense curve of DS9's docking ring and up to the Operations Module, as if there were viewports there through which he could see the major. "I'm running a level-six diagnostic," O'Brien explained. "There's not a lot I can do while the computer's working."

"Which is why I was wondering if you'd like to lend a hand to the PTC work crew," Kira said. The humor had gone from her voice. O'Brien thought he could detect the slightest undercurrent of concern.

"Have they run into trouble?"

"It's not trouble yet, Chief. They were almost ready to lift off a hull plate, but then they got an anomalous density reading."

Kira's news hit O'Brien like a shock of transtator current. "Tell them not to touch it!"

"I'm confident they know enough not to do that. Rom's leading the team."

"Ah, well, all right, then," O'Brien said, his sudden concern subsiding to a more tolerable level of wariness. Rom was one of the best junior technicians he had ever trained. The hardworking Ferengi could be counted on to take a conservative approach to repairs—and to O'Brien, the conservative approach was always the best. "Let me seal this bay and I'll join them." O'Brien tapped his thruster controls to move closer to the *Defiant*'s hull and the open coupling bay.

"Want me to beam you over?" Kira asked.

O'Brien gazed up through the top of his helmet, admiring the towering spires of the station's curved docking arms, picked out against the fathomless black of space by brilliant running lights. That a machine—an artificial construct built by intelligent hands—could even exist in this universe, could even dare to shine as brightly as the timeless stars, frankly thrilled him at such a visceral level that he couldn't care less if those hands had been Cardassian or human. "That's all right, Major. Looks like a nice day for a walk. . . ."

As DS9's chief engineer, O'Brien was well aware that, according to regulations, untethered spacewalks from one section of the station's exterior to another were strictly forbidden. The massive station's slow stabilization spin, almost imperceptible even at the outer edge of the docking ring, could induce in inexperienced personnel violent attacks of debilitating spacesickness. Poor Worf almost had to be prodded into his environmental suit for EVA drills.

But O'Brien had no such trouble with an exterior traverse of the station. In his mind, he saw the huge structure simply as a giant cog, moving within its perfect circle, wholly predictable, reassuringly stable. Thus, after the transionic coupling bay was safely sealed and the diagnostic readers placed on standby, he oriented himself to the station's local coordinates, correctly pointing his feet at the *Defiant*'s hull, and tapped his thrusters. Then he smoothly slipped above the ship, effortlessly adjusting his vector so he would rise above the gentle slope of the docking ring beside the pylon, level out, then drop over the ring's inner edge as if taking a ski jump into an infinite valley filled with stars.

O'Brien sighed with pleasure. He loved this view, the sensation of this movement. In an old-style system of measurement he had mastered in order to be able to read old engineering texts, the distance to the far side of the ring was almost a mile. Certainly, he now reflected, he had seen larger artificial structures in his career in space. The planet-sized Dyson Sphere, for instance, which Captain Picard's *Enterprise* had encountered when they had rescued the legendary Montgomery Scott. Contemplating that engineering feat still kept O'Brien awake at night, as he struggled to comprehend the staggering mechanical stresses on its hull components. But a Dyson Sphere was so enormous, he knew, that there was only one way to truly make sense of its size and scope, and that was through mathematical abstractions.

A mile-wide space station, though, that was something concrete, something that could be seen and felt. In fact, Deep Space 9 was about as large as an artificial structure could be built and still be comprehensible to unenhanced human senses. It was part of the reason he had enjoyed this assignment so much. In some ways, DS9 was the ultimate machine. And its size and complexity were just below the level at which engineers were forced to rely on artificial intelligence and data reduction in order to grasp the structure of what they built. But DS9—well, by now, O'Brien felt he knew it well enough that he could almost have built a duplicate of it by himself.

As he dropped, O'Brien's line of sight cleared the interior habitat ring. Now he could see the red glow of the fusion reactors' exhaust cone at the relative bottom of the station. There, the saucer-shaped module containing the station's main fusion reactors—of which only four had been certified safe enough to remain operational—was attached to the main core by a constricted airlock linkage. That airlock connector was what allowed the quick jettisoning of the module in an emergency with minimal loss of interior atmosphere.

The airlock connector, though, was strictly designed to allow only the passage of turbolift cars and life-support services. The end-product of the fusion reactor—power—was delivered to the rest of the station through six exterior power transfer conduits that extended from the top hull of the fusion module to the bottom hull of the lower habitat. Again, in an emergency they were designed to be quickly separated from the station. A single conduit could supply the station's minimal power needs for weeks.

But yesterday, when Odo's murder-investigation team had detected an inexplicable modulation in the output of power-transfer conduit B almost exactly where it entered the main station, jettisoning the conduit had fortunately not been required.

No Dominion warships were reported within tens of parsecs of the Bajoran system, so emergency conditions did not apply. O'Brien had called for a by-the-book shutdown of conduit B, using the remaining five to supply the station without requiring any power rationing. And once the conduit was cold, he had assigned an engineering team to open it up and remove all the exterior hull plates, so that they could conduct a visual inspection in addition to the molecular scanning. It was a time-consuming procedure to be sure, but also a conservative one. A chance to make repairs without danger of attack or risk of catastrophic disaster was something that came to O'Brien less and less these days. He found he was actually looking forward to helping Rom and his team.

There were three other engineers with Rom, floating by the top of the power conduit where it entered the lower hull of the main station. O'Brien could see they were each attached to the station by a memory tether— without them, DS9's rotation would move the conduit away from anyone in an environmental suit within sixty seconds.

O'Brien expertly maneuvered himself into position beside Rom. Rom was easy to identify among the engineering team because he was the shortest of the four, and he wore a modified helmet that provided more room for his Ferengi skull.

"Chief O'Brien," Rom said in greeting as he took O'Brien's arm, "I didn't mean for Major Kira to call you away from your important work."

"That's all right, Rom." From any other Ferengi, O'Brien knew that those words would be a reflexive and meaningless expression of the 33rd Rule of Acquisition. But in Rom's case, O'Brien believed that the Ferengi technician, gratifyingly enough, did consider anything the chief engineer of DS9 did to be of crucial importance to the station. Of course, it also was true that Rom always believed anything a chief of engineering did to be more important than what a mere assistant did. Unsure whether the Ferengi technician's belief stemmed from something in the Ferengi tradition of apprenticeship or from Rom's admiration for his chief's skills, O'Brien rather hoped it was the latter.

Grateful for Rom's steadying grip, O'Brien fired a memory tether from the mobility module around his right forearm. At once, the tether's tip sought out the nearest spinward positioning cleat on the hull and magnetically attached itself to the metallic surface. Now, O'Brien knew, the tether would automatically adjust its length and tension to keep him in position over the very same point—power-transfer conduit B, hull plate B-OF-186-9776-3. The Cardassians were nothing if not impressive record keepers.

"So what do we have?" he asked Rom.

Rom tapped some controls on his forearm padd, and they watched as a holographic display of a tricorder screen sprang up and took shape a half-meter in front of O'Brien's helmet.

O'Brien whistled as he interpreted the shifting, false-color display of a hull-plate scan. On a typical plate, the scan would show thirteen distinct color bars representing the thirteen composite layers used to form the station's skin. But on this display, O'Brien noted with a frown, several segments of the hull plate's interior layers were mixed together as if sections of them had melted into each other.

He checked the coordinates of the display. "You're sure this isn't reversed?"

"Yes, sir," Rom said earnestly. "See the outermost layer? Pure plasma-sprayed pyroceramic trianium."

Rom was right. The PSPT layer was for micrometeoroid protection, a final fail-safe for the station in case the station-keeping deflectors went off-line. Even more importantly, it was always and only applied to the exterior of the hull plates. Which meant the mixing of layers was definitely on the inside.

"Good attention to detail," O'Brien said. Even through his helmet he could see Rom's broad smile in response to his compliment. "A lot of engineers would have automatically concluded that the sensor was in error."

The smile left the Ferengi technician's face as quickly as it had appeared. "Oh, no, Chief—the whole team agreed that this was an anomalous reading."

O'Brien nodded. He didn't know if that were true or not, but he appreciated the fact that Rom took responsibility for his team—two Bajorans and a new Vulcan ensign who had just been assigned to DS9 from the Academy. "Well done, people," he said, with a glance that encompassed Rom's three assistants.

This time, all except the Vulcan smiled back in acknowledgment of the praise.

"All right, Rom," O'Brien said. "What do we do next?"

Though obviously startled that O'Brien wasn't taking over the operation, Rom rose to the challenge. "Well, the final decision will have to be based on an understanding of what has caused the mixing of the hull layers."

"Very good. What possibilities should we investigate?" O'Brien effortlessly reassumed his role as instructor for the station's engineering staff. It gave him real pleasure to see someone grasp and apply engineering concepts for the first time. Somedays, he even thought he might enjoy teaching at the Academy himself. Once the war was over, of course.

"Um, um . . ." Rom said as he gathered his thoughts. "Well . . . if we had found this kind of mixing on the *exterior* layers of the hull, we could conclude that . . . it was the result of an energy discharge. Maybe a stray . . . phaser hit from an old battle."

"That's one," O'Brien confirmed.

"And . . . if we open up the plate and find that the innermost layer is not disturbed—that is, it *appears* to be undamaged, then . . . we might conclude the mixing of layers is a manufacturing flaw."

O'Brien decided to challenge Rom once again. He frowned. "The Cardassians? Miss a manufacturing flaw as prominent as *this?*"

A look of momentary panic contorted Rom's face. From long experience, O'Brien knew that many students folded at this point, unwilling to appear to contradict their teacher's pronouncement.

But Rom swallowed hard and blurted out. "I really don't mean to argue but. . . ."

"But what?" O'Brien prompted, trying to keep a smile from his face.

"Well . . . Cardassian manufacturing standards fell drastically during . . . the last few years of the Occupation and if this hull plate was manufactured during that period and Bajoran slave workers were part of the quality assurance program then . . . then there's a chance—a little tiny barely-worth-mentioning *chance*—that a manufacturing flaw like this could slip through." Rom audibly gulped at his own temerity and the remainder of his words tumbled out in a rush. "But . . . you're probably right. Don't pay any attention to me."

O'Brien shook his head. "Rom, never be afraid to question the chief engineer."

Rom blinked in surprise. "Never? Really?"

O'Brien reconsidered. "Well, maybe not when you're under enemy fire. But this is a stable situation, so we might as well enjoy the luxury of exploring all the possibilities. In this case, you're right. It *is* possible we're seeing a manufacturing flaw."

Rom brightened like a puppy who'd been given a brand-new chew toy. O'Brien couldn't help himself. He had to smile.

"Thank you, Chief."

"But let's not get carried away." O'Brien was the teacher again. "I think there's one more possibility we should consider. What about you?"

Rom nodded quickly in his helmet, making his entire weightless body rock slowly back and forth around his center of gravity.

"And that possibility would be . . . ?" O'Brien said.

"Oh, uh, a power conduit rupture!"

"Exactly," O'Brien agreed. "Though because the hull plate surrounding the conduit isn't deformed. . . ."

Rom got it at once. "It would be a very small rupture."

"So given those three possibilities, what procedures do we follow to identify which one is the actual cause of the layer distortion?"

Rom looked off into space and recited the steps to be taken next, beginning with shutting down the power conduit—which had already been accomplished—to the final step of setting up a portable forcefield in order to keep any possible debris contained once the damaged hull plate had been removed.

Timing his actions to coincide with the completion of Rom's list, O'Brien activated the memory tether override and used his thrusters to slip to the side. "Well, what are you waiting for, Rom?"

O'Brien chuckled at the expressions first of surprise and then delight that washed across Rom's face as the Ferengi technician realized he was being permitted to continue with the examination.

With renewed confidence, Rom efficiently directed the others in setting up the forcefield generator that Kira now beamed to the engineering team. Then he positioned his team at the connection points of the hull plate they were about to remove.

Elapsed time for these preparations was approximately twenty minutes, and O'Brien took full advantage of his position as an observer to use the time to watch the incomparable parade of the wonders of space: the steady shine of the untwinkling stars, the subtly shifting colorful filaments of the Denorios Belt, and the distant pure light of Bajor's sun, Bajor-B'hava'el—the brightest star in space for DS9, though distant enough from the station that it was simply a brilliant point of light, not a blazing disk.

"We're ready, Chief," Rom announced.

Even from his position, floating five meters away, O'Brien could see that Rom's team had properly installed the forcefield emitters and that the four engineers were correctly in position. "You're in charge, Rom."

Rom nodded and turned his attention to steadying himself on the multitorque defastener he had attached to the plate bolt, then gave a quick glance to reassure himself that each of his team members was also poised to use their own. "All right, everybody, on the . . . count of ten. One—"

"Uh, Rom?"

"Yes, Chief?"

"Why not make it the count of three?"

"Good idea. Everybody, forget what I said about going on the count of ten. That would take too much time and slow down the—"

"One!" O'Brien prompted.

Rom got the hint. "Uh . . . two . . . and *three!*"

O'Brien carefully monitored the spinning bits of each defastener as they counterrotated, detaching the hull-plate fasteners.

"Slowly . . ." Rom cautioned nervously. "Standing by to activate the forcefield . . . as soon as the hull plate is free. . . ."

Then a few puffs of gas vented, as the hull-plate seal was broken and the plate itself began to drift away from the curved pillar of the conduit structure, propelled by the centripetal force imparted by DS9's rotation.

O'Brien's attention focused on what would happen next—in the next minute or two. When the plate had drifted about a meter away from the surface of the conduit, Rom would activate the forcefield so that any debris behind the plate would remain in place. Then, when the plate was about ten meters from the conduit, Jadzia was standing by in Ops to grab the plate with a construction tractor beam and hold it safely out of the way.

As far as O'Brien was concerned, his credits were on the cause of the distorted layers being a tiny rupture in the power-transfer conduit that had allowed plasma current to leak out and melt the inside of the hull plate. And a ruptured energy conduit would certainly explain the anomalous readings Odo's people got from the lower levels when they were investigating the death of that Andorian businessman.

Then the loudest, highest-pitched Ferengi scream O'Brien had ever heard shoved every other thought from his mind as he slammed his gloved hands to the sides of his helmet in a useless attempt to block out the din.

"Computer!" O'Brien shouted. "Lower helmet volume!"

Instantly, Rom's squeal dropped to a more tolerable level, and O'Brien swiftly detached his memory tether and thrusted in to see whatever it was that had so upset Rom.

Dead bodies.

Two of them.

Cardassians.

Crammed into the insulating buffer zone between the power-transfer conduit's inner and outer hulls.

The arms of the two corpses were stretched out as if desperately reaching to freedom. Their black, shrivelled lips were drawn back exposing startlingly white teeth, their jaws agape in terror.

O'Brien shivered. The dessicated gray flesh still coating what could be seen of the two skeletons was fractured by deep-cut purple fissures, the result of prolonged exposure to the absolute vacuum of space.

"It's all right, Rom. Calm down. Breathe normally." O'Brien stayed out of Rom's reach in case the Ferengi panicked and started flailing. "O'Brien to Ops, lock on to Rom and prepare to beam him in on my order."

"What is it, Chief?" Kira asked.

"I'm locked," Jadzia's voice added.

O'Brien kept his voice deliberately neutral, setting a proper example for his staff. "There are two bodies in the insulating space between the hulls. Cardassians."

"Construction workers?" Kira asked.

O'Brien thrusted in closer. One of the skeletons was missing its hand—it had been severed cleanly at the wrist. "Don't think so, Major. They're not in environment suits. In fact, they look to be civilians. Been here quite a while, though. All the moisture in them's sublimated long ago."

O'Brien puzzled over the missing hand. He looked around to see if it had floated free.

It had. He could see it attached to the inside of the detached hull plate, as if it had been welded in position, exactly where scans had detected that strange mixing of the plate's interior layers.

"Chief," Kira asked carefully, "any chance they might have been put in there when the conduit was manufactured?"

O'Brien understood what the major was suggesting.

The two Cardassians might have been victims of the Bajoran resistance—walled up in the conduit to die when it was carried into space. They certainly looked as if they had been in vacuum long enough to have been killed during the Occupation.

But the theory didn't hold because of one critical detail. "Probably not," O'Brien said. "These conduits were all assembled in space when the station was constructed. I don't know how the blazes they got in there."

Jadzia's voice came over the comm link next. "Chief, we should transport the bodies to the Infirmary for Julian. But I can't get a good lock on them. Is that conduit still live?"

"Dead cold, Commander. If you can lock onto Rom, there's no reason why you shouldn't be able to lock onto the Cardassians."

"Well, I can't," Jadzia replied, and O'Brien could hear her annoyance.

"How about I pull them out into the open?" O'Brien suggested.

"What a good idea," Jadzia said, with more than a hint of sarcasm.

O'Brien looked back at Rom. The Ferengi engineer seemed calmer now. "Okay, Rom. Best thing to do is to climb back on the horse."

Rom's grimace of distaste was clear behind his faceplate. "There's a *horse* in there, too?!"

O'Brien didn't have the strength to explain. "Just give me a hand pulling them out so Jadzia can transport them."

O'Brien could see that the Ferengi engineer would rather start a fight with Worf than handle dead Cardassians, but he gamely tapped his thruster controls and moved into position beside his teacher.

"You get the one on the right," O'Brien said as he moved in to grab the arm stump of the Cardassian on the left. "And be gentle. They're apt to be a bit . . . brittle."

"Shouldn't a medical team come out to do this?" Rom asked as he tentatively reached for the Cardassian on the right.

Exercising caution, O'Brien took hold of the other corpse's arm. For a moment, he was disconcerted because the insulating gap was only about a meter and half deep, and he couldn't see where the dead Cardassian's legs were. But before he could stop to analyze the significance of what he saw, his hand reflexively gave his thruster controls a tap for reverse, and he abruptly tumbled away from the conduit, pulling the upper half of the dead Cardassian with him.

At the very same moment, Rom's renewed screaming in O'Brien's helmet informed him that Rom had discovered where the missing legs were.

He could see it for himself.

The corpse he'd been reaching for was only half there.

Severed at the waist, the truncated body spun around in empty space, slipping away from the conduit with the momentum O'Brien had transferred to it.

And the fate of the lower half was now apparent.

All that remained of it was a shiny discolored patch of merged flesh and metal on the inner hull of the conduit.

The lower half of the Cardassian's body had been fused *within* the metal hull plate of the station.

No wonder Dax couldn't get a clear lock on them, O'Brien thought. The poor devil must have been caught in the worst kind of transporter malfunction imaginable.

So bad that fifteen separate fail-safe systems made certain that such a tragedy could never happen by accident.

Which meant only one thing to O'Brien, as the gigantic station wheeled around his tumbling form.

Odo had two more murders to investigate.

CHAPTER 6

AN ENTIRE WORLD lay before Captain Benjamin Sisko.

Its visage was smooth and pristine, like the all-enshrouding ice caps of a frozen planet. And its unmarked surface held no hidden secrets, nothing lost or obscured in deep caves or folded valleys.

Only smooth, featureless mountains broke the Platonic ideal of that perfect sphere. One long, unending line of regular red stitches, interlocking the two halves of the skin of the world to make a single whole.

Yet from that unblemished perfection, from that balanced mass and absolute symmetry, unending diversity was born in unending combination. Like an omega particle exploding to become an entire universe of possibilities in which—

"Captain Sisko . . . ?"

Sisko looked up from the baseball he held in his hand to glance across his desk. He saw the questioning expression in Commander Arla Rees's eyes and instantly knew this was no time for excuses. This very serious young Bajoran Starfleet officer deserved the absolute truth.

"I apologize, Commander. I must have tuned you out and—"

"That's quite all right, sir. I read the report of your mission to save Captain Cusak. I understand it might take time to recover from such an encounter."

Sisko regarded the attractive young commander with new interest. He had returned from the *Defiant*'s latest patrol—and the mission to save Cusak—to find that Starfleet had unexpectedly assigned him a new second-in-command to coordinate with Major Kira.

Kira's reaction had been explosive. She believed Starfleet was passing judgment on her performance, or the perceived lack of it. Fortunately, Sisko had been able to quickly confirm that Commander Arla was here only on temporary assignment. After more than a decade of intricate negotiation and elaborate construction, the Farpoint Starbase on Deneb IV was finally about to be activated and Arla was slated for the number-two position on the base's command staff. Given the complexities of Starfleet's relationship with the Bandi of Deneb IV, the staffing wizards at headquarters had decided that Arla could benefit from experiencing life on DS9, a living laboratory of cross-cultural complexity.

She'll need the benefit of a few other experiences, too, if she's to survive out here, Sisko thought as he contemplated the Bajoran newcomer before him, whose sharp edges had yet to be blunted by the realities of routine. But he remembered what he had been like when he was a freshly minted commander. He was willing to give her the benefit of the doubt. Jean-Luc Picard had done the same for him when Sisko had taken this assignment, though the captain of the *Enterprise* might not have realized it at the time.

"Thank you, Commander," Sisko said. "But that's no excuse for not listening to your report."

Arla offered him a padd. "You could read it later."

Sisko was tempted. The last thing he needed to hear right now was yet another report on Starfleet–Bajoran cultural referents in the workplace. But why was Commander Arla suggesting that she would be willing to forgo the official schedule? The scuttlebutt had it that Arla wasn't allowing anyone on the station to bypass standing Starfleet orders. Why was she willing to bend the rules for him?

"I appreciate the offer," Sisko said. He put his baseball back in its display stand on his desk and pushed it away so he wouldn't be tempted to reach for it again. "But you've worked hard on that report. I would like to hear it."

Arla nodded, and looked back to the padd, as if trying to find her place. Sisko was momentarily caught by the particularly elegant line of the epinasal folds on the bridge of her nose. There was a slight downward curve to them, which gave her an intriguing expression, as if she had just thought of a sly joke and was keeping it to herself.

Careful, Sisko cautioned himself. She had looked up without warning and caught him staring. Second time in this meeting alone.

"Captain? Is there something you wanted to say?"

Sisko shook his head, making a deliberate attempt to ignore her expression of shy amusement. "Please—continue." Then he leaned back in his broad-backed chair, tugged down on his jacket, and forced himself to listen to every word Arla Rees had to say about the time-and-motion modification studies that had arisen from observations of Bajoran and Starfleet personnel working together.

Regrettably, but inevitably, the thirty-minute presentation was followed by Arla's suggestions for overcoming the perceived difficulties of human-Bajoran interactions. Sisko struggled to give his full attention to each of her recommendations before responding.

"Very clearly thought out," he announced when she had finished. And he meant it. The new commander's report revealed exceptional intelligence. For just the briefest of instants, Sisko felt a rush of pride in knowing that someone with the potential of Arla Rees—who could have chosen virtually any career in the galaxy—had been inspired to join Starfleet.

"Thank you, sir."

"A most thorough analysis of the existing literature as well."

Arla's smile was tremulous, expectant.

Sisko wondered how far he'd have to go with this. "I'll definitely circulate it among the command staff." *That should do it,* he thought.

"And . . ." Arla prompted.

"And . . . I'll ask them to read it." Sisko didn't know what else she wanted of him.

Well, obviously that wasn't it, he thought as he saw Arla's crestfallen expression.

"Shouldn't we have a general meeting of all command staff to discuss implementing my changes? Sir."

Sisko leaned forward, trying to find the best possible way to put what he knew he had to say.

"Commander, truthfully, those are all very insightful

observations about working conditions on DS9. And your suggestions for improving things are just . . . fine. But they're not necessary." Before Arla could respond, Sisko quickly added. "And more than that, they won't work. Can't work."

The dismayed young commander shook her head as if to be sure she had heard him properly, making the chain of her single silver earring sway against her olive-gold cheek.

"I beg your pardon, sir, but how can you know without trying?"

Sisko firmly reclaimed his usual air of detachment, settled back in his chair with a patient smile. "I have tried them, Commander. Everything you've suggested and more. And really, when it comes down to a choice between forcing everyone to do their work according to Starfleet's textbook definition of perfection, or having everyone do their work in their own way, with respect for other people's traditions and work habits, I have found it's better for people to find their own way than to have it forced upon them by an unseen bureaucracy."

Arla's chin lifted, in a way that reminded Sisko of Major Kira when she was not at all convinced of someone else's argument. "But sir, the literature clearly suggests ways that humans and Bajorans could be more efficient as team workers."

With a sigh, Sisko rose to his feet and waved a hand past the closed doors of his office, down the stairs to the lower level of Ops. "I have no doubt that's true, Commander—for humans and Bajorans. But look out there. What about Commander Worf? Commander Dax? And I have a half-dozen other races staffing this station. Should we make Bolians adhere to some form of Bajoran-human work ethic? Should we force Martians to celebrate the Bajoran Days of Atonement instead of Colonial Independence Day?"

Arla's almond-brown eyes met his. "Well actually, sir, one of my suggestions is that all group religious celebrations be banned from the station. Not personal expressions of faith," she hastily amended, as his look of consternation and lack of comprehension registered on her. "I'm not suggesting that. But for the good of the group, religious events really have no place in what is, after all, a military environment—which is what DS9 will be for the duration of the Dominion War."

Sisko concentrated on keeping his voice calm in the face of Arla's surprisingly insensitive conclusion. "Commander, war or no war, this station is first and foremost a civilian installation run by the Bajoran government. Starfleet's presence as an administrative authority is temporary, and strictly limited to security operations. In no way would we *ever* infringe on the religious rights of any culture—which makes your suggestion totally out of line."

Arla's face reddened. "Sir, I'm not suggesting Starfleet outlaw religion, just relegate it to private expression, off-duty. I . . . I don't think there's anything out of line with my suggestion."

"No," Sisko said slowly. "Not as a suggestion. But what surprises me, frankly, is that you—a Bajoran—are making it."

"We're not all religious fan—" and Arla hesitated, apparently rethinking her choice of words. "We're not all religious to the same degree, sir."

"So it would seem."

"I don't mean to offend you, sir. I mean, I know that

many Bajorans believe that the wormhole aliens you've encountered are their Prophets."

"And you don't," Sisko said, not bothering to make it a question.

"Sir, with all due respect, I'd be much more inclined to believe that the Bajoran wormhole was a celestial temple if it didn't form with verteron nodes. I mean, if it's truly a home for gods, shouldn't it operate outside the normal laws of physics, instead of appearing as a natural phenomenon?"

Sisko sat down again and reached out for his baseball. He decided he was going to have to take a closer look at Commander Arla Rees's personnel file. He had met many Bajorans, with many different degrees of belief and many different traditions of worship. But he had never met one who so obviously rejected the idea that the beings in the wormhole were the Prophets.

"I have heard that argument," Sisko said, noncommittally, tossing the baseball from one hand to another while he waited to see what else the surprising young Bajoran would come up with.

Arla didn't keep him waiting, apparently most reluctant to accept such a neutral stance from him.

"Sir, do *you* believe the wormhole aliens are the Prophets? I mean, I know some people call you the Emissary, and I don't mean to offend you, but . . . you're an educated man."

"And as such," Sisko said lightly, "My eyes are open to the full range of wonder the universe contains."

Arla's spontaneous smile was full of quick, responsive humor. "You're not answering my question, sir."

Sisko stopped playing games. He placed his hands together as he thought for a moment. "Very well. What do I personally believe? I am sure there are entities who live in the wormhole. I have no doubt that these entities are the source of the Orbs which have had such a profound effect on your people's history and culture. I have no doubt that these entities are, indeed, what the Bajoran people call their Prophets. And I have no doubt that the Prophets are inextricably involved in the fate of your people."

"That's still not an answer." Now Arla, too, spoke in earnest. "And the question is so simple. Are . . . they . . . gods?"

"A wise man once said, 'Any sufficiently advanced technology is indistinguishable from magic.' Why should it be indistinguishable from the works of gods, Commander?"

"Sir, don't you think there's a difference—a *profound* difference—between having the *attributes* of a god, and *being* a god?"

If you only knew how many times I've asked myself that same question, Sisko thought wearily. "Yes," he said. "I do."

At that, Arla shot him a quick, almost triumphant look from beneath her improbably thick fringe of eyelashes. "So—what is the answer to my question?"

Sisko suddenly felt the need to bring an end to their conversation. "In all honesty, I don't know."

Sisko could see this disconcerting young woman didn't want their meeting to end with that pronouncement. But he could also see that she understood he did not wish to continue on this topic.

So, instead, she turned abruptly to look out the viewports in the main doors. Beyond her, in Ops, Starfleet uniforms mingled chaotically with Bajoran.

She glanced back at him. "So, ten races?"

Sisko reminded himself of his earlier resolve to give

the young commander the benefit of the doubt. In her way she was, perhaps, trying to change the subject, to bring their discussion back to the work at hand. "And that doesn't count the civilian staff," he said.

Arla turned away from the viewports, glanced down at her padd, then hugged it close to her, as if she no longer had any intention of turning it over to him.

"I'm sorry, Captain Sisko," she said quietly. "It's all new to me but I was just . . . trying to help."

"Believe me, Commander, I understand."

Arla took an impulsive step closer to his desk, and Sisko couldn't help noticing that the young commander's stiff military bearing, formerly so reminiscent of Kira's, had suddenly relaxed. "You *do* understand, don't you," she said with an open, frank look of approval that reminded Sisko of earlier days, of his youth, when he too had been capable of uncomplicated emotion. "I . . . I felt you would from the moment I met you."

Sisko might have been distracted before, but he was on full alert right now. There was only one way of dealing with what was happening, what might happen. "We should have dinner," he announced, rising to his feet to meet her gaze directly, though he had to look up to do so. The young Bajoran was a half head taller than he.

Arla's smile of pleasure was instantaneous. "I'd like that."

"So would I. I'd like you to meet two very important people in my life. My son, Jake, and Captain Kasidy Yates."

Arla regarded him quizzically. "I don't remember a captain of that name from the Starfleet personnel lists."

"Ah," Sisko said, as he stepped around his desk and toward the main doors, moving close enough to trigger their sensors. "That's because Kasidy is a civilian. A merchant captain." The doors slid open and the noise of Ops filled Sisko's office like a current of power. "She is also the woman I love," Sisko added deliberately, knowing no better way to set the record straight than by a blunt statement of the facts.

He was greatly relieved to see Arla's shoulders come back into square and her posture return to that of an officer. "I look forward to meeting them both," she said politely.

"I'll check with Kasidy, but I believe tomorrow night is open."

Arla stood beside Sisko at the top of the stairs to his office. She handed him her padd after all, and as he took it, her long, slender fingers for the briefest of instants grazed his, generating a current of another kind. "Tomorrow night," she said.

Startled by his own response, Sisko took the padd, promptly removing his hand from contact with Arla's. He was about to dismiss her when his communicator chirped, followed by a familiar voice.

"Bashir to Sisko."

Sisko tapped his communicator. "Go ahead, Doctor."

"I've completed my preliminary scan of the two bodies Chief O'Brien found."

Sisko could sense Bashir's unspoken conviction that his captain wasn't going to like what he heard next.

"What's the bad news?" Sisko asked.

"The Chief was right," Bashir answered. "I'd say we're looking at two more murders. And at least from a preliminary analysis, it appears both were killed by the same type of weapon that killed the Andorian."

Sisko's jaw tightened, and he felt his back stiffen as he reached a conclusion he suspected Bashir was about to share with him. "I see. Does Quark have a connection to the Cardassians?"

"I've asked Odo to bring him over to the Infirmary. I think you should be here."

"On my way, Doctor." Sisko paused for a moment, and then made a sudden decision. "Speaking of interspecies relations, Commander Arla, have you ever seen a changeling and a Ferengi interact?"

"Oil and water?" she asked.

Sisko shook his head. "Matter and antimatter. And you're about to experience it first-hand."

CHAPTER 7

"QUARK, QUARK, QUARK . . ." The expression in Sisko's eyes revealed such an unsettling combination of exasperation and pity that Quark couldn't hold the captain's gaze. Instead, he glanced furtively around the infirmary to avoid it—but everyone else present was looking at him too.

Everyone except the two very dead Cardassians on the examination table.

What was left of them.

"Can't you . . . cover them up or something?" Quark finally asked. "It's disgusting."

"Hmm," Odo said.

"What 'hmm'?" Quark demanded. "And don't say it's another sign of a guilty conscience. I've never seen them before. My conscience isn't guilty."

"I wasn't aware you had one," Odo said.

"Besides, Quark," Dr. Julian Bashir added, looking

up from his continuing inspection of the corpses, "after being blasted with microwaves, transporter-fused to hull metal, and exposed to vacuum for a few years, these two are so mummified that one of them could be Garak and you wouldn't be able to recognize him."

"However," Garak added with a polite cough from his position overlooking Bashir's shoulder, "one hastens to add that a simple process of elimination should serve to confirm that I am *not* one of the dear departed."

With open-mouthed disbelief, Quark watched the decidedly striking new Bajoran Starfleet officer who had entered the Infirmary with Captain Sisko turn to address DS9's sole Cardassian inhabitant. "Oh, are you Garak?" She held out her hand. "I'm Commander Arla. I've heard so much about you."

After a moment's hesitation, Garak shook the Bajoran officer's hand as if it were coated with a Brigellian nerve toxin. "I'm sure you have."

"Excuse me," Quark interrupted, "but can we get back to *me* for a minute?"

"That depends," Odo said gruffly. "Are you ready to make a confession?"

"That's it! That is absolutely it!" Quark bared his artfully stained fangs, which had cost his parents a small fortune in orthodontic bills to twist into such Ferengi perfection. "You people—oh, you take the spore pie, all of you. Two nights ago, an unexplained death, and what do you do? You play Let's Blame the Ferengi! And now, two more unexplained deaths—from *ten years ago*—and what do you do? *The same thing!* Well, I'm sick of it." He jabbed an accusatory finger at Odo. "I'm sick of being your one-size-fits-all answer to crime on DS9!" Then he pointed at Sisko. "And I'm fed up with Starfleet not standing up to Odo's lax standards and sloppy investigations!"

Odo bristled with predictable indignation. "Let's talk about 'sloppy' after we've discussed those Denevan crystals you sold to the Nausicaan last Saturday night. You thought I didn't know, didn't you?"

"Arrrghh! You're doing it again! Changing the subject! Every time I make a point in my own defense, it's as if you people don't even want to pretend you've heard me."

Quark turned to Captain Sisko. "When the Cardassians withdrew, *you* were the one who wanted me to stay on this station as an example to others. To keep the community together."

"As I recall," Sisko said calmly, "first I had to threaten to put Nog in jail."

Quark waved his hand dismissively. "Negotiations. That's all that was. The point is, I stayed, didn't I? Even in the middle of this war, the Promenade is thriving. Do you have any problem hiring workers to live on board these days? No. Because I've done exactly what you wanted me to do."

"Let's not forget you made considerable profit at the same time," Major Kira said pointedly.

Quark felt as if he were in a shuttle spiraling out of control. "Of course I'm in it for profit! I'm a businessman! But there are rules to business!"

"Two hundred and eighty-five. Isn't that right, Quark? Some of which have never been revealed to a non-Ferengi." Odo's condescendingly snide tone was utterly maddening to Quark.

Quark was so overcome by frustration, his voice almost rose to shouting level. "When the Dominion took over this station, I could have made immense profit by turning in the major and . . . and your son, Captain . . . and everyone else working in the Resistance. I could have become an honorary Vorta and ended up with a ship made of latinum. But I stayed here and I risked my life—and my business—for you people! And this—*this* is how you repay me. You should all be ashamed of yourselves."

This time, there was only silence in the Infirmary. Quark straightened his jacket, wondering if it just might be possible that he had finally managed to get through to these small-lobed, microencephalic aliens.

And then Sisko ruined it all by saying, "Why ten years?"

Quark sighed. "Didn't you hear a word I said?"

"Every one of them," Sisko confirmed. "And the two that concern me are 'ten years.' How do you know when these two Cardassians were killed?"

Quark's ridged brow crinkled in puzzlement. "Isn't . . . isn't that what Dr. Bashir said? That they were killed during the Occupation? That was ten years ago."

"Technically," Kira said, "the Occupation spans anywhere from six to sixty-six years ago. Though the station wasn't built until twenty-four years ago."

"All right!" Quark sputtered. "I confess! I took a number out of thin air! I was confused! I suppose the almighty Federation has laws against Ferengi businessmen being confused and I deserve everything I've got coming to me!"

"Calm down, Quark," Bashir said. "You're jumping to far too many conclusions."

"Me?!"

Bashir nodded. "The only reason I've called everyone in here is to see if we can't get some answers." He turned to Garak, who was still hovering behind the examination table on which the Cardassian corpses were displayed. "Garak, may I call upon your expertise?"

Garak regarded the doctor warily, the reptilian gray nobs of his forehead bunching together in deep furrows. "Oh, Doctor, I'm afraid that in matters of mysterious deaths, I am entirely bereft of experience."

Quark took some comfort in noting that no one in the Infirmary appeared to believe Garak any more than they appeared to believe him.

"I was speaking of your expertise as a tailor," Bashir clarified.

Now smiling expansively, Garak nodded graciously. "But of course. You'd like me to examine the clothes these two are wearing."

"Please," Bashir said. "They're carrying no artifacts, no currency, weapons, I.D. rods . . . all they have is their clothes."

Without further hesitation, Garak bent over the table as if he saw such grotesquely mutilated bodies every day of his life. The only reason Quark watched what happened next was because the thought had occurred to him that his freedom might be dependent on the outcome of Garak's examination.

Garak's sharp gaze traveled from one wizened corpse to the next. One body—the one truncated at the waist—was clothed in an undistinguished tunic of brown fabric. The other body, which had been severed approximately at the knees, wore a similar garment, this time of blue.

Quark held his position as Garak picked up a pair of medical tongs from the side of the examination table and pushed them through the slightly elastic resistance of the medical containment field that surrounded the bodies. No doubt Bashir had set up the field more to protect the sensibilities of his visitors than out of concern for medical contamination. That simple act, however, released a sudden and most unpleasant odor of charred flesh mixed with the sickly-sweet-smelling antiseptic spray the doctor had used to coat the bodies. Quark turned away, coughing and gagging, noticing that even the doctor held a hand against his mouth.

Garak, however, appeared impervious to the stench. Concentrating on his task, he delicately nudged the head of the body in the brown suit. Quark's eyes narrowed. The Cardassian tailor's handling of the tongs made it seem as if he was quite experienced with autopsy procedures. "Ah, here's your first clue, Doctor, and one doesn't have to be a tailor to see it."

Quark stopped breathing so he could take a closer glance at the gruesome mess on the table. He stepped back quickly, having seen nothing that told him what Garak was talking about. From his expression, neither had Bashir.

"His hair," Garak said. "See how long it is? The way it's tied? Very characteristic. This man was a soldier in the Invidian Battalion. They managed the southern provinces."

"Managed?" Kira repeated angrily. "They were a death squad."

Sisko put a hand on Kira's shoulder as if passing her an unspoken signal. "Then why is he in civilian clothes?" he asked.

Hew-mons, Quark thought, with a shake of his head. *Always changing the subject.*

"Perhaps he died on his day off," Garak said lightly,

directing his answer to Kira. "Whatever his reason for choosing this attire, I'm sure his DNA profile will be on file at Central Records. Determining his identity should make it easier to discover his date of death."

"What about the other one?" Bashir asked.

Garak glanced over at the slightly more complete body in the blue tunic. He used the tongs to lift up a tattered flap of cloth from the corpse's chest. "This one . . . I believe he might have been in a struggle. See how the fabric is torn on the shoulder?"

Now everyone crowded around the table to verify the tear in the body's tunic, then just as quickly reeled back. With all of Garak's movement through the surface of the medical containment field, the distressingly sweet, cloying odors of death and disinfectant had become even stronger.

"Any way of dating the clothes?" Bashir asked, with a hand shielding his nose. "The width of the lapels? Length of the sleeves?"

Garak cocked his head, as if puzzled. "Fashion is more a function of geography than time, Doctor. What is stylish on one world is hopelessly garish on the next. There are colony worlds in the Union right now where this brown tunic would be the latest word in male furnishings. And other worlds where a man wearing anything blue would be arrested for disrupting public morals."

"Can you at least make a guess as to *where* the clothes were made?"

Still holding the torn shoulder fabric in the tongs, Garak frowned in disapproval. "I'm afraid this tunic was replicated. It could come from thousands—tens of thousands of different suppliers across the quadrant." He released the fabric remnant, then turned his attention to the second corpse's brown tunic with an approving smile. "Ahh, but *this* is—or at least *was*—a hand-tailored garment of the finest quality." With his customary, fastidious touch, he manipulated the tongs to open up the tunic to examine its lining. "It should be possible to trace the fabric, and from there. . . ." Garak froze.

"Do you see something?" Bashir asked, though everyone, including Quark was aware that something had shocked the Cardassian tailor into utter stillness.

"The lining." The tone of Garak's voice seemed oddly flat to Quark.

The doctor looked over Garak's shoulder. "What about it?"

"I often used this fabric myself. It's from a very small mill on Argellius II. I . . . look at the exquisite workmanship of that cross-stitching . . . oh my." Garak looked up at the curious faces of the people who surrounded him. "This is one of mine."

"That's an enormous help," Bashir said to Garak. "Isn't it?"

"I'm . . . not absolutely certain that's true," Garak replied, almost haltingly.

Quark couldn't remain silent any longer. Did he have to do everything himself? "Are you kidding? The kind of records the Cardassians keep put Ferengi records to shame. And I guarantee you, if I had sold someone a hand-tailored suit *twenty* years ago, I'd still know the name of his mate, his offspring, *and* his pet vole."

Whatever honest reflection of mood that had been revealed in Garak's face disappeared as quickly as if an Ark had been closed on an Orb of the Prophets. From across the examination table, Garak delivered a withering cold glare in Quark's direction. "Ordinarily, I might say that the random sand scratchings of an unhatched *krimanganee* would put Ferengi records to shame, but alas, this is not the time for banter." Resentfully, Quark noted how the Cardassian tailor softened his expression as he turned to Bashir. "And again, ordinarily, I would have to agree with you, Doctor. It should be a simple matter to discover to whom I sold this tunic, because I, too, never forget a customer." Garak's face showed he was as in the dark as they were. "Unfortunately, though, it appears I have forgotten this one."

Kira voiced the next logical question before Quark could shout it out. "Is it possible someone else bought the tunic and gave it to this man as a gift? Or that he stole it?"

"No, no, Major, you misunderstand," Garak said with an exaggerated display of patience. "Obviously, I could not remember this customer by his features, given the condition he's in. What I meant to say is, I have no recollection of selling this tunic to anyone. In fact, I have no recollection of even making it. Yet it is unquestionably my handiwork."

While everyone else looked mystified, Quark suddenly saw the pattern that was emerging from the void of confusion. But before he could act to confirm his suspicions, he saw Odo looking thoughtfully at Garak.

Aha, Quark thought, *Odo sees it, too.*

The changeling's next question was proof enough.

"Garak, is it possible that you made or sold this tunic about the time of the Withdrawal?"

"The lining fabric is old enough. It's . . . possible," the tailor admitted.

But Quark had no intention of standing idly by

while Odo proceeded with his typically, time-consuming, step-by-step approach to an investigation. It was as if the changeling had never heard of the 9th Rule and the value of acting on raw instinct.

"Garak," Quark quickly said, "tell me—can you remember *anything* that happened on the Day of Withdrawal?"

"Of course," Garak said forcefully. "Every detail. Why are you smiling at me like that?"

Quark shot a sideways glance at Odo. The changeling was frowning, but Quark knew it was for the same reason that he himself smiled.

Garak was lying.

And Quark and Odo knew it.

"Would you like to try answering that again?" Odo asked Garak.

Garak looked at Quark, looked back to Odo, drew himself up rigidly. "I would not. And now, since I appear to have answered everything I can about these garments, I have a business to attend to."

Then Garak turned and left the Infirmary without another word.

Quark grinned at Odo, daring him to tell the others about what they both knew to be true. "See? The same thing happened to him."

"Am I the only one who's missing the point of this conversation?" Sisko asked.

Odo said nothing so Quark moved immediately to exploit the changeling's reluctance. "Captain," he announced, "allow me. Because unlike Odo, *I* have nothing to hide. You see, neither Odo nor I can recall anything about what happened to us on the Day of Withdrawal. And I think it's obvious that Garak doesn't remember anything, either."

"It *was* a long time ago," Sisko said.

"Not to me," Kira interrupted.

"Not to any Bajoran," Commander Arla added.

"And certainly not to any Cardassian," Quark said, "*or* Ferengi, or *changeling* who was on the station at the time. I'd say we've got a real mystery brewing here."

Sisko rubbed at his goatee. Quark suppressed a shudder of distaste. Even though the captain had worn the look for several years now, Quark still thought it made him look half-Klingon. "Quark, why am I feeling that *you're* changing the subject now?"

"It's the same subject, Captain. Two Cardassians dead from ten—I mean six years ago. An Andorian dead today. Dr. Bashir says everyone was killed by the same type of microwave energy discharge. Now what you have to do is find someone with a link to all three victims."

"We have," Odo said firmly. "You."

Quark turned in a full circle, appealing to the rest of them. "Does anyone else find it suspicious that Odo is going out of his way to blame these murders on me?"

Odo leaned forward and put his hands on the edge of the examination table. "You're heading into dangerous territory, Quark."

"See?" Quark said to Sisko. "See how defensive he is?"

Odo's voice actually shook with anger. "Quark, I'm warning you. . . ."

But, undaunted, Quark pressed the attack. "So, where were *you* on the Day of Withdrawal, Odo? In fact, where were you when Dal Nortron was killed? By a weapon that couldn't be detected by your own security scanners, I might add."

"That's it! You're going back to your cell." The changeling made a move as if to vault over the examination table and its grisly contents.

To Quark's relief, Sisko intervened again. He held up a hand. "That's enough, Constable. This is an open investigation."

"Not with Odo in charge," Quark complained through clenched teeth. He turned to Sisko. "Captain, I formally request you take him off this case because of conflict of interest. *He* should be a suspect, too."

"I will do no such thing. As far as I'm concerned, I agree with Dr. Bashir. Too many people are jumping to too many conclusions on too little information." Sisko looked at the doctor. "I want you to prepare complete DNA profiles for these two bodies so we can identify them."

"Through Cardassian Central Records?" Bashir asked.

"That's right."

"I'll prepare the records," Bashir said, "but aren't we at war with the Cardassians?"

"For humanitarian purposes, Starfleet and the Cardassian Union have established unofficial lines of communication to facilitate the identification of war dead and the repatriation of remains. You give me the profiles, I'll handle the rest."

Then Sisko faced Odo. "As for you, Constable, I want a complete report on Dal Nortron's death on my desk within the hour. And I don't want to read any conclusions not supported by incontrovertible evidence. Is that understood?"

Odo's initial reply was terse. "Yes." But then he continued. "Unfortunately, I will not be able to provide a *complete* report because Quark has refused to cooperate with my investigation."

"Is that right, Quark?

Quark squirmed under Sisko's intent gaze, but he remained defiant. "Why should I cooperate?" Quark said. "Odo's not interested in the truth."

The captain's reply was so loud, it echoed off the hard surfaces of the Infirmary walls and ceiling, and Quark reflexively covered his sensitive ear channels to protect them from the assault. "I am tired of this game you two are playing. Even if you don't think Odo's interested in the truth, you can be certain I am. Cooperate."

Quark knew a bluff when he heard one. "You can't order me to do anything," he countered.

"You're absolutely right," Sisko agreed. "But what I *can* do is decide that neither Bajor nor Starfleet has jurisdiction over the death of two Cardassian nationals. Which means, I could turn over these bodies to the Cardassians, along with our prime suspect, and let them settle this matter."

Quark swallowed. Hard.

"The choice is yours, Quark," the captain concluded. "You can either cooperate with Odo, or you can 'cooperate' with the Cardassians."

Quark frantically sought to extract some benefit from a deal he knew he would be forced to accept. "All right, but I want Odo to release me from custody, and to provide me with a bodyguard."

The look on Sisko's face told Quark that was the last thing he had expected the Ferengi to say. "What do you need a bodyguard for?"

"Dal Nortron's partners," Quark said. "The Andorian sisters."

Sisko looked at Odo for clarification.

"Their names are Satr and Leen. They claim to be representatives of a trade mission from Andor so they have limited diplomatic immunity. They both believe Quark murdered Nortron and have filed for the Andorian Rite of *Kanlee.*"

"And just what is the Andorian Rite of *Kanlee?*" Sisko asked.

"Roughly translated," Quark said darkly, "it means kill the Ferengi."

Odo ignored the interruption. "It's an old Andorian tradition," the changeling told Sisko. "They believe Quark killed Nortron. To maintain the balance of good and evil in the universe, they want to kill him. They are . . . a passionate people."

For a very long moment, Sisko stared at Quark, and Quark could tell the captain was making his decision. Quark felt almost sure he could predict what it was going to be.

"Here's my offer, Quark. You cooperate with Odo in the investigation of Dal Nortron's death, answer all the questions he asks, and instead of being confined to your cell, you'll be under station arrest, with a bodyguard."

Sisko's terms were exactly what Quark had expected. He took it as a minor victory. "Thank you, Captain."

But also as he expected, Odo didn't approve. "What about the murder of these two Cardassians?"

"For now," Sisko said, "I'll handle that investigation." He glanced around the Infirmary once, as if to make sure no one else had anything to say, then concluded, "I think we're finished here."

"But—but—" Quark protested, "what about the Day of Withdrawal?"

"One investigation at a time," Sisko told him. The captain looked back at the incomplete bodies of the unknown Cardassians. "This is one mystery where time is no longer of the essence." Sisko then nodded at Kira and the new Bajoran officer. "Major Kira, Commander Arla, you're with me." Then the captain and the two Bajoran officers left the infirmary.

Odo gestured sarcastically toward the door. "Come along, Quark. You're with *me*."

But it appeared Dr. Bashir wasn't quite finished with either of them. "Just a minute, you two. Is it true what you both said about not being able to remember what happened on the Day of Withdrawal?"

"A complete blank," Quark said emphatically. "I remember starting to pack up the breakables in the bar when the first reports of the troop transport launches started coming through . . . and then . . . next thing I knew, Rom and Nog found me asleep in the storage room and it was the next day."

Bashir looked at Odo. "How about you, Constable?"

"Nothing so mysterious," the changeling growled. "I've been thinking more about it, and I do remember breaking up a fight outside the chemist's shop. I was obviously hit by phaser fire, and woke up a day later when the Bajoran provisionals arrived."

"You're sure that's what happened?" Bashir asked. "I mean, someone saw you get shot, or you confirmed there *was* a fight at the chemists?"

Odo nodded. "Now that you mention it, yes. I do recall looking into it over the next few days. When the fighting broke out, I went to the Promenade, and the next thing I knew I was waking up and the whole thing was over—the withdrawal, Gul Dukat's departure, I missed it all."

Quark hid a smile of victory. Odo had just told his biggest lie of the day—one that would be easy to disprove. At a time when it would be most profitable to do so, that is.

"Well," Bashir said, "a phaser stun would certainly explain a loss of short-term memory."

But Quark wasn't willing to let Odo escape so easily. "Tell me, Doctor, would Odo's getting hit by phaser fire explain why *I* don't remember what happened that day? Or why Garak doesn't remember?"

Bashir looked confused. "Garak said he remembered everything perfectly."

Quark rolled his eyes at the doctor's incredible gullibility. "Dr. Bashir, Garak *says* he's a tailor. You don't believe *that,* do you?"

Bashir hesitated, then apparently decided to sidestep Quark's question. "There are techniques available, completely harmless, that I can use to see if either of you—or Garak—might be suffering from some type of post-traumatic stress syndrome, perhaps causing you to block out some kind of unpleasant memory of the Day of Withdrawal. I'd be happy to . . . see if I could help."

"Thank you, Doctor," Odo said. "But I doubt if I have anything to remember other than being in a phaser coma."

"I'll get back to you," Quark said drily. He would need many more details about how Bashir's techniques worked before he allowed himself to be in a position where someone might have access to his safe combinations and account passwords.

Bashir seemed disappointed by Quark's and Odo's lack of enthusiasm for his suggestion. "Well, you know where I am."

With that, Odo escorted Quark from the Infirmary, and they both made their way along the Promenade to the Security Office. Quark was only too glad to leave the unsettling smell of death and disinfectant and return to the bustling life of commerce the Promenade represented. Appreciatively, he sniffed the sweet tang of frozen *jumja* mixed with the incense from the Bajoran Temple, all overlaid with the exotic perfumes of twice a dozen worlds. It all was pure magic to Quark. Because to him, the combination of all these scents from all these potential customers gathered together to shop in one place invariably coalesced into the sweetest scent of all—latinum.

His snug jacket expanded to the breaking point as he breathed in deeply, happily. Then he saw the crowds in his bar to the left and instantly his sense of well-being evaporated. His eyes widened in alarm. There was no way his idiot brother Rom could handle that kind of crowd. He started toward the entrance. "I'm just going to check in with—"

But Odo grabbed him by the ear. "*After* you've 'cooperated,' " he hissed, and pulled Quark after him.

It was only with immense effort that Quark kept himself from squealing in public. Odo *knew* how much that hurt. But Quark continued without protest, because in just those few seconds he had had to look in through the main entrance to his bar he had seen three people who he did not want to notice him in his current state of custody.

Two of the people were those Andorian sisters, together at a small table and leaning so close together in intent and sibilant conversation that their blue antennae almost touched.

But the third person, sitting at the bar, trying and

failing to look interested as Morn prattled on and on and on to her, was far more important to avoid than either of the Andorians.

She was Vash, a human female who had traveled the galaxy not only with Jean-Luc Picard of the *Enterprise* but with the unfathomable entity known only as Q. She was also Quark's favorite archaeologist—the one potential business partner he constantly thought of with real regret, as the one who got away.

And if Vash had returned to Deep Space 9 ahead of schedule, then Quark had no doubt that the news of Dal Nortron's untimely end had already spread across the quadrant—and all of Quark's other 'special' customers were already on their way.

Unfortunately, for that exact same reason—Dal Nortron's death—Quark had been left with nothing to sell.

Which meant that over the next few days, the Andorian sisters were not the only ones on Deep Space 9 who'd be looking to kill a certain Ferengi barkeep.

CHAPTER 8

"ALL RIGHT," Sisko said to Kira and Arla as the turbolift began its short trip from the Promenade to the Operations Center, "who wants to start? The Day of Withdrawal."

Kira looked at Arla, who shook her head. "It only took a day on DS9," Kira said. "But it was more like a week of withdrawal on Bajor. The Cardassians pulled back to their garrisons and the spaceports in stages." She paused for a moment, clearly remembering scenes of devastating destruction, then doggedly continued. "Burning the villages, poisoning the land and the rivers. For the first few days, the Resistance didn't know it was happening everywhere. Each cell thought it was seeing the leadup to a concentrated regional bombing attack. The Cardassians had done that sort of thing before."

The lift rose up through the final deck and, as

always, Sisko felt a familiar sense of coming home. Ops was the heart of Deep Space 9, as much so as the bridge of a starship. Even the harsh angles and bare metal of its towering Cardassian components had become an oddly welcoming sight to him.

He exited the lift car with Kira and Arla close behind him and headed off in the direction of the science station, where Jadzia was on duty. She was running a metallurgical analysis on her screens.

"Dax," Sisko said, "join us." He nodded at the short flight of stairs leading to his office. Jadzia rose from her station to follow him at once.

As Sisko started up those stairs, he asked Kira if she could remember exactly where she had been on the Day of Withdrawal.

She shook her head with a rueful smile. "I missed it. Twenty years in the Resistance, and the week the Cardassians left I was in a triage center in Dahkur, burning with fever and pretty much delirious. Lake flu. It swept through the whole province that year."

"No lasting effects, I hope."

Kira shrugged. "So do I."

Behind them, Jadzia stepped through the entranceway, and the doors to Sisko's office slid shut.

"What about you, Commander?" Sisko asked Arla. He was pleased to see that whatever air of over-familiarity she had exhibited an hour ago, she was keeping it in check now.

"Oh, I was on the *Solok.*"

Sisko hadn't recalled that posting from his quick glance at the Bajoran newcomer's file. "The Vulcan science vessel?"

Arla nodded. "We were at *Qo'noS*. A very dull assignment to remap the Praxis Ring."

"So, you weren't involved in any of the events of Withdrawal either?"

Kira broke in. "She wasn't involved in the Occupation. Period."

As if a ship had just decloaked before him, Sisko was suddenly aware of the tension between the two Bajoran officers, and realized with a start that it had been there since he had first seen them meet.

He exchanged a quick glance with Jadzia and her subtle nod confirmed that she saw the same animosity. Sisko wondered how he had missed it. But he could guess what was behind it.

"Is that right?" he asked in as neutral a fashion as he could.

Arla kept her eyes on him, ignoring Kira. "My grandparents lived on B'hal Ta. A Bajoran colony world. When the Cardassians annexed Bajor, my family was able to relocate to New Sydney. That's where I was born."

"You were fortunate," Sisko said. He decided that that accident of fate was more than enough reason to account for the major's feelings toward Arla Rees. He knew that there were those on Bajor—especially those who had served in the Resistance like Kira—who believed that expatriate Bajorans who had not suffered through the Occupation, and who had not voluntarily returned to their homeworld or taken up arms against Cardassia, were only one step removed from being collaborators.

"Yes, sir, very fortunate."

Sisko decided to bring the conversation back to the less-controversial present. "So, from your experience, Major, and from any research you might have done, Commander, can you think of any reason why personnel on board DS9 on the Day of Withdrawal might have suffered from memory loss, selective or otherwise?"

"Benjamin?" Jadzia asked. "Who's suffering from memory loss?"

Sisko quickly summarized for his old friend Quark's claim to be missing memories of the day in question, and the Ferengi's suspicions that Odo and Garak were similarly affected.

"Fascinating," Jadzia said. "The old name for it is 'Missing Time Syndrome.' On Earth, it goes back centuries, before first contact, when the Reticulii were conducting their genetic profiling of humans and didn't want anyone in the sample group to know they had been transported to the orbiting medical ships. Today, the Federation's own First Contact Office uses the same techniques if a duck blind's exposed or a precontact investigator is detected."

"In this case," Sisko said, "I think we can rule out any involvement by the Reticulii or the First Contact Office. What other possibilities should we consider? Medical experimentation?"

Kira shook her head. "The Cardassians conducted a horrendous amount of so-called medical research on Bajoran prisoners. Some of it involved mind control. But that was mostly in the camps. Up here, they kept the slave workers in line with force and random executions. So I think it's unlikely anyone experimented on Quark—especially since, if the Cardassians *had* experimented on him, their protocols usually called for the experimental subjects to be killed when the experiment was finished."

Arla looked hesitant, but now offered her own theory. "I don't know how relevant this is, but starships use anesthezine gas to disable intruders, and memory lapses are sometimes reported as a side effect."

Sisko looked at Kira. "We have a Starfleet anesthezine system installed on DS9. But there're also the remnants of a Cardassian neurozine gas dispersal network which, as I recall, was kept on hand in case of worker revolt."

Kira's voice was bitter. "Crowd-control inhalants like anesthezine are nonlethal. And nonlethality was never a concern of the Cardassians. They used neurozine at fatal concentrations, and if they had used it up here on the Day of Withdrawal, there would have been a lot more than just four Bajorans dead."

Sisko turned to Dax, who had so many times in the past been able to share the wisdom and experience of her past hosts. "Old Man?"

But she didn't look hopeful. "Benjamin, there're so many methods of blocking memories that I wouldn't know where to begin without more information."

"What kind of information?"

Jadzia pressed her lips together in thought. "Well, I'd like to know how much time Quark believes he's missing. Is it the same length of time that Odo and Garak can't account for? Is it the exact same period of time? Were they together on the Day of Withdrawal? Were they exposed to . . . a radiation leak? An unusual subspace discharge?" Her face brightened as if she had just had a sudden insight.

"Something just occurred to you," Sisko said.

"I talked with Odo yesterday about his investigation into the Andorian's death. He thinks a microwave weapon was used, but I think it's possible some sort of accidental energy pulse could have caused similar injuries."

Sisko smiled at Jadzia. "Old Man, you've been

spending too much time in the holosuites with Worf. You were the reason we even found the Cardassians' bodies. Right after your talk with him, Odo sent a team down to the lower levels to look for energy anomalies. They found one where a power conduit entered the lower module. And Rom's team found that the cause of the anomaly was that the Cardassians had been transporter-fused into the inner hull plates, weakening the shielding."

Jadzia made a face at Sisko. After so many years of friendship, she was allowed more freedom with Starfleet protocol. "I knew that, Benjamin. I was standing by with the tractor beam when Rom found the bodies. I was just wondering if an anomalous *energy* event that resulted in microwave radiation could also be tied to an anomalous *temporal* event."

"An anomalous temporal event?" Arla said. "Those are incredibly rare."

"Not on DS9," Sisko said. "Unexpected time shifts are quite common in this region of space."

Jadzia confirmed it. "Actually, the odd temporal events we've experienced in the past almost all arise in some way out of our proximity to the wormhole. The structure of subspace is extremely twisted in this region. What's really surprising is that we don't experience even *more* jumps in time than we do. But on the Day of Withdrawal, the station was still in orbit of Bajor. And the planet's gravity well would have provided a great deal of shielding against almost any wormhole-related phenomena."

Sisko sat down on the corner of his desk, reached back, and picked up his baseball. "Okay, so we can rule that possibility out, too. But I still want this looked into.

"Major Kira," he said, rolling the ball back and forth in his fingers, feeling its comforting contours relax him as they always did, freeing him to think more clearly. "The constable seemed reluctant to discuss the Day of Withdrawal in the Infirmary. Perhaps he won't be as reluctant speaking with you. See if you can get him to talk about what he remembers from that day."

Kira seemed surprised by the request. "Captain, I'm not sure I feel comfortable doing that."

Sisko understood her reluctance. Everyone on the station knew about the love affair that had blossomed between Kira and Odo in the last month. And as their friend and colleague, Sisko was happy for both of them. "I'm not asking you to betray a trust, Major. Let Odo know that you're asking on my behalf. Let him know that I understand his reluctance to discuss what he remembers in front of Garak, but that I would appreciate a more forthright account that will remain confidential."

Kira nodded, accepting his argument.

Sisko tossed his baseball up a few centimeters, then caught it again. "Commander Arla, since I'm assuming you've had few if any dealings with Cardassians, I'm assigning you to question Garak."

Arla's eyes widened. "Question him about what, sir?"

"What Dax wants to know. I want a timeline of everything that happened to Odo and Garak *and* Quark on the Day of Withdrawal." Then he smiled winningly at Jadzia.

"Don't tell me," she said, pouting. "I get to talk to Quark."

Sisko's grin grew. "I can't imagine anyone else he'd rather open up to."

"Captain," Kira broke in briskly, "can I ask why something that happened six years ago is important enough for us to drop our other duties and—"

"No one's dropping their other duties," Sisko said. "There's a war on."

"Exactly," Kira agreed. "And I don't see the point of expending extra effort just to solve the deaths of two Cardassians, especially one who was in a death squad."

Sisko replaced his ball on his desk, then stood up to address Kira and the others, not as their coworker and friend but as their commanding officer and captain of Deep Space 9. "Major, those two dead Cardassians represent a mystery. And I will not have mysteries on my station. Because until we find out how those Cardassians died, and why Quark and perhaps two other people on this station had their memories interfered with, I can't be certain if any of it might happen again. And believe me, if an attack wing of Jem'Hadar fighters is bearing down at us, I want to know that my officers are not suddenly going to develop a case of amnesia and end up fused into the hull plates. Is that clear?"

Kira, Arla, and even Jadzia stood at attention. "Yes, sir," Kira said.

"Right away, sir," Arla added.

"Ben, I'll speak to Quark as soon as Odo's finished with him," Jadzia confirmed.

Sisko could see that there was more that Jadzia wanted to say. "Something else?" he asked.

"What about the Andorian?"

"Quark's many things," Sisko said reluctantly, "but he's no murderer. Though I do think Odo's enjoying this chance to make him sweat. And at the same time, I think that by appearing to be convinced that Quark is guilty, Odo's making the real murderer feel overconfident."

Arla seemed shocked by Sisko's statement. "Sir, do you honestly believe that the constable has the wrong man, and that the real killer is still free on the station?"

"That's exactly what I think, Commander."

"But . . ." Arla said, obviously disturbed by the thought, "isn't knowingly permitting the continued custody of an innocent man a violation of Starfleet directives concerning the application of local laws? And aren't you risking the real murderer escaping? Not to mention putting the other personnel on this station at risk of being killed?"

"Commander, Starfleet regulations are written by bureaucrats in comfortable offices back on Earth. As captain of this station, I do have the authority to . . . be flexible in how I choose to follow those regulations, whenever I feel a given situation is outside the parameters Starfleet considered when the regulations were written. Believe me, Commander, this entire station falls outside those parameters."

Jadzia smiled at Sisko, and then took the confused commander's arm. "Odo won't be through questioning Quark for a while. Why don't we get some *raktajino* and . . . we'll talk."

Sisko could see that Arla was flattered by Jadzia's request; she left the office with her, Major Kira following a moment later.

As Sisko stood in the doorway to his office watching the three officers head for the turbolift, he was pleased to unexpectedly see his son, Jake, just emerging from the lift on the main deck below. The love he felt for his boy, this anchor for him in the storm of events that regularly engulfed this station, filled Sisko with a transcendent joy.

But his sudden smile was undercut as he saw who stepped out of the lift behind Jake: Jake's best friend, Nog, and Chief O'Brien.

Jake looked up to wave at him, and Sisko returned the gesture, growing even more concerned as he noted Jake's half-hearted smile, Nog's nervous expression, and O'Brien's flushed cheeks.

"Hi, Dad," Jake called out as he took the stairs to the upper level, two at a time.

"Sir," Nog added crisply, just behind Jake.

Sisko frowned, and the three visitors froze where they stood. "You know, if this were six years ago and I saw you three coming up here like this, I'd think Chief O'Brien had caught you *boys* playing in the Jefferies tubes again. But you two young *men* are too old for that now, aren't you?"

O'Brien was wheezing slightly as he resumed climbing the stairs. "Funny you should say that, sir."

Sisko sighed. "Should we step inside?"

"Yes, sir," Jake said glumly.

Sisko followed the three into his office, suspecting he wasn't going to like what they had to tell him.

He was right.

CHAPTER 9

FOR THE second time in two days, Jake Sisko opened the small egress panel and slid it to the side of the cramped Jefferies tube.

"It's open," he said. Then he heard Nog's communicator badge chirp as his friend passed on the report to Chief O'Brien.

The chief's voice came back, echoing along the metal-walled tube. "According to your position on the station plans, you two lads should be facing another fifteen meters of unobstructed passageway."

Jake sighed. He and Nog had finally done what they should have done years ago, and told DS9's chief engineer about the hidden section of the station. Then, with an agitated O'Brien at their side, they had told Jake's father. And *then*—Jake was sure it was just to compound the humiliation he and Nog felt—Sisko and the chief had insisted they repeat their story to the forbidding, and strongly disapproving, Lieutenant Commander Worf.

But even though it was plainly evident through all the reporting that his father was keenly disappointed in him for having kept something like this a secret for so long, Jake could also see that neither his father nor the chief nor Commander Worf actually believed the story when they first heard it. So why were they upset? Not that they shouldn't be, because the story *was* true. It was just . . . Jake didn't know. He only hoped that in a million years or so, when he was his father's age, he would have a better grasp of a teenager's way of thinking.

Jake lifted his head to look back down the narrow Jefferies tube at Nog. "I don't get it. Do they still think we're making this up?"

Apparently, Nog's comm channel was still open because O'Brien answered. "No, I don't think you're making it up. I'm just telling you what's on the screen."

"Sorry, Chief," Jake said with a grimace. "I'm going to climb through the opening now."

Jake pushed himself up through the open access way just as he had before, then again swung his body around to free his legs so he could drop down into the dark section of corridor. Nog followed a moment later, much more quickly and smoothly than the last time. Once again, his palm torch was the only source of light.

"Tell them," Jake said.

Nog tapped his communicator. "We are in the corridor." Nog made it sound as if they were commandos who had just beamed in behind enemy lines.

A few seconds later, the short section of corridor lit

up with the golden energy of the transporter effect, and three sparkling columns of quantum mist resolved into Jake's father, O'Brien, and Worf. Each of them carried their own palm torch. Jake wasn't quite sure why Worf had his hand on the phaser he wore. But then, Worf was like that.

Benjamin Sisko's expression was unreadable. "Chief?" was all he said. Jake had noticed that his father had a shorthand way of dealing with his command staff, almost as if they shared some low-level telepathic link.

Chief O'Brien's attention jumped back and forth between the corridor and the large engineering padd he carried. The padd was similar to the kind Jake had seen artists sometimes use for sketching. "This makes absolutely no sense," the chief said. "Look at the deck plan for this section."

As Sisko and Worf stood on one side of O'Brien to study the engineering display, Jake stood with Nog on the other.

On the padd, Jake could see four yellow dots representing the team's active communicators tightly grouped together, blinking in the middle of what a label identified as a storage room.

"This is clearly not a storage room," Worf stated in his deep, somber voice.

O'Brien nodded, pointing to various bulkheads that surrounded the blinking lights on the padd display. "I think I can see what's happened here. The Cardassians' own official plans have been altered to show that these two storage rooms, here and here—" O'Brien's finger touched the surface of the padd, "—have back walls that extend an extra three meters or so. Notice this relay room extends two more meters. And this heat-exchange conduit is . . . maybe a half-meter wider than it has to be. And the two corridor sections running to either side are the same. So I'm betting the conduits that are supposed to be running right above us have been rerouted to either side, too, probably passing through the deck plates instead of running through that Jefferies tube that just isn't there."

Jake was surprised by how seriously the three men were reacting to the unmarked corridor's existence. His father, especially, looked grim. "Why weren't these deviations noticed when the first retrofit team went through the station to confirm the Cardassian plans?"

O'Brien looked apologetic. "I'm betting they were noticed. But there are lots of discrepancies between the Cardassians' plans for the station and how they were executed. A project this big, there would have to be. I've noticed little things over the years myself—pipes in the wrong order, a junction box on the left wall instead of the right . . . it gets so you come to expect it. But they're usually not major enough to bother altering the plans to fit."

"Yet this stretch of corridor is . . ." Sisko swung the beam of his palm torch from one end of the section to the other. ". . . at least ten meters long, Chief. That's a lot of station to go missing."

"No argument from me, sir. All I can say is that this is a noncritical section of the station, so with the war changing our priorities, we just haven't had a full refit team down here yet. For what it's worth, we would have found this . . . missing space . . . eventually."

Sisko levelled his gaze at Jake. "For what it's worth, we should have been informed about this missing space six years ago."

Jake was about to remind his father how many times he had apologized already, when Nog nudged him in the side. Jake understood. Nog had gone to great lengths to explain to Jake that their best defense was to behave like Starfleet cadets—limiting their responses to Yes, sir; No, sir; and most importantly, No excuse, sir. "It's a good way to avoid arguments," Nog had emphasized.

So Jake remained silent until his father said, "All right then, where's this . . . hidden holosuite?"

Nog hurried ahead. "Right down here, Captain. It's the only door in that bulkhead."

The team followed Nog until they were gathered together by the closed door. Worf and O'Brien immediately scanned the door and the area beyond it with their tricorders—one set for engineering readings, the other for security.

Jake shifted his weight from one leg to the other, impatient with the delay. He wanted this over with. "Dad, there's nothing dangerous in there. We've been inside a lot of—"

Sisko cut him off with an icy glare. "And maybe you've been lucky. Before they left, the Cardassians booby-trapped all sorts of equipment and facilities in this station, *especially* anything with a military function. And the only reason I can think of for putting a holosuite down here is for training purposes."

"Yes, sir," Jake said dispiritedly.

"I detect no explosives or triggering devices behind the door," Worf announced as he lowered his tricorder.

"Captain," O'Brien added, "I'm not even picking up any evidence of power flow. The tricorder's telling me there's a room beyond the door, about five meters by six. But I don't think anything inside is even connected to the station's power grid." The chief made an adjustment on his tricorder. "In fact, I'm not even picking up any evidence of holo equipment. Either projectors or microforcefield emitters."

Nervously, Jake looked up and down the corridor to see if there was any chance they could somehow be at the wrong door. But just as every time before, there was only the one.

"You're certain it *was* a holosuite?" his father asked him.

"Dad, it could run our fishing hole program perfectly. Water and everything."

His father looked back to O'Brien. "Then it has to be a holosuite, *and* for it to run a program from my own data library it has to have some type of interface with the station's main computer network."

O'Brien made more adjustments, then frowned. "If there is, sir, I'm going to have to make a more detailed scan. From inside."

Sisko nodded at Worf. Worf tapped the door control and the door opened.

Jake almost smiled as he heard Nog take a deep breath. His best friend was preparing himself for the embarrassment of having everyone see his adolescent modification of the fishing-hole program, complete with Ferengi bathing beauties.

But as the light from the palm torches stabbed into the room, it revealed . . . only a room.

Jake and Nog both tried to push ahead, but were held back by Worf.

"I've never seen that before," Jake said to his father.

"Sir, this holosuite has *always* been in operation," Nog added.

Sisko looked at O'Brien. "Any chance the holosuite

ran on batteries and yesterday's visit finally exhausted them?"

O'Brien was skeptical. "No battery powerful enough for a holosuite goes completely dead that fast. I'd still be able to pick up some residual charge somewhere. And even taking a direct reading from the far wall, there are *no* holoprojectors on it or in it."

Sisko nodded at Worf again and he and the Klingon stepped into the room together. Jake watched as his father and Worf reached the middle, then turned slowly, playing their palm torches around in a circle like all-seeing scanners.

"It appears to be a lab of some sort," Worf said slowly.

"Maybe," Sisko said. "It does look as if they were building things in here. Maybe a machine shop? Chief O'Brien?"

O'Brien stepped in next and Jake watched him make the same careful examination of the room, this time giving a running inventory of everything he saw. "Circuit testbed, communications console, a Type-IV computer interface. . . ." He gave Sisko a significant look. "That's identical to Dax's science station in Ops." He returned to his assessment of the room. "A few storage lockers, maybe for lab coats or tools or lunches . . . None of them locked."

"What about that?" Sisko asked, aiming his torch to a corner of the room Jake couldn't see.

"Well, it's a console," O'Brien said. "But I don't recognize the configuration."

Sisko looked at both O'Brien and Worf. "Gentlemen, any energy readings?" he asked.

Worf and O'Brien replied at the same time. "No, sir."

Sisko motioned to Jake and Nog. "You two. In here."

Jake and Nog stepped over the lip of the door and into the room. In this nonoperational mode it was completely unfamiliar to Jake, and he could see the same lack of recognition in Nog.

"Really, sir. We never saw it this way," Nog said.

"You two said you were able to change whatever program it was displaying," Sisko prompted.

"That's right," Jake said. "I'll give it a try." He cleared his throat. "Room, this is Jake Sisko. Show me my fishing hole."

Jake unconsciously braced himself for the sudden swirl of holopixels and the odd optical bounce that had always followed that command.

But nothing happened.

"Anything?" Sisko asked O'Brien.

"I've set this at full sensitivity, Captain. If there were a single acoustical pickup in this room, I would have detected the current flow created when Jake spoke." He showed the tricorder's flashing face to Jake's father.

Sisko answered his own question. "Nothing."

Jake winced at his father's tone of voice. "Dad, this *was* a holodeck. We played in my fishing hole. And Nog had a really great Ferenginar adventure playground." The playground had been at the edge of a dismal, rain-misted swamp, Jake remembered, but the programmable swinging vines *had* been a lot of fun.

"What else?" Sisko asked sternly.

Jake shrugged, perplexed by what he had no way to explain, or prove. "A couple of other programs from our personal library. You know, the theme park at Tranquility Base, the Klingon Zoo . . ." He glanced at Nog.

"We could only ever run programs that were in your personal files or my father's," Nog said. "I mean, we could customize elements of them with voice commands, but . . . we never really figured out the room's full operating interface."

Sisko looked again at O'Brien and Worf as if silently soliciting their opinions.

In response, Worf asked the next question. "Are you certain you never saw a holoprogram that was Cardassian in nature? A military training scenario? Cardassian history reenactments?"

Both Jake and Nog shook their heads.

"Oh," Nog suddenly added. "There was the moon. The Bajoran moon."

"Which moon?" Sisko asked sharply.

Jake stared beseechingly at Nog, who shrugged. "Dad, I don't know. One of the inhabited ones. That was the program that was running yesterday when we came in. That's what made us think that someone else had been in here."

Sisko rubbed his free hand over his clean-shaven scalp. It was a gesture Jake had seen his father make a thousand times, most often when Dax was forcing him into checkmate in three-dimensional chess.

"Chief," Sisko said, "if we don't know what that console is, is there any chance it could be some radically different form of holoprojector?"

Jake took a look at the unidentified console as O'Brien walked over to it and the four palm torches in the room converged upon it.

The console was definitely Cardassian in design—a large, jagged boomerang shape, tilted slightly toward the operator, finished with the familiar dull-gray bonding metal. The flat-panel controls were unlit, though the light from the palm torches showed that the controls were arranged in standard Cardassian logic groupings. About the only detail that made the console unusual was that in the center of its slanting surface, a section had been inset in order to hold a flat shelf about a half-meter square.

Even to Jake's untrained eye, it seemed obvious that whatever had been connected to the console on that shelf had been ripped out. Two power leads dangled to either side, their interior component wires roughly torn apart. Jake could even see heat damage on the console just beneath the lead ends, as well as in the center of the shelf.

"Now this is interesting," O'Brien said as he held his tricorder only centimeters from the damaged console.

"Was it a holoprojector?" Sisko asked.

"I doubt it," O'Brien answered. "But I don't think I've ever seen energy traces like this before."

"What kind of energy?" Worf asked.

"Hard to say, Commander. I don't think it's from a weapon. But . . . whatever was on this section here—" O'Brien pointed his tricorder at the console's inset shelf, "—it was radiating . . . something I haven't seen before."

Jake stepped back as his father moved in front of him and Nog as if to shield them from the console. "Dangerous?" his father asked.

"Not now, sir. And there's no way to know if what I'm picking up came about because it was a slow release of radiation over a long period of time—in which case, I don't think it ever would have been dangerous—or if it came in a sudden, explosive release, in a short time—in which case, it might have been."

O'Brien snapped his tricorder shut with a practiced flip of his hand. "Sorry, Captain. But that's the best I can do with this. I'm going to need a full team to take it apart. Couldn't hurt to have Dax take a look, too."

"Maybe in a day or two," Sisko said. "I've already got her helping out with the dead Cardassians."

Jake was surprised to hear Commander Worf snort.

Sisko raised his eyebrows. "A problem, Mr. Worf?"

Worf looked up at the ceiling. "Sir, it is not any of my business."

"But . . . ?"

"For Quark to say that he has lost his memory to provide an alibi for his actions at the time the Cardassians were killed is . . . ludicrous."

"You're right," Sisko agreed. Jake was as surprised to hear his father say that as it appeared Commander Worf was. But then his father finished his statement. "It *is* none of your business."

"Yes, sir," Worf growled grumpily.

Jake caught the lightning-quick wink and a smile that his father meant just for him. Then he watched as his father tugged down on his jacket and transformed himself from Jake's father into a Starfleet captain again.

"Anything else you feel we should know?" he asked Jake and Nog. "Any detail, however small, you think might help us out?"

Jake and Nog looked at each other, shook their heads.

Sisko accepted their answer. "All right. You two can—"

"I have a question," Chief O'Brien suddenly said. "How did you two find this room in the first place?"

"We used to explore the Jefferies tubes," Jake said.

"I can understand that," O'Brien replied. "But what possessed you to go to all the trouble of opening up that access hatch? It couldn't have been easy."

Jake looked down at the deck, trying to remember the first day he and Nog had found the room. "I think it was because we had never seen one so small. It's not exactly a standard size."

Nog coughed. "We were . . . looking for hidden Cardassian treasure, Chief."

"Ah," O'Brien said. "For a couple of twelve-year-olds, that makes perfect sense. But then, when you came in here, to the room, for the first time, how did you know it was a holosuite? It couldn't have been running any of your own programs without your having given it a command, right?"

"Right," Jake said with surprise. He looked down at Nog. "What *was* running when we came in?"

Jake felt his father's hand on his shoulder. "Jake, do you have any sense that you can't *remember* the first time you came into this room?"

"I don't think so," Jake said, wondering why his father suddenly sounded so worried.

"Wait! I remember," Nog said.

Everyone looked at him. He looked up at Jake. "You didn't want to go inside, remember?"

Jake laughed. "Oh yeah. I was . . . I was afraid. I remember now."

Nog looked back to Sisko. "So Jake dared me to go in first."

"And what program was running?" O'Brien asked.

"That's what was so great," Nog said excitedly. "It was Ferenginar. The swamp outside the capital city. It was dark, and wet, and raining. I was *so* excited. I came out to tell Jake it was just like my adventure playground program, and when we both came back in, we found the playground just a few hundred meters away."

O'Brien looked at Sisko. "The room recognized him. Called up his favorite program from his father's personal library. And all in the space of time it took to open the door."

Jake looked at the serious expression that his father, O'Brien, and Worf all shared now. "Why's that bad?"

O'Brien answered. "Jake, there's no power coming into this room. There's no computer link through that Type-IV console or through any other piece of equipment in the room. Yet somehow this room had the data-processing capability to identify Nog and call up a program from his father's personal library in seconds. Not even the holodecks they use at Starfleet Academy have that kind of processing ability." O'Brien turned to Sisko as if making a formal report. "Sir, with this new information, I think it's reasonable to assume that this was a top-secret Cardassian research facility, probably involving advanced computers and holo-replication technology far beyond anything we have."

"I agree," Sisko said. "So why did the Cardassians leave it behind?"

"Perhaps," Worf said in a voice full of grave concern, "the equipment in here was too complex to be removed in time during the Withdrawal, and was considered too valuable to be destroyed."

Jake could see that his father was definitely intrigued—and disturbed—by that possibility. "You know," he said softly as if talking to himself, "Starfleet has never been able to come up with a satisfactory explanation for why the Cardassians didn't activate

DS9's self-destruct system when they withdrew. I wonder if this room—this lab—is the reason. Did they achieve a breakthrough here that they hoped to keep hidden until they could return?"

"But they did return, Captain," Worf said. "Last year. Why did they not reclaim their equipment then?"

Sisko looked up, and Jake could see he was enjoying the challenge this room was presenting. "Perhaps the work being done here was so secret that only a handful of people knew about it. Perhaps they died during the Withdrawal, or shortly after. There could be a dozen reasons, Worf."

"But if the work was so secret and so valuable," O'Brien said, "then why was it being carried out *here?* In a mining station? In an occupied sector subject to attack by Bajoran resistance fighters?"

"I don't know, Chief," Sisko admitted, and didn't seem troubled by his lack of an answer. "But you can be sure there was a reason. We're dealing with Cardassians here, and they have a reason for everything they do." He looked around the room, deep in thought. "If this *was* a Cardassian research facility, then you can be sure that the reason it is *here,* is because this is the only place it *could* be."

Jake saw that O'Brien didn't share his captain's sense of urgency for the problem at hand. "But, sir, why would that be?"

Jake could see his father was in his element now. His face was alive with new purpose. "Who knows, Chief. But one thing's for sure—even after six years, this old place still has a few surprises left in it."

CHAPTER 10

THE ONLY THING worse than a Ferengi with a headache was a Ferengi with an earache. And at this moment, in his darkened bar in the middle of DS9's night, Quark suffered from both—unquestionably the aftermath of the past eight hours he had spent with Odo.

And now his woes intensified as he saw the after-hours condition of his establishment. The chairs had not been placed on top of the tables. There were still glasses on the dabo table. And behind the bar, the replicator had been left on.

"Why do I even bother?" Quark said to the empty room. He gazed up at the vivid orange, red, and yellow stained-glass mural that dominated the first floor of his bar. All its backglow panels had been left on, too. "What about you, Admiral? Do you have an answer?"

The mural kept its silence, which was no great surprise. Quark shuffled over to the bar to pour himself a very large drink.

Exactly what the mural was, Quark really wasn't sure. For years, that same wall had been dominated by a large Cardassian *galor,* courtesy of Gul Dukat.

Quark seldom cared about politics, and if the commandant of Terok Nor had wanted his grandmother hung on the wall, it would have been fine with the Ferengi. So the lurid green, pink, and yellow symbol of the Cardassian Union, which looked to Quark like some improbable combination of the hooded Smiling Partner of Ferengi legend and a short-handled screwdriver, had remained proudly in place—until Gul Dukat had swaggered in one day to announce he had just won a spectacular work of rare and valuable art in a late-night game of tongo. And since Quark's was the only public facility on the station with a ceiling high enough to properly display this great treasure, Dukat proclaimed Quark's would be its new home.

At the time, Quark had cared as much about his establishment's decor as he did about politics. His was the only bar on the Cardassian half of the station—indeed, it was the only bar on the entire station, the closest thing to competition being the Cardassian Cafe. And if a tired Cardassian soldier or Bajoran trustee would rather eat replicated Cardassian *neemuk* without benefit of *kanar* to wash it down or the company of luscious dabo girls, then Quark was just as happy not to have those lackluster, boring slugs taking up valuable space in his bar.

So, Cardassian *galor* or Dukat's esteemed art treasure, it mattered little to Quark at the time what was on the back wall of his bar. True, he had had to shut down for two days while a team of Bajoran artisans were brought up to install the mural, and Subcommandant Akris had not granted Quark's request for a matching percentage decrease in the weekly kickback—that is, licensing fee—that Quark had to pay the station management office. But Dukat had more than made up for Quark's initial lost profits by pretentiously buying endless rounds for his staff on the night the mural was grandly unveiled—to mostly diffident though polite applause.

As Quark had worked the tables that night, he had overheard the Bajoran comfort women saying that at least the orange light helped bring a more Bajoran flush to the cold gray faces of the Cardassian officers they were forced to entertain. Quark himself liked the orange light, because it made it easier to use short measures in amber-colored drinks. And Dukat got to proudly trumpet on about the addition he had made to culture on Terok Nor—making the station an uplifting beacon of Cardassian light amidst the primitive darkness of the Bajoran sector.

It was just that no one seemed to be sure what the mural was supposed to represent—until finally, that first night, when much *kanar* had been consumed and two glinns had already been dragged off to the Infirmary after a particularly brutish fight (which fortunately had lasted long enough for Quark to take bets and clear five slips of latinum), Dukat toasted the mural in such a way that it was clear what *he* thought it was.

"To a mighty enemy," Dukat had proclaimed, "defeated at last, now sentenced to look on the works of the Cardassian Union and despair! Ladies and gentlemen, I give you the portrait of Admiral Alkene, late of the Tholian Assembly!"

After Dukat and his guests had left that evening, Quark and Rom and two Cardassian mining engineers had closed the place, leaning on the bar, staring thoughtfully up at what was now called the Tholian mural.

One mining engineer drunkenly offered up the observation that Tholians had faceted heads.

The other, in an equal state of disequilibrium, disagreed, maintaining it was the Tholian helmets that were faceted, and that the shape of Tholian heads was closer to the long and pointed sections included in the mural. Except that he was positive the mural had been installed upside down.

Rom had volunteered that *he* was fairly certain the mural was actually a version of the traditional good-luck banners that were always hung over the drinking troughs in what he delicately referred to as Tellarite mud-pits of ill repute. "Yep, they . . . make them by the hundreds on Tellarus," Rom had sniggered. "And you see that same crazy design on Tellarite scarves and pill boxes and . . . lingerie."

Quark remembered glaring at his idiot brother, demanding to know why the Tellarites would put a portrait of a *Tholian admiral* on *lingerie!*

Rom had simply shrugged and gone on to explain in excruciatingly precise and clinical detail that the shape in the mural was not that of a Tholian head at all, but of an entirely different, but equally remarkable part of Tellarite male anatomy.

Even as he began to laugh at Rom's hilariously ribald description, Quark had felt his heart actually stop beating as he suddenly remembered the presence of the two Cardassian engineers. Fortunately, both were so drunk that they didn't hear Rom dismiss the Gul's great work of art as nothing more than a big Tellarite . . . well, even in private, Quark had not been able to say the word, though he relished the aptness of the image.

For at least a year after that, he and Rom had shared a rare moment of rapport in their guilty, private pleasure every time Dukat came to the bar with whoever his latest comfort woman was and regaled her with the story of Admiral Alkene, ending with a grandiloquent toast and salute to the mural.

Only Quark and his brother knew to what the gul was really raising his glass, and they kept that knowledge to themselves. And if any other visitors to Quark's during those last years of the Occupation recognized what was hanging on the wall for what it was, they also wisely kept their expert knowledge—and their laughter—to themselves.

Though Quark had never been able to confirm Rom's saucy identification of the mural's subject matter, and for that matter had never been able to determine how his idiot brother had come to have such deep knowledge of Tellarite mud-pits of ill repute, it was always in Quark's mind that if the day ever came that the Cardassians left Terok Nor, he would celebrate that glorious occasion by shattering Gul Dukat's mural into ten thousand shards.

But that day had come and gone, six long years ago, and the mural remained, with both he and Rom still referring to it, in private, as the Admiral.

But the Tholian mural was of no importance this night, and Quark tried not to think of the disarray the bar had been left in—or the overtime it would cost him to get it back in shape for Morn's arrival in the morning. Instead, he poured himself a *snoggin* of Romulan ale.

And since old traditions are hard to ignore, he did hold up the glass to the mural. "To you, Admiral—or whatever you are. Because you're still here, and I'm still here, and I have absolutely no idea why that should be." He gulped down a mouthful of the ale, shivering as the blue fluid sliced through him like a protoplaser. "Except, that is," he coughed to finish his toast, "as some twisted reminder of the 117th Rule: You can't free a fish from water."

"Actually . . ." a distant, muffled voice interjected, "that's the 217th Rule. A lot of people make that mistake."

The empty glass slipped from Quark's hand and shattered on the counter of the bar as he stared at the mural. For just a split second, visions of latinum came to his mind as he calculated the increased business he could attract with a talking wall decoration that knew the Rules of Acquisition. But only for a split second.

"Rommm . . ." Quark sighed. "What are you doing back there?"

"Uh, up here, Brother." Quark looked up. Rom was standing on the second floor, holding a large tray stacked with dirty dishes. He carried a server's billing padd in his mouth, accounting for the muffled nature of his voice.

"My mistake," Quark said in exasperation, "what are you doing *up there?*"

"Uh, cleaning up." Rom started down the stairs, eyes fixed on the precariously balanced dishes before him. "We had three different parties in the holosuites tonight, sooo . . . things are still a bit messy."

Rom made it to the bar and put down his tray just as Quark lunged to catch the first falling glass. "Where are the servers?" Quark demanded. "Did they all quit? Or did you talk them into going on strike again?"

Rom took the padd from his mouth and wiped the edge of it on his sleeve. "Well, no. I . . . sent them home."

Quark shook his head, having a hard time believing he was actually having this conversation. "How could you send them home when the place looks like this?!"

"Because . . . it takes longer to clean up when we've been this busy—and then we have to pay them overtime."

Quark blinked. Had his brother actually said something sensible? "Wait a minute. You sent them home—to save money?"

Rom nodded excitedly. "Well . . . yes. You see, tomorrow's my day off from station duty, so I can stay up all night to clean the bar, and that saves us the overtime charges for the serving staff."

Quark snorted cynically. "Sure. So you can pocket that money for yourself."

"Uh, no, Brother. If we can keep overtime to a minimum for the next two weeks, then when we get our next beverage shipment, we'll be able to pay on delivery, and that will net us a one-point-six-seven percent discount for cash. Which, when you multiply by our standard adjusted gross markup, works out to an additional profit of—"

"I know what it works out to," Quark said. "Who gave you that idea?"

Rom looked around the empty bar and shrugged. "Uh, . . . you've been saying we need to cut overhead, and that made me think of how Chief O'Brien tries to . . . optimize the station's engineering resources, so

I used his Starfleet scheduling programs to examine the bar's operations. And . . . it worked! Didn't it?"

Whether it was the headache/earache assault, the exhaustion he felt after Odo's interrogation, or—more probably—the Romulan ale, Quark ran out of things to complain about. "You surprise me, Rom."

Rom grinned. "Uh, you surprise me, too. I . . . heard you talking to . . ." He started to snicker. ". . . the Admiral."

Quark poured another *snoggin* of ale. "I didn't know you were eavesdropping." Quark went to swallow the drink, but stopped when he saw Rom staring at him. "What?"

"I heard what you said, Brother. Why *is* the mural still here? I mean, you always said you wanted to . . . get rid of it as soon as the Cardassians were gone."

Quark took a deep breath, realized he had no answer, so he made one up. "I got used to it. It's the same reason you're still here."

Rom's gap-toothed grin was knowing. "Oh, I know *that's* not true. You're just tired after being in that cell for so long. I sent a message to the Nagus!"

Quark felt as if he had just been slapped awake. "About what?!"

"Well . . . Odo told Leeta to tell me that you said that you needed a lawyer."

"Doesn't *anyone* on this station know about negotiations?" Quark exclaimed in disgust. "You know, when you make an outrageous demand that you know won't be met, in order to counter the outrageous demand made by the other party?"

Now it was Rom's turn to look confused. "You mean . . . you don't need a lawyer?"

"No."

"But—"

"But what?"

Rom shrugged. "You killed that Andorian."

"Rom! I did not kill anyone!"

Rom blinked innocently. "You killed that Klingon."

"An *accident!* What are you? Working for Odo now?"

"But, Brother, if . . . you didn't kill the Andorian, why have you been under arrest for the past two days?"

"Because Odo is one of those rare individuals on this station who is actually more of an idiot than you are!" Even as the words were leaving his mouth, Quark could see he had hurt his brother's feelings. "I'm sorry, Rom. Really. I didn't mean it. It's Odo who's put me in such a bad mood." Quark set up a second glass. "C'mon, have a drink to celebrate my release."

Rom watched carefully as Quark poured more ale. "But . . . wasn't it supposed to be a good idea that you were in protective custody?"

Quark handed the glass to his brother. "It was, until Odo decided I really was guilty and made it a real arrest. He still thinks I'm guilty."

The two Ferengi clinked glasses and toasted the Admiral. Then Rom gaped like a drowning fish as the Romulan ale scorched his insides. "I . . . I don't . . . understand . . ." he gasped.

"You drank it too fast," Quark explained.

"N-no," Rom wheezed. "If Odo still thinks you're guilty, then why did he let you go?"

"Captain Sisko listened to reason. *Hew-mons* do that occasionally, you know, Rom. He made Odo release me *and* give me a bodyguard."

"What bodyguard?"

Quark pointed out to the Promenade. "That body—oh, for—"

The Bajoran security officer he had left standing watch at the main door to the bar was gone.

Quark crouched down and waved his hand at Rom. "Check the other door. Hurry!"

Rom jumped back to look spinward at the smaller entrance to the left of the bar. "Uh, there's no one there either."

Quark's desperately racing mind tried to make sense of the situation. The bodyguard had been Bajoran, so he probably hadn't been bribed to abandon his post. And if Vash was making a move on him, she wouldn't kill an uninvolved party, so she had either stunned the guard and—

"The Andorian sisters," Quark hissed.

Rom nodded with a happy smile. "They're very pretty."

"They want to kill me!" Quark yelped from behind the bar.

Rom leaned over to peer down at his hiding brother. "But . . . that was only because they thought you killed Dal Nortron. And since you didn't . . ."

"But *they* still think I did!"

Rom nodded with understanding. "Oh . . . then you *are* in big trouble. Huge trouble. Gi*gan*tic trouble."

The only thing that stopped Quark from slapping his brother silly was his desire to stay down, out of the line of fire. "Thank you for figuring that out for me, idiot! Now listen carefully. . . ."

"Brother, I don't like it when you call me names. Chief O'Brien—"

"Shut up! Shut up and go to security. Get Odo. I don't care if you have to pour him out of his pail—"

"Uh, I don't think he lives in a pail anymore—"

"I don't care! It's not important! Just tell him his guard is gone and he needs to—"

A sudden series of swift knocks froze Quark in mid-command.

He mouthed the words, "Who . . . is . . . it?"

Rom mouthed back the words, "I . . . don't . . . know."

Quark made fists with both hands, and sputtered out loud, "Of course you don't know—you . . ." He caught himself, dropped his voice to a whisper. "You didn't look."

"Oh," Rom said, as if the concept of seeing who was at a door was startlingly new. "I can do that." He left the bar.

Quark sank deeper behind it, knowing there was nowhere to run. The closest entrance to his network of smugglers' tunnels was in a wall halfway across the bar. Then he brightened. The lights were out. Maybe . . . just maybe whoever was at the door who had come to kill him would think Rom was Quark, kill Rom, then leave. Quark chewed his bottom lip, trying not to jinx the possibility of good fortune by thinking too much about it. But it *was* possible. There could still be a happy ending to this tawdry mess after all.

"Hello?" Quark heard Rom speaking softly in the distance. "Is . . . someone there?"

Quark braced for the sound of a phaser. *My poor brother,* he thought. *How brave he is to risk his life for me.* He began to plan Rom's memorial party. He was sure he could get Chief O'Brien to pay for it.

"Hello?" Rom said again.

Quark heard the hum of the door inductors as they began to slide open.

"Is someone—*ah!*"

Quark grimaced as he heard his brother's death cry swallowed by the crackle of an energy discharge. *At least it was fast,* he thought. He'd be sure that his nephew Nog took comfort in that knowledge.

But then he heard footsteps—a sound so faint only Ferengi ears could perceive it.

Vash, Quark thought, outraged. She knew what he looked like. That *hew-mon* female had killed Rom out of spite. *You'd think spite would be enough for her.*

Then Quark heard a second set of footsteps. He stifled a groan. Two sets could only mean he was wrong about Vash. It *was* the Andorian sisters. They knew what he looked like too.

Who am I fooling? Quark suddenly thought. It was one thing to sit back and hope for disaster to strike others in order to save him. But the 236th Rule said it best: You can't buy fate.

I have to be brave, he told himself. *I have to avenge Rom's brave sacrifice. I have to stand up for what I believe in.*

Slowly, Quark craned his head around and reached for the bottle of Romulan ale, grabbing it by its neck. In his mind, he painstakingly choreographed the moves he would have to make to go on the offensive—a sudden leap to his feet, smash the bottle to create a jagged makeshift weapon, then prepare for victory. If there were any other result, he wouldn't know it until he was on the steps of the Divine Treasury bribing the Nagul Doorman.

So be it, Quark thought with utter finality.

And then in a brilliant burst of speed and grace, Quark thrust himself to his feet, spun around like a dancer, swung the bottle of Romulan ale against the edge of the bar and—

—screamed in high-pitched mortal agony as the *entire* bottle shattered, slicing his palm with shards from the fragile neck.

"Frinx!" Quark squealed, as he clasped his bloody hand to his chest and looked out across the bar to see the last person he expected to see—

"Rom?!"

"Uh . . . sorry brother . . . but there was nothing I could do."

Quark blinked through a haze of pain. Now his hand throbbed as badly as did his head and ears. "Nothing you could do about what?!"

"Well . . . he made me open the door."

Quark wrapped a bar rag around his bleeding hand, but that only drove the bottle shards in more deeply. And despite Rom's babbling, there was no one else present.

"*Who* made you open the door?!"

Rom looked down at something on his side of the bar. "*He* did. He . . . said you wanted to see him."

"Rom," Quark said as he rocked from foot to foot, "I can't see *anyone!*"

"Uh . . . because you're not looking?"

Quark sighed and trembled and wanted to cry, all at the same time. He leaned forward, looked over the edge of the bar, and saw—

—multicolored stars explode in his vision like the prettiest globular cluster he had ever seen.

As Quark fell into those stars, he heard what could

only be the laughter of the much-maligned Tholian Admiral echoing in his poor wounded ears. And he suspected that the basic underpinning of his personal philosophy had been proven true once again.

No matter how bad things look, they can always get worse.

CHAPTER 11

SOMETIMES Sisko felt that he had never left the wormhole after his first meeting with the aliens. That after his first encounter with the Prophets in their Celestial Temple, everything that had happened since—or that *appeared* to have happened—was somehow already a memory. A memory he was merely reliving.

Standing before the sink in the tiny kitchen alcove of his quarters on Deep Space 9, Sisko whisked at the eggs in their copper bowl, smearing out the streaks of dark pepper sauce, frothing the egg mixture into a whirlpool just as the wormhole frothed the quantum foam of normal space-time.

How many times had he done this—made an omelette? How many times had he made *this* omelette? Or could it be they were all part of the exact same moment in time and—

—he was a child standing on a low wooden step-stool in the kitchen of his father's New Orleans restaurant. His father—Joseph—stood behind him, his large, comforting hand guiding his son's small hand on the whisk as it swept through the eggs, teaching him as his father had taught him, and—

—he was a father looking over his own son's shoulder. Little Jake-O was standing on a low wooden step-stool in the cooking corner of that cramped apartment he and Jennifer had rented in San Francisco as they waited for the *Saratoga* to return to port so they could finally share their careers, and their dreams, as a family. He held Jake's small hand in his, guiding it as his father had guided him, as Jake might someday guide his own child's hand—

—all the *same* moment, these memories of things long ago and of things still to be, yet all bound up together in the soothing traditions of those kitchens.

He laughed, softly, caught up in his discovery.

"That sounds nice," Kasidy Yates said.

Drawn suddenly from all moments to *this* moment, Sisko turned to Kasidy Yates where she sat on a chair at the dining table set for breakfast. Her lithe form was draped in one of his caftans, a textured cotton with a bold brown and white blockprint pattern from Old Zimbabwe. Her long brown fingers gracefully cradled a cup of morning coffee, her soft dark hair still mussed from bed, her clear brown eyes not quite yet open. Her infectious smile transfixed him, as it had from the first day they'd met.

"I've missed that," he heard her say. "You laughing."

Sisko held the copper bowl against his hip as without conscious thought he continued to fluff the eggs. "I was thinking that the reason the Prophets made me their Emissary is because I already knew about nonlinear time."

Kasidy frowned, didn't understand.

Sisko's smile widened. "The kitchen!"

Kasidy nodded with sudden understanding. "Cooking does seem to carry you away," she said with an answering smile.

Sisko leaned over to give her a kiss on the forehead. "But it always brings me back to you." The light moment transformed when he did not move away.

Kasidy put down her coffee, Sisko his bowl, as Kasidy reached up to his face and kissed him as they had not kissed in weeks, in months, perhaps ever.

"I . . . thought I had lost you," she whispered, her breath soft against his cheek.

Sisko felt her body tremble, as if she were fighting back tears.

He knew why.

A week ago, they had been on the *Defiant.* Kasidy had volunteered to be a convoy liaison officer for Starfleet escort duty to Vega. So they could be together.

It had been a terrible mistake. And the mistake had been his.

In loving Kasidy, he had made her a part of his life that was separate from Starfleet and the Dominion War. In tearing down the barriers between his life and his duty, he had only succeeded in putting her in harm's way—at his side.

Once before, he had done that to the woman he loved, and it had cost her her life. Surviving the consequences of that mistake had taken him twelve years and the intervention of beings beyond human comprehension.

And he had.

Yet even now he could still see Jennifer, motionless on the deck of the *Saratoga,* her soul forever lost to him except in memory.

As protection from the cruel uncaring universe that might still end the existence of Kasidy Yates, Sisko now took refuge behind a different shield around his heart, a shield he had begun constructing the moment he and Kasidy had found themselves in active service together on the *Defiant.*

If Kasidy died under his command, the only way he could be certain he could still function to save his ship and his crew was to see her already among the dead, to mourn her before the fact, to be prepared for the awful day he might lose her. But even as he tried to reduce his vulnerability, Sisko knew it was impossible. He was in love and he was loved.

He stroked her hair, knowing how wrong it all was. First to put her at risk, and then to try to remove her from his heart.

"You can't lose me. Nothing will keep me from you," he murmured. For whether it was a memory of a past dream or a memory of something still to come, at the very end of whatever pain and whatever tragedy this universe and this war held for him, Sisko knew—*knew* with a conviction of faith and hope and love that would outlast the stars—he would *always* come back to the arms of Kasidy Yates.

And somehow, through some living bond still to be formed between them, he knew that Kasidy accepted his vow.

"Does this mean you're going to make me breakfast?" she teased even as her eyes told him she knew what he felt.

"Eventually." Sisko leaned down to kiss her again.

And as their lips met, their eyes closed, and time became nonlinear once again. Until—

A discreet throat-clearing cough.

Sisko opened his eyes at the same moment as Kasidy, brought back to *this* moment by—.

"Hey, guys."

Sisko couldn't resist reaching out a hand to tousle his son's hair as Jake, smiling sheepishly, skirted past them to the replicator. He remembered when he had had to bend down to touch the top of his son's head. Now it seemed he had to touch the stars to do the same.

"Hey, Jake-O," Sisko said as his son ordered and retrieved and drank in one gulp a tall glass of orange juice.

"I heard you went on a treasure hunt," Kasidy said.

Sisko saw Jake's swift glance at him, but he had no recriminations for his son. He and Jake had talked at length about Jake's actions—and his lack of action—last night. And Sisko had been deeply gratified to learn that almost everything he had to say to his son had already been in Jake's mind. Jake's and Nog's omission, not telling anyone about the mysterious Cardassian holosuite, was simply a leftover piece of business from when the two young men were little more than children.

Jake knew he had been wrong, and Sisko knew that doing the wrong thing and learning from it was what the process of maturing and growing was all about. All life was about such learning. What was important to Sisko, and what made him feel so proud of his son, was that for all the missteps the boy did make—and some days their number was truly astounding—he seldom made the same misstep twice.

As long as Jake kept that same spirit, Sisko could never really be angry with him—or disappointed.

"Buried treasure," Sisko said, picking up the copper bowl to give the eggs a final flourish. "Buried and forgotten." He set the bowl on the counter, cut a square of Imolian butter, and turned away to heat the empty omelette pan.

He could see that Jake heard and understood his tone of voice. The past was the past. They had moved on. They must always move on.

Jake pulled up a chair to sit down beside Kasidy at the table. "I was really surprised no one else had found that room by now."

Kasidy looked over at Sisko. "Do you think there could be other sealed-off sections in the station?"

Sisko dropped the butter into the hot omelette pan, then swirled it around to melt it evenly. "If there are, Chief O'Brien will know about them in a week. He's going to use the *Defiant*'s tactical sensors to conduct a full survey scan of DS9, then correlate that scan with the Cardassian's blueprints to look for deviations. He says he should have done it years ago."

"Any reason why the holosuite was sealed off?" Kasidy asked.

Sisko poured the beaten eggs from the copper bowl into the pan, tilting the pan expertly to lightly coat the top of the egg mixture with the melted butter. "We don't even know that it is a holosuite," he said.

"What else could it be?" Jake asked.

Sisko reached for a handful of grated jack cheese and trailed it perfectly along one side of the gently bubbling mass of eggs. "Just because we don't know the answer doesn't mean we have to settle for a guess." Biting his bottom lip in concentration, he sprinkled in chopped scallions, and then added a dusting of the secret ingredient in all the great recipes of Sisko's Creole Kitchen—the Cajun spices his father sent him on a more or less regular basis. "That would be too easy."

The door announcer chimed.

Sisko prodded the edge of the cooking eggs and glanced at his son. "I can't leave the pan now. . . ."

He heard the door to his quarters slide open just as he judged that the texture of his creation was perfect. With a rapid twist and a flip of the pan, he held his breath as he slid the golden disk toward the forward edge of the pan, then folded it expertly over on itself, achieving a half moon of Creole perfection.

"Uh, Dad . . ." Jake said.

Sisko looked up, saw Jadzia, was delighted. "Old Man! You're just in time for breakfast."

But Jadzia didn't share Sisko's enthusiasm—not today. She frowned. "Sorry, Benjamin, but . . . Quark's gone."

Sisko's sense of disbelief changed quickly to dismay, betrayal. "He's left the station?"

"I can't be sure. If he did, he did it in disguise. There's a chance he's simply hiding out here. But . . . well, maybe you should come down to the bar and . . . see for yourself. I think the situation's more complicated than we first thought."

Sisko's wrist jerked as he sharply snapped the pan again and the omelette flipped over with Starfleet precision. The bottom was an elegant combination of rich yellow and crispy brown. Sisko sighed. "Jake, it's up to you to uphold the family honor. You know what your grandfather always said." He slipped the omelette onto a plate already warmed by the inductor oven.

His son stepped into the alcove as Sisko stepped out. "No one leaves the table unsatisfied," Jake said.

"Do I have time to put on my uniform?" Sisko asked Jadzia.

She nodded. "This is going to be a Starfleet matter."

Sisko had been afraid of that. Somehow, when Quark was involved, situations always became more complicated.

Quark's bar looked normal for this early in the morning. The dabo table was silent. A rambunctious group of young Starfleet fighter pilots from the *Thunderchild* who hadn't yet switched over to station local time were ending their duty day around a large collection of bar tables they'd pulled together. A handful of the station's Bajoran morning-shift personnel were eating replicator breakfasts, a handful of night-shift personnel were eating replicator suppers. And faithful Morn was on his stool—so much a part of the place that he was sometimes easy to overlook, except for the nonstop droning of his voice.

"So far so good," Sisko said to Jadzia.

She gestured to the bar. "Let me buy you a *raktajino.*"

They chose stools as far away from the loquacious Morn as possible. "When did you find out Quark was gone?" Sisko asked.

"Odo told me he finished questioning Quark early this morning, around four. So I went to Quark's quarters at nine—I thought I'd let him get some sleep."

"And?"

"He wasn't there. Isn't anywhere."

"Anything missing? Signs of a struggle?"

"Nothing I could see. Odo's people are going through it now."

"That's not like Quark."

Jadzia almost laughed. "Not like Quark to run away from trouble? Benjamin, that's exactly like him."

Sisko shook his head. That wasn't what he had meant. "He and I had a deal. And . . . Quark usually keeps his deals. At least with me." He saw Jadzia's look of amazement. "Oh, he'll look for and exploit every loophole he can find. And just *making* the deal can be . . . an adventure in frustration. But when all is said and done, Quark, in his own Ferengi way, is one of the most honorable people on this station. *Not,*" Sisko added quickly, "that I would ever tell him that to his face. It could undercut me in future negotiations."

"Let's hope there are future negotiations," Jadzia muttered.

A sudden worrisome thought struck Sisko. "He didn't run into trouble with the Andorian sisters, did he?"

Jadzia shook her head. "Odo has them under twenty-six-hour surveillance. They've been keeping to themselves."

"Then what is it you suspect, Old Man?"

His old friend merely answered his question with another. "Do you have your *raktajino,* yet?"

Sisko looked around. Though the establishment was open for business—he recognized the usual servers managing the tables—no one was behind the bar. Yet he had heard the rattle of glasses in the recycler trays, and the hum of the replicator. That was why he hadn't noticed the absence of anyone—because it still sounded as if someone was present.

"All right," Sisko said, "I'll admit it. I'm confused. Care to enlighten me?"

Jadzia nodded. Tapped on the bartop. "Barkeep! We want to order!"

Sisko blinked with surprise as a Ferengi jumped up into view from behind the bar.

A very small Ferengi.

His skull and features were the size of any other adult of his species, complete with an unusual black headskirt, but the rest of his body was dramatically foreshortened. A meter tall at most.

"What do *you* want?" he snarled.

"Benjamin," Jadzia said, "meet Base. Base, meet Captain Benjamin Sisko, commander of Deep Space 9."

"Yeah, yeah, right, whatever," Base snapped. "You want to order? Or you want to stop bothering me?"

"Two *raktajinos,* please," Jadzia said.

"You actually drink that crap?" Base gargled in disgust, then whirled around and dropped below the level of the bar again.

Sisko couldn't suppress his curiosity. He stood up and leaned over the bar to see that a series of stools had been arranged behind it, presumably so the small barkeep could jump up to serve—if that's what such an unwelcoming manner could be called—the customers.

Sisko sat back down. "Base?" he asked Jadzia.

"Rom says he's an old friend of the family, helping look after the family's interests during . . . Quark's troubles."

"Does Rom know where Quark is?"

Jadzia rolled her eyes. "Here's where it gets interesting. Rom claims that he didn't know Quark had been released. Odo, on the other hand, says that Quark told him he was going directly here after he *was* released. And all the servers say that Rom sent them home early last night."

"Ah," Sisko said, rubbing the fingers of one hand against his temple to forestall the headache that Quark could so easily provoke. "So Quark could have come here, and the only witness would have been Rom."

"Exactly."

Sisko sat up straighter with a sigh. "All right. I see how this might complicate matters. But why do you think it might be a Starfleet matter?"

"Base isn't your ordinary Ferengi."

Sisko gave Jadzia a look of mock surprise. "No."

"Settle down, Benjamin. He's a smuggler."

"A Ferengi smuggler. That *is* unusual."

"Who operates in the Klingon Empire."

Sisko toned down his skepticism, recalling that the dismemberment and vivisection penalties Klingons assessed on captured smugglers tended to keep most Ferengi from becoming involved in illegal shipping in that region of space. "That makes him either the bravest Ferengi I've ever heard of, or the stupidest."

"Or," Jadzia added, "the most desperate. He has a number of warrants outstanding among the Ferengi Alliance, so by law he can't conduct business with any other Ferengi."

"Yet he's here," Sisko said, drumming his fingers on the bartop. There was still no sign of the *raktajinos*. "Presumably working for Quark."

" 'Helping Quark,' is what Rom said."

Sisko saw Jadzia staring at his fingers and forced himself to stop fidgeting. "Helping him do what, is the question. Clearly, he's not experienced in bartending. Is there any connection between Base and the Andorians?"

"Odo's working on it," Jadzia said. "Though I think he has other things on his mind." She nodded for Sisko to look down the length of the bar.

Sisko did, and this time he did not have to pretend to be surprised.

"Vash?!"

"The one and only."

The calculating archaeologist, known for her questionable ethics as much as for her beauty, was seated at the last stool at the bar, leaning forward and having an intense conversation with Quark's diminutive replacement.

"I bet she's not ordering *raktajino,*" Sisko said.

"Shall we?" Jadzia asked as she rose to her feet.

Sisko followed Jadzia down to the end of the bar, until they both stood behind Vash. At that same instant Base looked up and saw them. A fierce scowl darkened his face. "Go away, go way. I'll get your stupid drinks when it's your turn. I have other customers, y'know."

Her conversation interrupted, Vash turned around on her bar stool to see the cause of Base's displeasure.

Sisko caught the naked look of shock that illuminated Vash's pale face before she turned on her spectacular smile. *"Captain* Sisko, what a pleasure. I heard you'd been promoted."

His return smile equalled hers in sincerity. "And I'd heard the Siladians had put a price on your head for desecrating their burial moons."

"A misunderstanding," Vash said airily. "All the artifacts were returned."

"I'd heard that as well. Counterfeits, every one."

"They were counterfeits when I . . . retrieved them, Captain. The Siladians have been looting their own burial moons for generations, and replacing what they steal with replicas so they can keep the tourists coming. It's a rather clever operation."

"Or a rather clever story," Sisko said. He knew better than to trust a word she said. "Are you here on your own this time? Or . . . ?"

"No Q, if that's who you mean. He did come back a few times." For a moment, her face took on a strange expression, as if she were remembering things that were inexpressible. "But . . . I haven't seen him for . . . centuries, it feels like."

Sisko studied the wayward archaeologist thoughtfully. The way Vash said it, it sounded as if she really did mean centuries. He wondered what other types of adventures the superbeing known as Q had taken her on.

"Then what can we do for you?" he asked.

"I said, go away!" Base thumped the base of a glass tumbler on the bartop for emphasis.

"Why don't you look after your other customers?" Jadzia said with an easy smile.

"Why don't you and the captain take one of those barstools and—"

"Base!" Vash interrupted. "Captain Sisko is in command of this station. He can shut Quark's down anytime he feels like it."

"That barstool'd give them both something to feel," Base muttered, his small dark deep-set eyes burning into Sisko's.

"Why don't we take a walk?" Vash slipped off her bar stool and companionably took Sisko's arm in hers.

Jadzia locked eyes with the Ferengi barkeep. "Good idea, Benjamin."

"I'm still going to charge you for the stinkin' *raktacrappos!*" Base huffed as Jadzia and Vash walked out of the bar with him, one on each side.

Once out onto the Promenade, Sisko tugged at the collar of his duty jacket, puzzled by the Ferengi's anger—and over nothing. "How can anyone stay in business with an attitude like that?"

"He does business with Klingons," Jadzia reminded him.

"It's a bit more peculiar than that," Vash said as she quickly scanned the Promenade, both levels, right and left. "Did you notice Base's headskirt?"

Sisko thought back. "It was black. I don't often see that color."

Vash shot him a glance. "It isn't a headskirt. It's hair."

Sisko and Jadzia glanced at each other. "On a Ferengi?" Sisko asked. They had hair enough in their ears, Sisko knew, especially as they grew older. But he couldn't recall ever having seen a Ferengi that wasn't bald.

Vash's sharp eyes studied the customers at the gift shop. "Obviously neither of you is aware that on Ferenginar, the civil standardization authorities use Base as an example of what happens when pregnant Ferengi females travel in space and are subjected to radiation: They give birth to something like . . . well, Base."

"His mother left the planet?" Sisko knew that Jadzia's curiosity was warranted. Off-planet travel was still most unusual for a Ferengi female. Only in the past two months had Grand Nagus Zek introduced any gender-related reforms in Ferengi Society. Decades ago, when Base was born, it would have been almost inconceivable for a female to leave her family compound, let alone her homeworld.

Vash turned abruptly and began walking antispinward, leading Sisko and Dax toward what used to be the school, away from the gift shop. Sisko wasn't certain, but it was possible Vash had recognized someone at the gift shop. "Oh, Ferengi females leave the planet all the time," she said, in answer to Jadzia's question. "Always have. Otherwise, how would they have colony worlds?"

"By transporting their females in stasis," Jadzia said.

"And sometimes things go wrong." Vash gave Sisko a sly smile. "Stasis fields break down. A colony ship is raided on the outskirts of the Klingon Empire and one lone Ferengi female sets off on her own. Or, a lonely Ferengi businessman on a trip to *Qo'noS* decides to partake of the local pleasures. . . ."

"Are you suggesting Base is a Ferengi-Klingon hybrid?"

Vash innocently widened her eyes at him. "Captain Sisko, with the enmity between those two species, *and* their physical differences, that would be impossible. I'm surprised you'd even think such a thing."

"Then why go to such detail explaining Base's origins?"

"Just because something is impossible doesn't prevent people from speculating. You mentioned Base's attitude. Well, imagine how'd you feel if you were a Ferengi and everyone else thought you were half Klingon. You might have a bad attitude, too. Don't you think?"

"I *think* you're avoiding the question I asked back in the bar." Sisko looked at Jadzia and both of them stopped walking at the same moment. "How can we help you?"

Vash paused and Sisko saw her look past him, back in the direction they had come from. "Tell me, Captain, do you take such a personal interest in all the visitors to this station?"

"Only when they're thieves and scoundrels."

Vash nodded appreciatively. "Flattery will get you everywhere, Captain." She started forward again, turning toward the entrance to Cavor's shop.

Sisko put out a hand to hold her back, outside Cavor's display window. The featured floating antigrav balls were a popular attraction on the Promenade, and several other visitors were standing enthralled in front of the display. "I'm serious, Vash. We *are* in the middle of a war zone here, and I have no time for games. Either convince me that you are on DS9 for a legitimate reason, or you're on the next shuttle leaving for Bajor."

"Now who has an attitude?"

"You want to understand *my* attitude? Very well. Last week, three Andorians came to this station—Andorians with troubled legal histories involving smuggling. Then Base shows up in Quark's bar, and now you. The last time we had so many smugglers onboard at one time was, coincidentally enough, the last time you were here. When Quark was going to hold an auction of your stolen Gamma Quadrant artifacts."

"They weren't stolen," Vash said virtuously.

"Excuse me? What about the energy creature's crystalline offspring?"

"Well, not all of them . . ." she amended.

Sisko turned to Jadzia. "I think I see what's going on here. Quark was going to hold another auction. Which means that either he came into possession of something he thought would be of interest to the likes of Vash, the Andorians, and Base—" He looked at Vash. "—And whoever else it is who's on this station that you seem to be so concerned about. Or that you, the Andorians, or Base, or whoever, have come into possession of something you want Quark to sell."

Vash's studied silence told Sisko he was close.

"Ordinarily," he continued, "I really wouldn't care about what you people are up to. I'd leave you all to Odo and the Bajoran authorities. But in this case, I have one Andorian visitor dead, and one Ferengi inhabitant of this station missing. And that makes what *you're* doing here *my* business."

Vash turned away from her contemplation of the window display. "Who's missing?"

Sisko kept his expression carefully neutral. He didn't even risk looking at Jadzia. "Rultan. One of Quark's servers."

Vash shrugged. "Don't know him."

"When are you and Quark supposed to meet?" Sisko asked, as if he had just suddenly thought of the question.

"I had no plans to see Quark," Vash said.

"Not even for old times' sake?" Jadzia asked.

Vash looked at Jadzia, looked back at Sisko, and it was as if Sisko could hear isolinear circuits at work in her mind. "*Quark's* the Ferengi who's missing?"

Sisko didn't see the point in continuing the deception. He nodded.

"How missing?"

Sisko didn't understand.

"Any sign of foul play?"

"Nothing apparent," Jadzia said. "But he disappeared last night—which is when Base appeared."

Vash shook her head. "Base wouldn't hurt Quark. There'd be no profit in it."

"Vash," Sisko said, "this is your last chance. What's going on here?"

The way Vash looked at him, he could tell she knew at least part of the answer. This woman was maddening in her infernal duplicity. What would it take for her to share what she knew?

But, first, Vash had a question of her own. "The Andorian . . . Dal Nortron? How was he killed?"

"Lethal exposure to microwave radiation," Jadzia answered. "Odo believes it was a weapon. I think there's a chance it might have been accidental."

Vash nodded and turned back to Cavor's window display.

Though it was a struggle, Sisko succeeded in keeping his patience because it appeared Vash was in the midst of thinking something through. Finally, she turned and looked directly into his eyes. "Captain, do you believe what they say about Quark? That he killed Nortron?"

Sisko met her sharp gaze directly. "No." Believing that Vash was reaching her own moment of truth and would act on it momentarily, he offered no further qualifications.

"Do exactly as I say," Vash suddenly said in a low voice, confirming his supposition. "I'm going to walk away from you. I'm going to look angry. You're going to grab me and say that you don't believe me, and that you're taking me for questioning. Then do it, and make it look good. Understand?"

Sisko signaled his understanding by making no move to look around to see who might be watching. He felt certain that Vash knew who their charade was going to play for. So, he gave her the reason she needed to walk away. "That's not good enough, Vash," he said harshly. "I want answers."

Vash threw up her hands. "What's wrong with you

people?! I've already told you everything I know! Now leave me alone!"

She spun around and started to walk away.

Sisko took two quick steps and then took her arm.

"Let me go!" Vash shouted. "You have no right to hold me!"

Jadzia took Vash's other arm. "Yes, he does."

Sisko hit his communicator badge. "Sisko to security. I need a team on the Promenade, Main Floor South, *now.*"

Vash tugged back and forth between Sisko and Jadzia. "You can't be serious! I haven't done anything!"

All signs were good that they were putting on a convincing show. By the time two Bajoran security officers hurried around the curve of the Promenade, they were surrounded by an inquisitive crowd that was growing by the minute.

"I want this woman held for questioning," Sisko said loudly. He let go of Vash as the security officers took her. And just in that brief instant, Vash slapped a hand to the side of her neck and staggered, losing her balance.

Startled, Sisko caught her as she began to fall. On the side of her slender neck, he saw a small bronze-metal dart, no larger than a fingertip. He grabbed it, pulled, and a half-centimeter-long needle emerged from Vash's neck, dripping a fluorescent blue fluid.

Vash shuddered uncontrollably as Jadzia called Worf for an immediate transporter evacuation to the Infirmary. Sisko swiftly scanned the crowd, but there was nothing to see except the concerned faces of onlookers. Discovering whoever had fired the dart would have to wait until the station's security recordings could be studied.

"Quark . . ." Vash whispered urgently, her voice slurred. ". . . the auction. . . ."

Sisko bent nearer, cradling her as he waited for the transporter lock. "They're on their way, Vash. You have to hold on."

"Must listen . . . was going to sell. . . ."

Sisko leaned closer, put his ear to her lips. "What, Vash? What was he going to sell?"

Vash's eyes rolled up and her eyelids fluttered, and what she said next made Sisko's blood run cold.

". . . an . . . Orb . . ." Vash gasped. ". . . Jalbador. . . ."

And then the transporter took them.

CHAPTER 12

JADZIA SMILED as she watched Julian Bashir hold the neural dart up to a light and examine it closely by eye. It was so typical of him, and also what made him so endearing.

Here he was in DS9's Infirmary, a state-of-the-art Cardassian medical facility that had been fully upgraded with the latest Starfleet innovations, surrounded by scanners and sensors that could shuffle through the dart's composition molecule by molecule and more often than not identify the planet of origin for every mineral compound used in its manufacture. Yet Julian *still* had to look at the dart himself, using his own hands and his own eyes to be certain no detail had been missed.

It was so . . . well, Jadzia could find only one word to explain that kind of self-absorbed conviction in the superiority of his abilities, and that word was "cute."

Bashir glanced over at her and returned her smile, but seemed confused about why he was doing so. "What?" he asked.

"Nothing," Jadzia shrugged, lips still pursed in a smile. "Just remembering something Emony said. It was more than a hundred years ago."

"Ah." Bashir nodded as if that explained everything, and went back to peering at the dart.

That was one of the advantages to being a Trill, Jadzia knew. In fact, except for Lela, the first, all of Dax's previous hosts had known it too: A joined Trill could get away with the most outrageous behavior imaginable, and then simply explain it away by blaming it on a previous host.

Since most unjoined species could never even imagine what it must be like for two minds to share a single body and several lifetimes of experiences, they would accept such an explanation without question. What would be the point? To be honest, Jadzia thought, most people looked on joined Trills as some kind of zombie held in thrall to a neural parasite.

But the truth was that she herself had found that joining with Dax had been incredibly liberating. It was exhilarating to be able to decide to do anything at all—and that included indulging herself in harmless flirting with Julian right up to taking part in the most erotically charged physical challenge in the quadrant, euphemistically called 'wrestling' Galeo-Manada style—and because she was joined, anything she chose to do was *all* acceptable.

Of course, part of the trick of deciding which passions and pastimes to explore came from trying to think of something that none of the other hosts had been familiar with—which usually meant that the more lifetimes a symbiont shared, the more idiosyncratic and eccentric its hosts became.

Personally, before she was joined Jadzia had always had a particular curiosity about Vulcans, and had hoped that sometime during her career in Starfleet she'd have a chance to experience *Pon farr* on a more personal level than the textbooks allowed. But after joining, when she had instantly been able to look back on several *Pon farr* encounters—from both sides of the Teiresian veil, as it were—there was little there that remained mysterious to her, and that lost mystery had been the key to her fascination.

Oh, someday, a century or two down the road, the right Vulcan might come along at the right time for the Dax symbiont to decide it was time to travel down that road again. But for now, Jadzia was more than happy, deliriously happy in fact, with her sweet cuddly-bear of a Klingon mate.

Jadzia coughed to cover her sudden giggle, as she suddenly recalled the look on Worf's face when she'd startled him with the endearment at precisely the wrong moment—as if there were ever a right moment to call a rough, tough Klingon a sweet cuddly-bear. But fortunately, she'd been able to blame the transgression on her ever-useful past host Audrid.

Bashir gave her another perplexed smile. "Emony again?"

"Audrid. I'm sorry."

"No need." He placed the dart back in a small sample dish, then entered notes on his padd.

Jadzia admired the dark curls of Julian's close-cropped hair. *He was close,* she recalled with a sigh. If Worf had been unable to transcend his insular Klingon heritage enough to fully admit a Trill into his life,

Jadzia had little doubt that her heart could have been won by Julian Bashir. That was the other advantage to being a Trill. Life's choices that could last a lifetime for others were not necessarily a limiting factor. Other lifetimes and other choices waited to provide near infinite possibilities.

Bashir stopped writing on the padd, then tapped the small device against his hand.

"You've reached a conclusion?" Jadzia asked.

He had. "A linear-induction dart. Centuries-old technology. So primitive the launch tube would never show up on the Promenade weapons scanners. Cardassian design, of course, like most assassination implements, but its manufacture, interesting enough, is *Andorian,* as is the neural toxin inside: bicuprodyanide."

Jadzia frowned. "That's fatal to Andorians."

"And Bolians," Bashir added. "In fact, it has near one hundred percent lethality in any species with a bicupric-based oxygen-transport metabolism. Which means almost anything with blue skin."

"But . . . it's not fatal in humans," Jadzia said, perplexed.

Bashir dropped his padd on his medical work station in a gesture of finality. "In a high enough dose it can be, Jadzia. Just from ordinary metal toxicity. But Vash, mind you, would have to have ingested a coffee mugfull of the stuff, and even then we'd have a good ten to twelve hours to treat her. As it is, with the few milliliters that actually got into her bloodstream, she'll only have a bad headache for a day or two. Nothing more serious."

"In other words," Jadzia said slowly as she worked it out, "whoever used the dart against Vash either didn't know about human biochemistry—"

"Or," Bashir interjected, "was equipped to kill an Andorian and shooting Vash was an unexpected, spur-of-the-moment decision—"

"Which," Jadzia continued, getting into Bashir's rhythm, "could indicate that the attacker was desperate to stop Vash from talking—"

"—so he struck as quickly as he could to render her unconscious—"

"—and he—"

"—or *she*—"

"—plans on coming back to finish the job before Vash wakes up—"

"—which should be in the next thirty minutes!" Bashir grinned at her, quite obviously enjoying the chance to play detective. "I must say, Jadzia, we make a wonderful team."

Being a Trill, Jadzia simply returned Julian's grin and said, "I've always thought so. But for now," she went on, "maybe we should have Odo post more guards?"

Bashir nodded, "Good idea. I'll call—"

"Where is she?!"

Major Kira burst into the Infirmary like an avenging Pah-wraith, fury expressed in every line of her being.

Jadzia could guess what had caused Kira's reaction, and it seemed Julian had also, because at once he took on the manner of someone outside the jurisdiction of both Starfleet protocol and Bajoran laws. He faced Kira as a physician with a patient in his care—a patient no one would be allowed to harm.

"If you mean Vash, she's still recovering," Bashir said firmly.

Kira took a swift look around the Infirmary, saw the analysis bed was empty in the treatment alcove and started for the surgery. "I don't care. I'm talking to her."

Bashir immediately stepped in front of Kira, to block her advance. "Not until she's awake, Major."

They were centimeters apart, neither one willing to yield. Kira's hands were balled into fists at her side. Restlessly, she shifted her weight from foot to foot. Her voice was demanding, belligerent. "Then wake her, Doctor. Use some of those magic potions of yours to bring her around now."

Bashir held his ground, unconvinced. "There is no medical need to do so."

With that, Kira's military bluster gave way to a plea of personal indignation. "Julian! She is involved in trying to *sell* an Orb of the Prophets. That is an *outrage!* To me, my world, to ten thousand years of Bajorans who have sought to follow the Prophets' teachings. I *demand* to speak to her."

Bashir still didn't move, though Jadzia was pleased to see Julian's attitude soften. "Major, first of all, Vash isn't going anywhere. And second, any questioning you conduct might be more useful if you had a few moments to . . . gather your thoughts, so it won't be . . . as personal."

"How can it *not* be personal?"

Bashir sighed. "Listen, Nerys, whatever Vash said to Captain Sisko, you have to remember she had just received a jolt of a disruptive neural toxin, almost directly to her brain. Maybe what she said did make sense. Maybe it didn't. But in any case, the captain said he couldn't understand everything she said. The point is, we won't know for certain until she wakes up."

Kira stared hard at Bashir. "A 'disruptive' neural toxin? Not a fatal one?"

"Fatal to Andorians, not humans. She'll be fine."

Jadzia saw the major's rigid posture relax as she stepped back from Bashir, lowering the level of confrontation, but not ending it. "You're surprised by that," Jadzia said to her.

Kira nodded, taking a deep breath to further compose herself. "I thought . . . I didn't have much time. That I might lose her before. . . . Why would someone try to kill Vash with an Andorian toxin?"

"To make it appear as if an Andorian is the attempted murderer," Odo said, startling everyone as he suddenly entered the Infirmary.

"Did you find something on the scanner records?" Jadzia asked. She knew that was what Odo had been doing for the past ten minutes: analyzing the security tapes taken of the crowds on the Promenade at the time Vash was hit by the dart. Normally, she knew, visual scanners weren't used in the public areas of the station on an ongoing basis. But there were few things Odo hated more than an unsolved crime in his territory, and Jadzia was aware DS9's security officer was determined to use every means he could to solve Dal Nortron's death and erase what he would no doubt consider a personal affront to his abilities as station constable.

"No, I did not," Odo said gruffly. "Whoever the shooter was, he must have positioned himself just by the gym, under the banners. Precisely where there is a gap in the scanner coverage."

Bashir shot a sideways glance at Jadzia, clearly intrigued by Odo's reasoning. "That could indicate the shooter is someone with highly detailed knowledge of station security."

Odo folded his arms. "Just what are trying to suggest, Doctor?"

Odo's challenging tone seemed to unsettle Bashir. "I'm . . . suggesting nothing."

To divert Odo before he could directly accuse Julian of suspecting him, Jadzia bestowed a winning smile on the constable. "Odo, Julian and I were just trying to find a pattern to the . . . the clues in this case. So far, when you put them all together, they don't make a lot of sense, so any extra piece of information should be considered carefully."

"Of course they don't make sense," Odo said darkly. "Quark is involved."

Jadzia wasn't willing to let that stand. *"Maybe,"* she said.

Odo was silent, but the pained expression on his face conveyed his thoughts well enough.

"Well," Kira said, "the one person who might be able to make sense out of whatever *is* going on is still in there." She pointed to the surgery.

But Vash's doctor still wasn't ready to yield. "And she'll be waking up soon. Odo, just in case whoever attacked Vash tries to come back and finish the job, could you—"

"I already have three officers stationed outside the Infirmary, Doctor. And Worf has placed transporter-suppression shields around this section of the Promenade to prevent anyone or anything being beamed in or out."

"I certainly couldn't ask for more than that. Thank you, Constable."

Odo's stiff response told Jadzia that the constable wasn't swayed by Julian's attempt to create a more cooperative mood. "Don't mention it, Doctor. However, in the interests of full security, I would appreciate being in the room with Vash when she wakes up."

Before Bashir could answer, Kira added, "So would I."

"She's not going to be in the best of shape," Bashir warned.

But Kira was in control of her emotions now. "Julian, an *Orb of the Prophets.* Vash is no longer just a smuggler who can pay a fine and move on to the next system. Even an *attempt* to interfere with an Orb makes her liable to life imprisonment under Bajoran law. What she's done—or even planned to do—is so serious, I've reported it to Kai Winn. Three Vedek Inquisitors are already on their way."

"The Inquisitors function as a *war* crimes investigative tribunal." Bashir's voice betrayed his alarm.

Kira's jaw tightened. "Up until now, all missing Orbs were the result of Cardassian looting. We are talking war crimes."

Jadzia finally saw her chance to act as mediator. "Nerys, let's say Vash is involved in . . . oh, I don't know . . . some extralegal transaction involving obtaining an Orb from one of the Cardassians who stole it in the first place. If she were doing this so she could, say, *return* the Orb to the Bajoran people—the way Grand Nagus Zek returned the Orb of Wisdom—don't you think it possible that no charges would be brought? I mean, the Inquisitors didn't file charges against Zek."

"Are you defending her, Jadzia?" Kira's voice was incredulous.

"If she's done what you think she's done, not at all. But what I am trying to do is to point out that we don't know everything yet, and that there might be some alternate explanation. And if we keep that in mind, then maybe we'll be able to *talk* to Vash, instead of interrogate her. And maybe she can help us right now, instead of deciding to say nothing until her legal defender spends months negotiating an . . . accommodation with the Inquisitors. If we keep open minds, maybe we can get to the bottom of this much faster than if we jump to conclusions. That's all." Jadzia held steady under Kira's measuring gaze.

The major made her decision. She nodded to Jadzia. "All right, I won't threaten her with life in prison right away. And since you seem to be open to more possibilities than the rest of us, why don't you start the questioning—I mean, the conversation."

Odo cleared his throat. "In case any of you were wondering," the changeling said heavily, reminding them all of his presence, "I have no problem with Dax asking the questions. At first."

Now everyone looked at Bashir.

"Too much stress will delay her full recovery. A conversation will be much better than the third degree."

Kira blinked. "The third degree of what?"

"I'll explain later," Odo said.

But Kira wasn't willing to let it go. She frowned. "What are the first two degrees?"

"I'm sure 'interrogation' is what Julian meant to say," Jadzia said smoothly, glaring at Julian to stop him from adding anything else provocative. Jadzia could see that Kira was losing the fight to control her impatience. "So, Doctor, keeping our minds open, promising not to be a source of stress for her, is it possible you'll allow us to see your patient?"

"Yes. But . . ."

"But what?" Kira snapped.

Bashir raised his eyebrows. "Doesn't anyone think we should wait for Captain Sisko?"

"He's involved with Chief O'Brien," Odo said. "He'll be expecting a report from me, and from you, Doctor, when we're finished with the prisoner . . . that is, the patient."

"All right," Bashir shrugged. "Then just let me check on her first."

Odo bowed his head as if giving his approval.

Bashir went into the surgery.

Jadzia looked at Kira and Odo. "Why does it feel that we're on opposite sides all of a sudden?"

"We're not," Kira said testily as if offended even by Jadzia's question.

"I hope you don't think that Julian and I are insensitive to the Orbs, or to the Bajoran religion," Jadzia said.

Kira stared at a point over Jadzia's shoulder as she seemed to think over many different possible replies before she said, "Not intentionally."

Now Jadzia felt offense. "Then I apologize," she said tersely.

"No need."

"Well, obviously, something is needed."

Kira's gaze shifted. Her eyes met Jadzia's. Again, it seemed she struggled with finding the right answer before she muttered, "All right. It couldn't hurt for you to spend some time in the temple."

Jadzia felt her spots prickle, never a good sign when it came to her mood. "Major, since coming to this station six years ago, you know very well I have made the Orbs one of my chief areas of study."

Kira's smile was condescending, almost one of pity. "Dax, you've spent six years studying what you believe to be solidified energy vortices. And you can spend the next six hundred years doing the same, and you will learn absolutely nothing because they are not vortices, they *are* the Tears of the Prophets. And until you understand that, you won't—"

"She's awake," Bashir announced as he walked from the surgery. "Doing fine as a matter of fact." He looked around uncertainly, as if he sensed residual traces of the argument that had just begun between Kira and Jadzia. "You can . . . come in now . . . if you still want to, that is. . . ."

Kira pushed straight past Jadzia into the surgery. A moment later, Odo gave Jadzia a small shrug, and followed after Kira.

Bashir stared at Jadzia. "I was only gone a minute."

"Around here, that's all it takes," Jadzia said drily. Then she followed the good doctor into the surgery, wondering what the *next* minute would bring.

CHAPTER 13

O'BRIEN SHIFTED uncomfortably in the center chair of the *Defiant*. It wasn't that he had never taken command of the ship before. But he had never done so when Captain Sisko was standing at his side

"We're at 50 kilometers and holding," Commander Arla said from her position at the flight operations console. Beyond her, on the *Defiant*'s main viewer, Deep Space 9 was a distant, sparkling smear of jeweled radiance against the translucent lavender plasma wisps of the Denorios Belt. There was no atmospheric distortion in space to account for the constant flickering of the station's lights, O'Brien knew. Instead, it was DS9's slow rotation that caused lights to flare erratically from viewports and disappear behind defense sails and docked spacecraft, like the twinkling of stars.

"Um, what do I do now?" Arla asked.

It was obvious to O'Brien that the young Bajoran Starfleet officer was about as at ease as he was with their new assignment—which was to say, not at all. And for good reason. Apart from Captain Sisko, Arla and O'Brien were the ship's only crew for this mission. Arla claimed she hadn't piloted anything larger than a shuttle since she'd graduated the Academy, and now she was at the conn of one of the most overpowered, hard-to-handle starships in the fleet.

"Activate automatic station keeping," O'Brien told her. Reflexively, he looked up at Sisko to make sure he had said the right thing. The captain's nod told him he had.

"Relax, Chief. Worf is standing by at Ops. If anything even *looks* like it's about to go wrong, you can have a full crew beamed on board in less than a minute."

But the cause of O'Brien's unease wasn't the prospect of disaster. He couldn't resist the impulse any longer. He started to get out of the chair. *The* chair. "You sure you wouldn't feel more comfortable doing this yourself, sir?"

"The *Defiant*'s in good hands, Chief. Now sit down."

O'Brien sighed as he did. But it still didn't feel right.

"Are the tactical sensors reconfigured?" Sisko asked.

"As best they can be," O'Brien answered. "Though they really were never designed for this kind of detail. I mean, I had to modify the gravity generators to create an artificial inertial-matrix aperture for the—"

"I don't need a lecture, Mr. O'Brien," Sisko said

gently. "Just your assurance that they're going to work."

"Oh, they'll work, sir. Just not as fast as if she were the *Enterprise.*"

"How long then?"

O'Brien had already done the duration calculations, but he worked through them again just to be sure. "I'd say ten hours for the full sensor sweep. Maybe another hour for the computer to finish the comparison between the Cardassian schematics and the scan results."

"And then we'll have a complete interior map of the station—"

"—with all deviations from the original designs called out by the computer. If there are any more hidden rooms in there, we'll definitely find them."

"Very good," Sisko said. "Now I'm wondering if while you're conducting the station scan, you can look for something else that's gone missing."

O'Brien sat forward in his chair, apprehensive. "I can try, sir. What is it?"

"Quark."

O'Brien frowned at the viewer before him as he contemplated the computational effort that would be required by what the captain was asking of him. On the *Enterprise,* with her special-purpose science sensors and multiband hyperspectral arrays, O'Brien would have felt confident he could do a biosweep of Deep Space 9 and find an hour-old outbreak of mold on a single slice of bread in a neutronium-lined food cooler inside of fifteen minutes. Finding a full-grown Ferengi would have taken less than half that time.

But the *Defiant* wasn't built primarily for science.

Her scanners and sensors were designed to locate and analyze targets first and further humanity's understanding of the universe second. To tune and focus sensor emanations to ignore all living matter in approximately two cubic kilometers of space, *except* for one Ferengi. . . .

A sudden thought struck O'Brien. "Captain, are you sure Quark's even on the station?"

"That's what I'm hoping you will tell me."

O'Brien's brow became deeply furrowed as he calculated his chances of success. "Is there any chance you might get all the other Ferengi to leave the station for the day?"

"As I said, I don't want anyone to know that any kind of a scan or a search is under way. That's why you and Commander Arla got the job. And only you two. Do you think you can do it, Chief?"

O'Brien nodded, his head already filling with a list of the adjustments he'd have to make to the sensor scan rates, the density-overlap mapping algorithms, even the power-output waveguides. The subspace resonance patterns would have to be tuned to the exact salt content of Ferengi muscle tissue and. . . . He suddenly realized he hadn't answered the captain's question because he'd already become caught up in the *how* of his assignment. Not to mention the *why.* "Yes, I can, sir. Is Quark in trouble, Captain?"

Sisko nodded gravely. "He might be."

O'Brien found himself wondering if Quark had become the victim of a kidnapping. If so, then his sympathy was with the kidnappers. "Then should I scan the docked ships, as well? Just in case he's on one of them?"

"Good idea, Chief. And keep scanning them as they

dock, just in case someone's going to try to slip him onto one that's arriving later." Sisko tugged down on his jacket. "Anything else before I go?"

O'Brien reviewed the assignment again. "Well, it would help if I knew where Rom and Nog and all the other Ferengi staff from Quark's are, so I can rule them out as the sensors find them."

"Very well. I'll have Odo put someone on it. But I think it's a good bet that if Quark is on the station, he won't be on the Promenade. You'd be safe ruling out any Ferengi contacts you make there. At least, at first."

"Understood, sir."

"Carry on, Chief." Sisko touched his communicator. "Sisko to Worf. One to beam out."

O'Brien watched as his captain dissolved into light, and then the *Defiant* suddenly felt as if she were twice the size of any other starship he had ever been aboard.

But at least with no one around to tell him otherwise, O'Brien could finally get out of *the* chair.

He headed over to his familiar engineering station, settling into his own chair with a relieved sigh. He was home. "Computer," he said, "transfer command functions to the engineering station."

"Command functions transferred," the computer promptly acknowledged.

O'Brien took a few minutes to enter the standard biological assay parameters that would have to be implemented to search for Ferengi life-forms, then announced, "Activating sensor sweep," as if somehow the bridge was staffed by a full crew. He touched his finger to the 'initiate programmed sequence' control, and the display screen above his station changed its subspace-frequency-response graph to show that the scanning had begun.

"So that's it." He looked over at Arla.

The young Bajoran officer looked back at him. "Ten hours?"

O'Brien understood what she meant. "I'm afraid so."

"Afraid isn't the word for it. I mean, automatic station keeping, automatic sensor sweep. What are *we* doing here, Chief?"

O'Brien got up from his chair to walk over to the empty science station. He preferred to be on his feet anyway, rather than sit around waiting for things to happen. "Well, the one thing you have to expect in space is that nothing will ever go the way you expect it will. So, today we're the *Defiant*'s insurance and her last-ditch backup system."

As if restless also, Arla swung her tall form around in her chair to watch the Chief cross the bridge. "I want to run a starbase, not pilot a starship."

As if his hands had minds of their own, O'Brien leaned down to the science workstation and entered the commands that would start a level-four diagnostic running in the science subsystems. Just to be on the safe side. Couldn't hurt. He smiled as the science displays came to life, running through their paces. He glanced sideways at the young Bajoran officer, tried to remember what it was she had just said . . . Oh, yes. "It's good to know how to do different things, Commander. So in an emergency, everyone can trade off. Watch each other's back. That sort of thing."

"Would you call this an emergency?"

"I don't know what the captain knows." O'Brien kept his attention on the science displays.

"And that doesn't bother you?"

Arla's voice was serious. O'Brien sighed. "It's not my position to be bothered by it, Commander. But I can see that you are." He could see where this conversation would be going. He straightened up, deciding he might as well head back to his engineering station. If Arla was going to talk his ear off, at least he'd be comfortable.

Arla, it seemed, had come to a decision of her own. "Can I speak freely, Chief?"

Safe in his chair, O'Brien nodded, giving her a half-smile. "You're the commander, Commander."

"Captain Sisko, he's not the most orthodox commanding officer, is he?"

"Well, let me say that this isn't the most orthodox command. Y'know, before I came here, I served on the *Enterprise*—"

"Under Picard?" Arla asked, with true admiration in the way she said that famous name.

O'Brien appreciated that attitude. "The one and only," he said proudly. "And for a starship captain on the cutting edge of the frontier, out where no one's gone before, you need exceptional flexibility, because the situation's always changing. Picard was brilliant at that kind of give-and-take. Still is, from what I've heard. But, when I took this assignment at DS9, I thought I'd be settling back into a more normal routine, like being at a starbase."

"From what *I've* heard, I didn't think anyone ever got tired of serving on the *Enterprise.*"

"Oh, I didn't get tired." O'Brien chuckled. "I got married. Had a little girl. And all of a sudden, as much as I loved the *Enterprise*. . . ." He thought back to those agonizing days, when he'd debated endlessly with himself about putting in for a transfer. And the terrible nights, when he awoke from stomach-twisting nightmares in which the *Enterprise* ran afoul of Borg cubes, black holes, runaway warp cores . . . a thousand and one disasters that must never touch Keiko and Molly.

And how he'd felt when he read the reports of what happened at Veridian III, the ship blown from space to a terrifying crashlanding, with all its crew and its families and the children . . . at the same time that he'd said a prayer for the survivors he'd thanked the stars that he and his wife and their daughter were safe and not with them.

"You were saying, Chief—as much as you loved the *Enterprise . . . ?"*

O'Brien, still distracted, made an effort to retrace his thoughts. "What I meant to say was, Commander, as . . . as complicated as I thought commanding that ship was, I've found DS9 to be even more . . . challenging. I suppose that's the word. I mean, Captain Picard could take us to a planet in trouble, we'd show the flag, do what we could to resolve things, and then we'd move on, knowing that three other ships and half the Federation's bureaucracy would be in our wake to follow up on what we had done. But here," O'Brien looked at the young Bajoran officer, wondering if she could understand what he was trying to stay, with life experience so different from his own, "staying in one sector, dealing with the same worlds over so many years, there's no chance to move on. Captain Sisko has to live with the consequences of his decisions. It calls for . . . a very creative approach to command."

"Plus," Arla said carefully, "he's the Emissary."

"Ah, now, I wouldn't know about that." O'Brien knew his limitations, and this kind of discussion was not his strong suit.

"So you don't believe the wormhole aliens are gods?"

O'Brien knew the right way, for him, to answer this one. "When I was at the Academy, one of the best lessons I learned didn't come from a classroom, or an instructor. It came from Boothby."

Arla blinked. "The gardener?"

"Among other things. But he told me—Miles, when you find yourself locked up on a ship hundreds of light-years from nowhere and no chance of escape from your crewmates, there are three things you must never discuss: Politics, religion, and another crewmate's spouse." O'Brien stretched back in his chair. "So, right about now is when I think it's a good time for me to follow old Boothby's advice."

Arla tapped her fingers on the edge of her flight console. "There are a lot of cautious people on Deep Space 9."

"Goes with the territory."

Arla nodded. "I had a long talk with Dax about Captain Sisko."

That didn't surprise O'Brien. Dax was the most experienced member of the DS9 crew, and she was never reluctant to pass on whatever help or advice she could. All anyone ever had to do was ask. "They've been friends for a long time, those two."

"She wouldn't answer my question, either. About the wormhole aliens being gods."

O'Brien felt he was going to regret being sucked into this debate, but he didn't see as how the young commander was giving him any choice. If Julian were here, O'Brien knew, the doctor would view the situation entirely differently. Julian would relish the argument. O'Brien didn't. But it was either join the discussion or spend the next ten hours watching level-four diagnostics run. "I take it, then, that you don't believe the entities in the wormhole are gods."

Arla shook her head, and O'Brien thought he could detect a hint of unhappiness. "That's why I'm trying to understand how it is that Captain Sisko, an educated, intelligent man, an *alien,* brought up without any cultural influence from Bajor—how could *he* accept that they're gods? I mean, someone born on Bajor—fine, I can understand that. I don't agree with it, but I understand. They don't really have a choice. The whole primitive Prophet belief system permeates every aspect of our culture. There's no escape."

"You escaped."

"I wasn't born on Bajor."

That explains a lot, O'Brien thought.

After a few moments of silence, Arla leaned forward. "You're not saying anything."

O'Brien shrugged, looked around the unnaturally empty and quiet bridge. "I don't see that there's a lot I can say. Obviously, the type of environment someone's born into has a lot to do with what they end up believing in life. Vulcans embrace logic. Klingons find honor in battle.

"So what do you believe, Chief? Not about the Prophets. But about . . . whatever faith you were raised in."

O'Brien relaxed. This was one of the questions he could answer, one that rarely caused offense. "Oh, I'm a great believer in IDIC, Commander. Infinite diversity in infinite combination. The beauty of it is that nobody's wrong. Logic. Battle. They're all facets of the same thing. As if the true reality of the universe, whatever final answers there are to be discovered—if they can be discovered—is like a hyperdimensional string. Look at it one way it's an electron. Another way and it's a proton. Yet another one, you see a verteron. But it's all the same thing, just different ways of looking is all."

As pleased as O'Brien was with his answer, he didn't like the way Arla was staring at him, as if she had heard those exact words too many times before.

"Well, I'm not afraid to say when something's wrong."

Oh, oh, O'Brien thought. *This is where it can get ugly.*

"I think," Arla proclaimed, "that my people's delusional worship of the Prophets turned them into the galaxy's biggest victims."

"Now, that's harsh, don't you think?" O'Brien asked.

"No, I don't. Do you know how old Bajoran culture is?"

O'Brien wasn't sure. He thought back to that lost city the captain had rediscovered. "Twenty thousand years, I believe."

"Try *five hundred* thousand years," Arla said. "Think of that, Chief. Half a million years of almost unbroken continuity of culture. No notable worldwide disasters. No great empires fell. No dark ages. And no natural ebb and flow to history like on so many other worlds. But one, unbroken strand of culture that has lasted since before your species ever evolved."

"Quite impressive," O'Brien said.

Now Arla's sadness abruptly became disgust. "Quite a *waste.*" She stood up, started to pace. "Half a million years of utter, contemptible passivity! That whole time, we did nothing but pray and wait for the gods to guide us. And ten thousand years ago, when it finally looked as if some forward-thinking communities were at last going to throw off the yoke of stagnant religious belief, what happens?"

"I wouldn't know," O'Brien said nervously, though he could guess. He had heard the number ten thousand before. But somehow, he didn't think Arla was really interested in what he knew. She was working her way through some argument that had nothing to do with him. And one he wished that he knew how to deflect.

"The first Orb lands on Bajor." Arla's face twisted with loathing. "It was the worst thing that could have happened to my people."

O'Brien didn't like the hostility Arla was expressing. He wondered how anyone could get through the Academy with such negative views of an alien culture. Since Arla wasn't born on Bajor, he felt justified in thinking of the Bajoran culture as an alien one from Arla's perspective. "To be fair, Commander, I don't think you'll find a lot of Bajorans agreeing with you on that."

"Of course not," Arla said. "Because for the past ten thousand years, the wormhole aliens have been manipulating our culture, breeding us, in fact, to develop even greater passivity."

O'Brien couldn't believe what she had said. Even at the risk of provoking her further, he felt he had to object. "You're going to have to explain that, Commander. I've known too many Bajorans from the Resistance to think of you as a passive bunch."

"The facts are simple, Chief. Ten thousand years ago, humans were just getting ready to invent the wheel and the roads that go with it. Vulcans were bloodthirsty savages. Klingons were less than Vulcans.

And Cardassians? Ha! They were still swimming in swamps catching fish in their mouths. But we Bajorans were peaceful, advanced, and shared a world government."

"What's your point, Commander?" O'Brien wondered if it were too late to make a call to Worf. Just to check in. That sort of thing.

"My point is, ten thousand years later, every other race in the quadrant is busy carving up the galaxy—*except* Bajor. Instead, we've been brutalized, terrorized, occupied, and looted. And do you know why?"

"No," O'Brien said, his hand on his communicator, "but somehow I know you're going to tell me."

"Because for the past ten thousand years, the wormhole aliens have dropped their Orbs on us, deluding us into thinking that there are gods above managing our fates. And since the gods are taking care of us, why should *we* bother taking care of ourselves?" Arla now stood in the center of the bridge, arms spread wide in frustrated anger. "Honestly, can you think of a better way to cripple a species than by telling them that if they just wait peacefully, everything will be *given* to them? There's no need to study, to learn, to explore. Or even to dream. Just sit down, make yourself comfortable, and wait for the next dispatch from heaven." She shook her head, oblivious to O'Brien now, caught up in her own speechmaking. "You humans, and the Vulcans, and Klingons, and Cardassians . . . you reached *out* to the universe. You built starships and went looking for your gods. But on Bajor, with those hideous Orbs, the gods kept coming down to us, telling us not to worry, and not to try to better ourselves."

Arla flung herself down in her chair as if exhausted. O'Brien regarded her warily, wondering if she would settle down soon. "The Prophets occupied our world long before the Cardassians ever did," she concluded bitterly. "And that makes them the biggest enemy of the Bajoran people."

"Commander Arla, I don't mean any disrespect. But I certainly hope you know better than to go spouting off like that in public."

Her frown wrinkled her epinasal ridges. "I do know. But I asked if I could speak freely. . . ."

"You did that all right."

"Sorry, Chief," Arla said. "It's just that, coming to Bajor, seeing the shape my people are in, when I know how much more we could be capable of. . . ."

O'Brien nodded, relieved that her outburst was over, and that he hadn't had to alert anyone else. That he'd been able to handle the situation himself. Even Julian could not have done better. "That's all right. It's all off the record."

Arla nodded and turned her chair back to the board and the distant view of Deep Space 9.

"Someday, the Prophets are going to destroy us," she said quietly. "And the horrible thing is, sometimes I think I'm the only Bajoran who realizes it."

O'Brien didn't begrudge her having the last word, though he suspected there was something else the young commander wasn't telling him—whether about the Prophets, about her past, he couldn't be sure. But now was perhaps not the time to probe for it, not when the topic was so disturbing to her. There'd been enough emotional venting for now.

The Chief contemplated the next ten hours of silence with more equanimity than he had before.

It wasn't as if they had to be unproductive hours.

With his spirits already rising in pleasant anticipation, he asked the computer to run a level-*five* diagnostic on the engineering subsystems.

In all the confusing diversity of the universe, O'Brien knew he could always find his peace in the beauty of a well-constructed machine, operating according to the inalterable laws of physics.

He wondered where Arla and others who felt as she did would find their answers—their peace. And what might happen if they didn't find it soon.

CHAPTER 14

In the surgery, Vash was sitting up in the angled examination bed. She had shadowed circles under her large, expressive eyes and her lustrous skin was pale, but Jadzia could see no signs of trembling or weakness.

Vash's query was unspoken but obvious to all who observed her.

Kira started to speak but Odo coughed and she reluctantly turned to Jadzia.

"You're safe for now, Vash. Odo's using suppression screens to protect against unauthorized transportation." Jadzia moved to block Kira and Odo from Vash's line of sight. Julian was standing on the other side of the examination table with his hands behind his back, keeping watch on the Cardassian diagnostic displays above his patient. "And there are security officers standing guard outside the Infirmary."

Vash wasn't impressed. "Oh, I see. Being safe must be some new Starfleet term for being a prisoner."

Jadzia smiled. Sweetly. "You're not under arrest. Yet."

Vash's answering smile was just as sweet. "Why would I be under arrest? Is it against some Bajoran law to be the target of an assassin? Or did I obstruct traffic on the Promenade when I collapsed?"

Interesting, Jadzia thought. Of all the experiences of all Dax's previous hosts she had to draw on, the ones she usually found herself returning to least were those of Joran, her sixth. He'd been a mistake, his existence still suppressed by the Symbiosis Commission to avoid alarming the Trill public with the revelation that the selection process was not perfect. Joran had been unbalanced. He'd committed murder.

Jadzia now took the rare step of brushing lightly against the disturbing memories of that perverted mind and its hideous act. Because she sensed a similar lack of equilibrium in Vash.

But could Vash kill? Jadzia wondered. Not in self-defense, because almost anyone was capable of that. *Could she kill in the way that Joran had, merely for sport, or lust, or greed?*

"On Bajor," Jadzia said severely, "even the *attempt* to traffic in Orbs is one of the most serious crimes in their system."

Vash stretched and moved her shoulders as if verifying the health of her body. "I told him that, huh? The captain? About Quark being involved in selling the Orbs?"

Jadzia nodded, looking beyond Vash to see Kira now caught in an impressive struggle to remain silent.

The archaeologist bent forward, rubbed gingerly at

the side of her head. "On the Promenade, when I got hit . . . I thought I was dying, you know? I remember *wanting* to tell someone . . . the captain . . . something that might make it easier for him to find who killed me." She gave a sudden, rueful laugh. "My bad luck I didn't die." She twisted around to look over her shoulder at Bashir. "Why is that, Doc?"

Bashir looked away from the Cardassian readouts. "The dart contained an Andorian toxin."

Vash suddenly laid back against the angled table, as if all the strength had left her. "Satr and Leen. They've been after me for a long time. Ever since the Mandylion retrieval."

Jadzia saw Odo shake his head 'No' at the possibility that the two Andorian sisters were involved in the attack on Vash. But Jadzia had already deduced the improbability of that for herself. Even if Odo did not have visual records of whoever had fired the dart at Vash, Jadzia was aware the Andorian sisters were under constant surveillance. If they had been anywhere near Vash at the time of the attack, Odo's officers would have known it.

Right now there was no advantage to be gained in sharing that news with Vash. But if her cooperation were needed later, such information would be as valuable as latinum. So Jadzia did not contradict Vash's supposition. She merely said, "Odo's working on tracking the sisters' movements."

Then Jadzia added, as if the question were unimportant, "Anyone else who might be after you? Captain Sisko said he thought you saw someone you knew on the Promenade, just before the attack."

Vash stared up at the ceiling, frowning. "This'll sound crazy, but . . ."

"I know all about crazy," Jadzia murmured comfortingly. "Believe me."

"Yeah? Well, I thought I saw Dal Nortron following us. How's that for crazy?"

With that, Odo reached his breaking point. "Excuse me, ladies, but there are only two Andorians on the station, and had one of them been on the Promenade at any time close to the instant you were attacked, they'd stand out on the surveillance tapes like . . . well, like Andorians." Odo stepped back, a hand held up in apology. "I apologize for breaking in."

But the damage was done. Jadzia had seen a worrisome little flash of calculation in Vash, as if the archaeologist had just learned something of importance from Odo's outburst—such as the fact that the Andorian sisters had *not* been on the Promenade and thus could hardly be considered suspects.

"What I meant was, he was in disguise," Vash said, recovering smoothly, but not smoothly enough for Jadzia, who was on full alert, now. "Or altered or something. I mean, no antennae, sort of brown skin. He might even have had Bajoran epinasal ridges. Like I said, I couldn't be sure."

"We'll study the visual scans again," Jadzia said evenly, more and more determined not to let Vash control this interrogation. "But in the meantime—Quark and the Orbs. Let's talk about that."

"What's the point?" All sense of hesitation or unease gone, Vash sat up again and ruffled her hair into place. "If I do, I go to prison. If I don't, it's just something I said when I had a shot of bicuprodyanide bubbling in my brain. I think what I meant to say to Captain Sisko is, Damn, I'm sorry I'm dying before I ever got a chance to have Quark show me an Orb like he promised he would the last time I was on the station. There's one in the Temple on the Promenade, isn't there? Yeah," the archaeologist continued, staring brazenly right into Jadzia's eyes, betraying no guilt whatsoever, "I'm sure that's the one Quark said he'd show me. Did you actually think I'd deal in a stolen Orb when I know what they mean to the Bajoran people?"

Now it was Kira who was close to the breaking point. Jadzia heard her give a muffled exclamation, but the major said nothing more, keeping to her promise not to interfere.

Julian, on the other hand, was suddenly looking ridiculously pleased with himself. But all he did in reply to Jadzia's questioning look was grin foolishly, once again appearing much too cute for his own good. *A good Galeo-Manada workout would cure that in a hurry,* Jadzia thought.

"I can certainly see how your explanation of what you said to Captain Sisko *might* make sense," Jadzia told Vash. "Of course, part of the problem is that the captain didn't understand every word."

"I guess I was lucky to be able to say anything at all."

"One of the more interesting things he said you told him was that Quark was going to have an auction to sell an Orb."

"Did I say auction or action?" Vash suddenly seemed busy rearranging her tunic. "Sell an Orb, or see an Orb? I bet I wasn't too clear." She looked up and smiled brightly at her interrogator.

"And then there was a word you used, one he didn't quite get, maybe something . . . Bajoran?"

Vash stopped fussing with her clothing for a

moment, looked thoughtful for a moment, then shook her head.

"Let's try it this way, then," Jadzia suggested helpfully. "What Orb was Quark going to show you at the temple?"

"Oh," Vash said. She swung her legs off the side of the examination table. "Sure, that was it. The Orb of Jalbador."

"What?" Kira sputtered. She moved so quickly to Vash's side that she was between Jadzia and the archaeologist before Jadzia had even realized what she was doing. Odo moved forward but Jadzia quietly signaled him to hold back. Perhaps Kira could shake something out of Vash. It was worth a try.

" 'Jalbador'?" Kira said to Vash. "Is that what you said?"

Vash shrugged, unintimidated. "Yeah, so?"

"Not one Orb, but the Lost Orbs? The Lost Red Orbs of Jalbador? Is *that* what this is about?"

"You should talk to Quark," Vash said. "But, yeah, that's what he said he'd show me. A Red Orb of Jalbador."

Kira hung her head and shook it, as if berating herself for being a fool. "That's it, we're done here." She turned away from Vash, as if she had lost all interest in the archaeologist.

"I beg your pardon?" Jadzia asked.

"This is . . . more than ridiculous. I have to contact the Kai at once."

"Major, why?"

"Because, Dax, the Red Orbs of Jalbador don't exist. They are . . . I don't know a non-Bajoran example. But, they're not part of any of the legitimate teachings of our religion."

"Apocryphal?" Bashir suggested.

"That's as good a word as any," Kira said. "But more than that, they're something that . . . fringe people and fortune seekers and . . ." She waved a dismissive hand at Vash, who made a face back at her. ". . . and petty thieves go after all the time. I mean, at least once or twice a year there's some unbelievable story about the Lost Orbs being found, hidden in the ice on Mount Ba'Lavael. Or deep in the Tracian Sea in the sunken ruins of B'hala."

"But Major," Bashir objected, "B'hala didn't sink in the Tracian Sea. Captain Sisko found it under the Ir'Abehr Shield."

"Exactly, Doctor. But until the Emissary found it, B'hala had been lost for twenty thousand years! That's twenty thousand years of legends and lies and outright fraud. Do you know how many people on Bajor—and on a dozen other worlds, I'm sure—have been bilked by swindlers who claim to have an ancient map that shows the location of B'hala or the resting places of the Red Orbs?"

"The Brooklyn Bridge," Bashir suddenly blurted out. It made so little sense to Jadzia and everyone else in the surgery that they all turned to look at him.

"On old Earth," he continued, his expression somehow conveying the impression that he expected everyone else to know exactly what he meant. "The late 1800s. People newly arrived in what used to be called New York City were offered deeds to the Brooklyn Bridge—a spectacular public works built and owned by the local government. To buy the Brooklyn Bridge became a colloquialism for gullibility." Jadzia winced as Julian enthusiastically adopted a broad dialect as he quoted, " 'Well, if you believe dat, buddy, then I have a bridge in Brooklyn I wanna sell ya.' "

No one said anything right away. But Odo finally broke the silence. "Excuse me, Doctor, but is this the same Brooklyn Bridge that's installed at the big amusement park on Earth's moon?"

"Why, yes," Bashir said eagerly. "Taking it apart, moving it in sections, rebuilding it—it was one of the most phenomenal engineering feats of the twenty-third century."

"In other words, eventually, someone really *did* buy the Brooklyn Bridge?"

Jadzia tried not to laugh as Julian's face fell.

"Well, yes, Odo, but the point is. . . ." He looked plaintively around the surgery, loath as always to accept that no one was really up to appreciating whatever his point was. "Never mind."

"I really have to go," Kira said abruptly. "Odo, forget everything I sent you on Orb law. As far as I'm concerned, you can charge this woman with being a public nuisance, or you can . . . ship her out to wherever she's planning on selling her 'Orbs' next. Jadzia. Doctor." Kira left.

"That's it?" Vash asked, slipping off the examination table to stand upright, without any signs of ever having been affected by anything.

"Apparently so," Jadzia said.

Odo stepped around so that Vash could see him without straining. "Tell me, Vash, what *are* your plans now?"

"Staying alive is always high on my list of things to do."

"Then obviously, staying safely behind transporter-proof shields and being guarded by my officers is agreeable to you?"

"That depends on what the price is."

"Quark," Odo said. "Where is he?"

"Frankly, constable, I don't know. I was surprised to hear he had disappeared."

"Where were you going to meet him?"

Vash cocked her head at the constable. "I already had this conversation with the captain and Commander Dax."

"That's not an answer."

"At the bar, Odo. Where else would I meet him?"

"And what were you meeting him about?"

"According to the major there, not much." Vash sighed at Odo's poorly concealed look of exasperation. "All right. This is everything I know. Quark put the word out that he had been asked to be the broker for a transaction involving . . . the Red Orbs of Jalbador." Jadzia was impressed by Vash's attempt to make it seem she was embarrassed to even say the name of the Orbs. Vash was really good.

"The broker," Odo repeated gruffly. "So, presumably someone else had possession of the Orbs—"

"And Quark asked me if I knew of any prospective buyers."

"And did you?"

"Are you kidding? Half the antiquarian collectors in the Alpha Quadrant would bankrupt themselves for a chance to own a Bajoran Orb. Odo, seriously, this was shaping up to be the biggest transaction since the Fajo collection went on the block. I'm talking big."

"Did you put those interested collectors in touch with Quark?"

Vash drew back in surprise that seemed genuine even to Jadzia, who was increasingly fascinated by the archaeologist's behavior. Her performance, filtered as it was through poor Joran, seemed to Jadzia as if it were being dictated by an already written script. Somehow, the archaeologist had manipulated the situation so that Odo was asking all the questions Vash wanted him to ask. The performance was brilliant.

"Did you?" Odo repeated.

"Be serious," Vash said. "If I brought in my . . . clients, the bidding would . . . well, you could buy and sell planets for what some people would be willing to spend. And my cut would only be ten percent of Quark's commission." Vash sat forward, as if suddenly excited by the prospect of such a deal. "But, if I kept my people out of it, well, Quark doesn't have the connections I do. The bidding wouldn't go anywhere as high, and. . . ."

"You planned to buy it for yourself," Odo said, "and then hold your own auction for the people who could really pay."

Vash held up her hands as if surrendering. "Guilty."

"My sentiments exactly," Odo told her. "You know, of course, what the penalties are for trading in Orbs. Not just in Bajoran law, but under the Federation's own protection-of-antiquities statutes."

Vash curled a finger at Odo, asking him to move closer. "Odo, remember what the major said? There *are* no Red Orbs of Jalbador. If someone wants to buy something he only *thinks* is illegal, that's not a crime."

Odo rocked back and crossed his arms. "Oh, you are a piece of work."

"I'll take that as a compliment."

For a moment, Jadzia's Trill-constant swirl of consciousness paused and then coalesced into the pattern she'd been seeking as she realized what Vash was trying to do. There was now only one last question for Odo to ask.

As if on cue, she heard the constable say, "One last thing. If all of this . . . confusion was brought about by the potential sale of an artifact that you and whoever else was involved knew was a fraud, why would someone want to kill you?"

Jadzia caught her breath as Vash delivered her answer: "I'm not the only one who deals in rare antiquities. My clients buy from several different sources, so . . . any one of them could have decided that the potential payoff was worth taking me out of the picture."

Odo gazed down at the floor and Jadzia knew exactly what he was going to say next. The only thing a man like Odo could say after the story he had just been told.

"Vash, I have far better things to do with my time than try to stop criminals from killing other criminals. I'll keep all the security precautions in place while you're in the Infirmary, but as soon as Doctor Bashir says you can be released, I want you off this station. Is that understood?"

For once, Vash seemed truly serious. "Yeah, I understand. And . . . it may not mean much coming from someone like me, Odo, but thank you for . . . the transporter shields and the guards. I'll be on my way as soon as the doctor says."

Odo nodded his head once, said his good-byes to Jadzia and Bashir, then left.

Vash turned to Bashir. "So Doc? How long have I got?"

Bashir studied the Cardassian readouts. "How's your head?"

"Like I've got Gorns playing ten-pin behind my eyeballs."

Bashir nodded as if he knew exactly what that felt like. "I thought so. At least another twenty-six hours of observation, then I'll make a decision." He reached into a tray by the table and brought up a hypospray. "In the meantime, this should take the Gorns down to five-pin, at least."

Vash smiled as Bashir touched the hypospray to the side of her neck opposite to where the dart had struck. She still had a small dressing on that wound. Bashir had not wanted to use a protoplaser to speed the healing of the puncture because any residual toxin might have been trapped in the new tissue growth.

"Are you a bowler?" Vash asked.

"I'm afraid darts are more my game."

Vash laughed softly, seductively, and being a young attractive woman herself, Jadzia did not need to call upon the experiences of any of Dax's previous hosts to know exactly what Vash was trying to do.

"Maybe we should play sometime," Vash said.

"Darts or bowling?"

"Or . . . something else?" Vash's smile was sly, knowing. "You can choose. I'm open to just about anything."

Jadzia rolled her eyes as she saw the sudden flush that came to Bashir's cheeks as he *finally* realized Vash was no longer talking about the same indoor sports he was. "You get some sleep," he said.

Vash reached out to touch his hand. "Thank you, Doctor."

Jadzia had to admire Vash's technique. The touch had clinched it. Bashir was definitely on the hook, though she knew him well enough that he would do nothing to pursue this new opportunity until after Vash was no longer in his care.

Bashir eased away from her hand. "Uh, you're quite welcome. I'll . . . check in on you later, then."

"I'll be here."

I don't believe it, Jadzia thought as she started for the door. *The silly creature actually batted her eyelashes at him.*

Then Jadzia hooked her arm around Julian's and guided him to the door at her side. "Come along, Doctor. You have other patients."

"I do?"

The surgery door slid shut behind them, and they were in the main work area. Without Vash.

Immediately, Jadzia said, "Julian, I'm surprised at you."

"Why me? On the contrary, I'm surprised at you and at Odo."

"That woman was . . . wait a minute. Why are *you* surprised at *me?"*

Bashir headed over to the workstation where he had left the neural dart. "Because you—*and* Odo—were falling for everything Vash said."

Now Jadzia was doubly surprised. "I wasn't falling for everything she said. *You* were." She batted her eyelashes at Bashir. "Oh, Doctor, I'm open to anything. Really, Julian."

Bashir gave her a look of amusement. "Could it be you're jealous?"

"I am a happily married woman, thank you. I just happen to be concerned for my friend."

Bashir rolled the dart in his fingers, as if looking for something he and the most sophisticated collection of medical scanners and analyzers this side of Starbase 375 had missed the first time. "Well, your friend is equally concerned about you." He brought up his other hand and adjusted the position of the dart. "So you should know that everything Vash was saying in there was a lie." He began rolling the dart again, as if trying to feel for some slight imperfection.

Jadzia sighed with relief. There was hope for Julian yet. "Thank goodness you were able to sense it, too. I really was getting worried about you."

Bashir looked as if he hadn't quite understood what Jadzia had said. He continued to roll the dart in his fingers. Jadzia eyed him with renewed concern. She didn't like the way he was handling the dart, and she trusted he wasn't going to do something stupid, like accidentally prick himself with the dart's small needle. "I didn't have to *sense* anything, Jadzia. I knew what was going on the instant she made her mistake."

"What mistake?"

"Dax! You musn't have been paying attention. Now I'm even more surprised."

Jadzia put her hands on her hips. "Julian, unlike Miss Batty-Eyes in there, I am not fond of this kind of game. What mistake did she make?"

"Bicuprodyanide," Bashir said happily, entirely too happily in Jadzia's estimation. "She said she had it bubbling in her brain, if you recall."

Jadzia thought back. Yes, she could remember Vash saying exactly that. "But what about it? She did have bicuprodyanide in her system, didn't she?"

"Absolutely. Except . . . I never told her that's what it was. All I said was she had been exposed to an Andorian neural toxin."

Jadzia tapped her forehead with her fingers. It had slipped right by her. But then she thought she detected a flaw. "Just a minute, Julian. Maybe it was a lucky guess. I mean, how many Andorian neural toxins can there be?"

Bashir held up the medical padd he had been working with earlier. "In common use or easily replicated with nonspecialized equipment, one hundred ninety seven. I have no doubt that Vash knew exactly what was in this dart, and because of that, there was no possible way she thought she was dying when she told Captain Sisko about the Red Orbs."

Jadzia was struggling now to deal not only with what Bashir was suggesting, but with the fact that he had jumped so far ahead of her own assumptions. "But Julian, how could she take the chance that her accomplice would be able to shoot her at the right time, with the right toxin, without being seen?"

Then Jadzia felt Dax lurch within her abdominal pocket as Bashir suddenly slapped his hand to the side of his neck, driving the neural dart needle into his flesh. *"Julian!"*

But Bashir's only response was to seem to pluck the dart from his neck and then roll it forward in his fingers so that Jadzia could see the needle had been removed. It was in his other hand.

"What better way to make us believe she's telling us the truth, than by making us think that someone would rather kill her than have us hear what she had to say?"

To Jadzia, that moment of revelation was as powerful as if an Altonian sphere had just turned monochromatic. She had become so caught up in the idea that Vash was manipulating the truth in the surgery that she hadn't stopped to consider that that manipulation might have started much earlier.

"She's been lying from the beginning," Jadzia said wonderingly.

"I think that's likely," Bashir agreed.

"Which could mean . . . she does know where Quark is—"

"—and she knows who claims to have the Red Orbs—"

Then Jadzia and Bashir hesitated as they drew the ultimate conclusion from what they had discovered.

"And the Red Orbs themselves . . ." Jadzia said slowly.

Bashir nodded. ". . . could very well be real." He smiled at Jadzia's look of concentration. "As I said, we could be a great team."

Even his persistence struck her as endearing. But she deflected him by saying, "Julian, we already are a great team."

He stepped closer to her. "So what does the team do now?"

"Now . . . we go see Benjamin."

She could see it in his eyes: It wasn't what he had wanted to hear her say, but he knew it was the right thing for her to have said.

What a sweet hopeless romantic Julian is, Jadzia thought with real affection as they left the Infirmary together. *Someday, the woman who gets Julian is going to be the luckiest woman in the quadrant.*

She wondered who that lucky woman would be.

CHAPTER 15

"YOU'RE CRAZY," Nog said.

Jake shrugged. "My granddad says that's not so bad in a writer."

"Then may I say your grandfather is crazy, too."

Jake straightened up from the safety railing on the second level of the Promenade. Years ago, when he and Nog had first met and made the first tentative steps in forging a friendship that would transcend the traditional boundaries of their respective species, they would sit on the deck here, letting their legs swing over the side until Odo or one of his officers told them they should have something better to do and it was time to move along.

But now, Jake realized there *had* been nothing better for the two of them to be doing than watching the parade of life that had passed by beneath them. Because those long hours of observation, speculation, and just plain talking had helped them become the young men they were today—the writer and the Starfleet officer.

It was from this vantage point by the safety railing that Jake first began noticing the intricate details of people's behavior: how some couples walked close together, some apart; how some people smiled secretly to themselves, while others fought back hidden tears. He'd seen the confidence of the newly arrived visitor, fresh from the shuttle, striding in to face the challenge of Quark's dabo table. Hours later, he'd watched the defeated shuffle of that same person as he crept away with only the clothes he wore.

Nog had learned no less than Jake. He had explained the Great Material River to his *hew-mon* friend, and how the Promenade was a perfect tributary of that mighty cascade that shaped the universe. On the shores of the Promenade—that is, its shops and kiosks—were pockets of accumulation, areas that had too much of one thing or another. Flowing between those shores were the rushing waters of customers—that is, those who had too little of what the shops had too much of.

On the other side of the equation, the shopkeepers had far too little latinum, and so an endless rebalancing of accounts ensued as the waters lapped at the shores, eroding a little here, building up a little there, always working to achieve a balance that forever remained out of reach.

Jake had been brought up in a Starfleet home and was fascinated by the Ferengi outlook on the universe. Nog, who had been brought up to accept the Great Material River as the only reasonable way to see the universe, had been equally fascinated to learn about

Jake's alien perspective. The idea that it was acceptable—even desirable—to accumulate knowledge for no other purpose than to increase understanding, and the entire concept of helping others without *any* prospect of profit, were staggering to the young Ferengi.

But once both boys got over their initial dismissal of each others' viewpoints and began to truly try to see what the other meant, whole new vistas opened before them.

In Jake was born the need to see how other minds—not just human and Ferengi—viewed the universe, and then to illuminate those views for others through the written word. In Nog, a mad dream was born in which the precision of Ferengi thought could be applied to the romantic altruism of the Federation in order to create a new paradigm of galactic organization, one in which the most extreme imbalances in the Great Material River—meaning those that invariably led to conflict—would be forever eliminated, while still leaving ample opportunity for individuals to profit.

Thus Jake and Nog had set their lives' goals and directions, all in the idle pastimes of children, and all from this one corner of the Promenade.

Not that any of that made it easier for them to reconcile their differences today.

"You know what your problem is?" Nog asked.

"I don't get out enough?" Jake answered.

The Ferengi frowned. "No. It is that you are always trying to understand life in terms of a made-up novel."

"Nog, that's my job."

"How can it be a job if you make no money from it? Writing news articles is your job. Writing novels for no money, that is . . . an affliction."

Jake put an elbow on the safety railing and rested his head on his hand. "Nog, when you were at the Academy, did you make any profit?"

Nog reacted suspiciously to Jake's abrupt change of topic. "No. . . ."

"But someday you expect to profit from your Starfleet experience, don't you?"

Nog appeared to be selecting his words with extreme care. "I would hope that . . . many individuals, commercial concerns, and government agencies will profit from . . . what I will learn during my career in Starfleet."

Jake pounced as soon as Nog had cornered himself. "So you admit that—"

Nog realized the trap he'd been caught in and wouldn't let Jake finish. He did it himself. "Yes, yes, that I performed certain activities with no chance of immediate profit, but with the expectation of earning profit at a later time."

Jake's smirk let Nog know who had won this particular argument. "So, as I was saying, from the perspective of a made-up novel, there's something going on here on Deep Space 9. Something that your uncle's involved with. And something that's brought smugglers in from across the quadrant. And it's not what Vash told Dax and Odo."

"And as *I* was saying, you're crazy. You're drawing connections where none exist. You're trying to make my uncle into that Fermion character—"

"Higgs. Higgs is based on Quark. Fermion is based on Morn."

"—that *unbelievable* character in your novel. And he's not."

Jake stretched and straightened up again. A wave of

new visitors was arriving on the Promenade from the turbolifts and airlocks. Not too many were Bajoran, so Jake decided the commercial cruiser from Sagittarius III had finally arrived. The Sagittarians were neutral in the Dominion War, and as a result their cruisers carried cargo and passengers from most of the nonaligned worlds. Whenever a Sagittarian ship docked at the station, there was always a good chance a rarely seen alien might be on board, and Jake found himself watching the crowd closely, hoping he might catch his first glimpse of a Nanth.

But he hadn't forgotten his friend, and even as his gaze remained on the lower Promenade level he said, "Nog, if I gave you ten crates of stem bolts, self-sealing or not, your imagination would run wild thinking up new schemes for selling them, or trading them, or . . . somehow turning them into latinum. When it comes to business, you won't accept any limits."

"Of course not."

"Then why is it you have no imagination when it comes to how *people* behave?"

After a few moments of silence, Jake glanced sideways to see that Nog was just staring at him, as if he could think of nothing more to say.

Jake sighed. "Let's try it again." He held up a finger. "First of all, Quark called in a group of smugglers to take part in the sale of a counterfeit Bajoran artifact." He held up a second finger. "Then, one of the Andorian smugglers was murdered." He held up a third finger. "And then, someone tried to murder Vash." He held up a fourth finger. "And despite Vash explaining the whole thing to Dax and Odo, there are still at least four smugglers on the station—Vash, the Andorian sisters, and that guy, Base." Jake waved his hand back and forth, trying to emphasize the importance of those facts. "So put all that together, and what do you have?"

"Four fingers."

Jake closed his eyes. "Nog, use your imagination."

"All right. I will now imagine the impossible." Nog put his hand over his eyes, a thumb on one temple, a forefinger on the other. "I am imagining that you are giving up this stupid line of reasoning. I am imagining that . . . that you are buying me lunch at the Replimat. I am imagining that—"

But by then, Jake's laughter had become contagious and Nog began laughing, too.

"I am *not* buying you lunch," Jake laughed. "It's your turn."

"That is why I was using my imagination," Nog said.

They both began walking toward the closest spiral stairway.

"Anyway," Jake said, undeterred by his friend's resistance. "I still think I'm right."

"That the counterfeit Bajoran artifact isn't counterfeit?"

They came to the staircase, and Jake waited for Nog to go first. "If it were all a scam like Vash said, the smugglers would have left by now, right? After all, Odo knows all about it, so what's the point of sticking around?"

"To obtain the counterfeit artifact and take it someplace where potential customers don't know it's counterfeit," Nog said.

They arrived on the Promenade's main level, and Jake was surprised by the noise and bustle of the new arrivals. Many of them were looking around as if they had never seen a space station before.

"That still doesn't answer the big mystery," Jake said as he and Nog started for the Replimat. "Why would professional smugglers get involved with murder for a counterfeit artifact? I mean, I understand the idea of trying to make a profit for low risk—"

"I would certainly hope so."

"—but to commit murder?" Jake said. "That's a high-risk crime. Which means the potential profits have to be equally high. Isn't that one of your rules? The riskier the road, the greater the profit?"

This time when Jake looked at Nog, he could see the Ferengi looking thoughtful.

"All right," Nog said. "You have a point. A small one. And it probably has nothing at all to do with what's really going on here. But. . . ."

Jake grinned. "But what?"

"It is probably good enough for *The Ferengi Correction.*"

"*Connection.* The title is, *The Ferengi Connection.*"

"Whatever."

Jake stopped Nog by the directory monolith. "Okay. I'm being serious now."

"When aren't you serious?"

"I mean it, Nog. How am I ever going to be able to convince a reader that a story I write might be true, if I can't even convince *you* that what we're really seeing go on all around us *is* a story?"

Now Nog looked worried. "I do not have the slightest idea what you're talking about."

Jake took a breath, oblivious to the crowds of people passing by. "Given everything that's happened here over the past three days, what do *you* think is going on?"

"*Anything* other than what you think is going on."

"You're doing this on purpose."

"Jake, be reasonable. Let us say you are right. Let us say that Uncle Fermion—"

"Quark."

"—Quark is selling a real Bajoran artifact with a value worth killing for. First of all, what kind of an artifact is that valuable? I mean, the rarest Bajoran artifact that I have ever heard of was that icon of the city of B'hala. And nobody was trying to kill to get that. The Cardassians just . . . gave it back to Bajor."

Jake glanced up at the Promenade's high ceiling. Nog had a point. Even Jake had never heard of an artifact so valuable that—he had it! "Nog! It's an Orb!"

Nog reacted with outraged shock. "An Orb is not an 'artifact.' It is . . . an Orb. And my uncle would not be stupid enough to risk buying or selling an Orb, no matter how great the profit."

"But there would be incredible profit for someone not as . . . law-abiding as Quark? Like a real criminal?"

Nog clearly did not want to be having this conversation. "I suppose."

"All right. Then that's what it is. Thank you, Nog. You've solved an important story point. Quark—Higgs—is trying to sell an Orb. And since we haven't heard any news about an Orb being stolen, it's got to be one of the Orbs that went missing during the Occupation that the Cardassians haven't returned yet."

Nog looked disappointed. "So now you are suggesting that either a *Cardassian* is selling a stolen Orb or that someone with more lobes than brains stole an Orb from the Cardassians."

"Isn't there some Rule of Acquisition to cover this?"

Jake asked. "You know, Profit plus more profit equals temporary insanity for a desperate criminal?"

Nog screwed up his face in concentration. "Perhaps in one of the reform editions. But not in the . . ." He frowned. "You are not being serious. There is no such law."

"All I'm looking for is a possibility. A willing suspension of disbelief. What's it going to take to convince you?"

"Really?"

"Nog, if I can convince you, I can convince anyone. Now, let me have it. What do you need to believe the story?"

Nog looked around at the milling crowd. "More smugglers. If someone's trying to sell an Orb, there should be a great many more than four smugglers on board DS9. There should be dozens, if not hundreds."

"Okay, I can live with that. Quark put out the word a few days ago. The closest smugglers arrive in a day or two. With more continuing to arrive. So there will be more by now, we just don't know about them. What else?"

Nog shrugged. "Cardassians."

"Why Cardassians?"

"They're trying to recover their stolen property."

That was going too far for Jake. "Nog, there won't be any Cardassians coming to DS9. We're at war with them."

Nog shook his head. "The *Federation* is at war with Cardassia. Bajor is not a member of the Federation. Technically, it has been given neutral status by the Dominion. And technically, this station is Bajoran territory."

"But it's *in* Federation space."

Nog held his hands out as if he had nothing more to offer. "You asked what it would take. I answered. Now you really do have to buy me lunch."

Jake started walking again, with Nog hurrying to keep up. "I don't have to buy you anything. I asked for help. You set up impossible conditions."

The Replimat was full, every table taken. There was even a line outside. The Sagittarians did not have a reputation for palatable food. Too many of their flavorings were self-organizing slime molds, which often tried to reconstitute themselves and then escape from whatever dish they had been mixed into.

"Not impossible," Nog insisted. "Necessary. As in necessary for me to accept your premise. Should we try the Klingon Cafe?"

"Impossible, because there's no way anyone will believe that Cardassians will come to DS9. Why don't we try Quark's?"

Nog looked uncomfortable. "That little Base . . . he makes me nervous. Did you know he has hair? On his . . . scalp? Uh, no offense."

"We'll eat upstairs."

"All right." Nog suddenly brightened. "Maybe Leeta will be on duty. Then we can negotiate a family discount!"

The young men left the Replimat and started back toward Quark's. "You have to pay to eat at your uncle's?" Jake asked.

"Exploitation begins at home," Nog said, as if quoting another of the Ferengi Rules. "And if the Orb is really an Orb and you want your story to be believed, then you have to do something dramatic so the reader will understand the stakes have been raised."

"What are you talking about?"

"Cardassians on DS9."

"Forget it. I'm not writing a fantasy. I'm writing a heist novel and there are rules I have to follow. And one of them is. . . ." Jake hesitated. Couldn't quite believe what he saw—who he saw—stepping through the airlock across from Quark's, beyond the Infirmary.

"Is what?" Nog prompted.

"Cardassians," Jake said.

Nog sounded as confused as Jake felt. "That's a rule?"

Jake reached out, took Nog's shoulder, and pointed him in the same direction he was looking. "No," Jake said. "That's your proof."

Cardassians.

Three of them. Just outside the circular door of the airlock. One was female, the other two male. And one of them was unlike any Cardassian Jake had ever seen before: He was bald.

Jake felt Nog tense, and instantly the Ferengi tapped his communicator badge.

"Nog to Commander Worf. Security breach on the Promenade. Airlock Alpha. Three enemy personnel."

Jake wheeled to Nog. "Nog, they're not enemy personnel. Look at them—they're civilians. No weapons. No—"

Jake stopped talking as the crowd reacted to five columns of shimmering light that formed around the airlock stairs.

Jake stared in fascination as four Starfleet security officers beamed in with Worf and scattered the crowd. Each of the five had a phaser. Each phaser was aimed at the Cardassians.

"Isn't that a bit of an overreaction?" Jake asked.

"We are at war," Nog said.

Jake had tried, but he still didn't understand the military mind-set that had become so much a part of Starfleet in the past year. But the one thing he felt he did know was motivation, both in the characters he wrote about and in real life. And he understood the motivation that had led to the scene being played out before him right now.

"Okay, Nog—this proves my point," Jake said as Worf and his team took the Cardassians into custody. "What possible reason could three Cardassians have for risking a trip into *Federation* space to set foot on a *Starfleet*-controlled space station?"

Nog looked up at Jake, and Jake could see that this time his friend knew exactly what he was talking about.

"You said it yourself," Jake continued. "They want their Orb back. It's the only possible reason they could have for coming here."

Nog looked grim. "We shall see." Then he went to offer his assistance to Worf.

Jake remained behind. But as he watched the Cardassians being led away, he was filled with an overpowering sense of just being *right.*

He was the only person on Deep Space 9 who truly knew what was going on, and it was time to start letting people know it.

CHAPTER 16

"I AM LEEJ TERRELL," the leader of the Cardassian mission said in the relative calm of the Wardroom. "And these are our credentials."

Sisko accepted the articulated Cardassian padd she gave him. The excitement of the unannounced arrival of three Cardassians on a neutral cruiser had finally lessened throughout the station. But the security concerns remained.

As he took his seat across from his visitors at the conference table, Sisko studied the padd, comparing the identity dossiers it displayed as the station's computer automatically tested the authentication codes in the padd's memory.

According to the padd, Leej Terrell was the widow of a minor trade diplomat from Cardassia Prime. Her technical specialist, Dr. Phraim Betan, was a physician retired from the Cardassian Home Battalions. And her associate, Atrig, of no specified job function, was a businessman who ran an import-export company among the Cardassian colony worlds. The three Cardassians were, each dossier proclaimed, volunteers working for the Amber Star, with no official connection to the Cardassian government.

Sisko, however, didn't believe a word of the dossiers. For a diplomat's wife, Terrell was too clearly used to giving orders, not practicing diplomacy. Dr. Betan was too young to have retired from anything. And Atrig—perhaps the most striking Cardassian Sisko had ever seen—had not lost his hair nor been so badly scarred at the base of his neck and across one of his wide shoulder membranes ferrying goods from one world to another. Atrig had been in battle.

Decked out though they were with false identities, innocuous civilian outfits, and singularly hollow smiles, Sisko had no doubt he was seated across the table from three Cardassian soldiers. Three very active, and dangerous, Cardassian soldiers.

A Federation authorization window opened on the padd's display—the authentication codes had been confirmed. Terrell, Betan, and Atrig had been cleared for travel within the Bajoran sector.

But Sisko didn't really care. He placed the padd on the table as if it held nothing of interest or of value for him.

"So, you are traveling under the guise of a humanitarian mission," Sisko began.

"Not under the guise," Terrell replied easily. "We *are* a humanitarian mission, accepted by both the Federation and the Dominion during this terrible conflict."

Sisko folded his hands. "Then why didn't you make travel arrangements directly with this station? If you are permitted to travel through Federation space, why arrive unannounced?"

Seated directly across the table from him, Terrell matched Sisko's gesture, folding her own hands in a mirror image of his. "In times such as these," she said, "I often find it is more expedient to beg forgiveness than ask permission. If I had requested your approval to travel here, would you have given it to me?"

"No," Sisko said, registering Terrell's surprise at his decision not to hide the truth through the more standard practice of equivocation and diversion.

"Then I was right to do as I did," she said with a smile.

"Again, no," Sisko said, keeping his tone deliberately impassive and uninformative. "You have disrupted my station. You have raised many questions in the mind of my strategic operations officer. Whatever delay you might have expected if you had contacted me ahead of time you can be sure will now be even longer, as Commander Worf tries to uncover what you're hiding."

Sisko saw Terrell shoot a swift glance at Dr. Betan. And then as if the glance had been a signal for his action, the doctor spoke next.

"Captain Sisko, I assure you we have nothing to hide. We are volunteer workers of the Amber Star, private citizens aligned with no political group. We are merely here to repatriate the remains of the unfortunate Cardassians you discovered fused within the hull of this station. I'm sure you'll understand how this humanitarian act will at last bring closure to their families, as their fates are now known and the two unfortunates can be laid to rest according to their own customs."

"Ah, but I understand completely, Doctor," Sisko said. "And I am very pleased that the genetic profiles of the soldiers have allowed you to identify them." Hastily suppressed reactions from all three Cardassians informed Sisko that his statement had startled them, a suspicion Terrell quickly confirmed.

"I believe you have reached an incorrect conclusion, Captain Sisko. The dead whose remains we are recovering are not—were not—soldiers. Their identification files are in the padd, as well. You will see that they were civilian support staff for the Terok Nor mining operation. Low-level. Of course, they worked *for* the military in trying to restore order to Bajor—"

"Excuse me?" Sisko said, not sure he had heard Terrell correctly.

Undeterred by his interruption, Terrell proceeded silkily. "Captain, you know what a troubled world Bajor is today. Believe me when I say that in the past, it was even more so. Remember that the Bajorans endured centuries of petty political and religious squabbling. And almost sixty years ago, when we could see these poor people were about to allow those conflicts to erupt into the horrors of all-out world war, well, we had to act, didn't we? We're a compassionate people, Captain. If we had not brought order to these people—our closest neighbors in space, after all—when we did, Bajor would be a wasteland today."

Sisko clenched and unclenched his hands so vigorously during Terrell's vile tirade that the popping of his knuckles rang out in the Wardroom. "Parts of Bajor *are* a wasteland today, because of what *you* and your Occupation forces did to it."

"And we regret that," Terrell said. "If you could only

know how it pained us whenever we had to discipline these people."

Terrell paused as if to let him take part in the conversation. But Sisko remained silent because he knew if he opened his mouth to say a single word, he'd end up screaming at these sanctimonious monsters.

"I understand what you're feeling," Terrell said with infuriating condescension. "I know how attached one can get to Bajorans. In a way, they're so much like children. In fact, our research has proven without doubt that the reason they remain so backward, and so dangerously unable to consider the consequences of their actions, is that their brains are not as developed as most other sentient creatures. Those parts of the neural structure responsible for higher-order thought are stunted, more like those found in less evolved animals such as—"

"That is quite enough," Sisko said through clenched teeth.

Terrell waved her hand as if what she had to say was of no real importance. "I know, I know."

Sisko could hear his heart thundering in his ears. He wanted nothing more than to end this meeting and escape from Terrell's presence. He put his hands on the table, prepared to stand, to . . . he saw the padd.

He forced himself to relax back into his chair.

Terrell had almost succeeded in perfectly deflecting him off the topic they'd been discussing.

He looked at her with new respect—as an adversary.

He decided it was time to deflect *her.* "To return to the topic at hand, your identification of the bodies as those of 'civilians' does not match other details we've obtained from our investigation." Now Sisko stood to end the meeting. "I can only surmise that the Amber

Star has made some error, and so we will not be able to release the bodies until a more detailed analysis is completed."

Terrell was on her feet at once. "Captain Sisko, there is no error."

Sisko smiled. "I know an error would be unlikely coming from your military's Central Records. But as you said yourself, the Amber Star is a civilian organization. I'd prefer my medical staff continuing with—"

"I would be happy to be of assistance," Dr. Betan interjected. "There are subtleties to Cardassian biochemistry and physiology with which an alien doctor might not be familiar."

"Thank you, but it won't be necessary," Sisko said. "Our Doctor Bashir is one of the finest in Starfleet. And he has the advantage of working in a Cardassian medical facility." He gestured to the door. "I'm sure we'll clear this up in oh . . . a week or two."

Terrell gave no sign of leaving. Her voice turned harsh and her manner seemed more threatening. "Captain, do not turn this into a diplomatic incident. Whatever slim chance for peace exists now will be lost forever if the population of Cardassia believes the Federation would play politics with the bodies of Cardassian citizens. *That* they will not forgive."

"I don't understand," Sisko said.

Terrell's eyes narrowed. "That we care for and respect our honored dead?"

"No," Sisko said. "That you think Cardassia has anything to do with the disposition of this war." Sisko made no effort to disguise his pleasure at his Terrell's displeasure. "Admit it, Terrell, your world is as controlled by the Dominion as Bajor was controlled by you during the Occupation. In fact, I wonder how far down the evolutionary scale the Founders rank Cardassian neural structures."

"You are making a mistake," Terrell hissed.

Sisko actually laughed. "I'm not the one who's stepped into the middle of enemy territory." He turned his back on the Cardassians and walked to the doors. "The Sagittarian cruiser is departing tomorrow at fifteen hundred hours. You will be leaving with it. In the meantime, I'll have you escorted to guest quarters."

"Captain Sisko," Dr. Betan fluttered as he looked nervously at Terrell, "for the sake of galactic peace, please reconsider this deadly insult."

The doors slid open and Sisko looked up to see Major Kira approaching. He allowed himself a moment to contemplate what this meeting might have been like with Kira involved. The Cardassians would be badly injured or dead by now. Neither of which states would have been desirable.

"Captain," Kira said urgently, "we have a problem." Sisko was relieved to see that her attention was solely focused on him and not on his visitors.

"It's take care of, Major. I've dealt with the Cardassian delegation." It was safer not allowing the fiery Bajoran any contact with Terrell and her companions. If she did, a second front could open up right here on DS9.

But Kira was not interested in Sisko's visitors. She glanced back over her shoulder. "Not a Cardassian problem. A Bajoran one."

Sisko stepped out of the Wardroom to look down the corridor in the same direction Kira did. Past Worf's security detail. Where, surprisingly, four Bajoran monks were striding toward him in great haste.

"Didn't you say you contacted the Kai and the

Inquisitors?" Sisko asked Kira. "That they were no longer needed because the Red Orbs of Jalbador don't exist?"

"These aren't Inquisitors," Kira replied. "And they aren't here about Quark's Orbs." She frowned at Sisko, lowered her voice. "Word got out about the Cardassians arriving for the bodies."

"Captain Sisko," the lead monk called out in a booming voice. "I am Prylar Obanak. It is most urgent we speak."

Sisko was doubly taken aback. First, by the fact that a Bajoran monk had addressed him without calling him 'Emissary.' And second, by the narrow band of red cloth the prylar wore tied around his forehead under his hood. Recent events had compelled Sisko to study a wide range of ancient Bajoran texts dealing with the fallen Prophets known as the Pah-wraiths and he had learned that a strip of red fabric was often worn by those who worshiped them. When the red cloth was worn about the arm, Sisko knew, it was a symbol of a Pah-wraith cult which had been around for years, but which most Bajorans treated as a joke. What the fabric meant when tied around a monk's head—well Sisko wasn't actually sure, now that he thought about it—but each of the three monks accompanying Obanak was also wearing one in that position.

Sisko was not anxious to become involved in a new distraction. He still had O'Brien's search to contend with, along with the mysteries of the murdered Andorian and the dead Cardassians. He tried to deflect Obanak into Kira's care. "You can discuss anything you'd like with Major Kira and—"

"This does not involve Nerys," the prylar rumbled. Even though he pitched his voice at normal speaking level now, its timbre was still remarkably deep and resonant.

And once again he had surprised Sisko. For a monk, it seemed to Sisko that the prylar was unduly familiar with Major Kira, addressing her as he had by her given name. But then, even before he had uttered a word it was clear to the most casual observer that Obanak was not a typical prylar. He was a full head taller than Sisko, and despite the loosely fitted robes he wore, it was clear the monk had the musculature of a plus-grav powerlifter. Whatever kind of religious he was, Obanak did not appear to be living a life of quiet contemplation.

Kira offered her own explanation to Sisko. "We were in the Resistance together."

Obanak bared his teeth in a fierce smile, revealing less than a full set. Sisko wondered if the missing ones had been knocked out in battle and if so, in the past or more recently. "And my followers and I consider ourselves to be in the Resistance today."

Now Sisko was thoroughly confused. "Resistance to—" But that was all he was able to say before being cut off by a deafening roar.

"Murderer!" Obanak raised his arm and pointed accusingly past Sisko and into the Wardroom.

To Sisko, there was no doubt that Obanak meant one of the three Cardassians behind him and, as captain of DS9, he acted swiftly to prevent escalation of a potential incident that could involve the entire station.

Setting aside any consideration of how deserving his visitors might be of Bajoran wrath, Sisko twisted the enraged prylar's arm down and pushed Obanak back against the far bulkhead of the corridor. At the same time, Worf's two security officers held back the other three monks. Meanwhile, Kira stepped in to keep the Cardassians safely in the Wardroom.

As he held Obanak in position, Sisko became aware of the monk's improbably massive biceps. The only reason Obanak wasn't moving was clearly because he chose not to—it was doubtful even Worf would have been able to stop the Bajoran prylar.

With order restored, Sisko spoke sternly to the four Bajoran and the three Cardassians that he and his staff now held apart from each other. "You are all guests on this station. Do I have your word you will not disturb the peace again?"

"Of course, Captain," Obanak said thickly. "I apologize. I was unprepared for the sight of such *kheet'agh* in this place."

Sisko frowned, but he released his grip on the prylar, whose only response, fortunately, was to adjust the position of his robes. Though the term Obanak had hurled at the Cardassians was unfamiliar to Sisko, he could guess it was not a flattering one. His own attention, moreover, had been caught by the prylar's omission of a term that he was accustomed to hearing from Bajoran religious figures. It now seemed somehow wrong not to be addressed as 'Emissary.' But that was the least of his concerns at the moment.

Sisko turned back to Terrell, Dr. Betan, and Atrig, who had yet to give their word that they would not cause trouble.

Atrig had moved into position directly in front of Terrell, as if to shield her from attack. His legs and arms were in an unmistakable fighting rest-stance. Now Sisko was positive that the bald Cardassian was no more a civilian than the two dead Cardassians in the Infirmary had been.

"I assure you, you are in no danger," Sisko informed his visitors.

Terrell stepped out from behind Atrig, though Atrig was still poised to defend her. "So you say, Captain," she said. "Of course, we've come to expect this sort of overwrought emotional outburst from Bajorans. It's not their fault, you know, any more than a beaten dog is responsible for snapping at its rescuer. It's that the Bajoran neural—"

A powerful voice drowned hers out as Prylar Obanak intoned dramatically: "Leej Terrell. Prefect of the Applied Science Directorate, Bajor Division. Personally responsible for the deaths of over two thousand Bajoran citizens during the conduct of medical implant experiments. It was said that even the Obsidian Order feared her for her ability to make opponents simply disappear."

The silence in the corridor lasted only a moment.

"Is that all?" Terrell said, unperturbed and now in command of herself again. "Surely you're not finished. There are so many more crimes I'm supposed to have been responsible for. Prefect of medical research. Commandant of a work camp on a colony world. In charge of mining operations here on Terok Nor. I think once someone claimed I was even responsible for the assassination of Kai Opaka."

"Kai Opaka wasn't assassinated," Kira said grimly.

"Of course she wasn't," Terrell agreed soothingly. "And neither was I responsible for any of the other crimes I supposedly committed. It's just that your people have a great deal of displaced anger, and you—"

"I think you should leave it at that," Sisko warned.

"Good idea," Kira added.

Terrell looked past Kira as if she didn't exist. "Captain Sisko, again I appeal to your humanity. Given the unwarranted hostility you can see we're facing here, and the unfortunate consequences that might ensue if it's allowed to continue, would it not be to everyone's advantage if you simply let us receive the bodies of our fellow citizens with dignity and—"

"They cannot take the bodies," Obanak thundered.

Terrell's cold glance flicked off the prylar. "Sir, be reasonable. No matter how your mind's been twisted against us, you can only kill a Cardassian once."

"Unfortunately," Kira muttered.

"That's enough, Major," Sisko said firmly. He turned to the Bajoran prylar. "Why is it any concern of yours what happens to those bodies?"

Obanak nodded his head in the direction of the corridor. "May we talk in private?"

Sisko gestured to Worf and Kira to maintain the separation of the remaining Bajorans and Cardassians. Then, together with the prylar, he walked away from the Wardroom and down the corridor, until not even Obanak's deep voice could be overheard. And it was then that the prylar dropped his posturing and made the case for his position.

"Captain, I don't know how much you know about what happened on this station during Withdrawal, but there were many deaths."

Sisko knew that wasn't the case. He braced himself for other untruths. "The official death toll was four."

"Four Bajorans," Obanak said. "Among the Cardassians . . . well, certain Resistance members undercover on Terok Nor saw the confusion of Withdrawal as their chance to strike a final blow against the enemy. At least one hundred Cardassians were killed on that last day."

"That's never been part of any account I've heard." Sisko could not recall Major Kira ever alluding to such an event. But then she did not readily discuss the dark days before the Federation had taken over Deep Space 9.

"Why would it be? If the Cardassian people ever learned that their troops were slaughtered during a retreat, don't you think they would demand retribution? Either against the Bajoran people or against the Cardassian leaders who accepted the slaughter without retaliation?"

Sisko could see the logic in that, though it was still not a full explanation. "But then why didn't the Bajoran Resistance publicize their great victory against the oppressors?"

"Captain, think of the consequences." Sisko couldn't help noticing that the Bajoran prylar out of the presence of the Cardassians was a most persuasive fellow who presented his arguments in a reasonable, not a rigid manner. "In the past," Obanak continued, "it would be quite one thing for the Resistance to take credit for wiping out one hundred Cardassians on patrol in some desolate mountain region. Under conditions such as those, it was next to impossible for the Cardassians to be sure which cell was responsible. But up here, as I'm sure you know, the situation was more tightly defined. Consider this: The names of every Bajoran on the station at the time of the Withdrawal exist in Cardassia's Central Records. Among them, inevitably, are the Resistance members responsible for those last acts of righteous revenge. So my point is this: If the Cardassians show no signs of making an issue over what happened, then why would any Bajoran risk calling attention to it?"

"All right," Sisko conceded. "I agree that both sides have something to gain from hiding the truth. But what does that have to do with Terrell and the bodies we found?"

Obanak paused and took a particularly long, deep breath. The action reminded Sisko of a stress-reducing Bajoran meditation technique Kira had once recommended he try. "As of now, Captain, those actions, those deaths . . . they belong in the past. The two bodies you found, chances are they are two of the hundred from the Day of Withdrawal."

Sisko saw a shadow pass over the prylar's face as he gave name to the terrible last day of the Cardassian occupation of the station. "Now, what happens when those bodies return to Cardassia and an investigation begins? We on Bajor believe that witnesses will be tracked down, events reconstructed, someone will remember that a certain Bajoran was the last to see a certain dead Cardassian. A few days later, that Bajoran will be murdered in his home by assassins hired by the grieving family.

"And we can't forget the possibility of physical evidence as well," Obanak added. "A physical altercation during Withdrawal might have produced a fleck of Bajoran blood, a scraping of Bajoran skin under a fingernail, or a single strand of Bajoran hair caught in the fabric of a dead man's suit. Each body could provide hundreds of different ways for Cardassian investigators to identify a member of the resistance who may or may not have been responsible for a Cardassian's death." Coming to the end of his argument for Sisko's help, Obanak folded his arms within his robes. "If you allow that to happen, Captain, then the cycle of violence will continue."

Sisko studied the prylar. He still hadn't decided on a course of action. But he now understood Obanak's position. "What would you suggest I do?" he asked, truly interested in the Bajoran monk's answer.

"My followers and I will take the bodies and, in accordance with Cardassian rituals, we shall cleanse them, prepare them for their journey through their Divine Labyrinth, and then cremate them."

"Evidence and all?" Sisko asked.

Obanak nodded. "To keep the past in the past, where it belongs."

Sisko considered his options. Obanak seemed sincere but hopelessly naive. "Prylar Obanak, do you honestly believe I can convince Terrell and her people that you—a Bajoran monk—will perform any sort of Cardassian funeral rite with the proper respect?"

"We are incapable of doing anything except show the proper respect. Captain, my followers and I are not the type of religious with which you are familiar. I refer to the misguided ones who adhere to flawed texts imperfectly chosen from the long legacy of our world's relationships with the True Gods of Creation. Such misguided ones as might call you Emissary."

That explains his reluctance to call me by that title, Sisko thought. "You're right," he said. "I'm not familiar with your approach—"

"More than an approach, Captain. We follow the One True Way."

This encounter with Obanak was causing Sisko to feel both intrigued and uncomfortable. He was well aware that there were many sects on Bajor. Many different ways of interpreting holy texts, the Prophets, and their actions. But for all those different approaches, Bajoran religion was rarely, if ever, confrontational. All but a few Bajoran religions were based on the one central tenet of the Prophets' undeniable existence. But past that point, any group was free to go its own way. Most accepted the guidance and leadership of Kai Winn. Some did not. And, at least in Sisko's experience, Bajor was unique among most worlds of the Federation in that in the face of such diversity, religious intolerance did not appear to exist. Of course, he had also thought that given that the proof of their gods' existence was so tangible—in the form of the Orbs—there wasn't room for much argument.

"You will forgive me," Sisko began as diplomatically as he could, "but I have seen on Bajor that there appear to be many ways to worship the Prophets."

"Many ways," Obanak agreed. "But only one way that is correct above all others."

Sisko looked back down the corridor toward the door to the Wardroom. Obanak's three companions were still waiting there with Worf's security officers. Kira was standing with them, apparently having no desire to remain in the Wardroom with Terrell and the other two Cardassians.

Cardassians, Sisko thought. Cardassians back on DS9. A Bajoran monk from a sect he had never heard of. Two murdered Cardassians from six years ago—perhaps from the very same day Quark, Odo, and Garak could not remember. One murdered Andorian from four days ago. Quark missing. Smugglers everywhere. Counterfeit Orbs and . . .

Where is the pattern? Sisko asked himself. He could envision all the separate pieces swirling around like flotsam on the steep sides of a whirlpool or like tiny runabouts tossed by the negative energy flux of the wormhole. Yet he couldn't help but feel that somehow, in some way, all those pieces should fit together—if not among themselves, then around some missing final piece.

"Captain?" Obanak asked.

Sisko returned his attention to the Bajoran monk, not quite sure how long he had been staring blankly down the hall in search of answers.

"Were you with them?"

"You mean, with the Prophets?"

Obanak nodded.

"No," Sisko said. "But I thought you didn't believe I was the Emissary."

"Clearly, you are not," Obanak said. His thick brow suddenly deepened over his large, dark eyes. "Do you believe you are?"

Sisko paused before answering. It was ironic, but that was exactly what Commander Arla—a Bajoran of no religious beliefs—had asked him. And now he was being asked the same question by someone on the exact opposite end of the curve of religious possibilities—a Bajoran who seemed to believe that all other Bajoran beliefs were wrong.

"That is what the Prophets call me," Sisko said. "And that is what many Bajorans call me. So I accept that that is what I am—to them. What it means, though, I really cannot say."

Obanak regarded Sisko gravely. Almost, it seemed to Sisko, with respect. "I must say I hadn't expected you to be so open-minded, Captain. Usually, when the False Prophets cloud an innocent mind, that mind remains closed."

"False Prophets?" Sisko was certain he had never heard a Bajoran use the word 'false' in the same breath as 'prophets.'

"Those that dwell in the *Jalkaree.* The Sundered Temple. What the unenlightened call the wormhole."

It was then that Sisko realized why the prylar wore the sign of the Pah-wraiths. "I see: you consider the Pah-wraiths to be the *true* Prophets."

Obanak touched the thin red cloth strip on his forehead. "Oh, no, Captain. Open your mind even more. This compulsion that exists for people to choose only one path or the other—that of the Prophets of the *Jalkaree* or of the Pah-wraiths in their prison of fire—it is a deliberate obstruction of the One True Way."

"And what way would that be?" Sisko asked, wondering if he would ever truly understand Bajorans and Bajoran belief systems.

Obanak held the edge of his robe like an ancient orator about to deliver a speech. "Not so long ago, the misguided believed that a long-prophesied confrontation took place on this very station—the Gateway to the Temple. Is that not right?"

"The Reckoning," Sisko said. He still had nightmares about that horrifying event, when a Prophet had inhabited the body of Major Kira and a Pah-wraith—Kosst Amojan, the Evil One—had taken over the body of his own son Jake in order to fight an apocalyptic battle between good and evil.

"The Reckoning," Obanak repeated. "First prophesied twenty-five thousand years ago. Yet what happened?"

"Nothing." Sisko had trusted in the Prophets and had been prepared to let the battle take place, no matter the personal cost. But Kai Winn had flooded the Promenade with chroniton particles, creating an imbalance in space-time and preventing the noncorporeal entities from remaining within their selected corporeal vessels. Thus nothing had been resolved.

"Exactly. And nothing is all that will ever occur as long as the different sides remain in conflict. No progress. No enlightenment. No rest. And no end."

"I still don't understand," Sisko said. Just what did this sect of Obanak's believe in or want to have happen for the good of Bajor? "What is the True Way?"

Obanak beamed at Sisko with an expression of almost transcendental bliss. "The One True Way is that path which shall be revealed when no other paths remain to be chosen."

Sisko stared at the monk, mystified. For a moment, he had actually believed he might be about to learn something new about Bajoran religious beliefs. But instead, Obanak had responded with a typically obscure pronouncement so imperfectly defined it might mean anything.

"I see you doubt me," Obanak said.

"I don't understand you," Sisko said truthfully. "There is a difference."

"Understanding is simple to those whose minds are open, Captain Sisko. When the Temple is restored, there will be no false paths to chose from. No False Prophets. No Pah-wraiths. No good. No evil. Simply the one True Temple. The one True Prophets. And the one True Way to a glorious new existence beyond this one."

Sisko shook his head. "That sounds just like what was supposed to happen after the Reckoning."

But Obanak was full of even more surprises. "The Reckoning," he said sternly, "was a petty conflict between the False Prophets and the Pah-wraiths of the Fire Caves. The True Way will be revealed when the

False Prophets and the True Prophets are at last reconciled."

Sisko suddenly realized that Obanak might be referring to a *third* group of entities. He hadn't heard any discussion of that possibility before. "Are you saying that your True Prophets are *not* the Pah-wraiths?"

"Pah-wraiths and False Prophets and True prophets . . . they are all one and the same, Captain. And in a long-ago time beyond measure, their home—their Temple—was sundered, and they were driven apart. Some to dwell in the *Jalkaree.* Some in the Fire Caves. And some in the *Jalbador.*"

"The Red Orbs," Sisko said with abrupt understanding.

"I beg your pardon?"

"That's why you're here?" Sisko said. "For the Red Orbs of Jalbador?"

Obanak shook his head. "Captain, really, what do you take me for? The Red Orbs of Jalbador are a child's bedtime story. They don't exist, they never have. Don't tell me someone's trying to sell them to *you*—the Emissary!"

But before Sisko could say more, he heard loud footsteps in the corridor, and saw Kira's compact form hurrying toward him, urgency expressed in every stride.

He called out to her, "What is it, Major?"

"It's O'Brien, sir. He has to see you."

"Why?"

He's found something with the scan."

"What is it?"

"He's refusing to tell anyone but you, sir. All he'll say is that it's something that just shouldn't be."

CHAPTER 17

"I KNOW ALL ABOUT the Orb," Jake said.

Jadzia Dax looked up at him from her science station in Ops and thought again how much Jake reminded her of his father. "I see. And which Orb would that be?"

Jake leaned in close, dropping his voice to a conspiratorial whisper. "You know. The one that was stolen from the Cardassians. The one that Quark's trying to sell. The one that all the smugglers are after." His eyebrows moved rapidly up and down as if to signal her that he was telling her something particularly special.

Jadzia found the rather juvenile gesture endearing, and she adored the feeling it gave her—that she was joining a game in progress. Her love of play had not been a characteristic of any one of her past hosts more than another. She shared it equally with all of them, because after a few centuries of life it had become obvious to the full series of Dax's hosts that opportunities for fun must be exploited at every turn. Over the centuries, such opportunities came by far too seldom.

Thus, Jadzia leaned even closer to Jake, made her own whisper even softer, and attempted to move her eyebrows up and down as he had. "This is for your novel, right?"

"No," Jake said. "This is for *real.* I've figured it all out, Jadzia, but I haven't been able to tell my dad yet. Do you know where he is?"

Jadzia sat back. Jake wasn't playing a game after all. "You just missed him. He beamed over to the *Defiant.*"

"Beamed over? Isn't the ship docked?" Jake seemed troubled by her news.

Jadzia hesitated. She was well aware that Sisko made it a firm rule to never mislead or lie to his son. But Sisko's present mission was classified and he had left orders instructing that no one be given details about what O'Brien and Arla were doing with the *Defiant*'s sensors. So she compromised. "The Chief's testing some new equipment modifications," she said, neither lying nor telling the whole truth. "They're just fifty kilometers out."

"Can I beam over?" Jake asked.

"This wouldn't be a good time. Your dad's really busy."

"I know he is—because of the Orbs and the Cardassians and . . . well, everything. But I'm trying to help and—"

Jadzia held a hand up to forestall any further mention of the Orbs as she took a quick look around Ops. Again his father's son, Jake caught on right away and waited quietly for her next instruction. Jadzia's cursory visual sweep of the staff revealed to her that several of them were close enough to be half paying attention to what Jake was saying. Just in case he *was* on to something, she decided, his father's office would be a more prudent location for the details of whatever it was Jake had discovered.

Discreetly signalling that he follow her, Jadzia ushered Jake into the turbolift and then escorted him to Sisko's office. The instant the door had closed behind them, she asked Jake how he knew about the Orb. "Did your father tell you?"

"No. I figured it out on my own. At least, I figured it out when I was talking with Nog. I mean, I heard that Vash was supposed to be after some rare Bajoran artifact. And I figured that the only type of artifact valuable enough to motivate people to commit murder—well, it had to be an Orb."

Jadzia sat down on the corner edge of Sisko's desk as she mulled over what Jake had learned on his own and tried to decide how much she should reveal to him, in turn.

"Well?" Jake asked. "Am I right?"

Oh, why not? Jadzia thought. Jake's very intelligent. He's even able to work out the convolutions of *Vulcan* murder mysteries—the true test of intellect. Maybe it was time she started thinking of him as an asset to the investigation and not merely as Sisko's son.

"All right," she said, "let's talk about this. But," she cautioned the eager youngster, "you can't tell anyone else what we've discussed except for your father. He'll let you know if you can tell anyone else. And that means Nog."

Jake nodded vigorously. "So, it *is* an Orb!"

"Yes and no," Jadzia said. "Vash said it was an Orb, maybe more than one. Something special called a Red Orb of Jalbador."

"I was right!"

"But," Jadzia added, "Major Kira says the Red Orbs are just a legend. They don't exist."

Jake looked confused. "Why would Cardassians come to Deep Space 9 to get back something that doesn't exist?"

"The Cardassians say they are here to claim the bodies Rom and O'Brien found in the power conduit."

"A cover story," Jake said with a dismissive shake of his head.

"Maybe so," Jadzia allowed. "I didn't meet with them. But apparently a delegation of Bajoran monks also came aboard to demand that the bodies *not* be turned over, so *someone* thinks those bodies are important."

Jake's face took on a faraway look. He stared past her and through the large viewport behind his father's desk, muttering as if speaking only to himself. "So there's got to be a connection. . . ."

"Between what and what?"

"The Orbs and the bodies."

Jadzia sighed. A discussion of real facts and logical supposition was one thing. Making up fairy tales was another. "One major problem," she said as she eased off the desk and got to her feet. "The bodies are real, Jake. The Orbs still might not be."

Jake raised a triumphant finger. "Aha! My point exactly. A minute ago, you said that Major Kira said they *didn't* exist. But now you're saying they *might not* exist. What else aren't you telling me?"

Jadzia pursed her lips in admiration. The kid had her. "Well, you're not alone. Julian thinks the Orbs might be real, too."

Jake's shoulders went back and he straightened up to his full, impressive height. It was almost as if she were watching the actual inflation of Jake's ego. She could just imagine what he was telling himself—that he, a mere novice writer, had independently reached the same conclusion as DS9's genetically enhanced medical genius.

"Before you give yourself the Carrington Award," Jadzia said drily, "there might be a few more details to consider."

Jake's increased enthusiasm was all too evident to Jadzia. But it was too late to turn back. She had brought him into the investigation and now she would have to try to control his participation—for his own sake and hers. "Like what?" he asked, ready, it seemed, for anything she might ask of him.

"For one, where's Quark?"

"I've figured that out, too."

Jadzia sat back down, wondering if he had the ability to surprise her again, and half hoping he could. "Have you now?"

"Sure. My dad knows exactly where he is, or Odo does or someone like that. Because otherwise, everyone would be looking for him. And since they're not . . . I don't know, maybe they're using him for bait to catch more of the smugglers."

"Sorry to disappoint you," Jadzia said, getting up from the desk. Jake's ideas were at the predictable level after all. "And remember you can't talk about this with anyone except your father—but that's exactly what the *Defiant* is doing right now: a complete tactical sweep of the station looking for Quark. And any more of those hidden sections you and Nog found."

"Damn," Jake said. Then quickly added, "Sorry."

Jadzia accepted his apology without letting him see how sweet she thought he was for offering it. She started walking toward the door, Jake following her as he recited a list to himself, "Orbs, Cardassians, bodies, smugglers . . ."

Jake gave Jadzia an intent look. "As long as I've promised not to talk about this with anyone else, is there anything else you think I should know?"

Her hand already on the door, Jadzia paused, considering, then deciding no harm would likely come from telling him a bit more, she turned back to face Jake. "There is one other mystery your father's contending with. And again, it's like the Orbs. It might be real or it might be . . . just a mistaken recollection."

"Great," Jake said. "What?"

"Quark claims he can't remember what happened to him on the Day of Withdrawal. Odo claims he himself was knocked out by a phaser blast and missed the Withdrawal. And Garak says he remembers every detail, but . . . it's pretty clear there're some details he's completely forgotten."

"Whoa," Jake said. "Missing Time Syndrome."

Jadzia laughed. "You know about that, too?"

"Yeah, sure, I wanted to use it in a story some day. About a guy from way back in the twentieth century or so who gets involved in a Starfleet temporal operation and finds out about the future, so they wipe his memory, leaving him with Missing Time Syndrome. And the trick is," Jake said, the words all coming out of him in an excited rush, "the memory wipe isn't absolutely complete, and all these memories of the future come bubbling up in him, so he writes them down as if they're fiction. But they're real. And it's only now, looking back, that people today realize this guy actually did write about what was going to happen." He paused expectantly, as if waiting for her reaction.

Jadzia said the first thing that came into her head. "Sounds like a good children's story."

He frowned. "It's not for children."

Jadzia tried another approach. "The trouble is, the techniques the Department of Temporal Investigations use are foolproof. When they wipe a memory, it's gone. It won't even come back as a dream."

But Jake wasn't interested in talking about that story. "I'll think of some way around it. Tell me more about Quark and Odo and Garak."

"That's everything I know."

Jake clapped his hands. "Doesn't matter. I've got it! On the Day of Withdrawal, *they* killed the Cardassians and so . . . so the Bajoran Resistance wiped their memories so if they were ever interrogated, they'd really believe they were innocent!"

Jadzia put a hand on Jake's shoulder. "It's okay, Jake. This is real life. Not everything has to fit together that neatly. Sometimes things happen that just aren't connected to each other."

"Then why are all these things happening at once?" Jake asked. "There *has* to be some connection, Jadzia."

"Maybe the only connection is your imagination," Jadzia said, not wishing to sound condescending but definitely wanting to find some way to calm Jake down.

But Jake just shook his head, as if he'd just thought of something important. "No. The connection is the

Andorian. Dal Nortron. His murder is what started everything."

"If it was a murder." The door slid open and Jadzia walked out into the small landing. But Jake wasn't behind her. He was still standing in his father's office, the expression on his young face grim.

"What is it?" Jadzia asked.

"Nothing," Jake said, unconvincingly. He stepped out into the landing to stand beside her. "Can I see the file on Nortron's death?"

"That might be pushing research too far, Jake. I think that's up to Odo, and I doubt if he would approve it."

Jake nodded without protest.

Her interest caught, Jadzia couldn't help asking. "If you did have access to Nortron's file, what do you think you might find?"

"I don't know," Jake said. "I was just wondering where exactly his body was found. It's not important."

Jadzia began walking down the stairs with him. "Well, you're coming up with some good thoughts," she said encouragingly.

"Even if they're wrong." Jake gave her a wry smile which Jadzia found reassuring, under the circumstances.

They came to the turbolift. She gestured to Jake to enter first. "The only way we learn is by gaining experience. And the only way we gain experience is by—"

"—making mistakes," Jake said as he stepped into the lift. "So at least now I know where my dad got that saying."

Jadzia hid her smile as she joined him. "After three hundred years, believe me—I've made enough mistakes to know what I'm talking about. As soon as your father gets back, I'll—"

The sudden scream of a warning siren interrupted her, as at the same time all the main lights in Ops began flickering.

Jadzia ran from the lift. "Worf, what is it?!"

Worf looked up from his security station, sweat already glistening within the deep ridges of his forehead. "The main computer has been compromised. All security subsystems are off-line."

Jadzia rushed for her own station, Jake forgotten behind her. "What the hell does that mean?" she demanded.

"Only one thing," Worf growled. "It is a prelude to attack!"

CHAPTER 18

"THERE," O'BRIEN SAID. "That's the hidden stretch of corridor with the holosuite. The one Jake and Nog found."

On the *Defiant*'s main viewer, a small red dot flashed in the lower section of a three-dimensional wire-frame schematic of Deep Space 9. Only a third of the station's outline was filled with detailed depictions of bulkheads and decks, conduits and waveguides, turbolift shafts and structural support beams. The other two-thirds of the station remained featureless. But that was to be expected. O'Brien had been conducting his tactical sweep for only a little more than three hours, and it was still underway.

Sisko watched as another pulsing light joined the first on the screen, a few decks higher and closer to the station's core. "What about that?" he asked, pointing to a second red dot. "Over there, two levels up."

"Ah," the chief said as he rotated the schematic on the viewer. "That's a deficiency we already knew about. The original plans called for that section to hold about ten additional living units. But the Cardassians never got around to finishing them, so they left it as one large room. The dock management people use it as a storeroom for unclaimed goods. Odo checks it for contraband every week or so."

A third red dot began flashing. Sisko leaned forward to get a closer look. "What about that one, Chief?" He tried to place the third location's features from memory. "Is that the water-recycling plant?"

"Yes, sir. That's the one I called Major Kira about. That's the part that just shouldn't be there."

Finally, Sisko thought. "I need an explanation, Chief."

Sisko watched as O'Brien expanded the schematic of the station until the viewer displayed a section only three decks tall, the third red dot now an irregular rectangle pulsing precisely where a network of pipes seemed to come to an end.

"Well, first off, sir, it *is* the water plant. I'm in there at least once a month for inspection. I know the specifications of all the pipes, the filters, the evaporators. And after six years of me crawling all over this station, well, if there were a single deviation or deficiency from the schematics, I'd know about it. And I can vouch for that whole section being spot on to the Cardassians' original plans." O'Brien paused to qualify his statement. "Of course, it does have documented upgrades from when the Starfleet Corps of Engineers rebuilt it three years ago. But I can vouch for those, too."

"So," Sisko said, "if you know that the physical layout of the water plant is in perfect agreement with the Cardassian schematics, then why is that flashing light saying the two patterns don't match?"

"Because they don't, sir."

Sisko turned to regard his chief engineer with growing impatience. He was vaguely aware of Commander Arla standing nearby, but the young Bajoran officer was wisely choosing to observe, not take part.

"You're confusing me, Chief," Sisko said. "And I don't like to be confused." But from the look he now saw on O'Brien's flushed, red face, it was clear that the engineer was as mystified as he.

"Sir, according to the tactical sensor sweep I've conducted, DS9's water treatment facility no longer even exists. Somehow, and don't ask me how, it's turned into a large, empty room. And that's why the red light's flashing."

"Correct me if I'm wrong, Chief, but if the water plant had truly disappeared, shouldn't we know about it?"

"Oh, we'd know about it," O'Brien said, perplexed. "We'd have a thousand calls in from the habitat ring about no running water. We'd have transporter venting of all the water being spilled into the plant from the severed pipes. The whole station would look to be floating in a cloud of ice crystals."

"And since it's not . . . ?"

"Someone's got to be running a sensor mask in the treatment facility," O'Brien concluded with a frustrated frown. "Something small, tightly focused, no appreciable power signature. Intended, I'd say, to defeat any tricorders being used to conduct a search. A tricorder that encountered that mask wouldn't register that anything was trying to jam its sensors. All it would show is that there was nothing in the room."

"In other words, that's where Quark is."

"Frankly, Captain," O'Brien said, "there could be a hundred Jem'Hadar hiding behind that thing and we'd be the last to know about it."

That was all Sisko needed to hear. He activated his communicator. "Mr. Worf, we have a probable target. Prepare transporter suppression fields and arm the anesthezine dispensers for the following coordinates."

Sisko recited four groups of digits, each corresponding to a specific location's deck, ring, corridor, and door number in DS9. But each number was offset by a different, predetermined amount, so that anyone listening in to his transmission would not be able to determine Sisko's real target. Only Worf had the key to the code, and his reply, as usual, was to the point.

"Understood. Implementing security measures. I will beam you to the perimeter of the location."

"No," Sisko said. He wasn't looking forward to any type of violent encounter around the equipment that supplied water to the station. "The Chief and I will beam to Ops. We'll leave from there with a full security team."

"Excuse me," Arla said. "You're leaving me here?"

Sisko didn't even glance at the Bajoran commander as he replied. "Regulations don't permit me to completely abandon a ship."

"But . . . I'm not rated for this class of ship. Not on my own."

Arla's qualifications or lack thereof were not one of Sisko's priorities right now. "Commander, trust me, all you have to do is sit. As soon as we're finished on the station, I'll have a crew beamed out." Sisko didn't understand why the young Bajoran officer was so troubled by the prospect of being alone on the *Defiant.*

Most people in Starfleet dreamed of a chance to be the only person on a starship. It was a powerful experience, Sisko knew, to be the sole person in the presence of so much power and potential. But perhaps Arla Rees was better suited to flying a desk.

"Yes, sir," she said and made her way quickly toward the lone flight operations chair as if she expected the artificial gravity to cut out at any second.

Arla's disappointing reaction to opportunity slipped from Sisko's thoughts almost immediately. He was anxious to get moving. "Status, Mr. Worf?"

"Anesthezine systems are on-line. I am now reconfiguring the interior security fields to—"

A high-pitched squeal blared from Sisko's communicator.

Sisko hit his communicator twice to reset it, tried opening a frequency again, and got nothing. In an instant he was on his way to the *Defiant*'s communications console, even as O'Brien scrambled to the tactical station.

It took only seconds for Sisko to see that all of DS9's communications arrays were dead: No carrier waves. No navigation beacons. No subspace repeater signals.

Sisko turned to face O'Brien. "Report!"

The chief didn't take his eyes off the madly flashing tactical displays he studied. "I have no idea what's going on. Massive power fluctuations. All external *and* internal communications are down. They're on emergency lighting, life-support, gravity . . . unless a quantum torpedo hit Ops dead center, I'd say we're looking at a total computer failure." The screens stopped flashing. O'Brien looked stunned. "Sir, there's not a single automated system operating on the station. It's as if the computer's disappeared."

"This is not a coincidence," Sisko said angrily. "Worf was adjusting the security fields. They were waiting for us to make our move."

"Who was?" O'Brien asked.

"Whoever's got Quark. Whoever put up that sensor mask so we can't see what's behind it. But they couldn't know we'd be on the *Defiant*." Sisko rushed back to the auxiliary engineering console. "Chief! We need to shut down the *Defiant*'s computers."

"What?!" O'Brien and Arla said it together.

"If the station's computer has been infected by a programming virus, or some type of disruptive radiation, the *Defiant*'s computers might be vulnerable, too. Let's move it!"

With O'Brien at his side, Sisko transformed the *Defiant* into little more than an inert chunk of dead mass within two minutes.

"Now what?" O'Brien asked.

"Now we're beaming directly to the water plant. Or, at least to the edge of that sensor mask."

Sisko saw O'Brien glance over at Arla, who was staring at the screen in front of her. Her olive-gold face was pale, her mouth hung slightly open. "Captain," the chief said, "I think I should stay here and keep the ship under manual control."

"I need you on DS9," Sisko said. That was the end of the argument. "Commander Arla, you *are* going to drift. But as long as you're moving away from the station, there's nothing you have to do."

Arla's words were rasping as if her throat were bone dry. "What . . . what if I do start drifting toward the station?"

"Use the docking thrusters to alter your trajectory," Sisko said sharply. He wondered how he had thought just a short time earlier that Arla was exactly the kind of officer material that Starfleet needed more of. The young Bajoran was not behaving as if she were even worthy of the command rank she now possessed.

"Just don't try to reverse course," O'Brien added. "With the impulse engines powered down, you don't have enough thruster propellant to manage it."

Arla's nod was hesitant. Incredibly, it seemed to Sisko she could not even control her appearance of nervousness. "And . . . if I'm heading for the wormhole?"

"It's going to take you a couple of hours to drift that far," Sisko said, trying to sound reassuring, when all he wanted to do was shout at her to pull herself together. "This'll be over by then."

"Captain," O'Brien suddenly suggested, "what if I just set a course for her now? Steer her away from the station and the wormhole. Only take a minute."

But Sisko shook his head. O'Brien was a good man, but he was needed elsewhere. "If there's anyone on that station keeping track of this ship, I don't want them to see Commander Arla changing course, because that will make her a target. I want them to think she's either disabled or abandoned. Commander—you have the conn. I suggest you sit back and enjoy the ride."

Then Sisko headed at double speed for the main doors and O'Brien followed just as quickly.

The *Defiant* was a compact ship, designed for the efficient movement of information and personnel in battle. It took only seconds to run down the corridor and reach the closer of the ship's two transporter rooms.

Sisko pushed through the doors before they had finished opening and headed directly for the equipment locker. "Set the coordinates, Chief. I'll get the phasers."

"Not rifles!" O'Brien warned as he entered beaming coordinates on the console. "None of the pipes in the water plant is shielded. Take hand phasers and don't set them for anything higher than force three. Otherwise, one miss and we'll all be swimming."

Sisko knew better than to question O'Brien's technical expertise. But he took four hand phasers along with two tricorders. One phaser he attached to the holster strips on his uniform along with a tricorder. One he held in his hand. And the other two phasers he handed to O'Brien, along with the second tricorder, the moment his chief engineer joined him on the transporter pad.

O'Brien attached one of the phasers to his own holster strips. "We'll materialize just to the side of the equipment transfer doors leading into the main treatment room," he told Sisko. "And brace yourself, sir. I don't know what the gravity's going to be like."

Then Sisko felt a momentary tingle like that of a cool breeze, as the *Defiant*'s transporter room turned into a spray of sparkling light. Almost immediately, the light faded to reveal a dark corridor ribbed and ringed by Cardassian struts. He and O'Brien had returned to Deep Space 9.

It took a few disorienting moments, and slippage of more than a few centimeters, before Sisko's inner ear caught up to the fact that the deck was slanted by four or five degrees. For his part, O'Brien made a series of small jumps, rising up from the deck only a centimeter or two each time. *Trust the chief to come up with his own way to measure an artificial gravity field,* Sisko thought.

"Okay, not that bad," the chief engineer said, confirming Sisko's guess about the reason for his impromptu athletic performance. "The station's gone to emergency gravity, and I'm guessing the old units in section 3 are barely holding on at fifty percent efficiency."

"What can we expect if they fail?" Sisko asked, phaser held ready as he made sure the short stretch of corridor was deserted.

"If the old units shut down all at once, it'll feel like the station's suddenly lurched a few more degrees."

Sisko didn't like the image. "Like an old sinking ship."

"At least we won't drown," O'Brien said. He looked at the closed doors to the water treatment facility. "I hope."

Sisko frowned, tapped his communicator. "Sisko to Worf." No response. "Sisko to Ops." Still nothing.

There was no time to waste. Sisko moved cautiously along the slanted corridor to the edge of the oversize water-plant doors. They had been designed to allow large pieces of equipment to be moved in and out, so they and the corridor ceiling were twice the height of most other similar structures in the station.

Sisko flipped open his tricorder and scanned through the doors for life-signs. But the readings indicated there were no life-forms in the facility.

He flipped the device shut and put it back on its holster strip. "I don't know what to expect in there," Sisko said in a low voice, "but since we're only using heavy stun, feel free to shoot first and ask questions later."

O'Brien gave a quiet chuckle. "Careful, sir, you're starting to sound like Worf."

Sisko tapped the door control.

The doors to the water plant remained closed.

Sisko tapped in his command override code.

This time the doors opened.

Then Sisko and O'Brien both moaned at the same time as the overwhelming stench of raw sewage enveloped them.

Sisko blocked his nostrils with one hand, but his action did nothing to diminish the awful smell.

"Must have been quite a spill when the gravity generators switched over to the back-ups," O'Brien coughed. "We should get used to it in a few minutes."

Sisko had to force himself to open his mouth to speak. "You have such a way of looking on the bright side of things."

Sisko led the way into the huge facility—one of the largest open spaces in DS9. It was three decks high, forty meters deep, fifty wide, filled with a maze of pipes, metal vats, and overhead walkways.

It also reverberated with the deafening roar of rushing water.

Sisko hadn't been down here for years, but he didn't remember it being so loud. He stepped closer to O'Brien so the chief could hear him. "Is it supposed to sound like this?" he shouted.

O'Brien nodded, then shouted back. "The sound bafflers must be off-line, or—" Abruptly, the chief engineer pointed up to the left. "Captain, over there!"

Sisko saw what he meant at once.

What appeared to be a silver flower had sprouted on the top of a five-meter-tall vat of dull, copper-colored metal emblazoned with a Cardassian warning glyph. The 'flower' was perhaps a meter across, with three pulsing blue lights on the tip of each of its five gleaming petals.

It was not Cardassian technology. Neither was it Starfleet.

"The sensor mask?" Sisko asked.

"That's my guess," O'Brien confirmed, then he took aim with his phaser.

Sisko could only hope that a force-three setting would be enough to overload whatever the alien device used for circuitry. Any phaser blast more powerful would risk puncturing the vat.

"Here goes," O'Brien said.

Then an object flashed through the air. O'Brien grunted as something hit his arm and his phaser went flying. Spun around by the impact, he collided full force with Sisko.

Sisko staggered back. Without stopping to think, he pulled O'Brien into the shelter of an immense pipe that emerged from the deck and curved away overhead. Pushing the chief down to a sitting position against the pipe, Sisko immediately reached out to examine O'Brien's arm.

"Careful," the chief gasped. The sleeve of his black jumpsuit was wet with blood where a slender gold dagger, a kind Sisko had never seen before, impaled the chief's forearm. A rivulet of blood was dripping from his cuff.

The golden blade was edged with a series of angled barbs, making for easy penetration but near-impossible extraction. Sisko kneeled down and leaned closer. He yelled directly into the chief's ear to be heard over the thunderous roar of the water. "I'm not going to be able to pull that out."

O'Brien nodded, sweat mingling with tears of pain on his cheeks. "It's going numb," he murmured weakly, and Sisko was only able to understand him by reading his lips. He knew at once the blade had to have been coated with some type of poison.

"Chief—I'm going to take out the sensor mask," Sisko shouted. "Keep trying to get through to Worf on your communicator."

He didn't like the way O'Brien looked blearily at him then, as if the engineer didn't believe that Worf was ever going to appear, or that he'd still be alive when Worf did.

"I'll—come—back—for—you," Sisko shouted, emphasizing each word as if that made his promise more valid.

Silently, O'Brien mouthed his response, "I know you will. . . ." And then the engineer's head slumped forward, eyes closed.

Filled with furious purpose, Sisko leapt to his feet, edged around the pipe until he could just see the silver blossom of the sensor mask emitter against the dark edge of the vat.

With the tracking precision of the *Defiant*'s sensors, he checked each catwalk, each potential hiding place for the enemy. But there were too many shadows, too many dark corners. He realized there was no way he could know where a potential enemy was hiding until a knife struck him just as it had the chief.

Sisko frowned. That particular choice of weapon troubled him. *Why a knife? One phaser burst and the chief would have been killed. One wide burst, and we'd both have been stunned.*

Again he used the tricorder to scan for life-signs, but it was useless. This close to the emitter its displays flashed erratically.

Sisko made his decision. He set his phaser to force

six, medium dispersal. There was no time to take careful aim at the emitter as the chief had done.

He swung out and fired at once, ducking back behind the pipe even as a dagger clanged against it. The sensor mask emitter exploded in a shower of transtator sparks. The sensor mask was down.

Breathing hard, but feeling victorious, Sisko leaned back against the pipe, tried his communicator again. No response. But it didn't matter. Sisko knew that as soon as Worf was able to restore emergency communications in Ops, he'd be able to get through.

Suddenly, the thick odor of sewage intensified. Involuntarily gagging, Sisko stuck his head out to take a quick glance around the pipe and saw a gout of dark water spraying from the top edge of the vat where the sensor mask emitter had been. His phaser blast had obviously punctured the vat wall. And the vat had to be a waste separator, designed to send liquids to the recycling evaporators and solids to the replicator mass reclaimers.

Only now, both liquids and solids were splattering down on the metal deck of the facility, and because of the imbalance in the artificial gravity fields, the odiferous sludge from the vat was oozing toward the back of the cavernous water-plant room.

In a vain attempt to shield himself from the terrible smell, Sisko pulled the neck of his duty shirt up over his mouth and his nose. He had to keep going. At least now he knew where to go.

And with the emitter gone, his tricorder should be functional again. Sisko checked its display. It was. There were two life-signs twenty meters ahead.

Still keeping to the cover of the pipes, Sisko headed

in the direction of the indicated life-signs, not certain what he was looking for.

But what he found wasn't surprising.

Quark.

In chains.

Hanging head down.

Over an open collection tank filled to the brim with dark, bubbling sludge.

Quark's hands were tied behind his back and thick black wires were cruelly clipped to the edges of his prodigious ears.

And the only way Sisko was able to tell that the Ferengi was even alive was because the tricorder said he was.

Sisko checked the reading again. "Damn," he whispered. One of the two life-signs had disappeared. Now there was only one—Quark. The other had moved out of range, or else had—

Pain seared Sisko's back as he was thrown forward to the slippery deck, his phaser and tricorder both tumbling away.

Throwing off the shock of the attack, Sisko rolled to his feet, leaping up to face whatever, whoever, had felled him.

An Andorian female. Three meters away. Crouched in fight-ready position, the stark-blue tendrils of her antennae jutting from her distinctive blue-white, Vulcan-short hair. In one blue hand, she held a golden dagger like the one that injured O'Brien.

His attacker was one of the two sisters Odo had been watching. But which sister, Sisko didn't know.

The Andorian moved closer, hypnotically waving her dagger in circles, her dark, blue-rimmed eyes absolutely fixed on his own. Sisko could see muscles ripple in her bare blue arms and midriff. She was dressed more for a workout in a zero-G gym than she was for any trade mission, wearing only a snug black leather vest, black leggings, and low-cut gripshoes.

A spasm twisted Sisko's back where the Andorian had kicked him. The fact she hadn't stabbed him as she had O'Brien meant she didn't consider him a worthy opponent. She intended to toy with him.

But Sisko was in no mood to be toyed with.

He slapped his hand down to his second phaser, ripped it from its holster strips, and—even as the Andorian launched herself at him with an ear-splitting shriek—fired point-blank.

She collapsed at his feet, her eyes rolled back, her body unmoving.

Sisko kicked the dagger from her limp hand, then twisted her over on her back to keep her nose and mouth clear of the sewage whose level was still rising. The movement of her chest attested to the fact that she was still breathing.

Sisko checked to be sure she had no other weapons, then started for Quark, who was still trussed and helpless, suspended from the ceiling.

Quark's mouth was moving at warp ten, but saying nothing Sisko could hear above the increasing din in the vast chamber. Sisko muttered to himself as he studied the chains from which the Ferengi dangled over the sludge tank. "Quark, I don't know what you did to those people, but—" Sisko stopped suddenly, remembering. *People.* And he whirled around just in time to be thrown against the sludge tank, as the second Andorian sister's hand stabbed at his neck.

This Andorian female was even more threatening than her sibling. While only slightly taller, she was much, much stronger. She wore almost the same outfit as her sister, but her long blue-white hair was pulled back tightly and braided, and the smooth blue skin of her left arm was intricately tattooed in black from wrist to shoulder.

With a shriek even louder than her sister's, she launched herself at Sisko before he had a chance to regain his balance.

Sisko tried to feint sideways, but stumbled.

The Andorian changed her angle of approach in midair, transferring her momentum into a spinning high kick that struck Sisko's shoulder, knocking him back against the edge of the sludge tank, so that his arm fell back into it.

Then the Andorian dropped to one knee beside Sisko, raised her hand to deliver a lethal punch-down blow to his chest.

But Sisko summoned all of his strength to fling his arm up, splashing raw sewage in her eyes.

The Andorian screamed as she shrank back from him, her hands clawing at her face.

Sisko twisted away, swinging one of his legs under hers, tripping her, so that she fell to the deck.

Ignoring his still-twinging back, he staggered to his feet.

In a heartbeat, the Andorian's body flexed powerfully, and she was once again standing upright before him, her blazing, dark eyes intent on revenge.

Sisko reached for his phaser, but it was gone.

The Andorian threw herself at him.

Instinctively, Sisko tucked and rolled *toward* her, forcing contact before she had anticipated.

He lost his breath in one explosive moment as her foot slammed into his ribs, but then the pressure was gone and he looked up, gasping, in time to see her flailing form flip over him and land in the sewage tank ejecting a fountain of disgusting liquid that struck and soaked Quark as precisely as if the Ferengi had been its chosen target.

Slowly, clutching his side, Sisko struggled to his feet, trying not to laugh because it hurt too much as Quark maniacally spun and sputtered and sprayed droplets of a dark substance whose origin was too terrible for Sisko even to contemplate.

"Calm down, Quark," Sisko finally managed to shout. "I'll get you down."

Quark screamed something indecipherable—two words? Sisko couldn't be sure. But the Ferengi was shaking and swinging back and forth on his chains, clearly panicked by something. Probably the fear of falling into the sludge tank, Sisko decided.

"What?" Sisko called up to Quark. The Ferengi's neck veins were now bulging as Quark screeched again. But it was impossible to hear him over the incessant rush and roar of the liquids in the pipes all around.

The second Andorian sister was trying to pull herself toward the edge of the tank, to drag herself out. She was moving so slowly, Sisko doubted she'd cause him any more trouble. He decided to leave Quark to Worf's security staff, and instead to go back to get O'Brien and deliver him to the Infirmary. Quark might be uncomfortable but he wasn't in any danger now.

He looked up to wave at Quark to somehow signal him that someone would come back for him, when he finally realized that the Ferengi wasn't looking at him, but at something beyond him.

With a sudden flash of alarm, Sisko turned about.

A moment too late.

A black shape enveloped him like a tidal wave sinking a ship, and the roar of the room fell away into silence as he drowned in a sea of darkness.

CHAPTER 19

"BEHIND YOU," Quark muttered as Benjamin Sisko collapsed on the filthy deck of the din-filled water-plant room. "I was *trying* to say, behind you. . . ."

But, as usual to Quark's view of things, no one ever paid him any attention until it was too late.

And it was much too late for Sisko, just as it was too late for those ghastly Andorian sisters.

Quark had absolutely no idea who it was who had struck Sisko down. All he knew was that Sisko's attacker was outfitted in a shiny black, wrinkled, class-two environmental suit, one designed to operate within normal life-support pressure and temperature ranges, and that such a garment was worn usually to protect against biological or chemical contamination. Knowing this did not make Quark feel any better.

Or smell better, Quark thought bitterly. Ever since something had happened to momentarily interrupt the station's gravity fields a few minutes ago, the water treatment facility had begun to stink worse that he most likely did, thanks to that clumsy Andorian female and her spectacular fall into the sludge vat. In fact, now that he thought about it, this place smelled even worse than a Medusan moulting pit.

Quark hung motionless in his chains, shutting out the cacophony of the incessant sound of rushing liquid, regarding the floor and the latest interloper, as he stoked his internal fires of resentment. Trust the Cardassians to economize by treating waste water in a centralized location, instead of using personal recyclers. *I mean,* Quark thought indignantly, *there's an understandable desire for profit, and then there's being obsessed by it.* And right now, suffering the disastrous olfactory consequences arising from the imbecilic decision of whichever Cardassian genius thought he'd save some latinum on Terok Nor's waste-recycling system, he himself would actually be willing to trade a year's worth of profits from his bar for just one last lungful of fresh air before the stranger in black killed him as he had just killed DS9's chief executive.

Quark reconsidered the odds. After all, this close to the wormhole, one could never be too certain which prayers were going to be answered. *Better make that six months' worth,* Quark amended as he saw Sisko's murderer heading toward him, toward the sludge vat above which he dangled helpless, head first, and beside which Satr now lay, recovering her breath after climbing out of the vat.

Of the two sisters, Quark remembered thinking when he had first met them that Satr was the cute one. And that the other, Leen, was the smart one. But incredible though it now seemed to him, he had been willing to overlook that classic character flaw in a female. Instead, he had stupidly looked forward to seeing how long he might be able to prolong negotiations with both Satr and Leen. He'd been in the bartending business long enough to have heard what they said about females with blue skin. And the chance to feel four female Andorian hands on his lobes at the same time had always been a little fantasy of his.

But then Dal Nortron had gone and got himself killed and spoiled everything—he'd had to avoid the sisters instead of cultivating them. Before long Odo had him in protective custody, *and then* had arrested him, only to let him go just in time to be waylaid by that miserable excuse for a Ferengi—Base. And all to be dragged down here to meet Satr and Leen again.

Quark moaned just recalling the degrading treatment he'd been subjected to. His head hurt like the devil, and it wasn't simply because he had been left hanging by his heels like a Mongonian eelbat for the past day and half.

He'd been a perfect gentlemen with those two Andorian monsters. Even after that ingrate Base had dragged him in a sack through the smugglers' tunnels and dumped him out in front of Satr and Leen, he'd made the two sisters a completely reasonable request in his most charming manner. Something along the lines of: "Ladies, such a pleasure to see you again. Is it time to do some . . . business?"

Satr's reply had involved a sharp elbow in his stomach, and Leen had trussed him up in chains like the Friday night special at the Klingon Cafe. It was then that Quark knew for certain that he had been betrayed by them *and* Base.

Base. The name should have warned him. The little

insect had come into Quark's back office and launched into his oh-so-sincere sales pitch, about how he wanted to protect his investment in the Orbs, how he wanted to make sure Quark stayed safe before, during, and after the auction, how he planned to take care of Satr and Leen personally—and for only an extra eighteen percent of Quark's commission on the auction proceeds.

That percentage had been so out of line that Quark had actually spent twenty minutes negotiating a reduction, never once questioning why it was that Base should be on his side for eighteen percent, when the little gnat could kill him and have a shot at the full one hundred percent.

They had settled on nine-and-a-half. Plus Base could keep half the tips all the bar's wait staff earned during the days he replaced Quark as barkeep. In the meantime, Quark would be safe behind a sensor mask where no one could find him.

And worst of all, in Quark's recollection, was that the entire deal had been negotiated in front of his own idiot brother. Base had set the whole thing up so that when Quark disappeared, Rom would dimwittedly think that was part of the plan and would not be concerned. *No one* would be concerned.

As if anyone would anyway, Quark thought with a self-pitying half-sob.

And then, even more humiliating to recall, that conniving Base convinced him to put himself into the sack with an antigrav ballast, supposedly so he could be taken to a safe place deep within the station.

"Why the sack?" he remembered asking Base.

"For a stinkin' nine-and-a-half points," that little vole had squeaked persuasively, "no way you're going to find out about the perfect hiding place I figured out. But for twelve and-a-half. . . ."

It had been the perfect argument. No hiding place on the station was worth an extra three percent, and like a *targ* to the Klingon wedding feast, Quark had climbed willingly into the sack, hugging the antigrav, until Base tossed him out on the deck of the water-plant room—and the four female Andorian hands went to work on him in a terrible travesty of his fantasy.

Now, suspended directly above a dark substance which was as good a metaphor for his life as any, Quark mulled over those he considered his enemies as if he were fingering a pocketful of well-worn worry stones.

First, Rom, his idiot brother who betrayed him by letting that half-sized, half-son-of-a-Klingon into Quark's bar in the first place. Second, Base. Third and fourth, Leen and—

Quark saw the black-suited figure below draw a small phaser and shoot Satr with a soundless flash of energy, then splash through the sludge-strewn deck to dispatch Leen next.

Wincing in commiseration for their bad luck, Quark amended his list of enemies, at the same time wondering where the Andorian sisters had hidden their latinum. It would be quite a tidy sum for someone fortunate enough to find it.

But not for him. His own luck, no matter how poor it had been, had obviously run out. It was his turn now.

The black figure, face completely obscured by a wrinkled black hood and a full-face breathing mask, looked up at Quark, then adjusted the small phaser's setting and took careful aim.

Even though he was resigned to his fate and determined to face it as a rational being, Quark instinctively reached back to his childhood lessons from the weekly Celestial Market classes his loving parents had forced him to attend. Trying not to breathe in any more of the noxious fumes that he had to, he reflexively mumbled the Ferengi prayer that was his people's traditional ward against impending disaster. "All right, this is my final offer. . . ."

But the shooter below was in no mood to negotiate.

He fired.

In one timeless instant, Quark realized that the shooter's beam wasn't aimed at him but at the chain that bound his feet.

A second timeless instant later, as he felt his stomach fall *up* toward his knees, Quark *dropped*—the chains melted through—straight into the bubbling vat of—

"Frinx!" Quark gasped, as a strong hand grabbed him just before he hit the liquid sewage.

Still in midair, he kicked wildly to be free of what was left of the chains still loosely draped around his ankles.

The figure in black deposited him on the deck, standing upright on his own two feet, right beside the motionless body of poor Captain Sisko.

Quark opened his mouth and let loose with a string of invective in the Trading Tongue such that his moogie would have scrubbed out his mouth with carapace gel if she had heard a single syllable—swearing like a philanthropist his moogie would call it. Not that anyone could hear him in the roar of the outflow from the system pipes.

The figure in black regarded him impassively, then seemed to come to a decision, stepped back and pulled off his breather mask.

Just as Quark bravely barked out, "I don't care who the *greeb* you are. If you're going to shoot me like the rest of them, go ahead—kill me and be done with it." He realized that once again—big surprise—the Choir of Celestial Accountants had been braying his name in jest.

The murderer wasn't male.

He was a female.

Vash.

She delicately wrinkled her button-like human nose at the stench of the place, then yelled out the sweetest words Quark had ever heard—not that he'd ever admit that to her. "Is that any way to talk to your new partner?"

"Just what I need," Quark muttered as he looked at the sprawled bodies of Satr and Leen. "*Another* new partner. . . ." Then relief flooded through him. Vash was no murderer. The odds were very good that both Andorians were only heavily stunned, not dead.

Vash snapped her breather back into place, then motioned for Quark to follow her.

But much as he wanted to get out of this foul pit, there was something Quark had to do first. He reached down and got a good grip on Captain Sisko's jacket to drag the unconscious *hew-mon* toward an open metal staircase beside the sludge vat.

When Vash saw what he was doing, she tried to pull him away, but Quark refused to let go of Sisko. Maybe Satr and Leen deserved to remain in the muck where they fell, and maybe the captain wasn't the best friend a Ferengi barkeep ever had, but Quark wasn't about to leave him to drown in such an undignified fashion.

With Vash's reluctant assistance, Quark hoisted

Sisko up on a platform on the staircase, well above the steadily rising sewage.

Motioning to Quark to follow her across the room to the exit, Vash turned to look back at him, pulling aside her breathing mask long enough to shout, "I don't get it, Quark—what did *he* ever do for *you?"*

Breathing heavily as he dragged his boots through the disgusting deck debris—the *hew-mon* had been surprisingly heavy, and Quark's body was still telling him how badly abused it had been by its hanging ordeal—Quark looked back down at Sisko. "Nothing," he said, out of earshot of Vash. She'd never understand anyway. Not that anyone else ever had. Or ever would. "But he never did anything *to* me, either."

Even without looking at Vash, he could feel her suspicion, and he could almost hear her thinking, How could she trust someone who went out of his way to help a Starfleet officer?

Quark wearily cupped a hand to his mouth and yelled ahead to her, as he shook something unmentionable off his foot, "He owes me money!" The terrible thing was, he knew, that there had to be easier ways to earn latinum. But the even worse thing was that, all other things being equal, he hadn't found it. Yet.

"Stay still and keep your eyes closed," Vash told him.

In the dimly lit kitchen at the back of his bar, Quark did as he was told. "If you only knew how many times I imagined you saying those words to me," he murmured. Then he heard a frothy hissing noise and was suddenly engulfed in a thick foam. He started to protest, but the medicinal-smelling lather bubbled into his mouth the moment he tried to speak.

"And keep your mouth shut!" Vash snapped.

Quark suddenly felt cold. He started to shiver. As he did, he felt the foam begin to drop off him in clumps.

When his face felt free of bubbles, he risked opening one eye. Then the other.

Vash was in front of him, kicking off the last of her environmental suit, a large, carryall duffel bag beside her, along with a pressurized tank and nozzle, dripping foam. Quark could see that portions of her protective suit were covered in rapidly evaporating bubbles as well.

And then he realized with delight that the dreadful stench of the raw sewage was gone. "What *is* that foam?" He looked down at his suit jacket. It was still wet, but there wasn't a single stain on it. Neither was there any muck on his boots or on the floor beneath them.

Vash leaned back against an inductor stove with a sigh. "A cleansing agent from Troyius. Their pheromonal systems are so volatile, they need something that will break down all organic waste completely and instantly—otherwise, they couldn't leave their planet."

"Well, that's *fan*tastic," Quark said admiringly. "Tell me, do they have a good distribution network?"

Vash gave him an odd, measuring look. "Oh, it's not what you'd call a perfect product. There are a few drawbacks."

"Really." Quark grinned. Anything that could eradicate all traces of what he had just been through smelled like pure latinum to him. "I can't imagine what they'd be."

"That suit of yours—replicated from synthetics?" Vash asked, curious. "Or is it natural?"

Stung by the insult, Quark smoothed the multicolored fabric of his snug, tapestry jacket. "I am a successful businessman. Of course, all my suits are natural fiber."

Vash smiled. "You sure?"

Quark glanced down. *"AAAAAA!"* His jacket and trousers were in the process of melting, consumed by the same polyenzymic action that had neutralized the sewage.

The last curling streamers of his suit flickered out of existence just as he ducked for cover behind a food locker. Quark found himself facing the bulkhead whose small access door led to the unmapped tunnel through which he and Vash had escaped from the water plant.

Leaning out from behind the locker, ears flushed, as naked as a female in public, Quark blustered, "Well, don't just stand there, woman! Get me something to wear!"

Vash looked up at the lighting panels on the kitchen ceiling. They were dark. Only the emergency glowstrips on the walls were operating. "Bad timing, Quark. My guess is there's some trouble on the station. I don't think Garak's will be open."

Quark pointed imperiously to the locker behind her. "The locker by the door! Staff uniforms!"

Vash stuck her head in the locker and brought out a clothes holder with a few wispy strands of glitter cloth. "Not your size," she smirked, "but it'll bring out the yellow in your eyes."

Quark fumed. "That's a dabo costume. Give me a waiter's suit!"

"Oh, come on," Vash said as peeked at him through the almost transparent cloth. "You wear something like this, I might stay at the dabo table all night."

Quark couldn't help himself. "Really?" He ran the calculations comparing how much someone could lose at dabo in a single night against the irreparable loss of his self-esteem. It was a close call. As the 189th Rule had it: Let others keep their reputation, you keep their latinum. Maybe he had been hasty when he stopped having Female Nights at the bar. Even though Rom had put up such a fuss over wearing a dress the last time. . . .

"I'll take it under advisement," Quark said thoughtfully. "But now, a waiter's suit?"

Vash pulled one out of the locker and handed it over to Quark, making a show of covering her eyes. "Don't worry, I won't look," she said. "I just ate."

The pale-green jacket, brocade vest, and *ruksilk* shirt were too large, the trousers were too long, and the boots were so large they were almost unwearable. All in all, the lamentably unfashionable outfit reminded Quark of his years as a cabin boy on the old Ferengi freighter, the *Latinum Queen.* But it would do for now. It had to.

Decently covered, Quark emerged from behind the food locker, his steps necessarily mincing because of the unseen oversized shoes beneath the overlong trousers. "Now what did you say happened to the station?"

Vash looked him up and down with a broad grin as she hefted her strap-on carryall over her shoulder. But she merely opened the door leading to the main-level room of the bar without commenting on his appearance.

The room beyond was dark, but the light from the kitchen in which Quark and Vash stood revealed several overturned chairs, as if customers had run out of the bar in a hurry. There were still drinks and food dishes on the tables.

Quark stepped into the bar. He picked up a glass, sniffed it. Groaned. It had held a Deltan-on-the-Beach cocktail with a full measure of triple-proof Romulan ale. Was Rom trying to ruin him?

"Satr and Leen rigged a Pakled sensor mask in the water plant," Vash now told him, "so that if anyone went searching for you, you and they wouldn't show up as lifesigns on anyone's tricorders."

Quark looked around his bar. It looked to him as if it had been hit by something much more powerful than a sensor mask. "And that's not all they arranged," Vash said as she walked past him to open the closed doors of the bar.

Quark sighed. At least his idiot brother had remembered to lock up. Not that it mattered. Beyond the doors, the Promenade, lit only by emergency strips like his bar, looked deserted.

"I'm listening," Quark said, squinting to see what was in the shadows at the end of the bar, and frowning when he did.

"They also slipped a programming worm into the station's computer system," Vash said, turning to reclose the doors to the bar.

"Is that possible?" Quark began walking to the end of the bar.

"A little something they picked up on Bynaus," Vash said as she turned away from the door. "Until the worm detected someone setting up security screens around the water plant, trying to contain the area, the worm was dormant. The bad new is, once it was triggered, it reproduced so quickly it used up all available processing space. All the automatic systems locked up.

They'd have needed a cold start to reset all the computers. The good news is there's no permanent harm done. DS9 should be up and running in about ten minutes or so."

"Good," Quark said, reaching out to touch what he had noticed in the bar's shadows. "I'd like to see Satr and Leen talk their way out of Odo's cell this time."

Vash's voice suddenly became tense. "Is someone at the bar?"

"Just Morn," Quark chuckled, affectionately. He poked at the lugubrious alien's shoulder. His voice became a stage whisper. "Mor-ornnn? Hellooo? Are you in there?"

The huge Lurian snuffled something unintelligible and shifted slightly on the bar stool, driving his massive head deeper into the crook of his well-padded arm, as he remained slumped face-down on the bar. Very faintly, he began to snore, each exhalation accompanied by the pungent perfume of Martian tequila. And judging from the strength of each puff, Quark calculated that at two slips a shot for the extra-premium blend, Morn had had enough this evening to more than pay for a bartender's brand-new suit—even if Rom hadn't properly watered the goods.

"Look at him," Quark crooned. "Sleeping like a baby. A great big, wrinkled, prune-faced baby."

"Well, wake him up and get him out of here," Vash said sharply. "We have business to conduct."

But Quark stood defensively in front of his first, best, and most treasured customer. "I'm sorry, but even *I* have to draw the line somewhere. If Morn wants to sleep on my bar, well then—may the Divine Treasurer bless him and keep him solvent all the days of his life—I am not going to be the one who says no.

Besides, I can charge him half a bar of latinum for rent. *And* . . ." he added in a half-whisper, "if we wake him up now, he won't stop talking for hours." Quark smoothed his jacket, feeling better than he had since Base came into his bar. "If you want to discuss business, we can do it down there where we won't disturb . . ." His voice softened as he gazed down at the lovable lump of his constant and continuous consumer. ". . . the customer."

Vash eyed Morn's hunched-over and snoring body with distaste. She reached out to him, gave his bald scalp a sharp flick with one of her long nails. Morn's only response was to blow a series of small, quickly popping bubbles from his open mouth.

"Don't make him drool now," Quark warned. He took Vash firmly by the arm and led her to the other end of the bar. "Just think of him as part of the furniture."

"Now," Quark said as he took his usual place behind the bar, and placed both hands flat on the bartop. "What kind of business did my favorite archaeologist have in mind?"

Vash shrugged off her carryall, carefully lowering it to the deck, then rubbed at the spot on her shoulder where the carryall strap had been. "Not my business, Quark. *Your* business."

Quark blinked at her. "I'm not sure I follow. Would you like a reward for rescuing me? I'm sure I can work out an equitable payment schedule, though business has been slow and—"

Quark winced as Vash leaned over the bar and pinched one of his earlobes. Painfully. "Quark! I'm not talking about *new* business. I'm talking about the reason why I risked arrest in three systems to get here as soon as I did."

Quark's eyes widened nervously. He pulled back, but Vash did not release her grip on his ear. "You don't mean . . . ?"

"Yes, I do," Vash said. "The Red Orbs of Jalbador. You made it clear you were ready to deal. That's why I'm here. And that's why I saved your wrinkled Ferengi butt."

"You said you wouldn't peek!"

Vash increased the pressure on his ear. Quark had to stand on one foot, just to keep his balance, to spare his delicate earflesh. "Listen, Ferengi. I'm serious. When this station comes back on line, security's going to be all over the place trying to figure out what went wrong. And when they find out I'm not all cozy and warm in the Infirmary, they're going to come looking for me. And that's not going to happen, understand? Because I'm going to be on my way with what I came for. Now let's do it!"

Quark squealed as Vash suddenly yanked up on his earlobe, lifting him right off his feet. Then just as suddenly she released him, and he fell stomach first onto the bartop. His first thought was to look down the length of the bar at Morn, to make certain at least he wasn't disturbed. Then he flopped back, regaining his footing.

"It . . . it's not that easy . . ." he stammered, one hand to his injured earlobe.

Vash reached a hand inside a small pouch on her belt as if going for a knife. "Then I suggest you make it easy."

Quark waved his hands in a vain attempt to deflect whatever it was she was about to cut him with. "I'm just the middleman. The goods are with a . . . a third party."

"Then get him down here."

"I really wish I could. You have no idea. But, the fact of the matter is, he's dead."

Vash narrowed her eyes and Quark knew his other ear was doomed. Just knew it.

"Who?" Vash demanded.

"Dal Nortron. The Andorian who came here with Satr and Leen. Those heartless females were his bodyguards—and they killed him."

Vash snorted. "Bodyguards don't kill their clients. It tends to cut into repeat business."

Quark was outraged. "Base was *my* bodyguard, and he sold me out to Satr and Leen!"

Vash held the heel of one hand to her forehead and sighed. "Oh, *sleem* me. . . ."

Quark brightened. He sensed a slight lessening in her resolve to do something unspeakable to him. "Maybe your visit doesn't have to be a total loss. We can work out another deal."

"*Another* deal?" Vash leaned over, digging into her carryall from the sound of it. Then she straightened up and slammed a spindle-shaped chunk of dark crystal on the bar. It was maybe two-thirds of a meter tall, a quarter-meter at its widest, top and bottom. And except for the fact that it was oddly dull in the way it reflected what little light there was, it looked exactly like—

Quark choked.

". . . Oh, no . . ." he whispered.

"Oh, yes," Vash said. "A Red Orb of Jalbador."

Quark could scarcely draw a breath. Shocked. Unprepared. "You mean . . ." he gasped, "they *are* real?"

"*This* one is." Vash leaned over the bar counter and in the same moment, Quark leaned back, thus ensuring the continued health of his other, as yet uninjured, earlobe. "But without the other two," she said in disgust, "it's worse than useless."

Quark's business sense quickened. He felt a strong sense of finality within Vash. There would be no more negotiations. He was right.

"Time's up, Quark. I want the map."

A commotion behind Vash made Quark's heart flutter like a grubworm on a toothpick, with no hope of escape.

"You mean, this one?" Satr hissed.

Vash wheeled around, phaser already in her hand and aimed behind her.

But the danger was above her, not behind. Satr and Leen—clearly recovered from whatever miserably low-setting stun Vash had used on them—were on the bar's second level, and the golden dagger Leen now threw down knocked the phaser directly out of Vash's hand before she could even fire it.

Instantly Satr flipped over the railing, her lithe, tattooed body spinning through the air, to land like a feline in a crouch, braced by one hand. In the next instant, the Andorian spun around on both hands and reverse-kicked Vash, sending her skidding across the floor of Quark's bar.

By the time the archaeologist regained her feet, Leen had slid halfway down the stairway railing to the main level and flipped over to land on her feet, a golden dagger in each hand.

The spectacle of fully-clothed feminine physicality was too much for Quark, and he shivered with forbidden pleasure. Rather than slide the Red Orb off the bar, he continued to watch the action in anticipation of the three females' killing each other. Yet if even one of them survived, Quark had little doubt that he'd be the next victim.

Satr held up a slender cylinder of amber crystal. "We have the map, Vash. Without it, your Orb is nothing more than a sparkly rock. Let us buy it from you."

Vash was breathing hard, weaponless, holding her side where Satr had kicked her, but Quark suspected the resourceful archaeologist wouldn't admit defeat yet. And he was right again.

"Without an Orb, your map might as well be a Ferengi ear probe. Let *me* buy the map from you."

The one thing Quark never forgot was that he was Ferengi. He saw his opportunity and he acted upon it immediately. "Ladies, please . . . you each have something the other wants. What better situation could there be for striking a deal? A deal, I might add, I'd be glad to broker for just a small commission—"

Leen's bare blue arm flexed and a golden dagger flashed through the air to pin Quark's too-large jacket—with him inside it—to the wall.

"Or not . . ." Quark whispered.

Satr and Leen moved to flank Vash, one heading to either side of her. The archaeologist was forced up against the bar counter, with no way to escape them.

Leen drew a third golden dagger from the set of scabbards at her back, and once again held a wickedly sharp blade in each hand.

Satr tossed her crystal cylinder tauntingly, back and forth, from one hand to the other.

"You want the Orb, I want the map," Vash said, her eyes moving quickly from one to the other. "The Ferengi is right. We can work out a deal."

"Dal Nortron wanted to work out a deal," Satr

sneered. "He hired us, so of course we supported his decision. And then the Ferengi killed him."

"What?!" Quark protested. "I didn't kill anyone! I thought you were all lying! That the map was a forgery!"

"You were willing to be the broker at the auction," Leen said.

"I make no representations as to the suitability of the product for the use to which the purchaser intends—"

"Silence!"

Quark knew much better than to argue with a blue tattooed female. Each intricate black scroll on her arm represented a man she had killed—after having had her way with him. And though Quark suspected he would not necessarily object to the second interaction, he would definitely have issues with the first.

He nodded, not even risking a single word to say he agreed with her.

"If *you* didn't kill Nortron," Vash said, "and the Ferengi didn't, then who did?"

"Do I look like the changeling?" Leen snarled viciously.

"We don't care who killed him," Satr said quickly, with a sharp glance at her sister. "The fact is, he's dead. We're not. So now we do things our way. And we want your Orb."

"It won't do any good without knowing where to use it," Vash countered.

Satr brandished her crystal wand. "This map tells us which world we must take the Orb to."

"And when we get close enough to the second Orb," Leen said triumphantly, "the first will glow to lead us along the final path."

"You actually believe that *kragh?"* Vash asked.

Quark caught his breath as Satr's head jerked menacingly forward like a striking snake. "If you didn't believe it, you'd sell us your Orb."

"You wouldn't believe what I went through to get this," Vash said, undaunted. "I'm not selling anything."

The three of them faced each other, drenched in sweat, ready to fight to the death, taut muscles rippling beneath the Andorian sisters' glistening blue skin, Vash's long, lustrous hair a dark fountain against creamy-white shoulders . . . Quark trembled, took a calming breath. He was falling in love, and he didn't care with which one.

A moment before he had been on the verge of slipping to safety and obscurity behind the bar. But now he paused, unsure.

"We're not selling anything, either," Satr said.

"Which leaves us only one alternative," Leen added.

"Exactly," Base squeaked. "It means I'll take both!"

"Oh, for—" Quark snorted in disgust, as Base jumped up on the bar waving aloft his comically puny *bat'leth.* The little betrayer could only have been hiding among the crates of glasses across from the replicator, waiting for his moment to strike.

Moron, Quark thought. Base would probably last about fifteen seconds against the blue sisters. And Vash would—

"What are *you?"* Satr said.

"Your worst nightmare, bluecheeks," Base chirped.

Leen hooted at the thought, then suddenly threw both daggers at the minute Ferengi.

And then, to Quark's utter astonishment, Base twisted his *bat'leth* in an expert blur and deflected both daggers. He hadn't even tried to duck.

"I can throw this a *skrell* of a lot faster than you blues can run," Base crowed. "Now bring me the map crystal," he said to Satr. Then he glared at Quark. "And you, you lobeless hunk of greeworm castings, you bring me the Orb."

Quark tugged at his jacket where its shoulder was still fixed to the wall by Leen's dagger, trusting Base would see that he was otherwise detained.

But Vash provided distraction enough.

"You backstabbing little *hardinak,*" she spat at him. "You're supposed to be working for me!"

"Ha!" Quark said, much that had been unclear at last becoming clear to him. "He was supposed to be working for *me!*"

"You're both fools!" Leen snarled.

"We paid him off so he'd work for us!" Satr added.

"Which begs the question," Vash said. "Who the hell are you working for *now?*"

Base shrugged his shoulders. "What can I tell you half-wits? With all the latinum you slugs gave me, I finally had enough to go into business for myself." Base jabbed his thumb against his small chest. "You'd better believe it. I'm pure Ferengi, in it for the profit and nothing else!"

That was too much for Quark. "Oh, will someone step on him and crush him flat."

Base squealed, enraged, as he whirled around to confront Quark, holding his miniature *bat'leth* high—relatively speaking—above his head with both hands.

Quark fought to wriggle out of his borrowed jacket, still pinned securely to the wall. The only way that pitiful excuse for a Ferengi would actually kill him was if he died first from embarrassment.

But Vash got to Base first, knocking him straight off the bar to the deck.

Squeaking in outrage, Base rolled to his feet, still waving his *bat'leth,* but in the wrong direction. Because Satr and Leen now attacked him from behind, Satr sweeping him up in the bare, muscled arms Quark thought had definite potential, Leen drawing her own well-exposed arm back to slap him, and then—

—Quark moaned as everything went wrong. Again.

Even though Base's *bat'leth* didn't have the finely honed cutting edges of the traditional Klingon weapon—and he certainly didn't have the skill to slice an artery or bisect a key muscle group—all he seemed to need to do to cause havoc was make contact between the blade and any part of his opponent's body, and Ferengi plasma-whip circuits did the rest. Which is just what he did.

Quark watched in disbelief as Base swung the *bat'leth* wildly at Leen until he provoked her sufficiently to reach out to swat it away. At that precise moment of contact with Base's weapon, the blue Andorian flew back in a shimmering nimbus of disruptive neural energy.

Startled, Leen's sister dropped her prey; he took the opportunity to tuck, roll, and come up swinging, bashing Satr across the knees with his *bat'leth* so that she, too, collapsed in the throes of neural disruption.

Vash still hadn't regained her feet, and being at Base's level didn't have a chance. Quark covered his eyes with both hands, but peered through his fingers, appalled and fascinated at the same time.

After vanquishing his last female enemy with a glancing blow to the ankles, Base now threw back his head and cackled like a mad paultillian as he used his *bat'leth* like a vaulter's pole and sprang back up onto the bar.

He swaggered toward Quark.

Quark pulled and struggled mightily, but the barbs on the dagger just wouldn't let go. He was a sitting Grumpackian tortoise.

"Base, can't we talk about this?" Quark pleaded.

The little Ferengi spun his *bat'leth* around his wrist just like Bus Betar in the old Marauder Mo holos. The classic ones, not the remakes. "I don't think so, *frinx*-for-brains. For the first time in my life, it's winner-take-all." He stopped the *bat'leth* in midspin, tapped one pudgy finger against the tip of his weapon. "It's the 242nd Rule, after all . . . More is good, all is better. Prepare to meet your Accountant." Then Base raised his weapon. "The Orb is mine. The map is mine. *Everything* is mine! Do you hear me?! For the first time in my life, Base *wins!*"

"I don't think so, you miserable scrap of a sentient being!"

For a moment, Base stopped in midstride, staring at Quark as if those combative words had dared come from his intended victim's mouth.

Quark shrank down into his oversize green jacket, wondering if he *had* be stupid enough to utter those words. True as they might be.

And then, as the truth finally dawned on both hunter and hunted, Quark and Base both slowly turned to look at the person who had uttered them.

Morn.

No longer deep in his cups on the bartop.

Instead, the hulking Lurian was on his feet, a gigantic dark silhouette looming against the light filtering through the doors to the Promenade.

"Drop the *bat'leth,*" Morn growled.

"Make me!" Base squeaked back in defiance.

"I will."

Quark's mouth dropped open in awe and respect. Not only was Morn his best customer, he was about to senselessly sacrifice his life in a tragic and doomed attempt to save *him.*

What a noble gesture, Quark thought. *A totally ineffective, inadequate, useless gesture.*

If he lived, Quark decided, he'd retire Morn's stool. Or—even better—charge people extra to sit in it.

"Prepare to die," Base yodeled.

Morn grunted. "Not today," he said.

And then, even as tiny Base raised his *bat'leth* for the attack, Morn swung up his huge arm and—

—it snaked out along the bar like golden lightning, until Morn's immense hand closed on the *bat'leth,* and crushed it, dropping the shards to the ground, and then snapped back like a tentacle around Base's scrawny neck, still eerily flowing like the pseudopod of a *hew-mon*-sized amoeba.

As Base gargled helplessly in Morn's unforgiving grip, Quark recovered his senses.

"Why didn't you wait until the little monster had killed me?" he snapped. "Wouldn't that have given you an even better reason to act, *Morn?*"

Morn shook his huge wrinkled head once, then softened, melted, into a gelatinous amber statue before resolidifying as Odo, though one Morn-like arm retained its grip on Base.

"Ohhh, you enjoyed that, didn't you?" Quark accused the shape-shifting constable. "Seeing me almost killed."

"As a matter of fact, I did," Odo said. "By the way, Quark, nice suit."

"That's not funny."

"And you'll notice I'm not laughing. Whatever else is going on around here—and I assure you, I did hear *everything*—Dal Nortron's still dead. And if you didn't kill him, and the Andorians didn't kill him, then there's still a murderer walking free on DS9."

Quark threw up his hands. "Finding murderers is not my job," he said piously. With much relish, Odo gazed at Base's stumpy legs kicking frantically as he held the snarling little Ferengi above the deck just high enough to keep Base from connecting with anything solid.

"Fortunately," Odo said gravely, "it happens to be mine. And in this case, I think my job has just become much simpler."

Quark saw where Odo was looking—directly at the Red Orb of Jalbador, still sitting on the counter of Quark's bar. Shocked and appalled, Quark realized he'd forgotten what a Ferengi must never forget. Profit and the potential thereof.

"As a wise man once explained," the constable said, "all we have to do now to solve the crime is follow the Orb. . . ."

CHAPTER 20

EMPTY OF ITS lifeblood of people, the station seemed a melancholy place to Sisko.

After five cold restarts, Dax's computer team still wasn't rid of whatever type of Bynar code Satr and Leen had input into DS9's computers, and all internal automated systems remained off-line. Even the main gravity generators hadn't been brought back into service. As a result, the banners decorating the Promenade all hung at the same skewed angle, and the deck itself was at a slant as if, impossible though it was, the entire station were listing in space.

The litter on the carpeted sections of the deck was a sad reminder of the hasty evacuation of all nonessential station personnel into the habitat ring. And aside from the dim emergency lighting, some fixtures of which were finally beginning to flicker after having been on too long, the only signs of life that remained were the faint sounds of chanting coming from the Bajoran Temple and the opening and closing of the doors to Odo's office.

Sisko now headed for the Security Office to join the others assembling there.

His ears still rang from the twenty minutes he had stood within the sonic shower, ridding himself of the malodorous sludge of the water-treatment facility, and every muscle in his body still felt the effects of the stun Vash had fired at him. But the physical disorientation he still suffered was not his biggest problem; it was his continued mental confusion. With the uncovering of each new piece of the puzzle—the seemingly unconnected and unexplainable events on the station, the one key element that would make sense of them all, was still missing. And that was annoying the hell out of him.

Halfway between the turbolift and the Security Office Sisko turned to see Bashir striding quickly along the corridor toward him.

"How is he?" Sisko asked. Despite every other threat to the station, O'Brien was his first priority. Worf and his security team had been beamed into the water plant the moment the transporter systems had finally been manually tuned. They'd found Sisko, just coming to, and O'Brien unconscious. Sisko had given the order to evacuate the wounded chief to the Infirmary first.

Bashir's report offered more mystery. "Interestingly enough, there was another Andorian toxin on the dagger that hit him. Not the same one Vash used on herself, but one intended to incapacitate almost any species. But don't worry," the doctor said quickly, seeing the anxious look that Sisko could not keep from his face, "it's not fatal. At least, not to Miles. He's too stubborn."

The doctor glanced around at the unsettling state of the Promenade as they walked towards Odo's office. "I suppose you've already thought about this—but what happens if the Dominion hears about our condition?"

Sisko *had* thought about that, right after Worf's team beamed the chief out to the Infirmary. "Admiral Ross has already dispatched the *Bondar* and the *Garneau* to provide us support."

"*Akira*-class," Bashir said.

Sisko nodded. "They'll stand up to anything the Dominion can throw at us. At least for the time being."

They'd reached the doors of the Security Office. Sisko paused before entering, gathering his strength.

"Something wrong, Captain?" Bashir asked.

Sisko shrugged. "There's something going on here I don't understand. And, to be honest, it makes me uneasy."

"For what it's worth," the doctor offered, "when I heard Vash actually had one of the Red Orbs, I thought that explained everything. I mean, I had halfway figured out for myself that the Orbs might be real. So maybe we should look at this as just another one of Quark's scams—albeit blown up to immense proportions because of the potential for . . . mind-boggling profit."

Sisko understood, but was unconvinced. "I hope you're right. A simple explanation is always the best."

"Unless it's the wrong one, of course," Bashir added with a charming, self-deprecating smile. Then the door to the Security Office slid open and he stepped through.

Instead of following the doctor, Sisko wheeled about suddenly, aware of eyes upon him. He looked down the corridor to the right, toward the entrance of the Temple where the large, solid, unmistakable form of Prylar Obanak stood in the doorway, arms folded within bright saffron robes, watching.

Both men nodded to each other in silent acknowledgment.

Then Sisko turned and entered Odo's office.

He instantly wished he hadn't.

A wall of sound assaulted his still-ringing ears. Odo and Quark were heatedly arguing in the front office. Satr and Leen and Vash were shouting at each other and at anyone who was close to their holding cells. And a particularly irritating high-pitched howl that Sisko had never heard before seemed to be coming from all directions at once.

To save what was left of his hearing, Sisko issued an immediate command prerogative.

"BE QUIET! EVERYONE!"

In the sudden silence, the fluctuating siren-like howl seemed even louder.

"Is there something wrong with a wall communicator?" Sisko struggled not to sound as cross as he felt.

"That's Base," Odo said gruffly. "Apparently he's claustrophobic."

Sisko lost his battle with his nerves. "Tell him if he doesn't stop that infernal squealing, I'll have him hauled off to an escape module. And then he'll know what claustrophobia really feels like."

Odo almost smiled as he headed for the holding cells off to one side of his office area.

"All right," Sisko said brusquely to Quark, "where's the Orb, and where's the map?"

Quark led Sisko and Bashir to the other side of the constable's office, where a small doorway led to a secure storage room. The outer wall of the storage room was lined with stasis safes, and one of the safes was open.

But Sisko's attention was on the storage room's center scanning table. On it was a spindle-cut chunk of what appeared to be randomly faceted red glass, and a small amber cylinder.

"That doesn't look like an Orb," he said, referring to the red glass-like object. All the Orbs of the Prophets Sisko had seen resembled shimmering hourglass shapes of solid light. They were so breathtakingly compelling, so disorienting, that ages ago Bajoran monks had fashioned jewelled arks to shield and hold them so that they could be carried among the faithful.

"Word has it, it's only supposed to glow when it's close to the next Orb," Quark explained.

Sisko picked up the faceted artifact to examine it more closely. "The next Orb?"

"Actually, there're supposed to be three," Quark said. "You use one to find the next one, then use those two to find the third."

Sisko touched the edge of the artifact, felt nothing, sensed no trace of the Prophets. "I see." He put the artifact down with a sigh. "And how much were you going to make by allowing this travesty of the Bajoran religion to take place?"

"Captain Sisko," Quark said emphatically, "I swear I had no idea the Orb was real. I thought I was going to be selling a map. This thing!" He picked up the amber cylinder from the screening table and held it out to Sisko. "That's all. I make my living from the Bajorans.

Do you really think I'd risk my livelihood by insulting them?"

Sisko took the cylinder from Quark, turned it over in his fingers, still skeptical.

So, apparently, was Bashir. "Vash told Dax and me that an Orb could fetch the kind of money that can buy and sell planets."

Quark's eyes widened and he swallowed hard. "Really?" Then he recovered. "But I wasn't selling an Orb! Just the map! A treasure map! I must sell a half-dozen of them every year!" He faltered, then quickly added, "Not for Orbs, of course. But for the lost planet of Atlantis, missing ships, T'Kon portals, *Qui'Tu* and *Vorta Vor.* Classic stuff. Nothing more."

Bashir seemed to be convinced. "I believe him, sir. Especially since the penalties for dealing in Orbs cannot be plea-bargained."

"Exactly," Quark said with a shiver. "Why risk getting involved with a criminal-justice system that has such a rigid view of wrong and right when they're so many other ways to . . . uh, that doesn't sound right either, does it?"

"Quit while you're ahead, Quark." Sisko held up the amber map cylinder. "Tell me about this."

Quark shrugged. "I never saw it till Dal Nortron brought it to the bar the day he arrived. And I told that whole story to Odo just like you told me to."

"That's right," Odo said, making his appearance in the storage room just as Sisko noticed thankfully that Base's squealing had finally stopped. "According to Quark, the Andorian contacted him to arrange an auction for the map."

"Where did Nortron say he got it?" Sisko asked.

"He didn't tell," Quark answered. "And I didn't ask. There are some traditions in trade, you know."

"What's it a map of, Quark? Or did traditions prevent you from asking about that, too?"

"Captain, really. I had to write the promotional copy, didn't I?"

"And?" Sisko prompted.

Quark sighed dramatically. "According to the Jalbador legend, the three Red Orbs were scattered so they could never be brought together."

"Why not?" Sisko asked.

"It's a *legend,*" Quark said testily. "Why three wishes? Why a magic greeworm? Someone told a bedtime story once and it got taken way too seriously, if you ask me."

Sisko waved a hand, realizing it was probably unrealistic to demand much more depth from Quark's explanation. "Continue."

"So—whoever hid them made a map of where they were hidden. End of mystery."

"Well, that makes no sense," Bashir complained. "If the Orbs aren't supposed to ever be found, why make maps? Why not just launch them into the sun?"

Quark rolled his eyes. "Bajorans didn't have space travel back then, all right? Now, do you want to hear this story or not?"

"It gets better," Odo pointed out.

"Thank you," Quark said. "So, the point is, the map Dal Nortron obtained—from *whatever* source—apparently reveals the world on which the second Red Orb is hidden."

"A world's a large place to hide something so small," Sisko said.

"Exactly, Captain. Which means, you need the first

Orb to find the second. They react to each other, like a . . . a location beacon or something. And the thing is, I didn't know Vash had the first Orb."

Sisko handed the map cylinder to Odo. "Constable, is there any way we can see what's on this?"

Odo studied the transparent amber rod. "Looks like a standard Cardassian memory rod. . . ." He walked over to a wall display, pressed a control and a rod holder slid out.

"Quark," Sisko warned the Ferengi barkeep, "no games now. I'll accept that you're too smart to risk alienating the entire Bajoran population. But I need an honest answer." Sisko tried not to react to Quark's sudden look of panic at his use of the word, 'honest.' "Who else—smuggler or collector or buyer—is on this station who might have been responsible for Dal Nortron's murder?"

Only Quark could look contrite, worried, and embarrassed all at the same time. "Captain, I don't know. The Andorian sisters. Base, of course. Vash. Those are the only ones my inform—I mean, they're the only ones I've seen."

"Here it is," the constable said from his position by the display screen.

Sisko left Quark, who likely had nothing more to offer, and walked over to join Odo and Bashir.

The amber cylinder did contain a map, but not of an entire planet. Instead, it outlined a city layout, of streets and dwelling blocks.

And nothing was labeled.

"That's not going to do anyone any good," Sisko said.

Odo studied the schematics on the display screen. "Maybe the legend was wrong. Instead of showing a world, the map shows a place *on* a world."

"But, Odo," Bashir said, "there are millions of worlds in the galaxy."

"Maybe there's another map that goes with this one," Odo suggested.

Sisko tried a different approach. "How old is that cylinder?"

Odo tapped a few controls, read a line of Cardassian script. "According to the manufacturer's code, five years."

"So this is a copy," Bashir concluded.

"Of a copy of a copy of a copy," Sisko added. "And if this truly dates back to ten thousand years ago, when the first Orbs started to appear, then the first version of the map would probably have been carved into rock or—" He stopped and then smiled broadly. "No. It *can't* be hidden on any one of millions of worlds." He turned to the Ferengi and exclaimed, "Quark! You're right!"

"I am?"

"You said it yourself. Ten millennia ago, Bajorans didn't have space travel. So the Orbs *had* to have been hidden on Bajor itself."

This time it was Bashir who seemed unconvinced."But if the hiding place is Bajor, then why all the interest in a map that supposedly shows some *world* on which the orbs can be found?"

Sisko wasn't certain about that, himself, but he didn't think it was important. "The old Bajoran ideograms can be difficult to translate. They have so many meanings that change according to context. It could be as simple as the phrase, '*the* world,' meaning the known world of Bajor, having been translated as '*a* world,' a few thousand years ago."

Sisko shook his head to ward off any other questions that could sidetrack them again. "In any case, the mystery that should concern us right now is who killed Dal Nortron."

"Hey, Dad."

Sisko turned, automatically smiling at the sound of his son's voice.

Jake and Jadzia stepped cautiously into the storage room of Odo's security office, neither of them comfortable with the sharply slanting deck.

"Jake-O, Old Man—who's minding the store?"

"Worf," Jadzia said with a playful smile. "We're running another diagnostic on the computer and I had to get away from those screens for a few minutes."

Under current conditions, Sisko could accept Jadzia's presence. But not Jake's.

"You know you shouldn't be here," he told his son. "The whole station's on gravity alert and I want you back at our quarters to look after Kasidy."

Jake looked at him as if he were hearing a deliberately bad joke. "Like I'm supposed to look after the captain of an interstellar freighter. Sure, that's just the sort of job for a helpless female."

Sisko smiled but made his request again. "You know what I mean. I want my family out of harm's way."

Jake grinned. "Really? Family? Does Kasidy know about this?"

"Don't start," Sisko warned. "Now get moving, and don't use the turbolifts."

Jake hesitated, looked at Jadzia, and Jadzia coughed.

Something was obviously going on between them. "All right, you two," Sisko said. "I know a conspiracy when I see one."

"Benjamin," Jadzia said, "just before the computer

was compromised, when you had just beamed out to the *Defiant,* Jake and I were having a . . . talk."

"You were in Ops?" Sisko frowned at his son.

Jadzia answered before Jake could. "He's been helping out with the computer restarts, copying files, shutting down subsystems."

Sisko relaxed, reminded of what he sometimes forgot these days, of all the time Jake used to spend with O'Brien. He gave his son the benefit of the doubt. "I take it this 'talk' was important?"

Jadzia exchanged glances with Jake. "Well, the budding novelist here figured out on his own that someone was trying to sell an Orb, *and* that the Orb was real. He had a few other interesting conclusions, too, so I thought maybe you could use his input while you're trying to put all this together."

Sisko sighed. "Okay. But let's do that *tonight,* Jake. Right now, things are still too much up in the air." He could see the disappointment in his son's eyes, understood how the boy felt, but for now, the station had to come first.

Jake nodded without protest. He wasn't the only one who was disappointed, though.

"Don't give me that look, Old Man."

"A good commander makes full use of all his assets."

"I see. The conspiracy is turning into a mutiny." Not for the first time, Sisko observed that Jadzia and Jake were alike in that they both knew exactly how far they could push him, and when they reached that point without success, they backed off without recrimination.

Almost without recrimination.

Jadzia leaned closer and whispered into Sisko's ear,

"I'd watch out, Benjamin. Someday Jake's going to write a book about you and you do want to come off as one of the good guys, don't you?"

"Tonight," Sisko repeated firmly.

Jake said his good-byes to Odo, the doctor, and Quark and then, just before stepping out of the storage room, he glanced up at the display screen with a bright smile. "Hey, you got the interface going!"

Everyone looked at him in surprise, including his father.

"What interface?" Sisko asked.

"With the Cardassian holosuite." Jake pointed to the display screen. "Isn't what that is? It sure looks like the layout of the village Nog and I saw."

"What village?" Odo asked sharply.

"The one on the Bajoran moon."

Just for a moment, Sisko felt Deep Space 9 wheel crazily around him. And the effect had nothing to do with the canted slant of the deck or with failing gravity.

Without any logic or hard data, he suddenly was certain that the last piece of the puzzle had just fallen into place.

And the truly maddening thing was, it had been there all along.

CHAPTER 21

"THIS IS IT," Nog said. Then he looked up at Jake. "Wouldn't you say?"

Jake studied the holographic image that surrounded him and all the other onlookers in the holosuite at Quark's. As far as he could tell, it was a close reproduction of the primitive village he and Nog had seen in the distance four days ago, when they had entered the Cardassian holosuite. Fortunately, the computers that ran Quark's holosuites were separate from the station's, and were still fully operational.

The resolution, however, was low, the sky was an unreal shade of dark purple without stars or Bajor, and the recreation was missing details like an evening breeze and the flickering of lights in the windows. But from the arrangement of the buildings and the sweep of the landscape, Jake would have to say Jadzia had done a great job of turning the two-dimensional map on the Cardassian memory rod into a three-dimensional simulation. Best of all, she had adjusted the gravity in the suite to compensate for the station's list, so that for the first time in almost two hours everyone was standing on level ground.

"I agree," Jake said. "This is the village we saw."

He looked over at his father, secretly pleased to be able to make an important contribution to the investigation. Especially after being so publicly dismissed in front of so many people—who were now here to see that he wasn't just the captain's kid, who had to be kept 'out of harm's way.'

Even his father looked impressed. He turned to Odo. "Constable? Theories?"

"I think it's obvious, Captain. Dal Nortron somehow knew about the Cardassian holosuite in the hidden section of corridor. He used it to create a simulation of this Bajoran lunar village, no doubt attempting to narrow down the location of the second Orb."

"And he was killed for his trouble."

"Undoubtedly."

"Which brings us back to Vash, Satr, and Leen as suspects. But how could any of *them* know about the hidden section of the station?"

"You might as well ask how could Nortron?" Odo said. "And again, I think the answer is obvious. The map is recorded on a Cardassian memory rod. That implies Nortron obtained it from a Cardassian source, and that it was a Cardassian who knew about what was hidden on Terok Nor and then told Nortron."

Even though everything Odo had said sounded reasonable, somehow it didn't strike Jake as right. There had to be another explanation for what had happened. He tried to think about how he would make everything come out if this were a novel he was writing, but unfortunately all that kept springing into his mind was the usual shock ending in which the station commander is revealed to be the killer.

Jake suddenly stared at his father, who turned to him as if he sensed the intensity of his son's gaze. "What is it, Jake?"

"Um, Dad, are we . . . still following the Starfleet changeling-detection protocols?"

Sisko shrugged. "All the time." Then he grinned as if he could read his son's mind. "Anyone in particular you suspect?"

"No, not really," Jake said diffidently.

"Jake," Sisko said, "if the Dominion was behind any of this, a Jem'Hadar attack wing would have started pounding us the instant our computers went off-line. The fact that we're still here means this doesn't have anything at all to do with the Founders."

But that didn't sound right to Jake, either. "But it *does* have something to do with the Cardassians, right? And they're part of the Dominion, sort of."

Jadzia looked at Sisko. "See? That's a good point."

"No, no, no," Major Kira suddenly interjected. She had gone off to walk through the simulated village and had just returned. "This reconstruction doesn't match *any* village on *any* of the inhabited Bajoran moons. It's a fake. A typical Quark forgery."

"I resent that," Quark said huffily. "My forgeries are anything but typ—never mind."

"Captain," Kira said, "we're wasting our time with this."

But Jake could see that Kira's argument had made his father think of something else. "Just a minute, Major. Let's accept that this simulation *doesn't* match an *existing* lunar village. But could it match an *ancient* one?"

"Lunar villages aren't that ancient, sir. The oldest ones, even going right back to the first landings, would only be a thousand years old."

Jake understood the reason for his father's quick smile. It didn't mean that he was taking what Kira said lightly. His amusement stemmed from the fact that Bajoran culture went so far back that a thousand years to them was like a long weekend to anyone else.

"Forgive me, Major." Sisko's apology was sincere. "Rather than 'ancient,' let's say 'old.' Could this represent an *old* lunar village?"

Kira turned around to stare back at the simulation. "Well, the architecture is right, even if the layout isn't. But if the Red Orbs are supposed to have been split up ten thousand years ago, how could one of them have been buried on a Bajoran moon *one* thousand years ago?"

"Maybe someone's keeping track of them," Jake suggested.

Kira shook her head. "Oh, no, Jake, you can't have it both ways. Either the Orbs are hidden or they're not. It doesn't make sense for anyone to be moving around Orbs that supposedly can never be brought together."

"Of course," Bashir said slowly, "there is *one* way for everyone to be right."

That the doctor suddenly had everyone's undivided attention was an understatement. Jake felt a little envious that Bashir and not he might be about to solve the mystery, but he was excited, too, to be here on the spot, as his father's murder investigation proceeded to its solution, step by step. All of this was vastly preferable to being sequestered somewhere safe while all the really interesting activities on the station were going on without him.

The doctor gave a little bow toward Major Kira. "What if these Orbs *are* forgeries, but ones manufactured a thousand years ago which would give them a certain air of authenticity. This would make them rare Bajoran artifacts that could have been hidden a millennium ago, and would mean they could still serve as a motive for murder today. At the same time, they would then also *not* be the legendary, and possibly, apocryphal, Red Orbs of Jalbador."

"Makes sense to me," Kira said.

"Except for that Cardassian connection," Sisko said. "I wish we knew what moon this was supposed to be. . . ." He turned to Jake. "Where was Bajor in the sky?"

Jake and Nog both turned and pointed away from the village. "Up there," Jake told his father.

"We were beyond the terminator," Nog added, "but we could still see part of the sunlit side."

"Computer," Sisko said, "add Bajor to the night sky, as seen from the Bajoran moon of Baraddo."

Jake looked up as the purple sky suddenly rippled and turned black, now dotted with twinkling stars. A few moments later, a full Bajor appeared against the stars, green oceans sparkling with the brilliant reflection of Bajor-B'hava-el.

"Too small," Nog said at once.

"That's right," Jake said. "It was twice that size at least."

Sisko nodded. "Computer, which moon of Bajor would correspond to an apparent diameter of the planet twice the width of what's displayed now?"

"Unable to comply," the computer answered. "Library access has been temporarily interrupted."

Jake knew that meant the computer had tried to contact the station's central computer banks, which were still off-line.

Sisko gave the challenge to Kira. "Major, pick a moon. There're only five that are inhabited."

Kira looked troubled. "But some have eccentric orbits. . . . Computer, adjust the sky as seen from the moon of Penraddo."

Jake watched as Bajor seemed to jump closer in the sky, almost doubling in apparent diameter.

"That is still not quite right," Nog said, frowning. "Is there any moon that orbits the planet even closer?"

"Not habitable," Kira said.

"You mean, not habitable *now!"* Sisko's smile was triumphant.

Jake didn't know what his father was talking about. But Kira apparently did.

"Jeraddo?" she said.

"If I wanted to hide something so that it could never be found," Sisko said, "what better place than a moon that will kill anyone who tries to land there? Computer: Show Bajor as it would have appeared from the moon of Jeraddo before the moon's atmosphere was converted."

Instantly, Bajor jumped even closer in the sky.

"Now *that* is the right size," Nog said.

Jake nodded.

But Kira wasn't convinced. "Jeraddo was only converted to an energy source five years ago, not a thousand."

Jake had a sudden flash of inspiration. "Which means," he said excitedly, "someone could have hidden the Orb on Jeraddo five years ago! To keep it out of the hands of whoever's been trying to find the Orbs and bring them together!"

Kira suddenly developed a pained expression. "Jake, where did that come from?"

Jake could tell that his interruption had surprised her. He was getting more and more used to that reaction. It was hard for the adults on the station to stop thinking of him as the little kid they'd always known. And it was hard for him to suppress the ideas he had about just about everything around him.

"Well," he began explaining enthusiastically, "Jeraddo was converted into an energy moon five years ago. The memory cylinder the map is on is five years old. So maybe the map isn't a copy—maybe it's only five years old. . . ." Jake could see Kira wasn't buying a word. And neither was anyone else. *Too bad,* Jake thought. *It would make a great conspiracy novel.* He could even use his father's suggestion and call it *The Cardassian Connection.* He could write a whole series. He could . . . see the almost pitying look on Major Kira's face. "Never mind," he said.

"I won't," Kira replied. She turned to Sisko. "Shouldn't we all get back to work?"

Jake could see his father wasn't ready to let go of this latest lead that he and Nog had provided. "Don't you have any curiosity for making an even more detailed simulation from the map? Maybe find out exactly where the Orb is hidden?" Sisko asked.

"Absolutely none," Kira said. "That Orb will never be found because it either doesn't exist, or if it does, because it's hidden on Jeraddo. Either way, that map means nothing."

Jake watched as his father's glance polled the rest of the group in the holosuite—Odo, Bashir, Quark, even

Nog and him. No one else offered an objection to Kira's conclusion, so neither did Jake.

"All right," Sisko said. "We move on."

Jake braced himself for the return of the station's unbalanced gravity field.

"Computer," Sisko said, "end program."

But nothing changed.

"Computer," Sisko repeated, "*end* program."

The simulation remained.

"That Rom" Quark sputtered. "Computer, this is Quark. Implement safety override in holosuite C."

But again, nothing happened. Quark looked frantically back and forth at the unchanging Bajoran lunar village. "We're doomed," he said.

"Not yet," a disembodied voice replied.

Jake looked at Nog as everyone else scanned their surroundings, trying to find the source of the voice.

"Stay calm, and no one will get hurt," the voice said again.

Jake saw his father and Major Kira turn to look at one another at the same moment.

"Leej Terrell." To Jake, the way Kira said the name, it sounded like she was cursing.

Then something even more unusual happened. Jake was amazed to see the distant landscape shimmer just for an instant, as three Cardassians—one female and two males, including one who was bald and badly scarred—stepped *through* the holographic simulation to join the group in the holosuite.

Except they weren't here to play games.

Each held a Cardassian phaser.

"Thank you, Captain Sisko," the female said. "You finally found our missing Orb."

CHAPTER 22

SISKO STEPPED between Terrell and his son. *If she so much as aims her weapon in Jake's direction—*

The Cardassian seemed to recognize the reason for his move. "Noble, Captain, but unnecessary."

"How did you get in here!" Quark demanded of Terrell. "I demand to see your admittance receipt!" And he slapped at her bald associate as Atrig roughly searched through Quark's ill-fitting green brocade waiter's suit for possible weapons.

At the same time, Dr. Betan retrieved all communicators, along with Jadzia's tricorder and Jake's note padd. Sisko's holosuite party was now completely cut off from the rest of the station, captives of the three Cardassians.

Terrell stared at the indignant Quark. "You don't recognize me?"

Sisko saw the sudden flash of fear that moved

through Quark, as if the Ferengi barkeep did recognize her, but was somehow terrified to acknowledge that fact.

"Should I?" Quark asked.

"I'm not the one to ask," Terrell said. She turned her attention to Odo. "How about you, shape-shifter?"

"What about me?" Odo growled.

Terrell seemed only amused by his attitude. "Some things never change." She casually lifted her phaser and shot Odo point-blank.

As the constable fell, Kira's attempt to run to his side was aborted by Betan's menacing sweep of his phaser in her direction.

Bashir knelt quickly beside Odo's fallen form to use his medical tricorder to check the constable's condition. He looked up at Sisko as Atrig relieved him of the device. "Just stunned."

"You had no need to do that," Sisko told Terrell.

But all the Cardassian said was, "You'd be surprised, Captain. Whenever Odo permits himself to be captured, I can't help but be suspicious."

Terrell spoke as if she knew Odo. That meant to Sisko that it was possible that she had been on DS9 before. Perhaps during the Cardassian Occupation of Bajor. He realized it was also possible that he was looking at yet another piece of the puzzle that involved his people and his station.

Sisko caught the eyes of the rest of his staff and shook his head, to instruct them not to try what Odo had done. He was aware of the frustration that tormented all of them—Jadzia, Bashir, Nog, Jake, and especially Kira. But even Quark would realize it was suicide to risk a frontal assault on three phasers.

Terrell approached Sisko. "We've been listening to

everything you've discussed in here," she said. "All this talk about Orbs. Do they exist, don't they exist? Are they a fraud? A forgery? Apocryphal? You've been so caught up in the search for the real story about the Orbs that you've completely neglected the greater truth."

Sisko watched her closely, waiting for her to show the slightest inattention to her weapon. If he could get it, then the odds would be closer to even.

"What greater truth?" he asked. He didn't care what she gave as an answer. He only wanted to keep her talking, to increase the odds she'd be distracted. Having Jake here under these conditions was just as harrowing as when Kasidy had been with him on the *Defiant.* One way or another, these threats to his family had to end.

"Captain Sisko . . . *Emissary,*" Terrell said mockingly. "You're familiar with the Orbs the Bajorans call the Tears of the Prophets. Tell me, where do those Blue Orbs come from?"

Sisko stared at her, measuring her, judging her. He would not play her game.

"That's right," she said, as if content to conduct both sides of the conversation herself. "The Celestial Temple. *Jalkaree.* The wormhole." Her narrow, gray face twisted into an unpleasant smile. "So, where do you think the *Red* Orbs come from?

"Correct again," Terrell said, without even waiting for Sisko to respond. "See how easy this is? They come from *another* wormhole. You see, Captain, it turns out you weren't the first to discover the wormhole in the Bajoran system. Or, rather, should I say, you weren't the first to discover the *first* wormhole. Because there are *two* of them. Care to make a comment now?"

Sisko shot a glance at Jadzia, but the scientist shook her head, her expression of disbelief confirming what he already knew. "That's impossible," he said.

"There can't be two," Jadzia added. "The entire Bajoran sector's been subjected to one of the most intensive subspace structural analyses the Federation has ever undertaken. I helped design the project. There *is* no second wormhole."

The Cardassian sneered at Jadzia, "I don't suppose that thorough analysis of yours included the effects of the three Orbs of Jalbador? No? I didn't think so."

"You're lying," Kira cried. "There is only one Celestial Temple and the Prophets are those who dwell within it!"

Without even glancing at her target, the Cardassian swept out her arm and smashed her phaser across Kira's face, knocking the Bajoran officer down beside Odo's still form. Blood trickled from the ridges of Kira's nose.

Sisko lunged forward, ignoring his own order, only to be stopped by a phaser burst at his feet and the realization that Atrig's next shot would hit Jake.

Bashir helped Kira to her feet as Terrell said coldly. "Spare me the superstitious prattle, Bajoran. Do you think yours is the first planet of simpletons who have been toyed with by a more advanced species? Your Prophets are exploitive aliens and they've treated your world like their own personal chess board for twenty millennia. You people are nothing but their pawns. You've all been bred for ignorance and servility and—for all you know—pure entertainment."

"That is *enough!*" Sisko shouted. His voice was oddly flat in the dead air of the simulated holographic village, but it was loud enough to make his point.

Terrell's phaser swung back to cover him. "Of course it's enough. This dismal creature doesn't have the mental capacity to understand the truth. But you, Captain, and your Federation . . . you understand. You've always known about the corruption poised to consume the souls of those races that dare to think of themselves as gods. Why else would you have your Prime Directive except to spare yourselves that fate?"

Sisko shuddered as Terrell favored him with a look of approval. "That's one of the few things we Cardassians admire about your kind, you know. The Prime Directive. It shows that at some point you were like us—an ethical race. Your downfall, though, is that you lack the moral strength to distinguish between true sentient beings—like the Vulcans—and simple stock like the Bajorans, who have been so debased by their Prophets that—"

Kira pushed Bashir aside, launched herself at Terrell, arms outstretched, her hands her only weapons.

She almost reached the startled Cardassian. But Dr. Betan caught her in time, spun her around, and shoved her forward, where Atrig stunned her with his phaser.

Kira collapsed instantly, her body sprawling awkwardly across the holographic rocks.

"The rest of you. Get down on your knees," Dr. Betan ordered crisply. "With your hands on your heads."

No one in Sisko's party moved, their eyes all on Kira. The stun had been a heavy one.

Dr. Betan pointed his phaser at Bashir's head, close enough that even a stun would be fatal. "We only need one of you to answer our questions. No loss to us if the rest have to die."

At that moment, Kira stirred and faintly moaned.

Thanking the Prophets, Sisko took action. He had to learn what questions the Cardassians needed answered. If there was anything he knew that they didn't, then in some small way he would have power over them.

Knowing his people had to be his first priority, Sisko knelt on the stones then, beneath the night sky and the brilliance of a full Bajor. And he placed his hands on his head.

The others immediately followed the example of their commander.

"Ask your questions," Sisko said to Terrell.

She looked pleased at his compliance. "You and I are alike, you know. You've seen the Blue Orbs. You've contacted the wormhole aliens. In my way, I've shared those experiences."

"If you really had," Sisko said, "you would find it impossible to behave as you do."

Terrell cocked her head. "You surprise me, Captain. You know that's not true. You've devoted many of the scientific assets of this station to the study of the Blue Orbs. Each month I read an intercept of the latest installment of the never-ending report this Trill scientist of yours is compiling. And I want you to know, I understand. The Orbs are the artifacts of an advanced civilization. You're compelled to study them, just as we were when we discovered them on Bajor. But then again, we found more than just the Blue Orbs. We also found a red one. And do you know one of the things that distinguishes a Red Orb from a Blue? Other than the color, of course."

Sisko remained silent as before. The more she talked the more chance he had to learn what he knew that they didn't.

"Verteron traces," she said proudly. "That's what gives the Red Orb its color—a subspace-particle collision that traps chromic oxide atoms in a solidified energy vortex."

The sound of her voice rattling on while Major Kira lay untended not a meter away, made Sisko's head ache. How soon would it be before Worf would wonder why the meeting in the holosuite was taking so long?

"Not actually *solidified* energy, of course," Terrell said with a chuckle, "but one with a relativistic rate of temporal decay a billion times slower than the local inertial frame of reference. Am I boring you, Captain?"

"You'll never be able to leave this station," Sisko said challengingly. The safety of his people depended upon his keeping her off-balance, distracted until Worf could make his move.

Terrell's harsh, barking laugh was scornful. "My people *built* this station. We know more about it than you ever will."

The Cardassian waved her phaser at Quark, who ducked forward, lowering his head to his knees, his eyes tightly shut, expecting the worst. When it didn't come, he opened them one at a time to find Terrell regarding him with amusement. "Those smugglers' tunnels that you use for all your petty crimes, how do you think they came to be built, Ferengi? Because the designers of Terok Nor made an error? Or at the command of the Obsidian Order?"

Quark whimpered at the dreaded name and closed his eyes again.

"There is no Obsidian Order anymore," Sisko said.

Terrell shrugged, as if she were beginning to lose

interest in their conversation. "They had outlived their usefulness. But rest assured a dozen other groups are now battling to see who will emerge as the Order's replacement on the Detapa Council."

Sisko strove to regain her attention. "Do you honestly think the Dominion will allow *any* group to attain the power of the Obsidian Order?"

Provoked, as he had hoped, Terrell threw the question back at him. "Do you think Cardassian patriots will allow their home to be enslaved by the Founders forever?" She shook her head in contempt. "In one guise or another, Captain, the Order *will* be reborn. Just as Cardassia will throw off her oppressors. And the key to this great new victory is the second wormhole in the Bajoran system."

"But what you're saying is impossible!" Sisko said quickly. Inwardly, he sighed with relief as the Cardassian picked up the challenge and began talking rapidly, intensely.

"Captain, *I* studied the Red Orb. Right here. On this station. That single Red Orb had verteron traces different from those of the Blue Orbs. We were able to tell from those traces that it had been exposed to multiple bursts of negative energy—exactly the energy signature created by the sudden intrusion of a wormhole into normal space-time. A form of hyperdimensional Cerenkov radiation, if you will. But where the Blue Orbs contained very slight verteron tracks—almost impossible to measure—the Red Orb had multiple tracks. And that meant that though it was possible the Blue Orbs might have passed through a wormhole once—whatever the Orbs were, wherever they had come from—there was no doubt the red one had been close to an opening wormhole *many* times.

"You can see why that Orb captured the interest of everyone in the rarefied assemblage of the Order's science directorate. Somehow, that Red Orb could be the key to actually *creating* a wormhole."

Sisko's eyes widened with her next words. He tried not to look at Jake and Nog, praying that they would not speak or draw the Cardassian's attention to them.

"I set up my lab right here on Terok Nor," Terrell said. "In that hidden section of corridor you found. But it wasn't hidden from *you.* It was hidden from Gul Dukat, who never had a clue as to what I was doing here. And it was in that lab, with that Red Orb connected to a . . . well, let's just say, the right equipment, that I was able to release just enough of the solidified energy trapped within it. What I am saying, Captain Sisko, is that *I* was the first to create a wormhole precursor field—a thinning of the surface tension of space-time such that only a small push would be required to break through into a nonlinear realm. The realm of—"

Sisko's arms dropped to his side. He regarded Terrell with amazement. "Are you saying you made contact with the Prophets?"

"The *aliens!*" Terrell snapped. She gestured with her phaser and Sisko placed his hands on his head again. "Wormhole aliens. Not face to face, but oh, they were in there. And they contacted us before we could contact them. Some of us could hear their thoughts. Almost all of us could see the images they created for us, enticing us into their realm as they opened doorways to whatever place it was we each most wanted to go. Disturbing, wouldn't you say? An alien race reaching into our minds, knowing our deepest desires like that?"

"Sounds like something only the gods would know," Sisko said softly.

Terrell's response was harsh and blunt. "It's also something that could be known by telepaths. Telepathic *aliens* with a perverted desire to make less-advanced beings worship them."

The Cardassian looked away from him, up to the holographic image of Bajor in the simulated night sky. "But even knowing what we were dealing with, there were those on my research team who heard the aliens' voices and . . . obeyed them, stepping through the precursor membrane."

Terrell closed her eyes for an instant. Sisko saw Atrig and Dr. Betan look at her with concern. "Most never came back."

Sisko seized the opportunity to make eye contact with Bashir and Nog, who gave him imperceptible nods of agreement. Even though they were on their knees, they were ready to move the instant he judged the Cardassians' weapons would not be a threat. Sisko wished there were some way he could signal Jake to run for cover ahead of time.

"And then, when we were so close—" Terrell was now so caught up in completing her story that she had begun to pace back and forth. The gaze of her two associates followed her as she continued to speak, "—when *I* was so close to finally controlling the Red Orb's energy, the order came to *withdraw* from Bajor. Who knows the reason? I think it was because the patience of the Cardassian people had reached an end. Here we had spent decades and the lives of so many good soldiers and trillions of bars of latinum to help restore some semblance of order to this ungrateful world, and still its pathetic natives resisted us. What was the point of continuing? If the Bajorans wanted to remain the playthings of the alien telepaths they called the Prophets, then at some point we had to say, 'Enough.' We can't save everyone. We couldn't save them from themselves. Anymore than we can save you from yourselves."

Sisko shifted his knees against the rough stones, getting ready, still forced to listen to the Cardassian's self-serving, offensive recollection without objection.

"I knew I couldn't leave my lab behind for the Bajorans to discover," Terrell mused thoughtfully. "As challenged as they are, some of them have a certain natural, Pakled-like aptitude for machinery. They would never have understood the subtle complexities of subspace manipulation, but they might have been able to duplicate my equipment and quite by accident stumble upon a method for completing it. For that reason, the Obsidian Order gave the command to have the station self-destruct once all Cardassian personnel had been evacuated."

Sisko couldn't help the retort that rose to his lips. "So the station's continued existence is yet another example of the Order's effectiveness."

Terrell paused for a moment in her pacing, idly rubbed her thumb against the force selector switch on her phaser. Sisko heard the series of faint clicks that indicated the selector was dialling through its possible settings, like the spinning of a dabo wheel. "Captain, you're an intelligent being. The ability to open an artificial, stable wormhole between *any* two points in the galaxy, perhaps in the universe, would be the ultimate defense against aggression. Cardassian fleets could take off from Cardassia Prime and in minutes be in the atmosphere of any enemy's homeworld, having completely bypassed all that world's defenses."

Though he did not comment on what Terrell was saying, Sisko was perfectly aware of what wormhole technology offered the galaxy—or, in the eyes of some within Starfleet, how it threatened the galaxy.

"In a day," Terrell said calmly, "the Dominion would cease to exist. In a week, the Alpha and Beta Quadrants would begin an era of peace unsurpassed in galactic history."

Terrell now crouched down beside him. Sisko suppressed the urge to draw back from her in distaste. "You see, I know what drives humans to join Starfleet. I even know what you are, Captain. You're an explorer, a dreamer, someone who *needs* to propel his species beyond all limits of knowledge. In other words, you are just like *me* . . . like any other Cardassian."

"Don't count on it," Sisko said grimly. Surely Worf had had enough time to make his realization. He could feel the eyes of his own staff on him, expectant.

Terrell gave his shoulder an indulgent pat, and then stood up again. "You'll see. When the Dominion has been crushed. When the *Pax Cardassia* embraces all our worlds. When a bold new age of peaceful exploration and development of the galaxy has begun. I've no doubt you'll be there. On the bridge of a Cardassian science vessel or one of your own, it doesn't matter. Because we will all be joined in a common cause—"

"Never."

But Terrell was no longer listening to him. She was looking up once again at the simulated Bajor. "Computer, download current program to memory channel Alpha Prime. Authorization, Terrell, level 9, Green."

When the computer responded, Sisko was surprised

to hear not the voice of Quark's holosuite management unit but the station's own synthetic voice.

Terrell smiled at his reaction. "The Andorians weren't the only ones to augment your station's computers with their own codes," she said. "Terok Nor will remain nonoperational until I have completed my mission."

"What *is* your mission?!" Sisko demanded. There was no time left for subtlety.

And, as if she felt the same way, Terrell finally told him. "The one thing that held back my work," she said, "was the fact that I only had one Red Orb. After all, Bajoran legends say that the doorway to Jalbador shall be opened only when all three are brought together. But in sixty years, the entire might of Cardassia could only locate one of those three. Until Quark so helpfully announced that he had a map to sell."

"This is not my fault!" Quark said vehemently.

"Calm down, Ferengi. You'll be a hero to my people if to no one else."

"So what?" Quark grumbled. "That and a slip of latinum aren't even *worth* a slip of latinum."

"So," Terrell continued for Sisko's benefit, "with the chance to find a second Red Orb—which could possibly provide the means to recover the Orb lost on the Day of Withdrawal—it was time for me to return to my old home.

"And that is my mission, Captain Sisko. To obtain the three Red Orbs. To wrest from them the secret of creating a translocatable wormhole. And then, finally, to destroy the aliens within it so its full power will be in the hands of the greatest force for galactic peace ever imagined."

Sisko heard the station's computer voice again. "Program-transfer completed."

"End program," Terrell said, and the crude reconstruction of the Jeraddon lunar village began to dissolve.

The familiar hardness of the holosuite's smooth deck replaced the rough stones previously beneath Sisko's knees. The lighting brightened. In the green glow from the standby holoprojectors, the three Cardassians resembled supernatural beings emerging from some alien pit.

But all Sisko was conscious of was that at last he knew what Terrell's weakness was. "You lost an Orb," he said, making his statement an accusation.

"I prefer to think of it as . . . misplaced," she said, her attention alarmingly now focused on Jake. "But the fact that your internal reports are full of references to the 'lost Cardassian holosuite' leads me to believe that the Red Orb is nearby, its residual power still with enough of a contact to my old lab to maintain the precursor condition."

Terrell poked Jake's shoulder with her phaser. "You weren't in a holosuite, young human. You were looking at visions of what you wanted most, created by the wormhole aliens to lure you into their realm." She looked back to Sisko, whose heart was pounding at the Cardassian's closeness to his son. "And if the Red Orb had still been connected to my equipment, your son might have stepped through the boundary layer into that realm and been lost forever."

And as quickly, as unexpectedly as that, it all came together for Sisko. Everything Terrell had said and, more importantly, what she had not said. He took a deep breath. "I know the questions you need answered," he said. He nodded at the other prisoners. "Let them go."

"And you'll tell me everything I want to know?"

"Yes," Sisko said. It was not a lie, and it was not capitulation. The truth was, he *could* answer her questions now, but she would not be able to use what he told her.

"Very well," Terrell said. She aimed her phaser at Jake. "But you will tell me everything I want to know *before* I let everyone go. Or I will kill them all, starting with this one."

It took all of Sisko's self-control not to respond automatically. He told himself her threat was hollow. After all, she could have killed everyone but him the moment she and Atrig and Dr. Betan made their presence known. But she didn't. *Could it be she actually does see herself as a force for peace?* he asked himself. *In her twisted mind, is there really some ethical compunction not to kill?*

He made his decision. "You don't want to kill them, Terrell. You told me yourself. You're a scientist, an explorer. All you really want is information. And I *will* give it to you. Once I know my son and the rest of my people are safe."

His eyes met hers without flinching.

"Terrell," Dr. Betan warned. "You can't trust him."

Terrell didn't turn away from Sisko's steady gaze. She motioned him to rise to his feet. "I believe I can. Computer: Run Odo Ital, One."

At once, the holosuite became a duplicate of the station's security office. Sisko looked around carefully, noting that it was not an exact duplicate. Some of the wall displays were different. And the Promenade beyond the transparent door panels was drab, washed out by dim blue light. Then he realized where he was, and when.

"Odo's office from the time of the Occupation," he said.

"Fitting, don't you think?" Terrell said. She gestured to Atrig and Dr. Betan to move the rest of their prisoners into the simulated holding cells.

Sisko heard Quark's indignant protest, "This is not one of my programs."

"The systems of Terok Nor are integrated in ways you can't imagine," Terrell said to Sisko in explanation.

"The Obsidian Order?" Sisko said, rather than asked.

"Precisely, Captain. As you know, to observe everyone all the time requires immense computational ability. Even these holosuites are connected to the station's main computers, though not by links any of your engineers would ever suspect."

The last prisoner to be locked up was Odo. By now, the constable had regained consciousness, though he was still groggy. Atrig and Dr. Betan pushed him into the last cell, then activated the force field.

Now, only Sisko and the three Cardassians were free.

Sisko stood outside the force field sealing the holding cells. He looked at Jake.

"Satisfied?" Terrell asked.

"How long will this simulation run?" Sisko asked.

"Thirteen hours. More than enough time for me to go where I need to go next, and for you to tell me what I need to know."

Sisko stiffened. She was changing the rules on him

again. "Why don't I tell you what you need to know, and then you go wherever it is you have to go."

Terrell shook her head. "I'm willing to trust you, Captain. But only to a point."

She lifted her wrist communicator. "This is Terrell. Four to beam out. Energize."

And then, before Sisko could protest or even say a last word to Jake, he was lifted out of Deep Space 9, on his way to wherever it was that Terrell needed him to go.

CHAPTER 23

THE MOON OF Jeraddo was a seething crimson orb of gas wreathed in violent, thousand-kilometer filaments of blazing-blue lightning.

Three years ago, the moon's molten core had been tapped to produce power for Bajor, the world it orbited, an ingenious concept first developed by the Klingons. Decades ago, that initial concept's design flaws had caused the spectacular destruction of the Empire's main generation facility on the moon of Praxis. The flaws had since been corrected by assiduous Federation engineers focusing a low-level subspace inversion field on the moon's core. As a result, the normal convection of heat generated by the decay of natural radioactives had been accelerated a thousandfold.

In less than a year, the end result of the convection would have been to turn the entire moon into molten rock. But a clever feedback loop allowed the excess heat of the moon's core to be shunted into subspace and collected by orbiting conversion platforms. There, the enormous energy imbalance was transformed. Extremely high-frequency subspace waves were changed to more-easily-controlled midrange frequencies, which could be safely transmitted to Bajor's power grid.

The engineers who maintained the system likened it to setting off an antimatter bomb in a flimsy wooden box, and then only allowing the energy to escape through a very small hole in one side. The slightest miscalculation could result in the sudden release of *all* the energy at once, vaporizing the box—or, in this case, Jeraddo and whatever hemisphere of Bajor it was over at the time. But as long as everything performed according to specs, Jeraddo would be providing power to Bajor for the next thousand years.

And the only cost for that benefit was that what had once been an inhabited class-M moon, was now a class-Y demon world on which an unprotected visitor would live for less time than it took to draw a breath. Whether death would come from the toxic corrosive crimson clouds, the sudden atmospheric pressure waves of 1200-degrees-Celsius heat, or the wildly fluctuating gravity fields that were a byproduct of the subspace inversion at the moon's core no one could predict. Nor did anyone particularly care. All possibilities were equally unpleasant and equally fatal.

The ship that now took up a nonstandard orbit around the hellish moon appeared to be an ordinary Sagittarian cruiser, its gleaming yellow hull making electric contrast with Jeraddo's red clouds.

The cruiser was as long as the *Defiant* but no more

than half its width. For redundancy—not efficiency—its back third was ringed by four half-size warp nacelles. Its middle third was covered almost completely with pressure hatches for twenty-four escape modules—one for every five passengers and crew, though each had seating and supplies for ten. And the front third was thick with ablative shielding on its forward surfaces. Any impact with an unexpected body would first be absorbed by the hull, then by the "crush zone" provided by the forward cargo storage holds. All was designed to protect the all-important passenger cabins amidships.

In short, it was a typical conservative, civilian ship, designed for safety above all else.

Which is why it looked so out of place this close to Jeraddo, a world where even establishing a standard orbit risked the survival of a ship.

Inside the cruiser, though, Sisko had a better sense of the vessel's survivability. Though it looked Sagittarian on the outside, it was pure Cardassian within.

"A *Chimera*-class vessel" Terrell had called it. She and Sisko both knew that in times of war, a neutral vessel could be a much safer means of transportation. Especially when it was liberally outfitted with hidden weapons and capable of outrunning almost any other ship in the sector.

"You actually plan to beam down there?" Sisko asked as he watched a false-color image of the moon's hidden surface scroll across the main bridge viewer of Terrell's cruiser. Though the thick clouds of the moon prevented any direct visual observation of its surface, the cruiser's sensors had no difficulty picking up ground detail.

"We've found the abandoned village," Terrell said. She was in the command chair—an imposing black structure that had the silhouette of a looming bat. Atrig was her navigator, seated at a forward console. Sisko didn't know where Dr. Betan was. "And from the details on that map, we can narrow down the Orb's location to perhaps a square kilometer of surface area, and search."

"I'm curious," Sisko said.

"I should hope so," Terrell replied.

"How did you manage to misplace an Orb on the station and have it turn up on this moon?"

Terrell stood up from her chair. Typical of Cardassian design, the chair was mounted on a meter-high platform so that the commander would always be above the crew. "It's not the same Orb, Captain. It's the second. When I find it, then I can return to Terok Nor and find the first."

"And then what?"

"And then, with Vash's Orb I will have all three, and I will not need equipment to open a wormhole. According to the ancient texts we've deciphered, I merely have to bring the three Orbs together . . . anywhere I choose." She stepped down from her command platform and walked forward to Atrig's navigation console to check the readings on his display. "We're coming up on the village now."

On the viewer, Sisko detected a grouping of primitive, blocky structures slide into view, arranged just as he recalled seeing on Dal Nortron's map. Though the crisp layout of the village seemed to be obscured, somehow.

"Is that debris?" he asked.

Terrell made more adjustments on the console and

the sensor image of the village expanded on the screen and became more detailed.

"Some of the buildings appear to have collapsed," Terrell observed. "But with the winds and the gravity fluctuations, that's to be expected."

A door slipped open, and Dr. Betan walked slowly onto the bridge. He was wearing a bulky Cardassian environmental suit, shiny green-black in color, made up of curved segments to look even more like a beetle's carapace than any other Cardassian uniform Sisko had seen.

In his gloved hands, Dr. Betan carried the red hourglass-shaped crystal which Vash had brought to DS9. Sisko was startled to see that it wasn't as impenetrably dark as it had first appeared to be.

"See that?" Terrell said. "That glow inside?" She looked at Sisko. "It means it's getting closer to its missing mate."

"You seem to have everything under control," Sisko said.

"Not quite," Terrell said curtly. "You still have to answer my questions."

Sisko had known that was coming. "You won't like the answers."

"I think I will. Because if you're thinking of disappointing me, remember that Terok Nor is still running under manual-control conditions, and it will be several hours before anyone goes looking for your missing staff and your son. They are right where I left them—which makes them easy for me to find."

"All right. You want to know how to negotiate with the wormhole aliens," Sisko said.

Terrell nodded. "I know the science of wormholes. But the aliens are an X-factor. You've dealt with them and returned. My people never did. What's your secret?"

Dr. Betan pressed a small control on a side bulkhead and a panel beside a small transporter platform slid open to reveal four environmental suits in storage racks. Terrell gestured to them. "We don't have much time."

Sisko went to the suit Dr. Betan pointed out. It seemed to be the right size.

"There is no secret," he said. "The Prophets—the *aliens*—are in complete control the entire time. They initiate contact. They control the length of contact. And then they terminate contact." He stepped into the trouser section of the suit, and then watched as the imbedded pressure rings expanded to extend the legs to the proper length.

Terrell's voice was tense. "Then under what conditions could you see them refusing to let a traveler leave their wormhole?"

Sisko held up his arms so Dr. Betan could slide the chest piece over his head.

"Terrell, you told me I was too caught up in thinking about the Orbs. What if you're too caught up in thinking about the wormhole as simply another dimension?"

Terrell was more used to the suits than was Sisko. She was already dressed, needing only to attach her helmet. "Explain."

"The Bajorans believe their wormhole, the Blue Wormhole, is the home of their gods. In a sense, it's their heaven. But if you've truly discovered a second wormhole . . ."

"Don't even suggest it," Terrell threatened. "Heaven and hell, as you call them—supernatural realms of eternal reward and eternal punishment—are not worthy of scientific discussion or consideration." She strode over to Sisko and lifted a helmet from the rack behind him. "Life is everywhere in our universe, Captain. In the most unlikely ecological niche, on almost every world, we find something that qualifies as living matter. Why can't you accept that different dimensional realms also harbor life, without having to invoke superstition?"

"Just a suggestion," Sisko said. "The Prophets or aliens or whatever you'd like to call them can be unnerving, I'll admit. And I don't usually have any idea what it is they want when they contact me. But they've never kept me in their realm against my will. Why they, or beings like them, didn't allow your people to return, I can't say."

"Keep thinking," Terrell said tersely as she snapped Sisko's helmet closed and sealed it. The helmet was a hemisphere of something transparent that curved from a shell-like shoulder unit. At once, all sound was muffled except for the rasp of Terrell and Dr. Betan breathing over the suit's comm link, and Terrell's voice. "I'm sure you'll come up with something more useful in the next hour."

"Why an hour?"

"Because that's just about how long these suits will stand up to the corrosive atmosphere down there." She stepped up on the transporter platform at the side of the bridge. Sisko saw Dr. Betan do the same and followed.

Here we go, Sisko thought.

"Atrig," Terrell said tensely. "Energize."

And then Sisko dissolved into light, and reformed in absolute darkness.

CHAPTER 24

QUARK DIDN'T KNOW what made him feel worse. The fact that Captain Sisko had been kidnapped by crazed Cardassians who might soon have the means to conquer the galaxy, or the fact that his holosuites were wired into the station's main computers and apparently had far more computational capability than he had ever dreamed of, let alone charged for, in the past ten years.

He lightly moved his finger toward the open area at the front of his holding cell and marveled again at the sudden shock of the simulated security forcefield. "Amazing," he said.

"Oh, be quiet," Odo grumbled.

The changeling was sitting on the edge of the bunk at the back of the cell, holding his head.

"Well, I see you're back to being your old self," Quark said.

"Quark, I'm warning you . . ."

"No need. No need. In fact, I'm going to be especially nice to you while we're in here."

Quark loved the way Odo looked up at him then. The constable was so easy to bait.

"And why would that be?" Odo asked, sounding as if he already regretted saying anything at all.

"Because we're finally in a position where everyone will have to listen to me, and you can't walk out, or threaten to haul me off to your office."

"You're babbling, Quark."

Quark went back to the cell opening and called out to the others. "Excuse me! Can I have everyone's attention, please?"

The cell across from Quark's held Bashir, Kira, and Jadzia. Jake and Nog were in the cell to the right. They all stepped forward to the limits of their own security forcefields to look at Quark.

"We're listening," Bashir said. The doctor sounded exhausted. Or frustrated. Or hungry. With *hew-mons,* Quark knew, it was difficult to tell.

"Well, I just wanted to remind everyone what Odo said about what happened to him on the Day of Withdrawal."

Quark heard Odo get to his feet and come up behind him.

"Let it go, Quark. I got stunned by a looter. I missed the whole day."

But Quark shook his finger at his nemesis. "Uh, uh, uh. Not so fast. When Dr. Bashir asked if you were sure, you launched into a most convincing story about how one of the things you missed was Gul Dukat scurrying off like a vole deserting a ship seized by bailiffs."

Odo glared at him, but said nothing. Quark knew it was because there was nothing he *could* say. Not now.

Quark finished the conversation by calling out to the others. "But even I remember when Gul Dukat left, because it was early in the day, *before* the fighting broke out. So if Odo remembers coming down to the Promenade to break up a fight, then he *has* to remember Dukat's leaving, so one way or another, he's hiding something—which means he's *lying* to us!"

"Happy now?" Odo asked.

"I'll be happy when you admit you can't remember what happened to you on the Day of Withdrawal."

"Then you'll never be happy again," Odo said, and walked back to the bunk and sat down with a grunt.

"Quark!" Jadzia called out to him. "This might not be the time to revisit the past. We should try and find a way to shut down this simulation."

Quark put his hands on his hips, thoroughly miffed. "Oh, I get it. I get caught in a small white lie like, I thought you *wanted* me to keep the change, or, I logged the payment into your account yesterday—it must be the computer, and what happens? Everyone points their fingers at me like . . . like suddenly my pants are on fire. Typical Ferengi, you say. Isn't that just like Quark, you say.

"But catch Odo, our constable, our shining exemplar of truth, justice, and the Federation way, in a lie of supernova proportions, and what do you say?" Quark raised his voice in a not very convincing parody of Jadzia. "This isn't the time to revisit the past." He turned his back on everyone. "Well, I'm sick of it."

His ears tingled as he heard Jadzia sigh. Then she called out, "Anyway, Quark, you must have some kind of override on your holosuites. Can't you try shutting it down?"

Quark raised his hands to the simulated ceiling. "Don't you people get it? This isn't one of my holoprograms. *My* prisons have chains on the wall, metal rings on the floor, a complete selection of whips and restraints for every taste, and your choice of beverage. I have no idea where this came from."

"Could you at least *try?"* Jadzia asked.

Quark huffed with impatience. "Computer, end program. There, are you happy?"

"Try an override, please."

"Computer, this is Quark. I need an emergency shutdown in holosuite A."

"Please state your password," the computer voice replied.

Quark froze. How could he reveal his password to . . . *everyone?*

Odo seemed to be able to read his mind. "Quark, you can change your password later. We need to get out now."

Quark cleared his throat. "Computer . . . this is Quark. Password . . . and I don't want to hear any snickering," he suddenly warned his audience. "Password . . . Big Lobes."

Quark rolled his eyes as Nog covered his mouth and seemed to go into either a gagging or a coughing fit, Quark really didn't care to think which.

"Big Lobes authenticated," the computer confirmed. "Emergency shutdown procedure is not available."

"What?! Why not?" Quark demanded.

"Priority override is in effect during state of emergency. This simulation will run for an additional two hours, thirty-three minutes, or until terminated by Prefect Terrell."

Quark shrugged, totally defeated. His lot in life. "Well, that's that. The station's computer is controlling mine."

"But it can't be in *complete* control," Nog said with sudden inspiration. "For this simulation to exist, the station's computer *has* to be using subroutines from your computer."

"So?" Quark said.

"So," Nog answered as he stepped to the back of the holding cell he shared with Jake, "maybe one of those subroutines is the safety override, which means these forcefields might be just for show."

Quark wasn't impressed with his nephew's idea. "And how do you expect to find out if—"

"Nog!" The shout came from Jake as the young Ferengi charged forward to test his theory and—

—hit a full-power forcefield that threw him back against the far wall of the cell with twice the force with which he had launched himself.

Quark saw his nephew slide unconscious to the deck with a soft moan as his headskirt slid up the back of his head until it flopped forward to cover his face like a baby's sleeping bonnet.

Quark sighed. "That's Starfleet initiative for you."

He looked out past the Security Office to the doors to the Promenade. As gloomy as it was out there, in the abnormal blue Cardassian lighting Quark remembered so well and hated so much from the old days on the station, he could see simulated people walking back and forth. Bajoran slave workers and Cardassian soldiers, mostly. It was a very realistic effect, but it was still only window dressing. "If this simulation is so accurate, I wish we could get one of those pedestrians out there to come in," Quark sighed.

Odo snorted. "If it's an accurate simulation from the Occupation, no one will. This wasn't the favorite place on the station for Bajorans *or* Cardassians."

"Or Ferengi," Quark said.

And then the main doors slid open and someone entered.

"Anyone home?" a familiar voice shouted.

Quark stared in amazement, along with everyone else in the holding cells, as a human in a tuxedo four hundred years out of style strolled into the cell area, smiling with blinding white teeth.

"Vic!" Quark burbled.

"Hey, gang," the holographic mid-twentieth-century lounge singer said as he gazed around the room. "Looks like you cats could use a cake with a file baked in it."

"I don't know what you're talking about, but I don't care," Quark said. "Ya gotta get us outta here!"

"I know, I know," Vic said calmly. "You're innocent, right?"

"We're more than innocent," Odo said. "We've been put here by the real criminals who are now running loose."

"Oh, I believe it, Constable. A straight arrow like you'd never end up in a joint like this." Vic looked over to see Kira and smiled at her. "Unless it was on accounta some dame. How ya doin', sweetheart? Stretch still treating you right?"

"Vic," Kira said, "how can you be here?"

Vic shrugged. "Ya got me, dollface. There I am, up on stage at my joint, singing my heart out for the blue-rinse set, next thing I know the lights start flickering and the power goes out. Well, management's not too upset, 'cause they've got lots of battery lights to keep the gaming tables going, but me, I got no mike. And the ice is starting to melt."

"Vic," Odo said, "I'm sure this is all fascinating, but could you go back to the center office, and open the little drawer to the left of the chair, right under the display screen."

"Is that going to help get the power back on?"

It was suddenly all too much for Quark. "How can you care about power when your program wasn't even running? When we came up here, all the holosuites were off except for this one."

"Quark, bubeleh, I keep hearing you people say the holosuite's off, how can I keep hanging around? But I gotta tell ya, Vic's is the original we-never-close baby. Now how that works, I don't have clue one. I'm just a hologram remember, and it sounds like you have issues you need to take up with the big guy upstairs."

"The big guy upstairs?" Quark asked.

"Felix," Vic explained. "My programmer."

"Vic," Odo pleaded. "The drawer."

"You got it, pallie. What exactly am I looking for?"

"An optolithic data rod," Odo said.

Vic held up his hands. "Whoa, slow down, Stretch. I'm strictly a twentieth-century hologram."

"It's going to look like a pencil," Jadzia suddenly said. "A fat, transparent, green pencil. Like it's made out of . . . oh, what was it . . . *plexiglass!*"

"That new space-age plastic. Sure, I'm with ya." Vic stretched out his arms to make his white cuffs show against his black jacket. "Little drawer, ya said? On the left?"

"If you would be so kind," Odo said.

"Always willing to do a favor for the customers."

Vic walked out of the holding-cell area. Quark heard him whistle one of his twentieth-century songs. Something about "that old black magic . . ."

"How can this be possible?" Kira asked wonderingly.

"Vic's stepped into other holographic simulations before," Bashir explained. "If his program's being affected by all the computer disruption that's going on, it seems to make sense that he might go looking for a cause."

"The important thing is," Jadiza added, "that however he got here, he's going to get us out."

"Don't be too sure about that," Vic said. He was standing back in the doorway, holding the optolithic crystal in his hand. "I mean, this is something cats like me can only dream of." He paused, smiled at everyone until Quark almost screamed with frustration to have him get to the point. "A real captive audience," Vic said. "Badda bing!"

"Put the fat green pencil in the slot by the door frame," Odo said.

"*Captive* audience?" Vic asked. "Anybody? I know you're out there. I can hear ya breathing."

"Vic," Jadzia said. "If we don't get out of here as quickly as possible, there's a chance that the station's entire power grid could fail and—"

"I get the picture, Spots. The Big Lights Out." Vic went to the security operations control panel beside the door, held up the data rod. "Here?"

"That's it," Odo said. "Slide it in, then punch in this number."

Vic slid the rod into the memory reader, then scratched his head as he stared at the Cardassian control pad. "Punch it in where?"

Jadzia came to the rescue again. "What's the number, Odo?"

"Fifty-five, twenty-two, eight. Alpha," Odo said.

Quark repeated it to himself, then noticed Odo frowning at him.

"It's an *old* passcode. Big Lobes."

Then Jadzia carefully described the Cardassian symbols Vic would have to touch to input those numbers. "It's all Greek to me, doll," Vic said as he entered the final Alpha designator.

But at once the security forcefields flickered and Jadzia and Kira and Bashir jumped out of their cells to join Vic, while Jake carefully carried the still-unconscious Nog. Quark hung back to let Odo walk through their cell opening first. Once he knew it was safe, he quickly followed. By then Odo had left the others and hurried into the center office.

Vic rubbed his hands together. "So, whaddaya say you all come back to my place—drinks are on the house."

"We can't just yet," Jadzia said. "We still have to shut down this simulation."

Vic looked alarmed. "Hold your horses. You can't shut anything down while I'm in here."

"Can't?" Jadzia asked. "Or shouldn't?"

"Ya got me, Spots. I just said the first thing Felix put in my head. You people going to be okay, now?"

Odo appeared in the doorway holding a Cardassian phaser. "We will be soon."

"What kinda crazy pea-shooter is that?" Vic asked.

Odo adjusted the power setting on the weapon. "A Cardassian Model III phase-disruption weapon."

"Well, I'm glad you cleared that up," Vic said.

"Stand back everyone," Odo said, then aimed the weapon at the far wall.

"What good is a simulated weapon going to do?" Kira asked.

"You don't spend enough time in the holosuites," Odo said. "Small props like these are usually replicated, not simulated. This should be a fully operational phaser, and as Nog was good enough to demonstrate, all safety protocols are switched off."

Quark groaned. "There goes my insurance. . . ."

"You might want to avert your eyes," Odo warned. Then he fired.

At first, it appeared as if the lance of energy shot out eight meters to hit a wall. But then, that half of the holding cell area began to waver, and finally winked out, as it now appeared that the phaser beam had hit a wall only half that distance away.

Quark grimaced as three clusters of green holoemitters exploded and the entire simulation of the security office disappeared.

"Someone's going to pay for that," he complained.

"Oh, be quiet, Quark."

Quark couldn't be sure who had said that, because almost everyone did. Then Quark saw Vic. It was not a pleasant sight.

The hologram was wavering, sparking with holographic scan lines, and going transparent.

"Y'know, gang, all of a sudden, I'm not feeling so hot."

Bashir went to Vic as if his medical skills might have some use for a hologram. "Maybe you should head back to the club, Vic."

"You're not just whistlin' Dixie."

"Uh," Bashir said, "is that a Yes?"

Vic nodded. "And I thought Rocket to the Moon at Disneyland was an E-ticket. . . ."

Quark looked at Odo who looked at Jake who looked at Kira who looked at Jadzia who looked at Bashir . . . but it was unanimous. Nobody knew what Vic was talking about.

Vic shuffled toward a wall of functional holoemitters and Quark was surprised to see a gray metal door materialize, with a red sign reading EXIT just above it. "See ya in the funny papers," Vic said, then opened the door and stepped through it. At once, his holographic body stopped shifting and he stood upright. From beyond him, Quark could hear laughter, the clinking of coins, and the sound of a twentieth-century band.

Vic spun around and pointed a finger at Quark. "Next time, pallie, pay the man the light bill." Then he gave them all a casual salute, the door swung shut, and he was gone.

"I have *got* to talk to Felix," Bashir said.

"That can wait," Jadzia told him.

It was Jake who explained why to Quark. "Now we rescue my dad."

CHAPTER 25

SISKO WAS IN HELL. It was the only way to describe what Jeraddo had become.

The ground was nothing more than stone and shifting ribbons of storm-driven dirt. The air was like something alive, one moment so thick that all Sisko could see was his own reflection in the curve of his helmet, then thin enough that the lights mounted on his shoulders stabbed ahead a few meters. He cringed as roiling crimson swirls and eddies of corrosive gas appeared like entrails, twisting all around him.

Sweat poured from Sisko's face and dripped from his beard. He tried to tell himself that the environmental suit had been set for Cardassian temperatures, but the temperature indicator on the narrow status display board at the bottom of his helmet showed an outside temperature of more than 800 degrees, with wild swings of several hundred more degrees every few minutes. He utterly failed to convince himself that the suit's insulation was as robust as the type Starfleet used.

"Stop, Captain!" Terrell's harsh voice crackled at him through his helmet speakers. The same subspace distortions that caused Jeraddo's gravity to intensify and weaken, as if Sisko were on the deck of a madly pitching sailing ship, also interfered with the suit's communicator. In the twenty minutes they had already spent on the surface, Sisko had calculated that the communicators wouldn't work past ten meters, and even then he and the Cardassians had to shout to make themselves heard over the static. He doubted Terrell's tricorder could extend past that range, as well. And the only way they could be beamed back to Terrell's disguised ship was because of the high-power, tight-beam transporter beacons they each wore.

But even if he managed to run off and get out of range before Terrell could fire at him, what good would it do him? Right now, his suit had forty minutes' worth of life in it. If he pulled off his beacon so he couldn't be traced, he still wouldn't be able to beam back to Terrell's ship. In less than an hour he'd become another featureless mound of Jeraddo debris.

Terrell and Dr. Betan stepped up on either side of Sisko, their own shoulder lights blinding as they converged on him.

Terrell pointed to the left. "In that building," she said.

Dr. Betan held up the Red Orb and swung it slowly toward the ancient stone wall to which Terrell pointed. The pale red light within the Orb intensified slightly, then died down when Dr. Betan moved it away again.

Sisko trudged ahead. By now, he didn't need to be

told that he must always lead the way. Terrell had made it clear that she was not willing to turn her back on him. The building, perhaps a craft hall or a farmers' market a millennium ago, was larger than most in the village. The wind-eroded outer wall was made of giant blocks of local stone fitted together only with exceptional skill, not mortar.

The doorway through the wall was still in perfect condition, and Sisko did not have to duck down as he stepped through it, though he half-bent at the waist to aim his shoulder lights on what lay before him.

As he had suspected, the ground was littered with stones and tiles from the collapsed roof. There might have been wooden beams involved in the building's construction, but anything organic had been eaten away by the corrosive atmosphere years ago.

"Watch your step!" he shouted to the two behind him. "The floor is covered with roofing tiles." Then he stepped aside to let Terrell and Betan enter.

Though billows of red cloud still roiled through the building, the windblown dust and debris seemed lessened by the shelter of the walls. Sisko noticed that his shoulder lights reached a bit farther, and the buffeting of the gale-force winds that had threatened to topple him from time to time was no longer in evidence.

Terrell and Dr. Betan were discussing something. They had a comm-link channel separate from the one Terrell used with Sisko.

The glow of the Red Orb was much stronger now.

Sisko watched as Terrell used a tricorder, aiming it at the ground and showing the results to Dr. Betan.

"There's a chamber under this floor," she informed Sisko. "Dr. Betan's going to find a way down." Then Sisko and Terrell stood and waited while Dr. Betan walked carefully back and forth across the rubble-strewn floor, using the Red Orb as if it were some primitive dowsing tool. Sisko appreciated the chance to rest.

He looked over at the tall Cardassian, studying her through the flare of light reflecting from her helmet. Her dark eyes were wide. She was chewing on her bottom lip. But he didn't know if the gesture betrayed anticipation or nervousness. He wasn't at all sure that he could even come close to what was going through her mind, no matter how much she thought that he and she were alike.

"You don't need me down here," he shouted with some difficulty. His throat was becoming more and more raw. But he wanted to learn if she had any intention of allowing him back to her ship. If she didn't, then that might make it easier to . . . make sure no one else made it back, either.

"I will," Terrell shouted back. "Dr. Betan will keep Vash's Orb, but I need you to carry the second."

"Why?"

"Because you've survived contact with Orbs before. You of all people must understand the danger these artifacts represent."

"The Orbs of the Prophets have never put me in danger," Sisko shouted. The exertion provoked a brief coughing jag. For a moment, he wondered if his suit might already be leaking

Terrell peered at Sisko through her helmet. Its transparent surface was already clouded from the corrosive atmosphere. "The Red Orb claimed seven of my researchers. I won't risk touching them."

"What about Dr. Betan?"

"He handled the first Orb years ago on Terok Nor.

After that, he became addicted to neural depressants. By taking them, he can't hear the voices. But it has left him with . . . certain other deficiencies. His temper, among them."

"Have any of you thought that perhaps these Orbs aren't shaping up to be the best transportation system?" Sisko asked. "Especially if they're driving the people who use them insane or to drugs."

"There're ways around the Orb's psychic effects," Terrell said enigmatically. "That's why I had my soldiers save Quark from hanging on the Day of Withdrawal. That Ferengi owes me his life."

Sisko didn't understand. Terrell gave him the explanation.

"Because he's a Ferengi. They're resistant to most forms of telepathy. Even Betazoids can't get past those four brain lobes. Too complex? Too simple? Who knows? Who cares? But I needed to get my Orb out of my lab before the station self-destructed. So I told Atrig to bring me one of the Ferengi from the Promenade, and he brought me Quark—and Odo."

Quark and Odo on the Day of Withdrawal, Sisko thought. He saw another pattern forming.

"What about Garak?" he asked.

"Very good, Captain. Garak came on his own. He and I never really got along but Gul Dukat and he were involved in something . . . it's not important." Terrell frowned, as if remembering something unpleasant. "But he and Odo and Quark did enter my lab that day—along with the two soldiers whose bodies you found fused to the hull. I always wondered what happened to them." She fell silent, as if lost in thought.

Sisko touched her arm. "What happened to Quark and Odo and Garak?"

Terrell roused herself, checking ahead for Dr. Betan, who was still wandering back and forth with the Orb, then turned again to Sisko. "Twenty-two minutes before the self-destruct went off, the three of them staggered out of my lab. The precursor effect had already faded, and when I looked inside, the Red Orb was gone. At first, I was certain Quark had stolen it and hidden it somewhere. But then, why would he have come back to me? There wasn't any time for an investigation so I stunned them again and left the station. I thought everything would be lost when it autodestructed."

"But it didn't."

Even through her clouded helmet, Sisko could see Terrell's terrifying smile as she bared her teeth at him. "And if you knew how much time the Obsidian Order spent investigating why the autodestruct system failed . . . the record number of executions. . . . Even for the Order."

"Starfleet could never understand why you left the station behind."

"Well, now you know," Terrell rasped. "We never intended to."

Then Terrell turned sharply away from him, and Sisko realized she must have received a transmission from Dr. Betan, who was about fifteen meters ahead of them, pointing down at the ground and—

Sisko blinked as he saw Dr. Betan fire a phaser blast into the ground. Then he heard Terrell again.

"He's found a way down. The Orb's not far."

Terrell began trudging toward Dr. Betan. Sisko walked beside her. He checked his suit display. Thirty-two minutes of life remaining. If the Cardassian suit design could be trusted.

Halfway to Dr. Betan, Sisko caught sight of the liquid wave of rock that rose up behind the Cardassian, then swept forward, heading directly for him.

Instinctively he cried out, "GRAVITY WAVE!" then spun around to see Terrell beside him, screaming silently in her helmet to warn her associate.

Sisko dropped to his knees and wrapped both arms tight across his helmet. A moment later he felt as if he were falling, as the local gravity gradient dropped by at least ninety percent and then shot up by an almost instant tripling.

He was driven into the rubble so hard he felt stones push up into his flesh through all the insulating layers of his suit. Sisko lay unmoving on his back, instinctively holding his breath as he listened for the telltale hiss of atmosphere that would mean his death. But finally, all he heard was Terrell's harsh voice telling him to get up and hurry.

Apparently, Dr. Betan had also survived the sudden gravitational anomaly, but the hole the Cardassian had blasted into the stone floor of the building was now half-filled with rubble. Under one arm, Dr. Betan still held the Red Orb Vash had brought to the station. It glowed steadily now. The red light within seeming almost to pulsate.

"Down there," Terrell ordered as she aimed her shoulder lights into the pit Dr. Batan had created.

Sisko moved cautiously to the side of the opening, then peered down, awkward in his stiff suit. There was another stone floor about four meters below. Dr. Betan had already thrown a rope down to assist Sisko's descent. The other end was attached to an anchor loop on his belt, and Terrell stood beside him, coiling the rest of the rope in her gloved hands.

"Dr. Betan says that according to the way the Orb is glowing, the other Orb is no more than five meters in that direction." She pointed, and Sisko found a reference mark on the floor below. He took the rope in his clumsy Cardassian gloves and slowly edged himself off the side and into the hole.

Sisko dropped the first two meters at an alarmingly rapid rate before Terrell and Dr. Betan steadied him. A few seconds later, he was standing on the floor and looking around at—

Sisko gasped.

Across from him, in the direction in which the second Orb was supposed to be found, was a pristine wall carved with the largest Bajoran mural he had ever seen.

"What's wrong?" Terrell's voice crackled in his helmet.

"Nothing," Sisko shouted back. "If the Orb's down here, it might be hidden in a wall. I'll check it out."

Then he walked slowly over to the mural and lightly traced its exquisite details with his gloved fingers. He recognized some of the older word-forms that ran along the top and bottom of the mural and felt an odd combination of relief and disappointment when he could not find any reference to "the Sisko." But still, whatever events were depicted in the carving, they involved the Bajoran wormhole and the Prophets. Those word-forms and symbols he was able to read easily.

"Twenty-five minutes," Terrell's voice announced.

Sisko couldn't let this opportunity go to waste. He fumbled with the Cardassian tricorder built into his suit and programmed it for a full spectral scan of the mural. At the same time, he stepped back to see if he could find any place that an Orb might be . . .

There. In the mural. The distinctive Bajoran spiral that signified the opening of the Celestial Temple. Though this spiral curved the opposite way from most others Sisko had seen.

"I think I might have found something," Sisko called out. "Just a minute."

He moved closer to the stone block in which the spiral was carved. It didn't fit tightly to the other stones in the wall. He pressed his body against it.

The stone block swung up, little more than a slender slab of rock.

And behind it, in a hollow chamber no larger than an Orb Ark, a second Red Orb glowed brightly, throwing off small flares of red light, almost like the Blue Orbs Sisko had seen in the past.

"I've found it," Sisko reported to Terrell.

Her only answer was, "Nineteen minutes."

Carefully, Sisko removed the Orb from its protective shelter. As he did so, he felt no ill effects. Heard no voices. Sensed no sudden disorientation, the way he usually did at the start of an Orb experience. Whatever this thing was, it was not an Orb of the Prophets. At least, there was nothing in its behavior to suggest it was one.

Sisko carried the Orb back to the point at which he was below the opening Dr. Betan had made. He paused, half-expecting to hear Terrell tell him to tie the Orb to the rope for them pull it up, to be left here to spend the rest of his life—all eighteen minutes of it—to contemplate their betrayal.

Instead, Terrell told him to tie the rope to his belt, so they could pull both him and the Orb up.

Sisko did, keeping a tight grip on the Orb.

By the time he had emerged from the hole in the

floor, both Orbs were blazing brightly enough that they couldn't be looked at directly. The brilliance of their internal light also made it clear how badly his own helmet had been scarred and etched by Jeraddo's atmosphere.

Terrell's helmet glowed as if lit from within by flames. Sisko couldn't see her face. "Excellent," he heard her say before she called out for Atrig. "Lock onto our beacons and energize."

In that split second, as he waited for the transporter effect, Sisko suddenly knew that Terrell couldn't be allowed to control the Red Orbs.

Almost without thought, he swung the Orb he had retrieved directly at Dr. Betan's helmet.

As the Cardassian doctor stumbled backward, horrified, dropping Vash's Orb to press his gloves to the rapidly growing network of cracks that spread across his corroded helmet, Sisko yanked his own transporter beacon off and threw it away.

Terrell was still fumbling for her phaser as she began to dissolve in the transporter beam.

Dr. Betan's helmet suddenly exploded like fine crystal an instant before he was beamed away as well. And then, a moment later, Sisko saw the pale glimmer of his own discarded transporter beacon as it also disappeared.

Sisko didn't stop to ask himself what he thought he had done. Instead, with only fifteen minutes of life remaining, he concentrated only on what he still had to do.

He tucked Vash's Orb under one arm, secured the second Orb under his other arm, then began to run.

He knew he had only fifteen minutes in which to hide the Red Orbs so they could never be found again. Not by Terrell, not by anyone.

Within seconds, Sisko was through a breach in the wall and onto a narrow path between two collapsed buildings. The Orbs, so close together now, were throwing off almost the same amount of light as his shoulder lights. But visibility was still less than a handful of meters. By now, he knew, with the subspace distortion Terrell's ship would never be able to scan for him.

In fact, Sisko realized, if he were Terrell, he wouldn't come chasing after him at once. Instead, he'd wait the fifteen minutes for his target to die and use the time to put on a new environmental suit, knowing that when his target's suit finally succumbed to the atmosphere, the Orbs would not be going anywhere.

Reasoning that he would not be pursued at once, Sisko paused to get his bearings, recalling that there was another large building to his left. One with a single standing wall. If he could place the two Orbs near that wall and somehow topple the wall onto them, with any luck he'd shatter one or both Orbs, or at least make certain they were buried under tonnes of rubble.

Terrell's cruiser couldn't remain in orbit of Jeraddo for too long. All Sisko had to do was introduce a delay.

This last mission would become his life's work. All twelve minutes of it.

Sisko hurried through the ground-level twisting, crimson clouds, the red of the atmosphere swirling around him merging with the red nimbus of the glowing Orbs he carried.

Finally, he located the wall, and made out the shape of a relatively flat paving stone on which he could place the Orbs. All that he needed now was some way to dislodge the wall, get it started falling in the right direction.

He decided to check out the far side. He couldn't afford to waste the time it would take to make his way around it. So he risked tearing his suit as he half-clambered over a pile of rubble at its side and—

—wedged his boot.

Sisko groaned.

He was trapped two meters above ground level, visible from any direction, with no place to hide the Orbs.

To die for a cause was something every member of Starfleet had to prepare for. It was part of their oath.

But to die for nothing?

Sisko trembled with frustration as he tugged at his boot. He picked up another rock and bashed the offending boot with it. But all he managed to do was wedge it in deeper.

"Warning," his suit's computer suddenly announced. "Loss of atmospheric integrity in three minutes."

"No!" Sisko roared. "You're wrong. I have ten minutes at least!"

But there was no arguing with his internal displays. The insulation field was within five minutes of failing. His backup air supply was completely exhausted, its tanks probably already dissolved by the acid air.

He wondered how far he could get if he took off his boot and decompressed. Maybe he could last thirty seconds. But would he even be able to move with his exposed foot contacting 800-degree rocks?

"No," Sisko whispered. And then there was nothing for him to do but to lift up the rock in his hand and smash it against the Red Orbs of Jalbador.

Again and again he brought the rock down.

His suit informed him that only two minutes remained before loss of atmospheric integrity.

Again he smashed the Orbs.

But the simple matter of normal space-time was no match for the solidified energy vortices of a nonlinear realm.

The Orbs withstood his attack. Untouched.

"One minute . . ." his suit announced.

Sisko absolutely refused to give up without achieving his last mission. He lifted one Orb over his head and with all his strength brought it down on the other Orb.

The light they both shed did not change in the least.

Sisko girded himself to try again. *Maybe I didn't do it hard enough,* he told himself. *Maybe it will work the next time.*

Again he lifted the Orb above his head, swung it down.

Again, nothing.

"Thirty seconds . . ."

The next time . . . it has to work the next time . . .

Once more he lifted. He swung. He lifted. He swung.

"Five seconds . . ."

With a cry of hope, rage, determination, he lifted that Red Orb as high as he could possibly stretch and—

—he couldn't swing it down.

His arms were locked in position. Something was holding them.

He twisted around in the bulky Cardassian suit to see a white shape glowing in the brilliance of his shoulder lights.

A luminous being.

Sisko gazed up at that form, at that being, and in that moment, without knowing what he saw or how it could be that he saw anything on this hellish world on which he was destined to die within an instant, he knew the Orbs were safe.

The luminous being moved closer to him, leaned down, details of its existence impossible to see through the clouded corroded surface of his helmet.

The luminous being put its arm around Sisko's shoulders, tapped itself once, then all was still.

And an endless eternity later, an endless moment later, a new light played over him as he stood locked in the embrace of the luminous being, in the depths of this inferno.

In the light of a transporter beam, Sisko could finally see through his helmet and the helmet of the angel who had come to save him.

Everything would be all right now.

It was Jake.

CHAPTER 26

"EMISSARY," KIRA SAID, "are you absolutely sure this is what you want to do?"

Sisko stood on the Promenade, outside the entrance to the Bajoran Temple. In each hand he carried a simple cloth bag. And in each bag was a Red Orb of Jalbador.

Less than twenty-six hours after his dramatic rescue on Jeraddo, Deep Space 9 was nearly back to normal, if not yet fully recovered. There was still a slight slant to the deck, but O'Brien had been released from the Infirmary and was now leading the gravity-repair teams himself.

While most automated computer systems were still off-line, Jadzia, with an unexpected assist from Garak, had finally located the long-hidden Cardassian override programs Terrell had activated, and was replacing all the individual isolinear rods on which they had been encoded. Nog was fully recovered from his run-in with the holographic forcefield and was in Ops with Jadiza and Garak, helping them with their restoration efforts.

Of Terrell's fate no one knew. There was no record of a Sagittarian cruiser breaking orbit of Jeraddo. The Bajoran Lunar Power Commission had searched its records and had found sensor traces of the ship's arrival. But preliminary evidence seemed to indicate a gravity disturbance might have pulled it into a deadly descent.

Sisko had told Quark, Odo, and Garak what Terrell had told him about what had happened to them on the Day of Withdrawal. Garak and Odo flatly refused to believe her account. But Quark had started talking to Jake about collaborating on a novel based on the incident—*Marauder Mo and the Treasure of Jalbador* Quark wanted to call it. Jake had already warned Quark there might be some copyright problems with his main character.

The *Defiant* was safely in dock again, after fielding the massive search party that had led to his discovery at the very last moment. Sisko had since learned that more than forty Starfleet personnel had taken part in the intensive search of the abandoned village.

Moreover, Sisko reflected thankfully, in the time since the *Defiant*'s return, Commander Arla Rees hadn't engaged him in a single discussion about Bajoran religion. Nor had she taken him up on his dinner invitation to meet Kasidy Yates. And Prylar Obanak and his followers appeared to have disappeared just as thoroughly as Terrell had managed to vanish over the clouds of Jeraddo. Though no doubt the group of monks had gone back to ground on Bajor.

"I'm sure," Sisko now said to Kira, satisfied that he was doing the right thing. "It's time to end it."

"We still don't know who killed Dal Nortron."

"Or who hid the Orb on Jeraddo," Sisko agreed. He lifted the bags. "But with these in safe hands, we'll have time to sort it all out at our leisure. The important thing is, the Orbs won't be in Cardassian hands."

"I'd still feel better if Vash were off the station."

"And Satr and Leen. And Base. But Odo's dealing with them. When it comes down to it, those four scoundrels are just petty thieves, led astray by what these Orbs represent."

Kira suddenly looked serious. "What *do* they represent?"

Sisko smiled at her. "Let's leave that to the experts." He entered the Temple, once again marveling at how each time he stepped through the doorway, it felt like the first time.

Kai Winn was there to greet him, and she bowed her head much too graciously. "Welcome, Emissary. It is always a pleasure to receive your summons and put aside all that I am doing to come and see you here. I find the long ride from Bajor to be an especially productive time for meditation and prayer."

Every once in a while, Sisko was sorely tempted to just tell the Kai to stow it, but he let her play out her little game.

"And you, my child," Kai Winn said ingratiatingly to Kira, "how fulfilled you must be to stand at the Emissary's side during these important events, watching all that he does."

"Very fulfilled," Kira replied, not a trace of conviction within her voice.

"And these are the artifacts?" the Kai asked, looking at the bags.

Sisko carefully pulled the Orbs from their wrappings and placed them on a small table. The steady glow they had developed on Jeraddo had now become a gentle pulsing, slowly dimming, slowly brightening, three times each minute.

"Oh, my," the Kai said, "they are clever, aren't they? I could see how many people might think they are somehow related to the Orbs of the Prophets."

"I beg your pardon?" Sisko said. "These are the Red Orbs of Jalbador."

The Kai smiled beatifically at Sisko. "Oh, Emissary, I know you are new to our ancient traditions. Indeed, sometimes I wonder if anyone not born on Bajor could ever come to grasp the rich complexities of our beliefs. But I am not here to discuss the wisdom of the Prophets. Still, these . . . Red Orbs of Jalbador, they are but a legend from a troubled time in our past." She shook her head. "And since they do not exist, I do not believe that I, as a humble servant of the people of Bajor, can accept them. It might lend an unwanted credence to their existence, and to other unfortunate legends best left in children's storybooks."

Kira was outraged. "Kai Winn, you knew why we asked you up here. These are the Orbs. Look at the way they're glowing."

"Child, though my ways are simple and I am certainly not as worldly as some who look to me for guidance, I am no stranger to the wonders of our age. I have seen many things glow, from phaser beams to a child's glitterball. I am sure that as much as you and the Emissary might want to believe in the tales of Jalbador, a few days of study would reveal the secret of these objects to be nothing more than some novel chemical reaction."

"Then perform that study," Sisko said. "In fact, I hope you do. Nothing could make me feel better than to know that these are some ingenious forgery."

"Emissary, again I think you overestimate my abilities. Which is not to say I am not flattered by your high esteem. But really, I believe it is here, on Deep Space 9, in a temple of secular science as it were, that the objects should be studied."

Sisko took a breath to calm himself. "Kai Winn, I am asking for your help."

The Kai was barely able to look at Sisko, as if she were embarrassed beyond words. "Emissary, you do me an honor for which I know I am not worthy. But in this matter, I truly have no help to give." She glanced disapprovingly at Kira. "May we speak in private?"

"Major Kira has my full confidence and trust."

The Kai's false smile became exceptionally brittle. "Very well. I only wish to point out that many people look up to the Emissary as a role model, a person who sets an example which can help them find their own paths to the Prophets. And, with all humility, Emissary, to express your belief in the legends of Jalbador, and in these so-called Orbs, well, that is not an example right-thinking Bajoran people would want their children to follow."

"I would think," Kira said angrily, "that the best role model for Bajoran children would be one who encouraged the search for truth."

The Kai blessed Kira with another blindingly insincere smile. "Why, yes, my child, that is what you'd think."

"Kai Winn," Sisko said before Kira could escalate

the confrontation, "I'll make this simple. Take these Orbs to Bajor and subject them to examination, or I will find some other religious leader who will. And if these prove to have *any* connection to the Prophets, I promise I will make the Bajoran people know that you tried to stand in the Prophets' way."

That was the end of any pretence on the part of the Kai. She drew herself up, the perpetual smile gone. "Your acceptance of those objects as the Orbs of Jalbador marks your first step on the path to heresy. Do you understand? Do you think you can remain Emissary with half the population of Bajor believing you've become a religious fanatic?"

But Sisko knew this was an argument he couldn't lose. "You forget, Kai, I wasn't *elected* Emissary. For whatever reason, the Prophets *chose* me. And as their Emissary, I'm saying you don't have a choice. Take the Orbs."

The Kai's chin lifted in defiance. "Very well, if you are so certain these are the legendary Orbs, prove it. Find the third."

"It took sixty years to find these two. I have better things to do."

"But it cannot be difficult, Emissary. Look how they're pulsating with the fabled light of Jalbador."

Sisko wasn't sure what she meant and he could see that she knew it.

The Kai's cruel smile was predatory. "You mean you claim these are the Red Orbs—without knowing the whole legend?"

"Enlighten me," Sisko said.

The Kai clapped her hands together in delight, almost laughing at him. "Two Orbs *glow* when coming close to each other. But three Orbs *pulse*. It has been years since I read the legends, Emissary, but I would say that from the behavior of these . . . Orbs, the third one is quite nearby."

Sisko looked at Kira. "The one Terrell lost."

Kira couldn't resist adding, "You mean, the one Terrell thought Quark had stolen."

Sisko looked back at Kai Winn. "So if we find the third Orb, you will take them back to Bajor for study?"

The Kai's ingratiating smile returned in full force. "Oh, that will hardly be necessary, because you will be able to prove they are real right away. You see, when the three Red Orbs are brought together, the doors to Jalbador open freely, and then . . . well, it is all in the legends, Emissary."

"And then *what,* Kai?"

"Why then . . . the world comes to an end." This time the Kai really did laugh at him. "So you can see where a great deal of study would not be necessary. Either the objects are frauds, or they are real. And if they are real, Emissary, you will have the singular pleasure of knowing you have brought on the apocalypse." She sighed with pleasure. "Now you know why the stories of the Red Orbs are so popular with children and the unenlightened. They are quite . . . lurid, wouldn't you say?"

"I'm sure you'd know better than we would," Kira said. She gave Sisko a conspiratorial wink. "What do you say? Shall we go on a wild Orb hunt?"

"You're not worried about the end of the world?" Sisko asked with a smile, accepting the Bajoran major's challenge.

Kira looked directly at the Kai. "Somehow, I don't think the Prophets would spend twenty thousand years trying to teach us about the universe and our place in it, and at the same time leave a big 'off' switch lying around."

Sisko picked up a Red Orb in each hand. "Kai Winn, we'll be back."

"Of course you will be, Emissary. Because there are no such things as the Red Orbs of Jalbador."

A few moments later, Sisko was standing on the slanted deck of the Promenade, slowly moving the Orbs back and forth.

"That direction," Kira said, pointing spinward toward Quark's. "The pulsing seemed to speed up a bit."

"Why, Major, I think you're enjoying this."

"What I'm going to really enjoy is helping the Kai carry three of these things onto her shuttle."

Then it was Sisko's turn to laugh as he walked up the center of the Promenade, swinging the Orbs to the left and to the right.

And he didn't need Kira to tell him that the pulsing increased the closer they got to Quark's

Kira looked at Sisko. "Do you think he really did steal the third one?"

"Only one way to find out," Sisko said lightly, and he carried the Red Orbs of Jalbador into Quark's, where they proceeded to pulse faster than Sisko's suddenly racing heart.

CHAPTER 27

"OH, NO," QUARK SAID. "Not so fast! I don't want any of that in here!"

But he was too late, because Captain Sisko walked straight up to the bar counter and put both Red Orbs side by side on it.

"Captain, please, those things are more trouble than they could ever be worth. Things are—" Quark gave a strangled cry as he saw one of the most terrifying sights he had ever seen in his life!

Morn was running out of his establishment of business!

"Morn! Wait! Come . . . oh, for . . . now look what you did!" Quark threw his dish towel down on the bar, in disgust. "My holosuites are broken. My replicators are off-line. This stupid gravity imbalance is making people dizzy without the need to consume any drinks, no one wants to play dabo because the wheel won't spin straight, and now you chase off my best customer. If you've got a phaser on you, you might as well just shoot me now."

"Glad to see you, too, Quark," Kira said.

Sisko pointed to the Orbs. Quark had a hard time even looking at them because they were flashing like emergency strobe lights on Port Authority inspection shuttles. And that just unleashed too many bad memories.

"We have reason to believe the third missing Orb is in your bar and we want to take a look," Sisko said.

"I don't think so," Quark told him. "Unless we'd like to discuss compensation for what Odo did to my holosuite."

"Maybe we'd like to discuss an increase in rent instead?" Sisko suggested.

"For what?!"

"For what your inviting so many smugglers onboard is going to cost us." Sisko looked up at the ceiling. "Let's see now, we could begin with the bill for Odo's investigation. Then there's the replacement of the damaged hull plates."

"Oh, no—you can't blame that one on me."

"Oh, yes he can," Kira said.

"Oh, yes I will," Sisko added.

"This is blackmail!" Quark protested.

"Then we're in complete agreement," Sisko said. "You give us what we want—a few minutes to search the bar. And we'll give you what you want—peace and quiet."

"And no rent increase."

Sisko picked up the flashing Orbs again. "May I?"

"Oh, go ahead," Quark said. "And I hope if you find it, a Prophet jumps out and bites you."

Then Quark did the only thing he could do in the circumstances. He put an elbow on the bar, rested his head in his hand, and watched his customers leave in droves.

At any other time in his life, Quark might have found what Sisko and Kira were doing amusing. The *hew-mon* and the Bajoran were walking back and forth through the bar as if Odo had asked them to walk a white line.

But what wasn't amusing was that even Quark could see that every time Sisko passed through the center of the main level, the Orbs flashed faster and faster.

In less than ten minutes, all of his regular customers were gone. Instead, the bar was packed with Starfleet types. Dull, boring, root-beer-swilling slugs who wouldn't know a good time if M'Pella invited them up to her room for a nightcap. And they were all on duty, too.

Then, just to make matters worse—and lately, someone or something was always making matters worse—his idiot brother Rom chose this moment to walk in. With a construction team.

"Is it too much to ask what's going on?" Quark called out to anyone who might care to pay any attention to him.

Sisko came back to Quark. He pointed to the backlit glass mural on the wall facing the bar counter. "How long has that been there?"

"You mean the . . . uh, Admiral?" Quark asked, looking at the colorful artwork that was the centerpiece of his bar.

"Admiral?"

"Gul Dukat put it up. He said it was Admiral Alkene of the Tholian Assembly. Go figure."

Sisko studied the admittedly abstract portrait with a frown. "So it was here on the Day of Withdrawal?"

"You're not going to do something stupid, are you?" Quark asked nervously.

"I hope not," Sisko said.

Quark was getting the definite impression that the captain was deliberately tormenting him. Well, it took two to play that kind of game and, he wasn't one of them.

He closed the till, locked the order padds, then left the bar to join the Starfleet types at the base of the mural. The Orbs were now on the deck in front of it, flashing madly. Chief O'Brien and Rom were kneeling to either side, waving tricorders around like they knew what they were doing. Jadzia stood behind them, looking exceptionally lovely as always, Quark thought.

"Is there a problem?" he asked plaintively.

"I don't know," Sisko said. "According to the way these two Orbs are reacting, the third Orb is behind that mural. But according to the tricorders, it's just glass, plasma lights, and a cheap metal frame."

"It wasn't cheap, believe you me."

O'Brien got to his feet and joined Sisko and Quark. "If I didn't know better, I'd say there was a miniature sensor mask in there, just like the one Satr and Leen used in the water plant."

That was too much for Quark. "Why would anyone put a sensor mask inside a mural of a Tholian. . . ." He couldn't finish the statement. All he could think of was how much he hated the mural. How he had sworn he would tear it down the moment Gul Dukat left the station. And how, six years later, he still hadn't brought himself to do anything about it.

Almost as if he *couldn't* do anything about it.

"Something wrong, Quark?" Jadzia asked.

Quark shook his head. Wasn't there something Terrell had told him . . . not recently, but before . . . ?

"I'm so confused," Quark said. "I think I need to sit—"

A near-ultrasonic Ferengi scream pierced the bar.

Quark recognized it, and shoved aside Sisko and O'Brien to peer around the back of the mural to see—

Rom, on his knees, staring into a small open access panel at the back of the mural, his face bathed in a rapidly flashing red light.

"I . . . found it!" Rom squealed. "I . . . found the third Orb!"

Suddenly, Odo was behind Quark, arms folded, his attitude letting Quark know he was ready to make an arrest.

"Anything you'd like to tell me, Quark?"

"Odo, I didn't know it was there. I swear I didn't know!"

"According to Dr. Bashir, next you're going to try to sell me the Brooklyn Bridge."

But then Sisko was at Quark's side. "That's all right, Constable. I don't think he did know the Orb was there."

Odo snorted, disbelieving. "How could he not?"

"For the same reason," Sisko said, "you *and* Garak don't remember what happened to *you* on the Day of Withdrawal. Both your memories were tampered with. And so were Quark's. And before you ask why, I'll tell you right now I can't give you an answer. All I know is that it has something to do with Terrell and these Orbs."

"Hmphh," Odo said.

Quark stood closer to his new best friend, the great Captain Sisko.

"Well?" Kira asked, puzzling Quark but apparently not Sisko.

"Put the three orbs together?" Sisko suggested.

"Maybe that's not a good idea," Kira said.

"You think they might actually cause the end of the world?"

"What?!" Quark exploded.

"Calm down, Quark," Sisko chided him. "It's part of the legend of Jalbador that when the three Orbs are brought together, the Temple doors open and the world ends."

"I don't want the world to end in my bar," Quark said. "Talk about being bad for business."

"Probably not a good idea to get them *too* close together," O'Brien said. Quark could see the chief's attention was fixed on his tricorder. "I'm picking up a lot of neutrino flux. Almost as if some type of feedback loop is starting. That might explain the source of the light those things are producing. I don't think the world's going to come to an end, but we could get a blast of radiation that might do some harm."

"All right," Sisko said, holding up a hand that silenced Quark. "You call it, Chief. Five meters apart? Two meters?"

O'Brien made an adjustment on his tricorder, then showed it to Jadzia. "What would you say, Commander? Four meters should be safe?"

"Sure," Jadzia said. "And if you're going to send these back with the Kai, I'd recommend sending at least one on a separate shuttle. Just so an accident doesn't force them together."

Sisko smiled at Kira. "The *Kai,*" he said. "Major,

why don't you go back to the Temple and invite Kai Winn to visit Quark's."

Kira grinned fiercely. "With pleasure." Then she marched out into the Promenade.

"The Kai," Quark muttered. "In my bar. Might as well close early."

He watched anxiously as Sisko lifted the newly discovered Red Orb and carried it to the bar, keeping it well away from the other two still on the deck in front of the mural.

While everyone else packed away their tools and prepared to leave, Quark walked around behind the mural again. He looked inside the access panel.

"Uh . . . I never knew about that tunnel, brother."

Rom's sudden, without-warning appearance was enough to make Quark bang his head against the top of the opening.

"Neither did I," Quark said under his breath.

"But, it's a . . . good one to know about now," Rom said happily.

"Why not?" Quark said. "Everyone else knows about it now, too."

"Oh . . . yeah. I forgot."

Quark walked back to the front of the mural. He couldn't believe there was another maintenance tunnel coming into his bar that he didn't know about. Especially one that would have been so convenient for . . . he shook his head. For a moment, he thought he *did* remember the tunnel after all. But if he did, then why hadn't he been using it? And why hadn't *he* discovered the third Orb?

He was standing behind the bar when Sisko brought the second Orb up to the counter.

In a gesture of good will he knew would come back

to haunt him, Quark started pouring mugs of root beer and passing them out to everyone for free. For Jadzia, he even hand-mixed a *raktajino.*

Then all three Orbs were on the bar, one at each end and one dead center, all of them flashing so rapidly that they almost appeared to glow with steady lights.

"I . . . think they're pretty," Rom said, beside him.

"I think I'd like them out of my bar."

"You know, brother, you . . . really should learn to take time to appreciate the wonders all around us every day."

"That's easy for you to say. You're married to Leeta."

"I'm serious." Rom pointed to the Orb in the middle of the countertop. "Just look at how . . . gloriously the light comes alive in that."

"Are you feeling all right?" Quark asked. Whenever Rom's babbling began to veer toward poetry, Quark worried about his sibling.

"You're not paying attention, brother. Look more closely." Rom started to push Quark forward, toward the Orb.

"Careful there, Rom," O'Brien warned. "Don't want to knock one of those things over."

Quark pushed himself away from his brother. "See the trouble you almost caused. These aren't play-things." Quark turned to the Red Orb directly in front of him. "They're . . ." He stopped as he tried to see what was inside the Orb.

There definitely was something inside. He knew because there had been the last time he had . . . "Oh, this is feeling too strange," he whispered.

"Brother?" Rom said.

Quark peered deep within the Orb. Yes. He could

see it now. The city in the swamp. The glowing light approaching through the trees. The . . .

Quark popped open his eyes in Ferengi alarm.

"You're not moogie!"

He struck at the hideous monster before him, only at the last moment dimly realizing it was a reflection within a reflection within the sparkling red facets of the Orb.

"QUARK, NO!"

It could have been Captain Sisko who shouted. Or Jadzia or Chief O'Brien.

It might even have been Terrell or Odo or Garak, because they had all been there that day, in one way or another.

But by then it was too late, and Quark held the Orb in his hand and felt himself swung around through the air, as if he were dangling from a length of ODN cable stretching down from an antigrav high above the Promenade and then, when he let go and fell to the deck and looked up . . .

He had no idea what he was seeing.

Besides the Orbs, of course.

The three of them were floating in midair, just a meter or so above the deck, spinning and glowing, each just like an Orb of the Prophets, except their lights were crimson red, flame red, blood red.

The Orbs seemed to have moved themselves to the points of an equilateral triangle, and now twisting tendrils of light snaked out from each Orb to link up with the others. Defining the triangle's edges. Creating a . . . glow. A darkness. A distortion of some strange type. Exactly in the middle of their formation.

Quark felt Rom drag him to his feet.

He saw O'Brien try to touch one of the Orbs and be flung back in a flash of red lightning.

He saw Jadzia standing close to the floating Orbs, aiming a tricorder at them, a sudden strong breeze tugging at tendrils of her hair, which fluttered past her face as if flying right into the center of the Orbs.

"Do you feel that, brother?" Rom asked.

Quark braced himself against the deck. Somehow, it felt as if the deck were sinking in the center of his bar, drawing everything toward it.

The breeze was getting stronger. Now the flow of air blew *into* the bar, swirling napkins and debris into the center of the Orbs' pattern.

And that debris wasn't being blown back out.

"We've got intensive neutrino flux!" Jadzia called out over the intensifying wind. "A definite wormhole precursor!"

"Here?!" Sisko shouted.

Quark saw someone in a Starfleet uniform fire a phaser at one of the Orbs, but the beam suddenly doubled in width and flashed back at the shooter, disintegrating him.

And then Kai Winn and Major Kira were at the doorway of the bar, the Kai's saffron robes billowed around her.

"Emissary!" she cried. "What have you done?!"

And then Quark heard the deck creak as it seemed to distort even more and the station's pressure-failure sirens began to sound.

Quark could see Sisko tapping his communicator, giving orders, looking wild.

His brother Rom pulled on his arm, dragging him around the bar, giving the floating Orbs the widest possible berth.

Then the lights went out, as if the entire power grid had blown.

For a moment, the torrential wind died down and the red glow of the Orbs diminished. Quark and Rom stumbled and ran to join the last Starfleet stragglers fleeing his bar.

Outside in the Promenade, in the dim red glow that came from the three floating Orbs in the bar—the only source of light in the station, it seemed—Quark could see he was near to Captain Sisko. Without the roar of the wind, Quark discovered he could hear again, as well. O'Brien, at Sisko's side, was saying that the Red Orbs were drawing power from the station's fusion reactors. With the power failure, they too had lost power. If they could just shut down the reactors, the Orbs would be powerless.

"It's worth a try," Sisko said.

And then a dark shadow passed between Quark and Sisko, and Quark saw Sisko go down, struck by a sudden blow to the head by some crazed assailant.

"Abandon station!" Sisko suddenly shouted. "Chief! Jadzia! Pass the order on to abandon station!"

"What about the reactors?" O'Brien's voice was urgent.

"Now, Chief!"

Then the pressure alarms were replaced by a siren that Quark had only heard during drills. And never thought he'd live to hear.

Two long bursts. Two short ones.

The order to abandon the station had been relayed to Ops.

In the dim light and shadows, Quark saw Sisko push himself to his feet, rubbing at his jaw. The captain looked around in confusion, then tapped at his chest as he shouted more orders.

Suddenly new sources of light appeared on the Promenade.

Golden columns of quantum mist.

Emergency beam-outs.

"Uh . . . hold on to me, brother."

Quark felt Rom's fingernails dig into his arms. The wind began to rise again. The whole station seemed to creak and flex. The glow from the bar became brighter.

"Rom!" O'Brien shouted. "You're with me!"

Quark saw O'Brien lunge for Rom and grab his brother's arm just as Rom held onto Quark's

"Chief!" Quark shouted. "What's happening?"

"There's a wormhole opening *in* the station!"

Quark felt his heart stop. A wormhole was opening in the *station?* A wormhole was opening in his *bar!*

Quark looked past Rom and O'Brien as it seemed his bar was lit by the literal flames of hell. Gul Dukat's pride and joy, the ridiculous mural of Tholian or Tellarite design, suddenly exploded into a spray of splintered glass, each glittering shard spinning madly as it was sucked down into the center of the triangle formed by the floating, glowing Orbs.

It was the last thing Quark saw before the station flickered out of existence before him in the swirl of the transporter.

But then, since he had lost everything, it was the last thing he ever wanted to see.

As far as he was concerned, the legends of the Red Orbs of Jalbador were true.

His world *had* come to an end.

CHAPTER 28

SISKO JUMPED DOWN from the *Defiant*'s transporter pad and ran into the corridor and to the bridge. He could already hear the ship's impulse engines coming on line as she prepared to undock from the station.

Worf was in the command chair and he stepped out as soon as Sisko appeared. On the main viewer, Deep Space 9 stretched out to the stars. But it was only a dark silhouette against the Denorios Belt. All station lights were out.

"How did you get the order to evacuate?" Sisko asked, slipping into his chair.

"It came into Ops through Jadzia," Worf said. He was already at tactical. "More than one thousand people are already away."

Sisko knew just how fortunate the inhabitants and crew of the station were. With the two *Akira*-class starships Admiral Ross had dispatched to help with the evacuation, more than twelve banks of transporters were operating at once. And the main personnel banks on the *Garneau* and the *Bondar* could retrieve more than one hundred evacuees every minute between them.

Jadzia and O'Brien were next on the bridge, followed by Bashir and Kira.

Bashir held a medical tricorder to Sisko and Sisko winced, suddenly realizing his jaw hurt.

"How's that feel?" the doctor asked.

"You should see the other guy," Sisko quipped. He didn't know with whom he had collided during the evacuation, but this wasn't the time to worry about it.

"Oh, Prophets!"

Sisko leaned forward with a smile. The exclamation had come from Commander Arla at flight operations, the least religious Bajoran he had yet to meet.

But before he could say anything to her about her apparent change in faith, he saw what she saw on the viewer and all sense of amusement fled.

A large glowing sphere of red energy blossomed over a section of the Promenade, just below Ops.

"What is *that?*" Sisko asked.

"The wormhole precursor," Jadzia replied. "It must have found a new source of power, because it's continuing to accelerate."

"Worf! What's the status of the evacuation?"

"Fifteen hundred people away," Worf reported. "But there is growing gravimetric distortion interfering with—"

Worf fell silent as a chorus of gasps filled the bridge.

The section of the habitat ring closest to the growing red sphere of energy was beginning to buckle, bending like a broken wheel.

Sisko stared at the screen in sickened fascination. "How many people are still on board . . . ?"

"Communications are down, sir. We must withdraw."

"Release the docking clamps," he ordered.

Arla fumbled with her console until Kira touched the young Bajoran commander on her shoulder and swiftly took over the position.

On the viewer, three escape modules launched from the habitat ring, but instead of flying free of the station they were drawn on perfect arcs into the red sphere.

"This can't be happening," Bashir said in shock.

The impact of the three modules set off a series of explosions that ringed the Promenade, and in a chain reaction they traveled up the central core to Ops.

"Jake . . ." Sisko whispered, as if an icy hand clutched his heart, then spoke more strongly, "Did anyone see Jake?"

"He's on board," Bashir said at once.

"What about Kasidy?"

Sisko's heart sank. No one had seen her on the *Defiant.* His hands tightened on the arms of his chair. Surely with the combined might of all the vessels using transporters now, Kasidy had been among the lucky ones.

A new wave of horrified gasps escaped those observing the viewer as a section of the habitat ring broke off and fell up into the red sphere.

"We are beginning to experience tidal distortions from an intense gravitational source," Worf announced.

Then Jadzia made her report. "It's a wormhole, Benjamin. For some reason it's opening about a hundred times more slowly than the one we're used to, but it *is* opening."

"Get us out of here, Major."

"Aye, sir."

On the viewer, the image of Deep Space 9—what was left of it—angled abruptly as the *Defiant* banked away.

And then the starship shook violently as the viewer flared with blue energy.

"We are under attack!" Worf shouted.

"Full power to shields!" Sisko ordered. He knew it had to be the Jem'Hadar. The Dominion had finally reacted to—

"You're not going anywhere," Leej Terrell said from the viewer.

Sisko leapt to his feet to face her. He recognized the bridge of her Sagittarian cruiser. "Mr. Worf, lock on all weapons," he said.

"I cannot acquire a target."

On the viewer, Terrell was a study in triumphant rage. She pounded a fist on the arm of her looming command chair. "Go back to your station, Captain. You found the third Orb. Now you must join it."

"I thought you wanted the Orbs for yourself," Sisko said, trying to goad her, as he had so recently, so long ago.

"If Cardassia can't have them, then no one can. Fire!"

Instantly the *Defiant* shook under another fusillade of phaser fire.

"Worf! Where is she!"

"Her ship is cloaked, sir! I can pick up a slight modulation when she fires, but not enough to extrapolate a course."

"Where did a Cardassian ship get a cloaking device?" Sisko demanded to know.

The *Defiant* trembled as another round of phaser fire found her.

Then Sisko heard the ship's own capacitors discharge with return fire.

"I believe I hit her," Worf called out. "I will continue to—"

The biggest blast yet hit the *Defiant,* and the ship spun on her axis.

Each time DS9 slipped past the viewer, the red sphere was larger. Now Sisko could see the rotating vortex was composed of red spiraling tendrils of energy. In form, it looked just like the wormhole he had seen open so many times. Only its color was different.

"Major Kira," Sisko said. "We need to be stabilized so Worf can return fire."

"She's picked her targets," Kira warned. "Our thrusters are off-line. Impulse is out. All we've got is warp and that's not powered up yet."

"Working on it, sir!" O'Brien volunteered before he had been asked.

"Can we get support from another ship?" Sisko asked.

"All channels are down," Jadzia said. "The other ships are withdrawing."

"How can that be? Surely they can see we're in difficulty!"

Jadzia turned from her science station to Sisko. "Benjamin, we're so close to that wormhole we could be within some kind of event horizon. Those other ships might not even know we're still here."

O'Brien chimed in. "That could explain why the

wormhole seems to be opening so slowly. Those other ships might have seen it move as quickly as the blue wormhole does. And we might have been sucked in."

Sisko tried to follow the reasoning of his two experts. "So we're in some kind of temporal bubble?"

"Not necessarily," Jadzia said. "It could be straightforward relativistic time displacement. We should be able to warp out when the engines are ready, just like jumping out of a black hole."

"Thirty seconds to warp," O'Brien reported.

The *Defiant* shuddered as another volley hit her, then rang with her own phasers as Worf once more returned fire. "I think I may have hit her again," Worf said.

"Twenty seconds to warp," O'Brien counted down.

On the viewer, the red wormhole now obscured more than half of DS9. Sisko watched as the station's upper docking pylons begin to twist down to the red distortion, hull plates popping loose like autumn leaves in a storm. Then one of the pylons broke free entirely as an explosion engulfed its base. It tumbled into the wormhole, visibly breaking up into still smaller pieces. Then it disappeared.

Another explosion shook the *Defiant.* Transtator sparks erupted from Worf's tactical station and the Klingon had to jump back as the automatic fire-suppression system engulfed his console with anaerobic vapor.

"Ten seconds," O'Brien said.

"Major," Sisko ordered, "prepare to get us out of here."

Another hit.

"Shields at thirty-seven percent," Kira announced. "We can't take much more."

And then on the viewer, as if it were no more than a crumpled piece of tissue being pulled down a drain, Deep Space 9 fell in on itself, shattering like brittle ice, each shard drawn spinning into the endless, infinite tunnel of the red wormhole at its heart.

Sisko felt a part of himself vanishing into that ravenous maw, to be lost forever along with his station.

"They all got off in time," he chanted softly to himself, willing his words to be true. "They had to get off in time."

"We have warp!" O'Brien announced.

On screen, the red wormhole continued to expand, continued to open, its unwinding coils of negative energy now reaching out for the *Defiant*.

Sisko fell back in his chair, gripped the arms. "Now, Major!"

"Never!" Terrell's voice echoed from all the bridge speakers at once.

And then a final blast of phaser fire hit the starship just as she went to warp. And the first tendrils of the wormhole brushed across her hull to claim her.

No one on board the *Defiant* had a chance.

They were all engulfed in a red flash of overwhelming intensity, the sheer magnitude of which exceeded anything in their entire experience of existence.

And then each moment dissolved into the next.

Until there was only the silence and the darkness of endless infinite space . . .

CHAPTER 29

SHE TUMBLED dead in space. No running lights. No engine glow. Her only signature a faint infrared glow which testified to a barely functioning life-support system, and the fragile lives of the thirty-three people who still survived onboard.

There was no wormhole near her now. No sun. No planets.

And no hope.

Sisko awoke to the cool sting of a hypospray.

The bridge was dark, but enough display screens functioned for him to see Bashir kneeling at his side.

"Casualties?" It was any captain's first thought, first worry.

"Five dead in engineering," Bashir said. "A coolant leak. A dozen injuries. Nothing serious. And Jake's fine. He's helping clean up sickbay."

"Thank you, Doctor."

Sisko reached out, found the edge of his command chair, and used it to brace himself as he rose to his feet.

He could smell smoke and ozone, and the damp soapy scent of the fire-suppression sprays. But there were no wailing sirens. The ship was in one piece. They had survived.

Then he looked at the viewer, saw only stars there.

Closed his eyes. Saw Deep Space 9.

He found Jadzia. A small medical patch on her forehead.

"Your hair's a mess, Old Man," he said.

Jadzia smiled up at him, tightly. "Thank you, Benjamin. You know exactly what to say to make a girl feel her best."

"Any sign of Terrell?"

Jadzia shook her head.

"Communications back on-line?"

"There's no subspace distortion, if that's what you mean. But I'm not picking up anything."

Sisko looked back at the viewer with a sudden rush of apprehension. "Did we travel *through* the wormhole?"

The last thing he wanted was for the *Defiant* to become another *Voyager,* tossed tens of thousands of light-years from home.

"No. Those are local stars," Jadzia said. "But we are having trouble getting a fix on exactly where we are."

Sisko was suddenly aware of Major Kira beside him. Her face drawn, her eyes dark. She held out a padd. "I found out why our navigation charts aren't working." She handed Jadzia the padd. "It's not a question of where we are. It's *when* we are."

Sisko squinted sideways at the calculations Jadzia scrolled through on the padd. "We've travelled through time?"

Jadzia nodded. "From the drift in star positions . . . twenty-four . . . almost twenty-five years." She looked up. Her face held the same haunted expression as Kira's. "Benjamin, we've come forward to the year 2400."

Sisko exhaled in shock. "How can that be?"

"It has to be the wormhole," Jadzia said.

"Captain," Kira asked, "we will be able to go back, won't we?"

"Of . . . of course," Sisko said. "We can . . . we can slingshot back around a star. . . ."

"Not really, Benjamin." Jadzia seemed apologetic. "If we didn't travel here along a slingshot trajectory, we have no path to follow back."

"But there *has* to be a way, doesn't there?" Kira asked.

Sisko mind raced with possibilities. "We'll find a way. We'll contact the Federation Department of Temporal Investigations. Twenty-five years is a long time. There must have been some major breakthroughs in temporal mechanics. They'll be able to help us." Sisko turned to address his bridge crew. "Just remember, we have to follow Starfleet regulations to the letter. We can't afford to learn anything about the time we're in, so we won't alter the timeline when we—"

Sisko flew through the air as the bridge echoed with thunder.

"We are under attack again!" Worf said. "Cloaked vessel dead ahead!"

Sisko forced himself to stand. He could taste blood in his mouth from his fall. "Terrell . . ." he said. "However we got here, she came with us."

"I do not think so," Worf said as a collision alarm began sounding. "The ship is decloaking, and it is not hers."

Sisko stared at the viewer as a strange rippling checkerboard effect, unlike any cloak he had ever seen, distorted the stars until a ship became visible.

And though it was a class he didn't know, his apprehension became relief as he recognized the hallmarks of Starfleet design: twin warp nacelles set back for safety, a lower engineering hull, an upper command hull. Each element was elongated to an extreme degree, and the command hull had what appeared to be two forward-facing projections that resembled battering rams, but overall it was a welcome sight.

"That's quite a ship, Benjamin. It's close to a kilometer long, and I'm reading *eighteen* different phaser systems onboard. At least I think they're phasers."

Sisko smiled. "That's all right, Old Man. At least it's on our side. Commander Worf, open a channel."

"Channel open, sir."

"Attention, unidentified Starfleet vessel. This is Captain Benjamin Sisko of the *Starship Defiant.* My crew and I have been displaced in time and—"

"That's impossible," Kira said.

Sisko saw it, too. Didn't understand.

The huge vessel had come about so that its forward hull filled the viewer. And from that angle, the ship's name was clear.

U.S.S. Opaka.

"How could a warship be named for a woman of peace?" Kira asked, incredulous.

Sisko was uncomfortable with even seeing the details of the ship's design and learning its name. "Dax, degrade viewer resolution by fifty percent and disable recording. We can't take any of these details home with us."

He returned to stand by his command chair. "This is Captain Sisko of the *Defiant* to the captain of the *U.S.S. Opaka.* We are displaced in time. Under Starfleet regulations, we request that you do not communicate directly with us in order to allow us to preserve our timeline. We will require—"

"Incoming message," Worf interrupted.

"They have to know better," Sisko said. "We can't risk receiving it. Jam it, Mr. Worf."

"No good, Captain. They're using a type of multiplexing I have not—"

And then a familiar face formed on the viewer. His hair and beard were pure white, his features lined and wrinkled, but he was unmistakable to everyone on the *Defiant* who had encountered him four years ago—or twenty-nine years ago.

"Captain Sisko," the commander of the *Starship Opaka* began, "this is Captain Thomas Riker. Good to see you again, sir. And welcome back."

Sisko tried to make sense of the uniform Riker wore. It seemed to be closer to a Bajoran style, though in black and rust colors. Yet on his chest he wore a version of the classic Starfleet delta in gold, backed by an upside-down triangle in blue.

"Captain Riker," Sisko said. "I appreciate the contact, and I'm glad to see you're no longer in Cardassian custody. But by talking to us directly, you're making it difficult for us to go back to our own time."

Riker laughed. "I wouldn't worry about that, Captain. You can learn all you want about the future—because this is where you and your crew are going to stay."

Sisko squared his shoulders. "No, Captain Riker, we are not. One way or another, we want to return to our own time and our own lives."

Riker leaned to the side of his chair as if his back was sore. "Captain, I don't care what the hell you *want* to do. Your place is here and always has been. As for your ship and crew, every resource is needed for the war, and I'm not letting the *Defiant* get away."

"What war?" Sisko asked. Could it be possible that the Federation and the Dominion were still battling for control of the quadrant?

"Sir!" Worf suddenly announced. "Three ships approaching on an attack vector!"

"Cardassian?" Sisko asked. "Jem'Hadar?"

Worf looked up at Sisko in surprise. "No, sir . . . from their identification signals, they are *also* Starfleet vessels."

Suddenly a barrage of explosions surrounded the *Defiant,* shaking her badly.

On the viewer, Riker vanished and was replaced by an image of the *Opaka* firing needle-thin lances of silver energy at the approaching ships.

"All three of the new vessels have locked their weapons on us," Worf reported.

Riker reappeared on the viewer, eyes afire with rage. "The War of the Prophets is coming! Choose your side, Emissary—because this is your war now!"

Then the bridge of the *Defiant* fell silent, as everyone turned to their captain.

And waited for Sisko to make his decision.

TO BE CONTINUED IN . . .

DEEP SPACE NINE®
MILLENNIUM
BOOK II of III
THE WAR OF THE PROPHETS

ACKNOWLEDGMENTS

None of the novels of the *Deep Space Nine: Millennium* trilogy could have been written without the magnificent store of *Star Trek* knowledge, insight, and good humor contained in the *Star Trek Encyclopedia,* by Michael and Denise Okuda, with Debbie Mirek, and the *Star Trek Chronology,* also by Mike and Denise.

In addition, in the writing of these novels we have benefited enormously from the exquisitely detailed and brilliantly illustrated *Deep Space Nine Technical Manual* by Herman Zimmerman, Rick Sternbach, and Doug Drexler, and from a hugely entertaining and informative advance copy of the coming-soon-to-a bookstore-near-you *Deep Space Nine Companion* by Terry Erdman.

In the spirit of the 33rd Rule, we would also like to offer our thanks and a shameless plug for Quark's own *Legends of the Ferengi,* as told to Ira Steven Behr and Robert Hewitt Wolfe, which offered fascinating insights into Ferengi culture.

We're also indebted to our editor, Margaret Clark, and to Liz Braswell, Scott Shannon, Dave Rossi, and Paula Block for their ongoing involvement and much-appreciated contributions to the development of the entire *Millennium* project.

And, of course, our thanks as always to Gene Roddenberry for setting the stage, and to Rick Berman and Michael Piller for creating such an endlessly intriguing arena for storytelling and such a compelling cast of characters.

Seven years was definitely not long enough.

—J&G

THE CHRONICLES OF GALEN SWORD #1: SHIFTER

Galen Sword is an aimless New York twenty-something with no friends, no family, and a multimillion-dollar trust fund. After a night of indulgence he crashes his sportscar, and the doctors in emergency write him off—his injuries are too extensive for him to survive. Then a mysterious man with blue glowing hands heals Galen, and as Galen's body is restored, so are long-buried memories of his early childhood, a childhood he appears to have spent in another world of exotic beings and magical forces. Filled with new purpose, Galen uses his wealth to become an investigator of the unknown and the unexplainable—not to disprove such things, but to find his way home.

Shifter *tells the story of his first success, three years later, as he captures a creature he believes to be a werewolf stalking New York, and is drawn into the violent political turmoil between a clan of First-World shape-shifters—the Clan Arkady—and creatures even more deadly: the elusive, formless Seyshen.*

ONE

Galen Sword had lost.

He kept his dark eyes fixed on the steady pinpoint lights of the dashboard video map display. Each dot on the glowing grid represented a motion sensor hidden at chokepoints in the web of alleys nearby. Each light was green. The werewolf had eluded him again.

Melody Ko's voice crackled in Sword's ear. He touched a finger to the tiny Mitsubishi transceiver there, to better hear her over the steady drumming of the night rain. The woman's words were crisp and to the point, as always.

"Four A.M., Sword. No previous sightings past three before." It was Ko's way of saying it was time to go back to the Loft. To quit. Sword sighed and stretched his arms against the leather-wrapped steering wheel. Maybe it was time to quit everything.

Another voice broke in, but it said nothing. It was only a long yawn triggering a VOX circuit in one of the transceivers each of the team wore on a job.

Sword recognized the yawn. "Still with us, Ja'Nette?" he asked, keeping his eyes locked on the unchanging display.

"Bore-*ing,*" the child answered sleepily. "How come you let me do this shit but you won't let me stay up to watch *South Park?*"

Sword didn't answer, didn't even smile. There was no humor in him this night. Three tedious months spent narrowing down the operating range of a werewolf in Manhattan, three long years spent trying to find some way back into the hidden world: and all that time, all that money, had come to this—another failure.

He looked out through the rain-rippled windshield of his Porsche. This far north in the city there were few streetlights still working. Only a handful of them were smeared into orange streaks through the windshield, dimly illuminating the deserted streets. Yet Sword was certain there was something beyond their light, in the darkness. It was only a question of knowing where to look, and when. He knew the answers were there. He knew he had been close enough to touch them in the past three years. He knew he had once been part of them himself, so long ago.

Sword leaned back and closed his eyes. He saw another rain-swept night, the werewolf in Greece, trapped in the ruins, close to speaking, felled by the swift whisper of a silenced silver bullet. Sword saw the woman again, atop the crumbling wall, her cloak billowing in the wild wind, rifle held ready as her quarry bled out its immortal life on marble twice a thousand years old, and shifted painfully back into its human form, taking its secrets into darkness.

Sword and the woman had faced each other in that night until the dying creature had raised a claw to the blackness from which the rain swirled, turned its now human eyes to Sword, and called out with its dying breath, "*Galen!*"

Lost in a country not his own, confronted by a creature others thought only a legend, Galen Sword had been *recognized* by his prey. He had seen that same flash of instant knowledge widen the eyes of the woman who had killed the beast, just before she had turned back to the night and leapt from the wall, and disappeared into shadow. Even now, safe in the dry, technological cocoon of his car, Sword felt the hairs on his arms bristle with the memory of that night and what it might have meant.

There *were* secrets in the darkness.

And other hunters.

He opened his eyes. He touched the transceiver in his ear. It was time to quit, but only for the night.

Then a green light on the display changed to red and began to flash. And in his earphone, he heard the familiar mechanical sound of a shell pumped into place as Ko cocked her weapon.

The hunt began again.

To the creature's eyes, the alleys were a jungle, the city a continent of secret lairs, hidden prey, sudden death. But tonight he had no need to hide, no need to fear. Tonight he ran with the force and the fury of the storm. Tonight he flew with the wildness of the cold autumn rain. Tonight, for just this little while, this tiny escape, he was free as no human could ever be.

His name was Martin and he was what he was. The false term "werewolf" meant nothing to him. And this night he had a destination. His favorite place.

Martin's heavy feet slapped over the filthy asphalt and paving bricks of the back alleys. His large hands, cold rain streaming from their sparse fur, smacked against the glistening walls and alley paths, propelling him forward with perfect balance and elegant gait. Freedom fueled him. He knew his clanmates were too busy with their preparations to realize his absence for hours.

Martin rounded a corner, transferring his momentum and motion so perfectly he didn't slip or slide. With a leap that seemed to require no effort, he was at the lip of a bent and buckled dumpster. But before the metal could even creak with the pressure of his landing, he had flipped up against the rain-slicked wall, pushed off with his feet, rolled twice through the air over an eight-foot-tall rotting wooden fence, and hit the ground on the other side with no greater sound than that of an ordinary footstep, and no break in the rhythm of his running. Yet the cloak of his silent progress was broken by his howl of delight because, for this night at least, he believed he ran without pursuit. He did not scent or see the motion sensors as he triggered them.

In the final alley, Martin came to a sudden stop, so still in the shadows that he became almost invisible. His nostrils flared as he scented the approach to his destination. Even through the rain and the city's perpetual stink of garbage, cars, and buses, Martin could tell that humans had passed by recently. The rotting stench of the fruit and vegetables that oozed through their pores clung to the night air, unavoidable to his refined olfactory sense. At least by now he was used to the foul odor enough that he no longer felt like gagging as he had as a child.

But the human spoor in the final alley was strong enough to keep him from moving again. His instincts were more than a match for his goal that night, no matter how rare and hard-won his freedom. If there were even a chance that humans were in the alley, he would not continue. Above all, Martin knew he must survive.

His nostrils flared again as he tasted the air with a sensitivity greater than two parts per billion. Then he smiled, his dark face split by perfect teeth which by human standards were marred only by incisors remarkably too long and too sharp. Martin recognized alcohol. Lots of it. Whatever human might be hidden in the alley would be unconscious, or too drunk to notice Martin's presence.

Martin pursed his lips and mouthed a silent howl of victory, then moved into the open alley on the last leg of his journey.

The old back door, battered wood splotched with flaking remnants of dirty green paint, was protected by a hinged black iron grill held in place by a thick chain and heavy padlock. Martin didn't pause. He reached out and took the padlock in both hands. His eyes rolled back in his head. A faint, electric blue glow sputtered between his fingers and palms and the lock clicked open. His clanmates called it a blue power, but to Martin it was just a legacy from his father, a way to get into places he wanted to get into. What it was or how it worked, he didn't know or care.

Carefully, he unthreaded the chain from the grill, swung it open, and touched the doorknob. It wouldn't turn until a second blue flash glimmered beneath his palm. He pushed the door open. He had arrived. The crudely painted delivery instructions on the door were topped by a sign that said, NOAH'S PET SHOP EMPORIUM, but Martin couldn't read them. His nose had told him what waited for him inside. Soft animals, small animals, young animals.

His favorite.

A moment after the back door to the pet store swung shut, Melody Ko stepped forward from the narrow inset in the alley wall opposite. The young Japanese woman's face was tense with concentration, not fear. Her eyes were narrowed not in apprehension, but for protection from the rain that ran without slowing through the short razor-cut bristle of her hair.

"It's in the pet shop," she said softly, then brushed at her nose to clear it of the smell of the whiskey Forsyte had instructed her to pour at her feet, to camouflage her scent.

She heard the rasp of Sword's breath in her earphone as he ran for his position. "I'll cover the front," he said, voice resonating with the impact of his running.

Ko frowned. Sword always stated the obvious. Of course he would cover the front. That had been Forsyte's plan. And Forsyte had never been wrong. Except that once.

"What have we got, anyway?" Sword asked, breathing harshly with his exertion. He never kept to the exercise program she had devised for him.

Ko scanned the dark alley. She heard Ja'Nette's footfalls approaching. "Humanoid. No pronounced snout. Sparse fur. Maybe five-four, five-six standing up." She guessed the creature was young. Some of Sword's sources had put the height of mature werewolves at over seven feet. But there were always so many contradictions among the observers who had survived, making it extremely difficult to formulate theories.

A small dark shape appeared at the corner of the alley: Ja'Nette. Ko held up a hand to silently stop the child, twelve years old but looking ten, no evidence of womanhood about her.

Ja'Nette instantly froze in position, and not necessarily because of Sword's incessant training. She treated whatever Ko told her to do as a command from heaven, or from the parents who haunted her dreams.

"Sword?" Ko said. Coming from her, it was a complex question.

His reply came through the transceiver. "In position . . . *now.*" She could hear that he had stopped running. Then he added, "Adrian, are you on-line?"

There was a long pause, then a flat mechanical voice answered, "Yes." Ko felt her stomach tighten as it always did when she heard Forsyte's voder, knowing the real voice that lay behind it, forever stilled.

"Is Ja'Nette in position?" Sword asked.

"We are proceeding," Ko replied. It was answer enough.

Keeping her modified assault rifle aimed at the back door of the pet shop, Ko turned to Ja'Nette twenty feet away and nodded her head, then pointed silently back to the door.

Ja'Nette pulled off the hood of her red nylon windbreaker to reveal her richly black features tense with expectation. Ko saw the girl cross her wrists and lift her clenched fists to her shoulders, then begin slowly rocking. Her soft humming came over the transceiver. An old Michael Jackson tune, greatly slowed down.

The falling rain quickened for a moment, sending a curtain of spray through the alley. Ko ignored it, turning back to the door, finger on the trigger, poised on the brink of sudden action.

The chain moved like a snake on the ground.

"Focus," Ko said softly.

Ja'Nette's humming rose. From the corner of her eye, Ko saw the child's rocking increase.

"Focus," Ko repeated like a mantra.

The chain became motionless. The doorknob moved. The door swung silently open.

There was nothing on the other side.

"Open and safe," Ko announced. She hefted the gun, knowing what would come next.

"Proceed," Forsyte's voder said.

"In position," Sword confirmed.

Even without the transceiver, Ko could hear the sound of Ja'Nette vomiting at the end of the alley. When would the girl learn not to eat before one of their excursions? But Ko did not turn to the child, nor speak to her. There was no time for that. Instead she held her rifle ready and moved toward the open door. It was time to make Galen Sword's day. It was time to catch a werewolf.

Pudgy fat puppies yipped with bellies round and swollen like berries about to burst. Puffs of kittens mewed as they tumbled over each other in a furry avalanche. Martin peered into the cages full of life and slowly licked his lips. His favorite place.

Without turning his head, Martin reached out and grabbed a package from a shelf, then crept back through the dark pet store until he came to the door that opened onto the room at the back of the cages. He needed no blue power to open it. It was unlocked, unprotected. He went inside and closed the door behind him. He didn't want a single one of them to get away.

The puppies were first. They always were. *Excitable,* Martin thought. That was the word his clanmates used for him as they laughed, as they hunted.

Martin opened the cage door. Eight-week-old beagles erupted in rush of high-pitched squeals. Martin's huge hand reached into the cage, found the first puppy, engulfed it, and Martin grinned in anticipation. Next would come the kittens.

Best for last, Martin thought. *Best for last.*

Ko moved through the back storeroom until she stood in the doorway to the main part of the shop. She could hear the muffled barking of puppies and mewing of kittens, but saw nothing moving in the shop except for the lazy passage of tropical fish in five softly-lit aquariums along one wall. But the rippling light from the tanks was weak and there was no way of knowing what was hidden in the shadows.

Carefully, precisely, Ko slipped a Raytheon thermal viewer from a loop on her black canvas equipment vest, and flicked the device once, scattering beads of rain from its slick casing. Then she flipped the switch on its side as she held the viewer to her eyes like binoculars, squinting at the bright multicolored image it produced.

A five-second scan revealed nothing hiding in the shadows, but she suddenly heard the puppies in the cages at the side of the store begin to howl. Quickly Ko slipped the viewer back onto her vest. There was a small room running the length of the wall of cages at the side of the shop. The door to it was closed. Ko didn't want to do it, but Forsyte had worked out the procedure as the safest, so she pressed the call button on her locator band three times.

She heard Ja'Nette answer, very tired now, "Comin'."

Twenty seconds later, Ko heard Ja'Nette behind her. Ko pointed to the cage room door, then moved into position five feet in front of it. Now, the cries of kittens filled the shop, high-pitched and plaintive. She tried not to think of what might be going on in there.

Ja'Nette hummed softly. Michael Jackson again.

The handle on the cage room door began to move by itself.

The cage room door slammed open.

Ko lunged forward and screamed in attack, bringing the gunsight to her eye and—

—there was nothing there.

Ko halted in the open doorway. She moved her head cautiously so she could see past the gunsight. The creature had been at least five-four. It *had* to be close to her eye level.

"What's going on in there?" Sword asked in her ear. But Ko shut him out. He always talked too much.

A kitten tottered into view on the floor. Ko looked down, gun barrel reflexively following the new motion. The kitten stopped, looked up at Ko and her rifle, and mewed. A gigantic dark hand with black nails and tufts of rain-soaked fur snaked out, scooped up the kitten and drew it back behind a row of cabinets.

"Melody?" Sword asked. "Ja'Nette?"

Ko could hear Ja'Nette retching behind her in the storeroom.

"Proceeding," Ko announced firmly and stepped into the cage room.

She heard a deep growl as she entered, a warning in any language, human or otherwise.

"Show yourself," Ko said. Her voice was steady and calm. What little emotion was in it was excitement. Sword had hopelessly screwed up the photographs he had taken of the werewolf in Greece—that incident had been before she and Forsyte had joined up with him—and Ko was eager to see what such a creature looked like. Electrophoresis of its DNA promised to be a blast, too.

The creature growled again. She heard one puppy yip, another bark.

A standoff, Ko decided, except she was the one with the rifle. She stepped further into the cage room, brushing against an open cage door and swinging it shut with a metallic clink. She heard another warning growl. Ko took a breath and prepared to—

"Hold your position," Sword said. "I'm coming in."

Ko heard a tremendous crash as the storefront window exploded inward. The creature hidden behind the counter howled deafeningly. "You asshole!" Ko shouted at Sword, but she leapt forward anyway, raising her gun barrel.

The creature, dark and squat, naked and muscular, was crouched on the floor behind the counter. Its eyes were wide and its thick arms and powerful hands encompassed a writhing armload of small animals.

"Nooo!" the creature shrieked at Ko.

But it made no move to stand up. No move to protect itself.

Ko stopped in surprise. The creature was more human in appearance than she had anticipated, and was definitely a *he.* And he wasn't attacking. Almost as if . . . as if he were worried about . . . She saw an open box of dog biscuits on the floor. Two of the puppies beside the creature were happily digging into it.

"Please," the creature said. "Don't hurt . . . don't hurt . . . "

Ko hated the unexpected, but she never denied it. "You mean . . . the puppies?" she asked.

"Kittens, too," the creature said, and dipped his eyes in supplication. "Don't hurt."

Ko lowered her rifle. Then Galen Sword was beside her, rivers of rain still dripping from the black leather jacket covering his equipment vest, gas pistol held ready at his side.

"You're not going to believe this, Sword," Ko said, "but—"

Sword fired.

The creature screamed and jerked back against the wall, sending his kittens and puppies flying.

He writhed and gurgled and in seconds was still, only the slow movement of the red tag of the tranquilizing dart giving evidence that he was still alive.

Ko clenched her jaw in anger. "Why the bloody hell did you do that?"

Sword glanced at her. "You okay?" Without waiting for an answer, he knelt down beside the creature and lifted its limp arm. "Look at that musculature," he said, shaking his head. He absently pushed a puppy out of the way as it tried to lick the creature's face.

"I said, why did you do that?" This time, Ko's voice wavered with rage. Sword was perhaps the only person who could affect her that way. "I had everything under control. He was just sitting there! He came to *play* with the animals. Look at the dog biscuits!"

"Good, good," Sword said, ignoring her as he forced open one of the creature's eyes and shone a penlight beam into it.

"For God's sake, Sword," Ko sighed.

Sword stood up beside her, studied her for a long moment. "Bring the van around and we'll load it in."

Ko cleared the tranquilizing charge from her rifle and snapped the gun's strap over her shoulder. "Ja'Nette was sick back there. I'm looking after her."

"Ja'Nette knows better than to eat before translocating," Sword said. He was almost six feet tall and he towered over Ko, but she refused to be intimidated.

"She's just a child, remember?"

"She's on the payroll," Sword said. He kept glancing down at the unconscious creature and Ko sensed an elation in him that she had never known before. "Just get the van, Ko. Adrian doesn't know how long the drug will last."

"Oh, go to hell," Ko muttered as she stormed from the cage room.

Behind her, almost softly enough that she didn't hear, Galen Sword said, "What makes you think I'm not already there?"

Fuming and grumbling all the way, Ko brought the van to the store before seeing to Ja'Nette. After all, this was Sword's big night. After three years of ineffectual effort, he had finally caught himself a werewolf. Now, as far as Ko was concerned, it was time to see which of the two was the bigger monster.

Presenting, one chapter per month . . .

The very beginning of the Starfleet Adventure . . .

OUR FIRST SERIAL NOVEL!

STAR TREK®
STARFLEET: YEAR ONE

A Novel in Twelve Parts®

by
Michael Jan Friedman

Chapter Eight

When Captain Bryce Shumar materialized in the transporter room of the Tellarite trading vessel, he did so with his laser pistol drawn and leveled in front of him.

As it turned out, his concern was unfounded. Outside of Shumar, Kelly, and the three armed crewmen they had brought with them, there was only one other humanoid in the room—a Tellarite transporter operator.

"Come with me," he said.

"It would be my pleasure," said the captain.

He gestured with his weapon for his team to follow. Then he stepped down from the transporter disc and fell in line behind their guide.

The corridors of the vessel were stark and poorly illuminated, but very wide. It wasn't surprising, Shumar reflected, considering the girth of the average Tellarite.

Before long, they came to a cargo bay. As luck would have it, it was on the same level as the transporter room. The Tellarite opened the door for them and plodded off.

Broj, the vessel's captain, was waiting for them inside. He wasn't alone, either. There was a tall, green-skinned Orion with a sour expression standing next to him.

Not that there was anything unusual about that. Tellarite traders often took on financial backers from other species, and there never seemed to be a shortage of willing Orions.

However, this particular Orion didn't look like a financier. He looked more like a mercenary—which inclined Shumar to be that much more careful in his dealings here.

In addition to Broj and his green-skinned associate, the cargo bay contained perhaps two dozen metal containers. None of them were labeled. They could have contained apricots or antibiotics, though Shumar wasn't looking for either of those.

Shumar nodded. "Captain Broj."

"This is an outrage," the Tellarite rumbled.

Shumar didn't answer him. He simply turned to Kelly and said, "Keep an eye on these gentlemen."

"Aye, sir," she assured him, the barrel of her laser pistol moving from the Tellarite to the Orion and back again.

Tucking his weapon inside his belt, Shumar crossed the room and worked the lid off a container at random. Then, still eyeing Broj, he reached inside. His fingers closed on something dry and granular.

Extracting a handful of the stuff, he held it out in front of him. It looked like rice—except for the blood-red color.

"D'saako seeds," said the Tellarite.

"I know what they are," Shumar told him. "When you run a starbase, you encounter every kind of cargo imaginable."

Taking out his laser, he pointed it at the bottom half of the container. Then he activated its bright blue beam.

Not even titanium could stand that kind of point-blank assault. The metal puckered and gave way, leaving a hole the size of a man's fist.

"What are you doing?" bellowed Broj, taking a step forward. He looked ready to charge Shumar, but couldn't because of the lasers trained on him. "I paid good money for that grain!"

"No doubt," the human responded, deactivating the beam and putting his pistol away again. "But I'm willing to bet there's more than d'saako seeds in this container."

After waiting a moment longer for the metal to cool, Shumar reached inside. What he found was most definitely not seeds. They were too big and hard. Smiling, he removed some.

"Gold?" asked Kelly.

"Gold," the captain confirmed.

There were perhaps a dozen shiny, irregularly shaped orange nuggets in his open hand, ranging in size from that of a pea to that of an acorn. Shumar showed them to Broj.

"Our informants say this gold is from Ornathia Prime."

The smuggler grunted disdainfully. "I don't know where it came from. I only know I was paid to take a cargo from one place to another."

"According to our informants," said Shumar, "that's a lie. You mined this gold yourself, ignoring the fact that you had no right to do so. Then you set out for the Magabenthus system in the hope of peddling it."

The Tellarite puffed out his chest. "Your informants are the ones who are lying," he huffed.

"In that case," said the captain, "you won't mind our checking your other cargo bay. You know, the one a couple of decks below us? I'll bet you we find some gold-mining equipment."

The smuggler scowled disdainfully. "Go ahead and check. Then you can apologize to my government for waylaying an honest businessman."

Shumar knew he would need the mining equipment as evidence, so he tilted his head in the direction of the exit. "Come on," he told Kelly and his other crewmen. "Let's take a look at that other bay."

"Aye, sir," said Kelly. She gestured with her laser for the Tellarite to lead the way.

But before Shumar had made it halfway to the exit, something occurred to him. He stopped dead—and his weapons officer noticed.

"What is it?" Kelly asked him.

The captain turned to Broj. "Where did those d'saako seeds come from?"

The Tellarite regarded him. "Ekkenda Four. Why?"

Why indeed, Shumar thought. *Because an immunologist at the University of Pennsylvania, back on Earth, is trying to cure Vegan choriomeningitis using the DNA of certain Ekkendan lizards—creatures whose entire diets seem to consist of adult sun-ripened d'saako plants.*

If Shumar could find some lizard cells among the d'saako seeds, he might be able to conduct some experiments of his own. Maybe he could even expedite the discovery of a cure. It was the kind of work that would make people sit up and take notice. . . .

And see the possibilities inherent in a science-driven Starfleet.

"Captain?" said Kelly, sounding annoyed at the delay.

"Hang on a moment," Shumar told her.

Returning to the open, laser-punctured container, he zipped down the front of his uniform almost to his waist. Then he scooped up a healthy handful of d'saako seeds, poured them carefully into an inside pocket and zipped up his uniform again.

If there were lizard cells present, his science officers would be able to detect them and pull them out. And if there weren't, the captain mused, he hadn't lost anything.

That's when he felt the business end of a laser pistol poke him in the small of his back.

"No one move," rasped the Orion.

Apparently, he had had a concealed weapon on him. Shumar's detour had given him an opening to use it—but he would eventually have used it anyway. At least, that was what the captain chose to believe.

"I'll kill him if I have to," the Orion vowed.

Shumar didn't doubt it. "Easy," he said. "Stay calm."

"Don't tell me how to feel," the Orion snapped. "Don't tell me anything. Just tell *them* to move out of our way."

"*Our* way?" the captain echoed.

"That's right," said his captor. "You and I are going to take a little trip in an escape pod."

"What about me?" asked Broj.

"You're on your own," the Orion told him.

So much for honor among thieves, Shumar thought. Feeling the prod of the laser pistol, he began to move toward the exit.

Then he saw Kelly raise her weapon and fire.

The flash of blue light blinded him, so he couldn't tell what effect the beam had had. But a moment later, it occurred to him that the pistol in his back was gone.

"Are you all right?" asked a feminine voice, amid the scrape of boots and the barking of a warning.

The captain blinked a few times and made out Kelly through the haze of after-images. Then he looked down and saw the Orion lying unconscious on the deck. Broj had his hands up, kept in line by Shumar's crewmen.

"Fine," he told Kelly, "thanks to you. I was surprised you were able to get a clear shot at him."

The weapons officer grunted. "I didn't."

Shumar's vision had improved enough for him to see her face. It confirmed that she wasn't kidding.

"What would I do without you?" he asked sotto voce.

"I don't know," Kelly said in the same soft voice. "Exercise a little more care, maybe?"

"Come on," said the captain, understanding exactly what she was talking about. "There was no way I could have known the Orion was armed."

"All the more reason not to leave yourself open."

Shumar wanted to argue the point further. And he would have, except he knew that the woman was right.

Taking out his communicator, he flipped it open and contacted his ship. "Commander Mullen?"

"Aye, sir. Did you find what you were looking for?"

The captain glanced at the Orion, who was still sprawled on the floor. His actions were all the justification Shumar needed to seize the *Prosperous.*

"That and more," he told Mullen. "Send a couple of teams over. We've got a smuggling vessel to secure."

Daniel Hagedorn watched the cottony, violet-colored walls slide by on every side of his vessel, missing his titanium hull by less than thirty meters in any direction.

He and his crew were traveling the main corridor of a nebular maze—a gargantuan cloud of dust and destructive high-energy plasma that dominated this part of space. Unlike other nebulae of its kind discovered over the last thirty years, this one was rife with a network of corridors and subcorridors, the largest of which allowed a ship like Hagedorn's to make its way through unscathed.

Hence the term "maze."

The captain's orders called for him to remain in the phenomenon's main passageway, where he would gather as much data as possible. Normally, he was the kind of officer who followed such instructions to the letter. Today however, he planned to diverge from that policy.

For the last several minutes he had been scanning the cottony wall on his right for an offshoot that could give him some clearance. Unfortunately, that offshoot hadn't materialized.

Until now.

"Lieutenant Kendall," Hagedorn told his helm officer, "we're going to change course. Take the next corridor to starboard." He consulted the readout in his armrest. "Heading two-four-two mark six."

Kendall glanced at the captain, his confusion evident. "Sir," he said, "that's not the way out."

"It is now," Hagedorn told him.

For a moment, the helmsman looked as if he were about to object to the course change. Then he turned to his console and dutifully put the captain's order into effect.

Instantly, the *Christopher* veered to starboard and entered the passageway, which was substantially narrower than the main corridor but still navigable. Satisfied, Hagedorn leaned back in his seat—and saw that his executive officer was standing beside him.

Her name was Corspa Zenar. She was an Andorian, tall and willowy, with blue skin and white hair. Her antennae were bent forward at the moment—which could have signified a lot of things, disapproval among them.

"You'd like an explanation," the captain guessed.

Zenar shrugged her bony shoulders. "That won't be necessary."

"And why is that?" Hagedorn asked, intrigued.

"Because I know what you have in mind," she said. "You're going to try to find the exit that will let us out near the Kryannen system."

He eyed her. "For what purpose?"

"During the war, the Pelidossians aided the Romulans. They sold them supplies, even helped them with repairs. Earth Command returned the favor by destroying a couple of Pelidossian ships."

The captain was impressed. "And now?"

"Now you want to reconnoiter—and you don't know when you'll again be in a position to do so." Zenar glanced at the viewscreen. "Of course, our orders call for us to chart the main corridor only. But if you're waiting for me to object, you'll be waiting a long time."

It didn't take him long to figure out why. "Because you're a scientist first and foremost, and the more prodding around we do in these tunnels the better you'll like it."

The first officer nodded. "Something like that."

Hagedorn grunted. "I believe you and I are going to work well together, Commander Zenar."

The Andorian allowed herself a hint of a smile. "Nothing would please me more, sir."

Hiro Matsura had never fought the Shayal'brun, but he knew some captains who had. They were said to be a vicious species, capable of unpredictable and devastatingly effective violence whenever they perceived that their borders had been violated.

The problem, as Matsura understood it, was that their borders seemed to change constantly—at least from the Shayal'brun's point of view. As a result, Earth Command had felt compelled to monitor the aliens' movements every few months, sending patrols out to the Shayal'brun's part of space even at the height of the Romulan Wars.

But now, with Earth Command turning so many of its activities over to Starfleet, responsibility for keeping track of the Shayal'brun had fallen to Matsura. That was why he was slicing through the void at warp one, scanning the aliens' farthest-flung holdings for signs of hostile intent.

"Anything?" asked Matsura, hovering over his navigator's console.

Williams shook her head from side to side. "Not yet, sir," she reported, continuing to consult her monitor. "No new colonies, no new sensor platforms, no new supply depots. . . ."

"And no sign of the Shayal'brun fleet," said Jezzelis, Matsura's long-tusked Vobilite first officer.

"Looks pretty quiet to me," Williams concluded.

Matsura straightened. "Then let's get out of here. The last thing we want to do is start an incident."

It was a real concern. The Shayal'brun were no doubt scanning them even as they scanned the Shayal'brun. The aliens would likely overlook a fly-by, as long as the ship remained outside their perceived borders.

But if the *Yellowjacket* lingered long enough, the Shayal'brun would attack. That much was certain.

"Mr. McCallum," said the captain, "bring us about and—"

Before Matsura could finish, his ship bucked and veered to starboard. The captain grabbed wildly for the back of Williams' chair and found a handhold there, or he would surely have lost his feet.

"What was *that?*" asked Jezzelis.

Williams examined her monitor again, hoping to give him an answer. But McCallum beat her to it.

"It's a subspace chute," said the helmsman.

Matsura looked at him. "A *what?*"

"A chute, sir," McCallum repeated, his fingers dancing across his control panel. The man looked excited, to say the least. "We ran into one on the *Pasteur* about a year ago."

"And what did you find out?" asked the captain.

"Not much, sir," said the helmsman. "Our instruments weren't nearly as powerful as the *Yellowjacket*'s." He looked up suddenly. "If I may say so, sir, this is a rare opportunity."

"You mean to turn back and study the chute?"

"Yes, sir." McCallum looked almost feverish in his desire to retrace their steps. "We may never come across one again."

Matsura frowned and turned to the viewscreen, where the stars burned brightly against the black velvet of space. He couldn't ignore the fact that some of those stars belonged to the Shayal'brun.

On the other hand, every captain in the fleet wanted to get a better handle on subspace anomalies, regardless of his background. Lives had been lost during the war because they hadn't known enough about such things.

And here was an opportunity to rectify that problem.

Jezzelis, who had enjoyed both military and scientific

careers, didn't say anything. But his expression spoke volumes.

"All right," Matsura told his helmsman. "You've got ten minutes—not a second more."

McCallum started to argue, to say that ten minutes might not be enough for the kind of analysis he had in mind. Then he saw the captain's eyes and seemed to think better of it.

"Yes, sir," said the helmsman. "Ten minutes. Thank you, sir." And he brought the ship about.

Matsura glanced at the viewscreen again and bit his lip. With luck, he thought, their little detour wouldn't be a bloody one.

Sitting at the compact computer station in his quarters, Aaron Stiles called up the message he had received a few minutes earlier.

Normally, he waited until the end of his shift before he left the bridge to read his personal messages. But this one was different. This one had come from Big Ed Walker.

The first thing Stiles noticed was that the admiral was smiling. It was a good sign, he told himself.

"Hello, Aaron," said Walker. "I hope you're well. I've been doing my best to keep track of your exploits. It sounds like you're doing good work, considering the adverse circumstances."

Naturally, the admiral was referring to the butterfly catchers. He just didn't want to mention them by name, in case his message accidentally fell into the wrong hands.

"I just wanted you to know that everything is looking good back here on Earth," Walker continued. "Our side is gaining the upper hand. It's looking more and more like one of us will get that brass ring they've been dangling in front of you."

The brass ring, of course, was the *Daedalus*. The upper hand was control of the fleet. And if the Earth Command camp was winning the battle, Stiles wouldn't have to worry about Darigghi and his ilk much longer.

In the captain's opinion, it couldn't happen soon enough.

"Stay well, son," said the admiral. "Walker out."

Stiles saw the Earth Command insignia replace the man's image. Tapping out a command on his padd, he dumped the message. Then he returned to his bridge, his step just a little lighter than before.

Bryce Shumar regarded the image of Daniel Hagedorn on the computer monitor outside his bedroom.

"So," said Shumar, "Councillor Sammak arrived safely?"

The esteemed Sammak of Vulcan was returning to his homeworld for his daughter's wedding ceremony. He had left San Francisco on an Earth Command vessel, which had transferred him to the *Peregrine* two days earlier. Now the *Peregrine* was transferring the councillor to the *Horatio*.

"He's being shown to his quarters now," Hagedorn told him.

"How are your missions going?" asked Shumar, because he had to say *something*.

"Well enough," said his counterpart. "And yours?"

"We're getting by."

Neither of them spoke for a moment. After all, if it was a war they were fighting over the future of the fleet, neither of them wanted to give away any strategic information.

It was a shame that it had to be that way, Shumar told himself. Hagedorn wasn't a bad sort of guy. And he had taken Cobaryn's side in that brawl back in San Francisco.

Maybe the time he had spent with a crew half full of scientists had softened his position a little. Maybe with a little urging he could be made to see the other side of the issue.

There was only one way to find out.

"Actually," Shumar remarked, "I'm glad we've got a chance to compare notes. I think you and I are a lot alike."

"In what way?" Hagedorn asked, his expression giving away nothing.

"We're reasonable men, I'd say."

The other man's eyes narrowed ever so slightly. "Reasonable . . . ?"

"We can see the other fellow's side of the story," Shumar elaborated. "Certainly I can."

"And what side is the *other* side?" Hagedorn inquired. He was beginning to look wary.

Shumar smiled in an attempt to put the man at ease. "I think you know what I'm going to say. That a strictly military-minded Starfleet would miss out on all kinds of scientific opportunities. That it would fail to embrace all the benefits the universe has to offer."

Hagedorn hadn't lodged an objection yet. Shumar interpreted that as his cue to go on.

"Mind you," he said, "there's a lot to be said for combat smarts. I've learned that first-hand. But two hundred years ago, when man went out into space it was to expand his store of knowledge. It would be a shame if we were compelled to abandon that philosophy now."

Hagedorn regarded him. "In other words, you would like me to rethink my position on the nature of Starfleet."

"I would," Shumar admitted, "yes. And believe me, not because I want to win this little internecine war of ours. That doesn't matter to me one bit. All that matters is that the Federation doesn't get cheated out of the advancements it deserves."

The other man leaned back in his chair. "You know," he said, in a surprisingly tired voice, "I like you. What's more, I respect you. And I sure as hell won't try to tell you that you don't have a point."

Shumar's hopes fell as he heard a "but" coming. Clearly, the other shoe was about to fall.

"But," Hagedorn went on, "I believe that this fleet has to

be a military organization first and foremost, and I can't tell you I'd ever advocate anything else. Not even for a nanosecond."

The scientist accepted the defeat. "Well," he responded in the same spirit of candidness, "it was worth a try."

The other man just looked at him. He seemed at a loss as to how to respond.

Shumar could see there was nothing to be gained by further conversation. "I ought to be getting on to my next assignment, I suppose. I'll see you around, no doubt."

Hagedorn nodded. "No doubt."

"Shumar out."

He was about to break the connection when the other captain said something. It was low, under his breath—as if it had escaped without his wanting it to.

"I didn't catch that," Shumar told him.

Hagedorn looked sympathetic. "I said it wasn't. Worth a try, I mean. The competition is already over."

Shumar felt his cheeks grow hot. "What are you talking about?"

"I mean it's over," Hagedorn said soberly. "I'd tell you more, but I've probably said too much already."

Shumar saw the undiluted honesty in the man's eyes. Hagedorn wasn't maneuvering, he realized. He really meant it.

"Thank you," Shumar replied. "I think."

For a moment it looked as if his colleague was going to say something else. Then he must have thought better of it.

"Hagedorn out," he said. And with that, his image vanished from the monitor and was replaced with the Starfleet insignia.

Suddenly, Shumar thought, he had a lot to think about.

Connor Dane made his decision and turned to his helmsman. "Take us out of orbit, Mr. Dolgin."

Dolgin shot a glance at him, his surprise evident on his florid, red-bearded face. "Sir?"

"Out of orbit," the captain repeated, with just a hint of derision. "That means *away.* More specifically, away from *here.*"

The helmsman blushed. "Yes, sir," he said with an undercurrent of indignation, and got to work.

"Captain Dane?" said Nasir, his tall, dark-skinned blade of a first officer. He moved to Dane's side and leaned over to speak with him. "Would you say it's wise to move off so quickly?"

The captain looked up at his exec. "*Quickly?* We've been here for two entire days. If the Nurstim are going to take note of us, I'd say they've probably done it already."

Nasir frowned. "Begging your pardon," he said, "but the Nurstim may simply be waiting for us to move off."

"At which point they'll attack the Arbazans?"

"Precisely, sir."

"In that case," said Dane, "maybe we should stay here forever. Then we can be *sure* the Nurstim won't start anything."

Nasir smiled thinly. "Another day—" he began.

"Is a day too many," the captain told him. "Our orders called for us to stay two days—no longer."

His first officer nodded. "That's certainly true. But I assure you, anyone with a military background—"

"Can go straight to hell," said Dane.

That brought Nasir up short. "All I meant—"

"I *know* what you meant," the captain declared. "That I didn't wear black and gold during the war, so I can't possibly have the slightest idea of what I'm doing. Right?"

The first officer shook his head. "Not at all, sir. I just—"

Dane held his hand up. "Spare me the denials, Commander. I'm not in the mood." He turned to the science console, which was situated behind him and to his right. "Mr. Hudlin?"

Hudlin, who was hanging around the bridge as usual, looked up from his monitors. "Sir?"

"Didn't we pass something on the way here that you wanted to investigate? Some kind of cloud or something?"

The white-haired man smiled. "An ionized gas torus," he said. "It was trailing one of the moons around the seventh planet."

"Sounds intriguing," said Dane, though it didn't really sound intriguing to him at all. "Let's look into it."

Hudlin looked at him askance. "What about the Arbazans?"

"The Arbazans are as safe as they're going to be," the captain told him. He addressed his helmsman again. "Mr. Dolgin, head for the seventh planet. Three-quarters impulse."

"Aye, sir," came the faintly grudging response.

Next, Dane turned to his navigator. "Chart a course for the eighth and ninth planets as well, Lieutenant Ideko. They might have some interesting moons too."

Ideko, a slender, graceful Dedderac, nodded her black-and-white-striped head. "Aye, sir."

Hudlin seemed unable to believe his ears. "If I may ask, sir . . . why the sudden interest in moons?"

The captain shrugged. "I've always been interested in moons, Mr. Hudlin. It's the scientist in me."

For Nasir, that appeared to be the last straw. He straightened and looked down at Dane with undisguised hostility. "It's only fair to inform you that I'll be lodging a formal protest."

The captain nodded. "Thanks for being fair, Commander. It's one of the things I like best about you."

The first officer didn't say anything more. He just moved away from the center seat and took up a position near the engineering console.

Inwardly, Dane cursed himself. Nasir was a strutting know-it-all he should never have hired in the first place—but still, he didn't deserve that kind of tongue-lashing. It wasn't his fault that his captain was a walking tinderbox lately.

It was Big Ed Walker's.

Dane's uncle was the one who had notified him that the Earth Command faction had carried the day. *As if I were one of them,* he reflected bitterly. *As if I had come around, just the way Big Ed always knew I would.*

Truth be told, Dane hadn't considered himself an ally of Shumar and Cobaryn either. But his uncle's message had sparked something inside him—and not just resentment.

It had made him realize that he had to take a stand in this war sooner or later. He had to choose between the cowboys and the butterfly catchers, or someone else would make the choice for him.

All his life, he had denied his family's glorious military history—but he hadn't embraced anything else in its place. *Maybe it was time to make a commitment to something,* Dane told himself.

Maybe it was time to start chasing butterflies.

Bryce Shumar watched the small, slender woman take a seat in the anteroom of his quarters.

"Well," said Clarisse Dumont, "here I am. I hope this is as important as you made it out to be."

The *Peregrine* had been nearly a trillion kilometers from Earth when Shumar had asked to speak with Dumont. Of course, it would have been a lot more convenient for them to send messages back and forth through subspace, but the captain had wanted to see his patron in person.

So Dumont had pulled some strings. She had made it to the nearest Earth base via commercial vessels. And now she was waiting to hear why she had made such a long and arduous trip.

Shumar found himself in the mood to be blunt. He yielded to it. "What's going on?" he asked unceremoniously.

Dumont's brow puckered. "What exactly do you mean?"

Shumar felt a surge of anger constrict his throat. "Don't play games with me," he said with forced calm. "I spoke with Hagedorn. He told me that the war for the fleet is over—that his side has already won."

He wanted Dumont to tell him he was crazy. He wanted her to say that Hagedorn didn't know what he was talking about. But she didn't do either of those things.

The only response she could muster was, "Is that so?"

"Was he right?" the captain pressed, feeling he knew the answer already. "Is the war already over?"

Dumont sighed. "Honestly, not yet. But it's getting there. Unless something changes—and quickly—Starfleet's going to be nothing more than Earth Command with a different name."

Shumar frowned. "You could have told me," he said.

"I could have," she agreed. "But then, you might have stopped fighting—and whatever slim chance we had would have been gone."

It made sense in a heavy-handed, presumptuous kind of way. He asked himself what he would have done if he had been Clarisse Dumont. It didn't take him long to come up with an answer.

"You should have left that up to me," the captain told her. "I deserved to know the truth."

Dumont smiled a bitter smile. "We seldom get what we deserve." She paused. "So now what, Captain? Are you going to pack it in, as I feared? Or are you going to keep fighting?"

Shumar grunted. "Do I have a choice?"

She nodded. "Always."

The woman was glib—he had to give her that. But then, she hadn't risen to such prominence by being shy.

"In that case," he told her, "I'll have to give it some thought."

"I hope you'll do that," said Dumont. "And I hope you'll come to the same conclusion you did before, odds or no odds."

He didn't pick up the gauntlet she had thrown down. Instead, he changed the subject. "Can I get you something to eat?"

She shook her head. "Thank you, but no. I should be getting back to the base. As always, I've got work to do." She smiled again. "Miles to go before I sleep and all that."

The captain nodded. "I understand."

He and Dumont talked about something on their way back to the transporter room—though afterward, he wasn't sure what. And he must have given the order for his transporter operator to return her to Earth Base 12, but he didn't remember issuing it.

All Shumar remembered was what Dumont had said. *Unless something changes—and quickly—Starfleet's going to be nothing more than Earth Command with a different name.*

It was a depressing thought, to say the least.

In the privacy of his tiny suite on the *Cheyenne,* Alonis Cobaryn viewed a recorded message from his friend and colleague Captain Shumar. It didn't appear to be good news.

"Dumont confirmed it," said Shumar, his brow creased with concern. "Our side is losing the war for the *Daedalus.*"

Cobaryn eased himself back into his chair. He was sorry to hear such a thing. He was sorry indeed.

"She asked me whether I intended to stop fighting," Shumar continued, "since our cause was all but lost." He chuckled bitterly. "I told her I'd give it some thought."

And what decision did you make? the Rigelian wondered.

Shumar shrugged. "What could I do except stick it out? I made a commitment, Alonis. I can't give up now."

Cobaryn nodded. *Bravo,* he thought.

"I'll expect the worst, of course," the Earthman told him. "But that doesn't mean I'll stop hoping for the best."

Cobaryn smiled. "And they call *me* a cockeyed optimist," he said out loud.

Shumar sighed. "Pathetic, isn't it?"

If it is, the Rigelian reflected, *then we are both pathetic. Like you, I will see this venture through to its conclusion.*

He had barely completed the thought when a light began to blink in the upper quadrant of his screen, signaling an incoming message. Responding to it, he saw that it was from Earth.

From Director Abute . . .

Aaron Stiles was peering at the tiny screen of a handheld computer, going over the results of his science section's analysis of the asteroid belt, when his navigator spoke up.

"Sir," said Rosten, a tall woman with long, dark hair, "I have a message for you from Director Abute."

Stiles turned in his seat to acknowledge her, glad for the opportunity to put the asteroid data aside. "Put it on-screen, Lieutenant."

"Aye, sir," said Rosten.

A moment later, the starfield on the forward viewer was replaced by Abute's dark, hawk-nosed visage. The man looked positively grim.

"Good morning, Captain Stiles," said the Starfleet administrator. "I have a mission for you."

Judging from the seriousness of the man's tone, Stiles guessed that it was a *real* mission this time. He certainly hoped so. He'd had enough asteroid-watching to last him several Vulcan lifetimes.

"I trust you're familiar with the Oreias system," Abute continued. "It's not far from your present position."

In fact, the captain *was* familiar with Oreias. A girl he had dated for a while had gone there to help establish an Earth colony.

"We have four scientific installations there, one on each of Oreias's class-M planets," the director noted. "Late yesterday, the Oreias Five colony was attacked by an unknown aggressor."

Unknown? thought Stiles. He felt his jaw clench.

"I know what you're thinking," said Abute. "That it may be the Romulans again. Frankly, I can't imagine what they would have to gain by such an action, but I concede that we cannot rule out the possibility."

Seeing a shadow fall across his lap, the captain traced it to its source. He found Darigghi standing next to him, his tiny Osadjani eyes focused on the Earthman's message.

"Fortunately," the director remarked, "no one died in the attack. However, the place is a bloody shambles and the colonists are scared to death—those on the other worlds as well as on Oreias Five. After all, whoever did this could be targeting the other colonies as well."

True, Stiles reflected. And if it *was* the Romulans, if he found even a hint that they were back on the warpath . . .

"Which is why we need a Starfleet presence there as quickly as possible," Abute declared, "to stabilize the situation, defend against further attacks, and try to determine who was responsible. Your vessel is the one closest to Oreias, Captain—"

Stiles smiled to himself. So I'll be the one who gets to check it out, he concluded. He was already beginning to savor the challenge when Abute completed his sentence.

"—so it looks as though you will be the first to arrive.

However, I am deploying the remainder of the fleet to the Oreias system as well. A threat of this potential magnitude clearly dictates a team effort."

The captain slumped in his seat. Six ships . . . to investigate a single sneak attack? If they had worked that way during the war they would never have had time to launch an attack of their own.

"Good luck," said the director. "I look forward to the report of your initial findings. Abute out."

Abruptly, the man's image was replaced with a starfield. Stiles frowned and turned to his navigator. "Lieutenant Rosten," he sighed, "set a course for Oreias Five. Top cruising speed."

"Aye, sir," said the navigator, applying herself to the task.

The captain leaned back in his seat. Then he looked up at Darigghi. "I don't suppose you've ever been in battle before?" he asked.

The Osadjani shook his head. "I have not."

"Well," said Stiles, "this may be your chance."

Look for STAR TREK Fiction from Pocket Books

Star Trek: Deep Space Nine®

Warped • K.W. Jeter
Legends of the Ferengi • Ira Steven Behr & Robert Hewitt Wolfe
The Lives of Dax • Marco Palmieri, ed.

Novelizations
Emissary • J.M. Dillard
The Search • Diane Carey
The Way of the Warrior • Diane Carey
Star Trek: Klingon • Dean Wesley Smith & Kristine Kathryn Rusch
Trials and Tribble-ations • Diane Carey
Far Beyond the Stars • Steve Barnes
What You Leave Behind • Diane Carey

#1 • *Emissary* • J.M. Dillard
#2 • *The Siege* • Peter David
#3 • *Bloodletter* • K.W. Jeter
#4 • *The Big Game* • Sandy Schofield
#5 • *Fallen Heroes* • Dafydd ab Hugh
#6 • *Betrayal* • Lois Tilton
#7 • *Warchild* • Esther Friesner
#8 • *Antimatter* • John Vornholt
#9 • *Proud Helios* • Melissa Scott
#10 • *Valhalla* • Nathan Archer
#11 • *Devil in the Sky* • Greg Cox & John Gregory Betancourt
#12 • *The Laertian Gamble* • Robert Sheckley
#13 • *Station Rage* • Diane Carey
#14 • *The Long Night* • Dean Wesley Smith & Kristine Kathryn Rusch
#15 • *Objective: Bajor* • John Peel
#16 • *Invasion! #3: Time's Enemy* • L.A. Graf
#17 • *The Heart of the Warrior* • John Gregory Betancourt
#18 • *Saratoga* • Michael Jan Friedman
#19 • *The Tempest* • Susan Wright
#20 • *Wrath of the Prophets* • David, Friedman & Greenberger
#21 • *Trial by Error* • Mark Garland
#22 • *Vengeance* • Dafydd ab Hugh
#23 • *The 34th Rule* • Armin Shimerman & David R. George III

Star Trek®: Invasion!

#1 • *First Strike* • Diane Carey
#2 • *The Soldiers of Fear* • Dean Wesley Smith & Kristine Kathryn Rusch
#3 • *Time's Enemy* • L.A. Graf
#4 • *Final Fury* • Dafydd ab Hugh
Invasion! Omnibus • various

Star Trek®: Day of Honor

#1 • *Ancient Blood* • Diane Carey
#2 • *Armageddon Sky* • L.A. Graf
#3 • *Her Klingon Soul* • Michael Jan Friedman
#4 • *Treaty's Law* • Dean Wesley Smith & Kristine Kathryn Rusch
The Television Episode • Michael Jan Friedman
Day of Honor Omnibus • various

Star Trek®: The Captain's Table

#1 • *War Dragons* • L.A. Graf
#2 • *Dujonian's Hoard* • Michael Jan Friedman
#3 • *The Mist* • Dean Wesley Smith & Kristine Kathryn Rusch
#4 • *Fire Ship* • Diane Carey
#5 • *Once Burned* • Peter David
#6 • *Where Sea Meets Sky* • Jerry Oltion
The Captain's Table Omnibus • various

Star Trek®: The Dominion War

#1 • *Behind Enemy Lines* • John Vornholt
#2 • *Call to Arms...* • Diane Carey
#3 • *Tunnel Through the Stars* • John Vornholt
#4 • *...Sacrifice of Angels* • Diane Carey